HIDING IN
PLAIN SIGHT

EOGHAN EGAN

RED DOG

UK

www.reddogpress.co.uk

For Theia Ellis Kirwan.

Born: August 24th 2019
Welcome to planet earth, young lady. May you be the best possible version of yourself and have a long, happy, exciting, fun-filled, book-filled life.

-

1

MONDAY 7 JANUARY

AFTERNOON

JUST BEFORE AFTERNOON coffee break, the art dealer decided to kill Roberta Lord.

He compressed a tennis ball, gazed out of the corner office window, and watched another heavy snow shower blanket the space between Tullamore's O'Carroll Street and Market Square. Snow was a natural enemy; it meant tracks and traces. But with more prolonged showers forecast for tonight, it would hide footprints and allow him to slip away unseen.

He'd noticed her at a gallery three weeks earlier and sidled close enough to breathe in her scent and learn the basics: a single mother and artist, employed part-time in a café, struggling to stretch her income. He overheard her ask where she could find a copy of a particular book, and later, he smelled her insecurity as she paused at a display and gave him a quick smile. No conversation. No phone number exchange. No swapped business cards. He'd taken the volume Roberta wanted from his library and kept it in his briefcase—an alibi, if needed.

He sat back and closed his eyes.

Yes. In a few hours, Roberta Lord will die.

He willed his body to trigger the intense hormonal surge that swelled and gushed like waves, followed by blessed peace of mind, and...

A desk phone buzz interrupted his reverie. He stabbed a button on the console. 'Yes?'

'Mrs Wilson's downstairs.'

'Get someone else to deal with her.'

'She specifically—'

'Ambrose, perhaps?'

'—asked for you. Won't talk to anyone else.'

Face muscles bunching, wishing he could throttle this new secretary, the art dealer glared at a digital desk clock as it blinked *2:49*. 'Be right there,' he said.

Ten minutes. Have to be out of here in ten minutes.

He pressed an external line and dialled a local garage. 'My car is due a service,' he told the receptionist.

'Of course. What day—?

'Now.'

'I'll transfer—'

'Twenty minutes. Have a replacement ready.' The art dealer dropped the receiver, shoved the tennis ball into a pocket, grabbed his briefcase and marched out. At the lift, he pressed the call button, lips curling in distaste when he saw the secretary totter towards him, teetering in tangerine high-heel courts. She gestured at the folder in her hand.

'I've typed and printed the file, sir.' The art dealer stared at her and the secretary blushed, wary now. 'The one you said was urgent. Will I leave—?'

'I'll take it.' The art dealer punched the lift button again, riffled through the pages, and scowled at a typo on page three. He gave up on the lift, pushed through an exit door and bounded downstairs. On the ground floor, he dumped the folder into a rubbish bin, patted down his hair, switched the scowl to a choirboy's smile and walked into the reception area, hand outstretched. 'Christine. *So* wonderful to see you again.' The handshake was warm and firm. The art dealer placed his hand on the woman's elbow and guided her towards a viewing room. 'Now—' his voice settling like smoke around the visitor '—prepare to be impressed...'

TWENTY-TWO MINUTES later, across town in Kilcruttin Business Park, the man exchanged keys with a garage mechanic, made sure all lights and taillights worked...
Faulty brake lights. That's how others got caught.
...and settled into a Toyota Avensis. He nosed the car onto the N52, passed by Charleville demesne, through Kilcormac village and signalled left after Fivealley. The car jounced along a narrow pot-holed lane and he glanced in at the empty farmhouse. When the road petered out, he stopped, opened a field gate and inched the car up a gravel road that gave access to farm sheds. Eastwards, dark cloudbanks hovered over Stillbrook Hill and Wolftrap Mountain, presaging more snow.

In a tool shed, he slipped into wellingtons, donned a hooded raincoat, pulled on a pair of latex gloves, and cased the Toyota boot with a piece of old black tarpaulin used to wrap silage bales. Housed cattle stuck their heads under feed bars, lowing in expectation. From a toolbox, he removed a wooden mallet and a steel-handled claw hammer with a rubber grip. He hefted each, judged weight and balance, decided on the mallet and put it in the briefcase alongside a new pair of rubber gloves. From a shelf, he selected a tin of black paint and an artist's rigger brush. Eight strokes changed the registration numbers from 10340 to 18848. He stepped away, inspected his handiwork...
Fine.
Dabbed on a small alteration...
Better.
...and placed a bottle of turpentine and a cloth on a shelf. He'd need them later. He left his mobile phone beside them, tore off the gloves, shoved them into an old fertiliser

bag, and glanced around once more. In a tin box, he found a rusted Stanley blade and placed it in the car's ashtray. A trickle of anticipation snaked up his spine. 'Number seven,' he murmured. 'Your time is up.'

THE ART DEALER retraced the route back to Tullamore, skirted the town and continued towards Kilbeggan. A quick glance at his wristwatch.

16:34.

To the left, spotlights cast a shadow on the big house stitched into a glade on Hattinger's estate. He hadn't set foot inside since marrying into the family. Linking up with the M6 motorway, he headed west amid a convoy of commuters.

16:41.

He needed to be in position by five-fifteen.

Pillow drifts reduced the motorway to a single lane. The procession of vehicles slowed his progress; he'd have to risk a shortcut rather than take the more circuitous route. Westwards, the orange glow of Ganestown's lights appeared tantalisingly close, before another snow squall, thick as duck down, obliterated the view.

A "Traffic Diverted" sign caused a holdup. The man growled in frustration. He took out the tennis ball, squeezed it tight, ignoring the darts of pain that coiled and dug like strands of barbed wire around his brain, and glowered at the silent council machines barricaded behind traffic cones. Further repairs of the road surface, chewed away by weeks of Arctic ice and frost, would have to wait.

He inched by, fury simmering…

16:58.

…gritted his teeth, and mind-mapped the quickest route to Oak View Lane.

If I turn left—

A van in front stopped. The art dealer jammed on the brake, skidded along the ice-crusted surface, his arms and body tensed, expecting an impact. He felt the pump-pump action in the pedal as the ABS system kicked in, tyres struggling for grip, and stopped centimetres away from a collision. Through narrowed eyes, he stared at a portable traffic light and willed it to turn green.

EVERYWHERE SEEMED SIMILAR in snowy suburbia.

It took eighteen minutes to find Oak View Lane, the cul-de-sac where Roberta Lord lived. The art dealer navigated into the dead-end, where a lone streetlight cast shadows in the gloom. Roberta's house was still dark. He steered around a snow-covered car, halted three-quarter ways around a traffic circle, cut the lights, set the wipers to intermittent, and stared through a fresh flurry of billowing snowflakes. Then, with the patience of a spider, he settled in to wait.

Her schedule had become a predictable pattern. Leave café by five. Collect boy at crèche—except on Mondays and Thursdays when the child got collected by a man, presumably his father, and taken to an apartment across Ganestown for sleepovers. Either way, Roberta was home by five-thirty. Lights out at eleven. There'd been several chances to kill her, but tonight felt right; a treat for his thirty-ninth birthday.

He glanced at dashboard clock.

She's late. There's been a crash.

His eyes followed the dipped headlights turning into Roberta's driveway. The trickle of anticipation became a torrent.

A tiny figure ran from the car to the front porch. The man's lips tightened.

Boy's supposed to be across town. Weather must've caused a change in plans. Should I wait? When will I get a better opportunity?

The pounding headache upgraded to a throbbing migraine. He needed relief. Impossible to suppress the urge.

And it's my birthday. It has to be now. If the boy sees me, I'll kill him too. That means I must stun the woman first. Otherwise, she'll cause havoc. Then deal with the child. One body or two doesn't matter.

The art dealer's eyes traced Roberta's progress. She draped a jacket over her shoulders, removed shopping bags from the back seat, fumbled keys, used a hip to nudge the hall door open and shepherd the child inside. She hadn't closed the driver's door.

Means she's coming back. Saves me knocking on the door.

He rolled the car forward, executed a reverse manoeuvre and positioned it boot-to-boot with Roberta's on the short driveway. He switched off the engine, pulled the waterproof hood over his head, opened the briefcase, snapped on the gloves, gripped the mallet and stepped out.

One, two, three…

Pushed the boot release and checked the tarpaulin was in place.

Light spilled from a front room window. A television screen flashed, and Roberta stretched to fasten the curtains.

Sixteen, seventeen, eighteen…

Roberta reappeared in the doorway. One hand held the jacket over her head, the other clasped a mobile. She peered at the screen, high-stepping through the snow. Shrouded by the snowburst, the art dealer waited.

Twenty-seven, twenty-eight, twenty-nine…

Roberta glanced up, saw the strange car, stopped, frowned, squinted at the motionless figure. 'Hello? Is there a problem? Has there been an accident?' She stepped closer. Then, a sudden flash of recognition. 'Oh, erm…the art exhibition, right?'

The figure stepped forward.

Thirty-five, thirty-six...

'No.' The word burst from Roberta, sharp as a sword swipe, and she stretched out a hand to defend herself.

With his left hand, the art dealer pressed the jacket over her head and face. His right hand arched and descended, the dull "whap" like bowling balls colliding.

Forty...

The thick jacket blunted the delivery. Stunned, Roberta sank to her knees.

Forty-three, forty-four...

Her arms flailed. The mobile fell. The man grabbed Roberta's shoulder, held her in position, adjusted his stance and launched another attack, using more weight. His arm jumped from the impact, and he tightened his grip on the wooden hammer.

Forty-nine, fifty, fifty-one...

Faint, up-tempo cartoon sound effects wafted through the doorway.

Better make sure in case the boy appears.

Third crunch. Harder now. The wooden head snapped off and disappeared into the snow, leaving him grasping a short piece of jagged wood. The art dealer snarled.

Fifty-five, fifty-six...

He threw the useless piece of wood into the boot, stooped, gripped the mallet's shortened handle that jutted from the snow, and struck again. This fourth blow sounded like a shoe squashing through soggy soil, and it shattered Roberta Lord's skull.

Sixty-eight, sixty-nine, seventy...

He crouched, poised, his sweeping glance taking in the house and driveway, prepared to kill again.

Nothing.

He swivelled towards the roadway, gazed through soft, silent snowflakes.

No voice.

Seventy-three, seventy-four...

No shadow.

Clear.

With ease, he pitched the body inside the car boot. The fingers on Roberta's right hand jerked, flexed, clinched, then relaxed.

Eighty, eighty-one, eighty-two...

He tossed the mallet on top of the corpse, slammed the boot lid, picked up Roberta's mobile and shut her car door with his knee. Within an hour, nature would obliterate his presence.

Eighty-seven, eighty-eight, eighty-nine...

NINETY SECONDS AFTER he reversed in, the art dealer drove away.

The migraine hadn't slackened.

Where's the rush? The release? Maybe I'll feel something after getting rid of the body.

At the temporary traffic light, he used the Stanley blade to prise open the cover of Roberta's mobile. He levered the SIM card from its slot, broke the chip and pitched it and the knife blade out the window. Sweat trapped inside the latex gloves made his hands itch. He opted to avoid the motorway and crossed a flyover to join a minor road. Swirling snow hampered his vision and neutralised landmarks. Within a kilometre, neither full nor dipped beams helped distinguish where the roadside ended and the water table began. He slowed, concentrated hard.

Near Ferbane, the art dealer lobbed Roberta's phone battery into a ditch. After Cloughan, the heavy snow shower suddenly turned light as lace, and he increased speed, relieved to have completed the circuit and be back in familiar terrain. A few kilometres later, he flung the mobile itself into the swollen Rapemills river. Time to take Roberta Lord to her burial place.

THE TOYOTA NOSED along the gravel road, tyres locked into the ruts they'd cut earlier, its undercarriage scraping the build-up of icy slush. A half-moon sloped over Wolftrap Mountain, punching a gap through clouds, its beam illuminating the galvanised farm sheds. The art dealer unbolted a double steel door, piloted inside and parked beside a Hitachi excavator. He switched on fluorescent lights and checked his phone. Three missed calls. If he ever needed proof of his whereabouts for the past few hours, satellite towers would have pinged and stored his phone's location at the farm. He soaked the old cloth in turpentine, scrubbed the paint off both number plates, started the Hitachi and manoeuvred it outside to a feed area. Dipper arms arched, and the bucket scooped up a half-tonne wrapped silage bale.

He returned to the car, unlocked the boot and tugged at Roberta's jacket, gummed to congealed blood. He wrenched the fabric away, unveiled the corpse and studied the mushy goo that gelled in clumps to her hair and coat. Her left eye had disappeared within the shattered side of the skull, the other remained wide open in an expression of eternal surprise. The tangy metallic aroma of blood compelled him to lean closer and inhale. He took a last look, folded the plastic cover around the corpse, used a length of electric fencing cable to secure the crude body bag and propped it alongside the silage bale.

No trophies. Another way others had got caught.

He unlatched an enclosure gate to one of the cow byres before climbing into the Hitachi cab. The caterpillar wheels tracked into a field, chewing up virgin snow. A dozen cattle followed the trail of sludge. Near a boundary ditch, he dumped the load and spun the turntable ninety degrees and toggled controls. The engine growl deepened as the blade edge on the six-foot wide mud bucket sank through snow, biting into the soil. He removed the clay, banked it to one side and angled the bucket into the opening again. Four scoops to make a grave.

One more for good measure.

The man hopped down from the cab, rolled Roberta's body over the hole, pushed it in, waited for the hollow thump before he ripped off the silage bale cover and threw most of it onto the corpse. Back at the digger controls he refilled the grave, then positioned the cattle feed across the clay. The animals arranged themselves in a semi-circle, eyes reflecting in the machine's beams.

The art dealer smiled.

By the time they'd finished eating, the combination of hoof tracks and the next snow shower would erase all signs of his activity.

Nothing beats natural camouflage.

At the sheds, he washed both the wooden hammer and its broken handle, shoved both pieces along with the raincoat into the fertiliser bag. The byre gate remained ajar; the cattle would return for warmth after their snack. He added the paint-stained cloth to the trash, replaced the turpentine on the shelf, then peeled off the latex gloves, stuffed them beneath the raincoat, and held both hands aloft, letting the polar air act as a balm. Then, slipping back into shoes, he added the wellingtons to the rubbish and placed the sack in the car boot. On the way home, he'd scatter the contents. He straightened his tie, ran a comb through his hair, and slid the mobile into a pocket. Now, he needed a shower.

The art dealer turned right in Kilcormac.

After Saint Cormac's Park, he pressed a fob to unlock cast iron electric gates. Noticed fresh tyre imprints.

Madeline's back.

He steered into the grooves cut by his wife's jeep and drove through the tree-lined avenue, headlights reflecting on the mock-Palladian mansion, and parked beside an Audi Q7. The hall door opened. A woman stepped into the entrance.

'When did you get here?' The man brushed by his stick-thin wife.

'An hour ago. This weather…Didn't think I'd make it. Happy Birthday.' Madeline leaned in and gave her husband a kiss on the cheek. A dry peck, more suited to greeting a distant cousin. 'Ugh, you're wet.'

'Had to check the farm.'

Madeline's nostrils quivered at the faint stench of silage and cow manure. 'Why bother? The part-time farm manager—'

His glare cut like the graze from a bullwhip. Madeline flinched, retreated a step, arms folded. 'I've booked Spinner's restaurant for nine.' Her timbre changed from bearish to benign. Anything to avoid another night marred by a mean mood. 'I wasn't sure what time you'd get here.'

The art dealer eyed a speck of mush on his shoe.

'I'll take care of that,' Madeline said. 'Have a shower. If you wish.' She squeezed out a tight smile. 'Good day at the office?'

'Fine.'

'What's new in the art world?'

'Sold a Paul Henry earlier. That was the highlight.' The art dealer crossed the hall to his library, removed the David Hockney book from his briefcase and slipped it back into its slot, lining the spine precisely with volumes on either side. Upstairs, he turned his face to the shower spray, expecting the cascade to wash the migraine away. This time, it didn't recede. He conjured up images of Roberta Lord's last moments, but they didn't generate any gratification.

Why? Is it because it was too fast? Too quick? Too easy? I need a different technique. A new challenge will boost stimulation. I want someone with spirit. Bolder. Sharper. Competitive.

A finger of expectation caressed his senses. Tomorrow he'd vacuum the garage car and begin another search. One more. In time for her anniversary.

2

TUESDAY 8 JANUARY

MORNING

'SHIT.' HUGH FALLON stared at the mobile phone screen. 'You won't believe this.'

'What?' Eilish's voice floated from the en suite.

'Denis Wiseman phoned. I'm included in the selection for redundancy.'

Eilish stuck her head around the doorway, curling tongs clamped to her long, Irish-setter red hair. 'But you said you —'

'I thought I was—'

'God, Hugh. That's…What'll you do? How—?'

'Denis said—'

'Ask for an individual meeting, Hugh. Ask him to—'

'—he said, on behalf of Pharma-Continental, thank you for your endeavours, and I wish to re-affirm our commitment to handling this process sensitively,' Hugh quoted.

'Christ. Over the phone?' Eilish left the wand down. 'That's cold. Sounds like he's reading from a prepared script. Forget Denis. Get Ferdia to—'

'I'll meet him in Mullingar, but—'

'I'm way late, Hugh.'

Hugh frowned. 'I get it. You're in a rush, but Jesus…' He pointed at the phone screen. 'Do you have to go now? Can we talk this through?'

'What can *I* do?' Eilish spread her arms wide. 'What do you want me to say when I don't know what to say? Mum's rung twice already. She's afraid the bargains…sorry.' Eilish shrugged, edged past Hugh and studied the contents of a free-standing wardrobe. 'Oh, Ciara McGuire and I arranged a meal out tonight. Could be late when I'm back.' She hand-flicked through half-a-dozen coats and removed a jacket from a hanger. 'Look, talk to Ferdia. He's got contacts. There must be someone who'll…We'll talk later if you're awake.'

'Course I will. How'd you expect me to sleep after—'

'I know.'

'Coffee?'

'Don't have time.'

'I'll clear the ice off your car.'

Hugh shivered in the freezing air and pushed a plastic ice scraper across Eilish's windscreen. Another snowfall had been dumped on the Midlands overnight. Eilish rushed out, air-kissed Hugh in case, he supposed, he messed her make-up. She studied his tall frame, from the jet-black hair that fell in little whorls above warm brown eyes, to the shoes covered in slush. 'Please tell me you aren't going to a meeting looking like that.'

'What?' Hugh finger-combed his hair.

'Not your hair. The clothes. You need a new suit.'

'I'm *jobless*, Eilish. Spending is officially on hold until—'

'Fine.' Eilish's hand sliced the air. She opened the Passat door, perched on the seat rim, and swapped high heels for flat pumps.

'Careful driving,' Hugh said.

'You too.' Eilish swivelled her legs into the car, shut the door and drove out.

Hugh sat into his own car, depressed the clutch and turned the key. Nothing. He pumped the accelerator, twisted the key again and the engine cranked once. Tried a third time, and it turned. An orange light he hadn't seen before shone from the dashboard. He left the engine running and went indoors for coffee.

A group of hunched smokers clustered outside Pharma-Continental.

They sucked in nicotine with aggressive, jerky movements, bodies tight as taut springs, ready to attack at the slightest provocation. Hugh wished he still smoked. Inside, he asked the switchboard operator if Denis Wiseman was available.

'Sorry, Hugh. He isn't here.'

'Human Resources?'

'In a meeting.'

'Ferdia?'

'On his way. Are you one of—?'

'Yeah.'

The canteen atmosphere was thick with tension. Anxiety and worry etched across furrowed brows, and expressions ranged from ashen-faced shock to red-faced rage. Hugh observed and listened to colleagues jostle for attention.

'Some reward for pay cuts, dude.' Ronan Lambe's usual boy-band smile had disappeared. An Iron Maiden T-shirt clung to his wiry frame. He'd joined the company before Christmas as a web designer and tech support. Now he sat hunched in a chair, another jobless statistic. From a quick headcount, Hugh estimated a third of the workforce were present: sales, customer service, marketing, IT. Every department had felt the redundancy knife's cut.

A Mercedes swung into a No Parking zone. Hugh watched Ferdia Hardiman uncoil from the driver's seat, a mobile phone clamped between his shoulder and ear. Ferdia flicked a cigarette butt into the sludge, stretched and braced himself against the car, coaxing cramped leg muscles to function, and to relieve back pain—a souvenir from years as a lock in Ganestown's rugby team. He'd worked in Pharma-Continental for thirty years, rising through the ranks and now, aged forty-eight, held the title of National Sales Manager. He'd appointed Hugh as a regional manager four years earlier, and even with a twenty-year gap between them, the two men formed a friendship. A year into his new position, Ferdia introduced Hugh to his young sister, Eilish.

Ferdia plodded towards the entrance and Hugh moved to intercept. Before he reached the inner door that led to reception, it sprang forward. Ferdia ducked under the lintel and barged through, his physique filling the door frame. A smell of cigarette smoke and peppermints wafted around him. He had russet-grey hair, wayward as a 1970s rocker, a boxer's hairline scars under both eyes, a badly realigned nose and a bruise the colour of eggplant on his right jaw. He ended the phone conversation and nodded at Hugh. 'Feckin' taxi drivers. Lookit the state of my trousers. There I was, motoring along nice 'n' steady, and there's this fella in a Mondeo, in the outside lane, chattin' a young wan in the back seat. Next minute, he crosses into my path and clipped my front wing, the gobshite.' Ferdia peeled off his tie, rolled it into a fireman's hose reel and stuffed it into his jacket pocket. 'Well, Jaysus, I swerved, blasted the horn an' tried to straighten the Merc. Dropped my sandwich, an' the phone landed in the coffee cup between my legs.' Ferdia rubbed his crotch. 'Big John and the twins almost got scalded. Feckin' taxi drivers.'

'Least of our worries, Ferdia. This redundancy—'

'Yeah. Caught me on the hop too. Only saw your name last night when I got the full list. You know what multinationals are like; they keep their cards close. Don't worry. You'll be grand.'

'Grand? WILL I? God almighty. I'm redundant. This is the complete opposite to grand. I need a wage. I'm stretched beyond breakpoint.'

Ferdia held up a hand. 'I asked Denis to reconsider, and—'

'That's it?'

'And I've—'

'Guess how that'll work out, Ferdia? Denis *phoned* me this morning. I mean, if you heard what he…Jesus.'

'So he still hasn't figured out a good way to deliver bad news, huh? But I've—'

'A face-to-face discussion with him would be a start.'

'Yeah, but I've—'

'I. Need. Money,' Hugh pushed closer to Ferdia. 'Whatever annual holidays I've left, I want them *now*. I *have* to find a job.'

'Willya listen?' Ferdia said. 'That's what I'm saying if you let me get a word in edgeways. I've had a chat with Charlie. We're meeting him in the morning. He's got a short-term gig for you.'

'Charlie McGuire?'

'Yeah.'

Hugh knew Charlie, Ferdia's brother-in-law. From a base in Mullingar he'd purchased premises in other Midland towns and changed the original hardware shop format to lifestyle stores. The double whammy of big-box competitors with buying clout, coupled with a recession, caused a backslide and McGuire's never recovered. Now, it was on the rocks.

'And I'll put out a few feelers,' Ferdia added. 'Bound to be something stirring. I'll book us into a hotel for tonight, and we'll have—'

'I'll drive back to Ganestown. I can't afford—'

'You're not driving thirty miles home and travel *back* here tomorrow,' Ferdia said. 'No point in this weather. And it'll suit if you drive me home afterwards. I'll borrow wheels from a friend for a few days. Relax, lad. I'll bury the hotel bill in expenses. We'll talk tonight over a jorum of single malt.'

'What's the job with Charlie? His stores are on the brink of...How can—?'

'Later. Look, I've no idea when I'll get outta here, and I need to get the motor to a garage. We'll get you sorted. It'll be grand. Trust me.'

Ferdia pushed open the canteen door and stood sturdy as an oak, while the braying hordes circled. Panic and survival instincts transformed docile employees into a feral mob. Ferdia lowered his voice, compelling the clamouring crowd to listen. 'It's a bad day. Hadn't a notion 'twould hit us to this extent. Soon as I get more information, I'll answer—'

'Fuck answers.'

'We want our jobs,' Hugh said. 'End of story.'

Other strident voices swamped Hugh's words.

'Why're you so anxious?' John McGinley, North-West's regional manager, fixed hostile eyes on Hugh. His body bristled with antagonism.

'What makes you say—?'

'Everyone knows Ferdia's got a wee soft spot for you, seeing as you're gonna marry Eilish. Hah. Guess who'll get a cushy number in the reshuffle? Keep it in the family.'

Hugh pushed his chair away. 'Piss off, John.'

'Where's the Wiseman dude?' Ronan Lambe asked.

'Off-site.'

'Why isn't he here? He sees us as a cost, dude, not a business asset. He's—'

'Yeah. He's a great man to tell us people are the company's biggest strength, and then this—'

'Wiseman my arse,' McGinley's focus diverted, and an outburst of voices erupted, unified against the CEO. 'Bet *he* hasn't lost his job.'

'Yeah. It's all his fault.'

'A monkey could run this place better than the current ape. When business is good, praise the captain. When the downturn comes, sack the team. Never a word about shite executive decisions—'

'Yeah, Wiseman needs to go…'

Hugh left an update on Eilish's voicemail and cancelled the car service he'd arranged. In the canteen, post-mortems got conducted in an atmosphere of benevolent hostility. Conversations became confrontational. Hugh spoke to and commiserated with members of his sales team, and by afternoon, he could see the early stages of a transformation from rage to acceptance, as axed groups clung together for support. They made assumptions and speculated how territories would get carved up. Rumours mutated into facts. Theories got debated, dissected, discarded and by evening, nobody was any the wiser.

EVENING

CHARLIE MCGUIRE'S MOBILE buzzed, breaking his concentration.

He picked it up. 'Hello, Dorothy.' His eyes returned to a spreadsheet and the column of figures he'd highlighted with a red marker.

'Charlie? Hope I'm not interrupting.'

Charlie sat back and looked at the peninsulas of folders scattered round the office floor. 'Not at all, Dorothy.'

'Good. You'll say I'm a forgetful old fuddy-duddy, but—'

'Never, Dorothy.'

'—you'll never guess what's happened. One of my paintings is missing. Stolen.'

'No. When? How?'

'Friday last. Right from under my nose.'

'Impossible? You must've mislaid it.'

'I know *exactly* where it was when Hattinger's people finished the inventory. I've spent all weekend and yesterday searching. My McKelvey's gone.'

'Perhaps it's—'

'I've already tackled Ambrose Hattinger and threatened him with legal—'

'Are you sure that's wise? Without proof or—?'

'*Course* I'm sure. And to shut me up, he's agreed to pay for an independent consultant to help locate the piece and authenticate it.'

'Why would he—?'

'Because A, I'm a good client. B, he wants to keep me sweet, and C, he expects to make a fortune when I decide the auction date. *His* people were the last ones near it. He's well aware I'll move heaven and hell to get my precious painting back. All my contacts are on holidays, away from this cursed weather. With your connections, Charlie, you *must* know someone who can liaise—'

'I don't—'

'—with Hattinger's and validate my McKelvey when it's found.'

'Dorothy, I bet the painting's in your house somewhere…Tell you what, Malcolm's girlfriend, Sharona Waters, she's an art graduate—'

'Perfect.'

'—works part-time as an exhibition co-ordinator and tour guide with the National Art Gallery—'

'I'm a patron.'

'I know. Sharona wants to set up her own gallery and—
'

'I like her already. When will she be free?'

'God, Dorothy, you've no patience. I'll *ask* her. Maybe she's not interested in—'

'Well, get her here as soon as possible, Charlie. She can link up with Hattinger's manager, Jana Trofimiack. That's J-A-N-A. T-R-O—'

'You can give Sharona the details *if* she—'

'Fine. Oh, did you give Ferdia his tickets for the Ball?'

'I'm meeting him tomorrow.'

'Tell him the first dance is mine. Must dash, Charlie. Say hello to Ciara and Malcolm for me. And call me the *minute* you hear from Sharona.'

'That's assuming she's—'

'Bye, Charlie. See you Saturday.'

Charlie sighed, scrolled through phone contacts and pressed Sharona's number.

NIGHT

EILISH'S MIND WAS miles away as she spun into Ciara McGuire's driveway.

From the garden, a barrel-bodied snowman stared from the grey gloam. Ciara's son, David, had been busy. Eilish sat, marshalled her thoughts, then marched towards the house, manufactured a smile and pressed the bell. Ciara opened the door, and Eilish pirouetted in front of the full-length mirror in the hallway: 'Mirror, mirror, on the wall, who's the fairest of them all?'

'Mirror, mirror, shiny glass, tell me that is not my ass,' Ciara replied. 'You look fantastic. Glowing. Nice dress.'

'Thanks. Bought it today in Galway. A simple LBD. Your basic black. God,' she studied her reflection, 'I'm so pale,' and breezed by her friend into the kitchen.

Ciara sniffed. 'New perfume?'

'Jo Malone. Like it?'

'Love it. And the jacket?'

'Cavalli. Feel it. Guess how much it cost?'

'A lot, I'd say. I should've been a teacher too. Or did you win the lottery? Wow. Nice shoes!'

Eilish lifted a leg and pointed her toes. 'My latest most valuable possessions. *These* are Jimmy Choos. Got them today too. Aren't they beautiful?'

'Yeah, but will they stop bloody blisters? Why can't a designer produce stylish low heels?'

'Bliss, not blisters. Beauty before comfort, Ciara. Time heals all wounds.'

'And stilettos wound all heels. Quick coffee?' Ciara offered.

'Okay.'

'What's new?'

'Hmm?'

'What's—?'

'Oh, not much.' Eilish slipped off her jacket, hung it on the back of a chair and left a red clutch bag on the counter. She leaned over the worktop and picked up a book. 'On a positive note, it looks like this weather will keep the school closed for another week. God bless burst pipes.'

'Lucky you.'

'Yeah.' Eilish riffled pages. 'Since when did you need to consult a diet book?'

'Last week. Payback for a month of too many chocolate Kimberleys.' Ciara spooned coffee into mugs.

Eilish appraised the slim brunette, dressed in palazzo pants, Lacoste shirt and a narrow shawl. 'Rubbish. You look smart, cool…Um, if you pack away that furry stole till next years' parties, you're good to go.'

'Then why am I still single, huh? I *never* want to go through Christmas bashes on my own again.' Ciara poured boiling water over the coffee. 'I'll have a partner by the end of summer; a keeper this time. But Jesus, the search to find someone decent around here has turned into a bloodsport; anything half respectable is taken, and what's on offer I don't want. No more hookups. Tinder swipes are over. New year. New me. New life.'

'What happened,' Eilish wiggled her fingers, 'to the last guy?'

'See? You can't even remember his name. Nothing happened.'

'Except?'

'Except nothing. Monotonous monochrome.'

Eilish sat on a stool, crossed her legs and picked a snag on her jacket. 'Blink your eyelashes and they'll fall in line. Oh, you won't believe—'

'Yeah, right. They call me Sinbad at work: Single Income. No Boyfriend. Absolutely Desperate.'

'And over thirty,' Eilish added.

'Ouch. Not quite. I'm twenty-nine for…eleven days. I'll either freeze my eggs or put them all into one basket.' Ciara stirred in milk and handed the mug to Eilish. 'Any gossip?'

'Not much.' She rummaged through her bag for her phone. 'You won't believe—'

'Biscuit?' Ciara lifted the lid off a tin.

'No, thanks.'

'Ah, go on.' Ciara pushed the treats across the counter. 'I can't start a health regime while these are here. You're doing me a favour.'

'Ta.' Eilish nibbled a marshmallow.

'What were you saying a second ago?' Ciara asked.

Eilish back-combed her hair. 'Jesus, I don't remember.'

'Twice you said, "you won't believe…" What won't I believe?'

'Did I? God, my brain, hmph? It's gone.'

Ciara sipped her coffee and studied her friend. 'Fair enough.'

Eilish wrapped both hands around her coffee mug. 'So, what restaurant did you book?'

'Gambadini's.'

'Nice.'

'And then before we go clubbing, I want to check out the new bar on Kelly's Corner. The Chicken Coop.'

Eilish wrinkled her nose. 'That side of Ganestown has become a wilderness of grime and graffiti. I'm overdressed for—'

'It's got brill reviews. Oh, I've invited Jill along too.' Ciara pushed an opal ring onto her middle finger.

'Jill?'

'It'll be fun. Girls united in gossip. She's looking forward to a chat. Said she hasn't seen you in ages.'

'I'd hoped we'd have a chance to—'

Ciara's mobile, lying on a windowsill, rang. She picked it up, looked at the screen. 'There she is now. Jill? What? Slow down. *What?* You're…No way. Aww, crap.' Ciara held the phone to her side and whispered, 'Richard's gone.'

'Gone where?'

'Left. For good.'

The mug slipped from Eilish's hand, and the liquid formed a lake on the worktop. She grabbed a kitchen towel roll, tore off a wad and mopped up the spill.

Ciara pressed a button and put the phone on the counter. 'Jill? Eilish is here. I've put you on speaker.'

'It's possible you're mistaken, Jill,' Eilish said. 'Richard's—'

'No mistake.' Jill's tinny voice shook with sobs. 'He met some trollop. Wants a divorce. He said…he said I'd be well taken care of. Bastard.'

'Did you have suspicions?' Ciara asked. 'Who's the other woman?'

'Didn't ask. Don't want to…God, life was fine 'til this bombshell hit me—'

'When did—?'

'An hour ago.'

Ciara's landline shrilled from the hallway.

'…Jesus, I *know* I've gained weight since Christmas,' Jill said, 'but come on, we don't cheat 'cos of their beer bellies. Three kilos is a we-should-join-a-gym talk. It doesn't give him free rein to slip his dick into some hussy's hole.'

Eilish flinched.

'I've given him the best years of my life. *Then* he throws me in the rubbish bin. When I *think* of the *years…nine* years, he's manipulated me into *believing* his wants were our wants.' Jill broke down again.

The landline stopped ringing.

'Come over,' Ciara said. 'David's on a sleepover tonight. We'll stay in and talk this through over a bottle of wine.'

Eilish coughed. 'I ought to get—'

The landline chirruped again. 'Christ,' Ciara said. 'Jill, my other phone's ringing. It might be David. Talk to Eilish for a minute.' She disappeared into the hall.

Eilish spoke into the mobile. 'Jill? Ciara's right. You'll feel better after—'

Jill's convulsive sobs reduced to hiccups. 'Should've seen this coming after the way he treated his ex-wives. They don't fuckin' change, you know.'

When Jill interviewed for a secretarial role with local haulage company, Western International, she'd caught owner Richard West's eye. Twenty years her senior and already on wife number two, Richard decided he wanted a younger model. He divorced again, and Jill Kavanagh became Jill Kavanagh-West.

The silence lengthened.

Eilish racked her brain for a thoughtful remark. Something sensitive. 'What'll you do?' She cringed as the words tumbled out. 'I mean, how'll you cope?'

This brought another onslaught of heart-wrenched sobs, forcing Jill to contemplate her disintegrated life. She relaunched her story, and Eilish supplied a stream of generic platitudes, with frequent glances at the hallway. What the hell was Ciara at? Clips of her friends' conversation trailed into the kitchen. Ciara's voice reached a higher pitch. 'NO, Malcolm. I *won't* fund your…It'll ruin…*Don't* put yourself through…after the effort you've made? What? I don't *care*—' Her tone became more placating. 'For me. Do it for…Please, Mal? Promise? Right. Call me tomorrow. Don't break your word.'

Ciara dashed back to the kitchen and picked up the mobile. 'Jill? Drop everything and come over now, okay? Okay. See you in twenty minutes.' She ended the call, leaned against the countertop and twisted the opal ring round her finger. 'Jesus.'

'Yeah.' Eilish saw Ciara's flushed face. 'What?'

'Two break-ups in one night. Malcolm and Sharona split up too. He's in another shit mess. That brother of mine. God. Bloody family.'

'Oh. Does your dad know?' Eilish stood and smoothed her dress.

'Not yet. I told Malcolm to phone. It'll—'

'Well, I'll head off.'

'Wait. What? Jill'll be here in…She needs support.'

'Hugh texted me. He's lost the house key.' Eilish grabbed her jacket and bag. 'I'll let myself out.'

'What about Jill?'

Eilish drained her coffee, grimaced and swallowed the gritty dregs. 'I'll try to make it back later. If not, we'll chat tomorrow.'

'Shit, shit, shit.'

Eilish parked in a lay-by, chewed her lower lip, fingers knotted on the steering wheel, her breath a grey mist in the frosty air. She delved into her clutch bag, found the phone, swiped the screen and pressed a number. When a voice answered, she said: 'In case you're interested, Jill's at Ciara McGuire's house tonight. Why'd you—?'

She listened for a moment. 'Richard. I don't understand *why* you decided it was a good idea to—'

She waited a beat. 'Stop, Richard. Whatever we had, it's finished. I can't continue this. Make amends with Jill and get on with your life.' Eilish disconnected and powered off the mobile.

At home, she sat on the stairs, clasped both hands around her head and rocked back and forth. Agitated, she pulled herself upright. A shoe heel caught and ripped the dress hem. She went upstairs, flung herself on the bed, and curled into a ball as spasms of guilt gnawed her gut. For the first time in years, she prayed: 'Please, God, let it be okay. Please let it be okay.'

3

WEDNESDAY 9 JANUARY

MORNING

JANA TROFIMIACK. THE Belfast office manager's name in the contact line caused the art dealer's good humour to evaporate. He tightened his grip on the computer mouse and skimmed the email. Following the art inventory, a McKelvey oil painting had disappeared from Dorothy Ridgeway's home. She'd made a formal complaint. Jana added a footnote: the canvas hadn't surfaced during their visit.

Surfaced?

His left eye twitched.

Stupid whores. Both of them.

His mood deteriorated further when Ambrose Hattinger appeared in the doorway. His brother-in-law had the bulging eyes of a person easily provoked, and the florid colour of someone with an excessive alcohol habit.

'Dorothy Ridgeway called me,' Ambrose said, his nose held at half-mast. 'A McKelvey's missing. We're blamed.'

The art dealer skimmed Jana's email again. 'Why? It's obvious she's mislaid it. With the amount of chattels that woman accumulates, I'm surprised she even remembers what's hoarded.'

Ambrose hitched up his trousers, leaned back and scratched a shoulder-blade on the door frame. 'Dorothy planned to ask the PSNI to investigate—'

'When was this arranged?' The art dealer hated when Ambrose supplied information he was unaware of. He detested this self-absorbed, insufferable man, with his air of superiority and a tendency to ignore anybody he regarded as inferior.

'She phoned me yesterday.'

'Dorothy Ridgeway rang you with an exclusive on her obtaining the full resources of the PSNI to investigate a misplaced canvas? Or to persuade you to take responsibility for her memory glitch?'

'No. Yes.'

'Well, which is it?' The art dealer power-gazed Ambrose.

'Dorothy rang me vis-à-vis the annual ball. It's—'

'And you conveyed we're not honouring her with our presence this year, didn't you?'

'I appreciate that was our intention.' Ambrose's voice whined. Under the art dealer's scrutiny, his pompous manner reverted to the nervousness of a junior executive.

'Was?'

'The main thing is, I persuaded Dorothy to change her mind about the PSNI. She's opted for an outside consultant instead. That's a better alternative for—'

'I'm certain the PSNI don't have the resources to investigate Mrs Ridgeway's little—'

'Dorothy carries clout.'

'Only with weaklings she can intimidate. Police have greater concerns than tracking misplaced paintings. Why should we care what…Incidentally, how *did* you make Mrs Ridgeway reconsider the PSNI involvement?'

'We've taken our usual tables for the ball. Saturday. Herbert Park Hotel.' Ambrose looked away from the art dealer's icy glare.

'I see. And consultancy expenses? Who pays them?'

'We do.'

'Let's recap.' The art dealer leaned his elbows on the desk, fingers steepled in front of his nose. 'Mrs Ridgeway threatens to phone the PSNI and ask them to please come and locate my lost canvas. In your haste to…to *pander* to that woman, you agreed to attend *and* donate another fortune to her fundraiser? *Plus* pay consultancy fees?'

'Dorothy's a friend as well—'

'We're not responsible for either her memory loss or the misplacement of a—'

'She's distressed.'

'You fell for it.'

Ambrose picked a speck of lint from a sleeve. 'I'd no choice.'

'Remind me again where we are in regard to scaling back overheads?'

'Dorothy's a special case, and—'

'You massage Dorothy Ridgeway's ego any way you want. Keep her out of my sight.'

'You should attend Saturday night's ball,' Ambrose said. 'Would look good if—'

'Anything else?'

Ambrose used the door frame as a back scratcher again. 'I, ah, I've written an article for February's Country Life and Garden magazine.'

'About what?'

'The company. When we started. Where we are now. Visions for the future, etcetera.' Ambrose waved an arm. 'They wanted to profile me. Don't worry, I've included you and the contributions you've made—'

'And *you* wrote it?'

'I met one of their staff. Over lunch. Attractive girl. I gave her the general blah, blah, blah. She'll add in the bells and whistles.'

'Name?'

'Amanda Curran.'

'It'll be a hatchet job. She's aiming for career promotion.'

'It's not like that. I—'

The art dealer turned his attention to the laptop. 'I'll consider allowing publication. Or not. When I read it.'

Ambrose slunk out.

The art dealer kneaded his head, satisfied he'd restored the balance of power. Visions of the future, he thought. Ambrose can't see past the next glass of brandy, but his name attracts clients, and that thin coat of university educated gilt, distracts them from his weak character. Saturday is the last time we're supporting Ridgeway's fundraising campaign, so for once, he's right. I'll attend. He debated whether to include Madeline and decided she'd be useful. It would remind people what a generous sponsor and considerate husband he was.

He punched an internal number and barked at the secretary: 'Get me on a flight to Belfast tomorrow evening and arrange client appointments for Friday. I'll be at Dorothy Ridgeway's fundraiser in the Herbert Park, Saturday night. Book two extra rooms in my name. Text Madeline and tell her be there. Contact that Country Life magazine and have them mail me the Hattinger editorial. And get the Trofimiack woman on the line.'

'Yes, sir.'

Whether she's right or wrong, Jana's made her last gaffe, the art dealer thought. *She's no longer essential. I'll force the illiterate bitch back to whatever unpronounceable Polish town she came from.*

The landline rang. 'Jana? Thank you for informing me of Mrs Ridgeway's concern.'

'I never saw the painting—'

'I'm sure you didn't. It's nothing to do with us.' The art dealer picked up a tennis ball and squeezed, imagining his hands around Jana Trofimiack's neck, thumbs digging into her hyoid bone, choking…'Nevertheless, Mrs Ridgeway has arranged a consultant to investigate. It may be wise to make yourself available. This person will want to meet with you.'

'I've nothing to add—'

'I understand. Keep yourself on standby, Jana. Just in case.'

The art dealer cut the call. The ice-pick was chipping at the base of his skull again. He'd collect his car, buy a pair of wellingtons, and visit the farm for an hour. Help to de-clutter his mind before he began the new search.

JANA TROFIMIACK'S HEART palpitated.

'Jezus! How did the old kurwa find out so soon?' She took a deep breath and dialled a London number. 'Cześć.'

'Cześć. Co słychać?'

'Tomasz, I *must* return the McKelvey.'

'It's sold. I—'

'It can't be. The deal's off.' Jana's stomach roiled. 'Get the painting back. TERAZ!'

'Can't talk now. Later.'

'I—' A 'disconnected' signal bleeped, and Jana was left grasping a dead phone.

MID-MORNING

THE AIR, CRISP as celery, hurt Hugh's head.

A steady throb beat a drum solo behind his eyes. He'd ordered breakfast to soak up last night's alcohol, but seeing Ferdia tuck into a full Irish made his stomach rebel.

Ferdia twisted into the passenger seat, belched and rubbed his chest. 'I'm gettin' fierce feckin' heartburns. I swear, they cut like a welding torch. Might hafta pay doc a visit.' His voice sounded raspy as sandpaper on rusty metal.

'You drank too much red wine,' Hugh said. 'Should've asked that German medical rep you disappeared with last night to check you out. What was her name?'

Ferdia scratched his head. 'All I remember is the amount of feckin' rings she wore. Moral of the story: No jewellery. 'Twas like raw meat on a cheese grater. Life lesson learned.'

'Christ, Ferdia.'

'Anyhow, I'm grand, thanks for asking. Plus, I picked up a few new German words. Might come in handy if Angela Merkel ever takes charge of this country.' Ferdia buckled up. 'Thought you were getting rid of this auld banger.'

'Twelve years isn't old for a Lexus. I said it needs a new starter and—'

'New engine, more like.'

'Engine's fine. I'd booked it in for a full service, but I cancelled it yesterday.'

'Should've changed it last year when I told you. Someday, when you need it most, it'll…What's that orange light?'

'No idea.'

'Feck sake, man.' Ferdia searched for the car seat adjuster. 'Does this not go back any further?' He ratcheted the seat to the end of its runners. 'I'm as cramped as Houdini in a glass case.'

'Don't break the—'

'Too late.' Ferdia tossed the broken lever onto Hugh's lap. 'Willya drive on before this pile falls apart. Charlie's waiting for us.'

CHARLIE MCGUIRE CROSSED the office floor to greet Sharona Waters. 'You shouldn't have come over in this weather.'

'Passing through on my way to Dublin.' Sharona, dressed in double denim, pushed back her dark curly hair. 'Sorry I missed your call last night.'

Charlie led her to a chair, then sat behind his desk. 'I found out after the call that it's over between you and Malcolm.'

'Malcolm's a great guy. Makes lots of effort—'

'His mother, God rest her, would be glad—'

'—and then spoils it all by sneaking away to a bookie's office when we're out together. Not good for my ego, knowing he'd prefer gambling to—'

'That's finished. He's learned an expensive lesson.'

'I'm twenty-three, Charlie. Life's too short.'

Charlie toyed with a letter opener. 'Did you loan him money?'

'I don't *have* money to give. I know he's borrowed from other people, though.'

'Hmm. I've drawn up a list.'

Sharona stood and leaned a hip against the desk. 'I've an appointment at twelve, so I won't hang around, Charlie. What was the phone call about?'

'Did I ever mention Dorothy Ridgeway?'

'Don't think so.'

'She's a friend. Lives outside Belfast. We're involved in a cross-border fundraiser. Her husband, Blake, died last year, which made her reflect on her own mortality. Dorothy wants to downsize her property and asset portfolios, so she's putting most of their art collection up for auction. Two experts from Hattinger's completed an inventory last week. You know Hattinger's?'

'I applied for a job with them a while back, but never got an interview. I've visited a few of their galleries. They do little for local artists, and that's where I see a gap in the market.'

'And you'll do well. Yes. I've bought several pieces from them over the years. When the appraisers left, Dorothy noticed a Frank McKelvey canvas had disappeared. She has a special grá for this piece, and is adamant she remembers where it was. Now it's gone. Hattinger's people say they didn't see it.'

'Stashed, maybe?' Sharona said. 'For security.'

'Dorothy's convinced Hattinger's people mislaid it. She spoke to Ambrose, the company chairman. Threatened to get the PSNI to investigate. Ambrose doesn't want police traipsing around, wouldn't be good for business, so he compromised: Dorothy hires a consultant to help locate the McKelvey, and Hattinger's picks up the tab.'

'Why on earth would they do that if—?'

'Oh, Dorothy can be persuasive. Salty as crisps one minute, sweet as sugar the next. She asked if I knew anybody who'd assist. You came to mind, with your art background.'

'I'm not a detective, Charlie.'

'You don't have to be. The canvas is in her house. Help her find and validate it. Get compensated for your troubles. Could be a golden opportunity for you. Dorothy and Ambrose Hattinger are best buddies. If Dorothy likes you, she'd be a great business contact. This may be your doorway into the art world. Win-win.'

'If it's straightforward, I *could* confirm the painting, and yeah, I'd love a change of scenery for a few days.'

'Brilliant.'

'Have you names of the people involved in the inventory?'

'She mentioned Jana…something. Hattinger's manager. Dorothy will fill you in.'

'I may throw this back at you if—'

'Go to Belfast. Find the McKelvey and send Ambrose Hattinger a fat expense claim.'

'Well, that'd come in handy.'

Charlie scribbled on a Post-It note. 'Here's Dorothy's mobile. Call her. Set up a meeting.'

'I'll be in touch,' Sharona said. She stepped into the corridor. A man gripping a wad of A4 spreadsheets bumped her aside. He pushed into Charlie's office, banged the door behind him. The force didn't give the lock time to engage, and it bounced ajar. His angry voice flooded the hallway.

Sharona sped around the curved corridor, passed Malcolm's office door, hesitated, then dashed downstairs via a fire door that squeaked shut behind her. In the reception area, she smiled at the two men signing in. 'Hi, Hugh. Morning, Ferdia.'

'Hiya, Sharona,' Hugh said.

Ferdia turned. 'The very woman. I'd planned to phone you, but between this and that...' he scrawled his initials on the visitor pass.

'Did you sort out the art gallery yet?' Hugh asked.

'I'm going to a meeting now.' Sharona's impish grin faded. 'You'd think landlords would be happy to reduce rent and lease units, but no.' She unpinned the ID badge, handed it to the receptionist, said 'thanks, Deirdre,' and turned back to the men.

'Funny,' Hugh said. 'Few years ago they couldn't give them away. Now they'd rather board them up and leave them idle.'

'That's what I wanted to ring you about,' Ferdia said to Sharona. 'That unit on the corner of Main Street and Bread Lane? It used to be—' he clicked his fingers, '— whatyamacallit...'

'Great location,' Sharona said. 'What about it?'

HIDING IN PLAIN SIGHT

'Later this week, I'm meeting a cousin of the man who owns it. If you're interested, I'll put in a word.'

'God, that'd be great, Ferdia.'

'There's separate living accommodation upstairs too.'

'Happy where I'm renting at the moment. Still, it's all a question of money.' Sharona's grin was back. 'Talk to your guy and get back to me.'

Ferdia turned to watch the woman leave. 'Nice girl.'

Deirdre smiled. 'Now, Ferdia. Sharona's young enough to be your granddaughter. She'd do well in business. Great personality. Charlie shouldn't be long.'

'Grand. Malcolm around?'

'He passed by a minute ago.'

'We'll find him.'

Upstairs, Warhol prints interspaced each office. Opposite, a bank of windows overlooked the town.

'I didn't realise Malcolm was here,' Hugh said. 'Thought he was still in university.'

'Finished. Took the scenic route, but he's got the business theory at last. Now he needs the practice. Has to get his hands dirty. This is where he parks his backside.' Ferdia opened a door and peeked around Malcolm's office interior. A jacket hung on the back of a chair, and a printer spewed out paper. 'Empty,' Ferdia called over his shoulder. 'It's like the feckin' *Mary Celeste* round here.'

Voices poured from another portal. One muted; the other loud. '...you've delivered a decade of bad decisions...'

Ferdia twisted his head. 'Huh. Bit of rí-rá 'gus rúille búille in Charlie's office.' He closed Malcolm's office door, wandered back along the corridor and looked out at Mullingar Business Park, the Grand Canal and the landscape beyond. 'Nothing beats it.'

'What?'

'The mystical, magical, mythological Midlands.'

Hugh looked across the foggy, snow-clad expanse. 'Misty too.'

More heated words spilled out from Charlie's office. '...yesterday you said tomorrow, Charlie. The figures are what they are. For God's sake, rein in your expectations.'

'Problem is,' Ferdia's raised voice cut through the angry tirade, 'tourists make a mad cross-country dash for the coast and miss the fifth province. They think the Midland's a feckin' bog.'

'And Electric Picnic,' Hugh said.

'It's the *Mid-lands*. Mid-point between this world and the next. And the Hill of Uisneach, the Cat stone, is the centre of Ireland. Has a record going back to Saint Patrick, *before* Saint Patrick.'

'I thought the middle of Ireland was in County Roscommon.'

'Aye. Roscommon people say that, but they're—'

The strident voice next door drowned out Ferdia's words.

'...interest should be the company, *not* employees, Charlie. Sell. Today. Or do you want an asset management company hammering down the door...'

Ferdia whistled tunelessly, took a wallet from his back pocket and removed a credit card. He pressed the card edge, and a knife blade sprung out. 'If you're not busy later, we'll—'

'I've paperwork to finish.'

'—we'll swing by Ciara's place on the way home.' Ferdia pared a thumbnail. 'Say hello to my godson.'

'Not heading into Pharma?'

'Nah. There are enough people in the hive today. Couple of suits, efficiency consultants, for feck sake, have flown in fro—'

'...we *have* no more paddles, Charlie.' The voice got louder. 'We couldn't *borrow* paddles to canoe our way out of this river of...' The man who'd been arguing shouldered by and stormed next door into his own den. The partitioned wall shuddered when he slammed the door shut with a heel kick.

Ferdia strolled into Charlie's office. 'Reckoned I'd have to act as referee.'

Charlie shrugged. 'Another day in Paradise.' He beckoned Hugh in. The remnants of the row radiated around the room.

Hugh hadn't seen Charlie McGuire for a few months. His grey-blond hair had become the colour of dirty steel, and he'd lost weight. Charlie looked at the bruise on Ferdia's face. 'How'd that happen?'

Ferdia folded the blade back into its credit card sheath and slotted it into his wallet. 'Argh, I was sparring with a few boxers last week and got tagged. There's this lad from Crumlin, even his feckin' beard hurts when he rubs against you. Caught me with a solid punch. His left fist's a sleeper. Spotted it coming, but hadn't a chance to react. Packs serious power in them meat hammers.' Ferdia rubbed his jaw. 'Sure, it's part of the tax every boxer pays.'

'Ouch. Sorry for the delay, Hugh.'

'No problem, Charlie. Ferdia gave me a history lesson.'

'Oh, don't wind him up. He can trace his descendants back to Niall of the Nine Hostages.'

Ferdia picked a random spreadsheet off an untidy pile covering his laptop keyboard. Numbers typed in red filled the page. He waved the sheet. 'Always a link between past and present. You gotta look back to see forward. Study the past, and it'll stop you making the same faults again.'

'Should, but doesn't.' Charlie nodded to the Excel sheet. 'Can't remember last time I read a column of black ink on a financial report. Whatever the powers that be think, this economy's still screwed. Bloody bankers have a lot to answer for.'

'I agree,' Hugh said. 'But there were multiple factors—'

'Not long ago, bank managers gave me whatever I asked for, seldom requested even a set of accounts. Now, guess what? They won't even take my calls.'

'No business is worth stressing yourself over,' Ferdia said. He sailed the spreadsheet back onto the desk. 'Close the feckin' place.'

'If life was that simple.' Charlie sagged back in the chair and rubbed his forehead. 'I've built this business on the backs of great individuals. Some are offspring of people my father hired. They've commitments. Families, mortgages...There's a burden of expectation I *have* to shoulder, and I'll move mountains to make sure they get a week's wage. I *owe* it to them. Letting a hundred and seventy-three people go is *not* on the agenda. Bloody politicians. Money earmarked for job creation is funding government debt. If it were me alone, I'd lock the gates, but I've got to prioritise staff.'

'Anything I can fix?' Ferdia asked.

'Thanks, but no.'

'You'll give yourself a heart attack, man,' Ferdia added. 'Pull yourself together. It'll be grand.'

Charlie exhaled. 'Fingers crossed, the business will improve by Easter.'

'That's the spirit, Chas. Every setback opens the door for a comeback.'

'I should plan a burglary,' Charlie said. 'Or a fire. Claim on the insurance.'

Hugh shot a glance at Ferdia. 'You'll survive and thrive, Charlie.'

'Huh,' Ferdia said. 'Long as you don't do something legal, like run the business into the ground and repurchase it from the liquidator at a fraction of its current price.'

'Yeah. Enough have done that. Anyway,' Charlie shifted attention to Hugh. 'You've had bad news.'

'Got word yesterday.'

'Wish I'd a management role for you, but all we've got at present is a part-time delivery job; our driver's gone home to Slovakia. More work there than here nowadays. Sign of the times. I'll pay you cash.'

'I've to sign on for Welfare.'

'Fair enough. We'll keep the arrangement between ourselves. Here's a thing: as a self-employed person, if I shut up shop today, I'm not entitled to claim dole. Isn't it madness? After the millions in taxes and...Don't get me started.'

Hugh hadn't considered hauling boxes, but he needed the wage. 'When can I start?'

'Soon as Ferdia lets you go.'

'Whenever,' Ferdia said. 'You're due holidays so it won't affect your redundancy.'

'I'll start in the morning, Charlie.'

'Won't be many deliveries until this weather clears, but our stores will need supplies. Tomorrow, I'll introduce you to Brendan, the back store manager. Something more in your line may arise in a few weeks. I've heard rumours our manager in Ganestown is leaving, nothing official yet, but if it happens, the position's yours.'

'God, Charlie. That's much appreciated.'

'You're welcome. Oh, stick Saturday night in your diary, Ferdia. Dorothy's Gala Ball, if you can fit into a dress suit.' Charlie tossed across an envelope to Ferdia.

'This Saturday?' Ferdia looked at his gut. 'Doesn't give me much time to lose this. Hafta use a weight cutting trick boxers use. Where's it held this year?'

'Herbert Park. She said to remind you to keep the first dance free.'

'Depends what humour I'm in. How's Dorothy?'

'Argh, she's had a squabble with Hattinger's, the art and furniture people. You know them?'

Ferdia cracked a thumb joint. 'Of them. They're a clannish crowd. I break bread an odd time with Ambrose on the nineteenth tee. Get the impression he'd prefer wading through clouds of cigar smoke in a gentleman's club and talking shite, than dealing with business.'

'Dorothy organised an appraisal, and—'

Ferdia looked at his watch. 'Land the feckin' plane, Chas. I've got a to-do list the length of your leg.'

'Me too. Anyhow, it's more or less sorted. We'll agree an hourly rate tomorrow, Hugh. Chat later, Ferdia.'

'Grand. Slán go fóil.'

Ferdia lit a cigarette, sucked in nicotine. A trail of smoke curled in the frosty air. 'That went well.'

'Last thing Charlie wants is another employee,' Hugh said.

'It'll be grand. Your foot's in the door. You've no idea where this could lead.'

'I'll be driving a van, not running the company, Ferdia.'

'Aye. Still, I bet you'll be so good they won't be able to ignore you. Step up and—'

'I don't mind stepping *up* to it, long as I don't step *into* it. Logistics isn't my forte. It'll be a challenge to—'

'God, but you're a mighty fella to see hitches. I see this as a lucky break. I've said it before: opportunities knock, but they don't notify in advance. In a month you'll be managing the place in Ganestown an' God knows where *that* might lead. No risk, no reward.'

'*If* the place is still open.'

'Give over, lad. This might be the step that'll get you from where you are, to where you want to be.'

'We'll see. Did you hear the bit about the asset management company?'

'Yeah, 'cept it wasn't a question. More an accusation and an insult dressed up as a question. Anyway, it's bullshit. I'd say those fellas have their sights set on bigger fish than Charlie's half-dozen retail properties. Still, 'twould be his worst nightmare, having an asset stripper tearing the heart outta the business, and putting people on the dole. Row in and do your best. Once you're on board, you'll figure out solutions. Either lead change from the front or push from behind. Simple as that.'

'I'll be driving a…Anyway, simple issues can become complicated. It'll take a lot of rowing to turn this ship.'

'Nothing's impossible. Use the six senses God gave you.'

'I think you'll find there are five senses.'

'Check again.'

'Sight.'

'Correct.'

'Sound, smell, taste—'

'Hmm-mm.'

'Touch.'

'Yep.'

'What's the sixth one?'

'The one everybody forgets to use. Common.' Ferdia threw the cigarette butt away. 'Best way to lead people? Give them direction and let 'em find their own path.'

'Company's in crisis, though,' Hugh said.

'Huh. The one thing wrong with Charlie is, he spends too much time working *in* the business, and forgets to work *on* it. You'll be good at leading that change.'

'Did you *hear* me? I'll be driving—'

'Jaysus, man. Embrace the challenge, willya?' Ferdia closed the car door, settled into the seat and closed his eyes. 'Now, take me to see my godson, an' quit acting like an auld granny. Nag, nag, nag.'

'Reality, reality, reality,' Hugh shot back.

AFTERNOON

SNOW CLOUDS MUSHROOMED above Slieve Bloom and Wolftrap Mountain.

The art dealer relished the effort it took to pull the wellingtons out of drifts. In the field where he'd buried Roberta Lord, the Hitachi tracks had disappeared. A tiny piece of black plastic wrap jutted from the snow, like a cigarette burn on a crisp white tablecloth. He looked at the grave, then inspected the field for burial spot number eight. Whoever she may be.

At the sheds, he forked silage, savouring the muscle strain. When he'd sweated the office stress from his system, he tramped to the farmhouse, had a shower and returned to Tullamore, mentally ticking off steps he needed to take. He ducked into an internet café on Church Street, set up a new Gmail account, clicked on free dating sites and spooled through the passport-sized photos. None stirred his interest. Combing through another search engine, he found a website offering a two-week free trial. He created a fictitious account and considered usernames.

Jewels, gems or diamonds would act as click-bait. The diamond merchant? The jewel designer? The jewellery collector? That's it.

He dipped into Shutterstock and grabbed a royalty-free photo of a male whose features vaguely resembled his own.

He downloaded, cropped and uploaded the image into his new webpage, studied the profile.

Perfect.

He saved the details and logged into the new account. The "how" part was set up. Now for the 'who' 'where' and 'when'. He foraged for faces that stirred interest.

Click, scan. Next.

Click, scan. Next.

She was here. Somewhere. This trap would expand his skill set.

Click, scan. Next.

Click, scan...

Bidingmytime:

I'm a twenty-eight-year-old female, hoping this will be a Positive alternative from drunken chat-ups. I won't set myself up for idealistic expectations, but I'm keen for exposure to fresh approaches, and I promise not to take rejection personal...

Confidence issues. Too easy.

Next.

Click, scan. Next.

Click, next.

Click...

BachtoBasie:

Hi,

First time on a dating site, so in the spirit of hope over experience, here goes... I'm a single working mother. So, how to write a summary that'll make me appear interesting? Does 'blonde' give the impression I'm ditzy, and 'bubbly' make me sound fat? Should I lie about My age, as most men appear to be on the lookout for 18 to 23 year-olds? Well, I'm neither chubby, blonde, or 23...

The art dealer's spine tingled. He read the profile: Brunette, 29, 5'8", slender, attractive. Ganestown area... His brain shot out alarm signals.

Ganestown? No. Too soon.

The high-end headshot made his skin itch.

Same hairstyle as Isobel Stewart.

The cursor jumped between "next" and "save."

Save.

He skipped a dozen outlines, skipping over any descriptions where he detected desperation. Stopped at Justme, Wicklow. Scrolled back. Read the summary again.

Sounds feisty. A possibility.

He stared at the picture, willing his body to respond.

No spark.

He whittled the wish list down to three, browsed these again; discarded one, then another.

BachToBasie. Ganestown.

It's asking for trouble, but...

The tingle spread to his nerve extremities along with a new feeling. The sense of danger excited him.

Risk plus impulse equals high reward.

He calculated the gamble versus consequence ratio, and made his choice.

Let gardaí continue their stupid inquiries and news bulletins. Good luck trying to catch me. I'm superior. The next one has to be special. Unique. And after this fresh fodder, after March, I'll take a break. She's in my sights. Let the deception begin.

From: thejewellerycollector@datingvista.ie

Sent: Wed., 14:09
To: BachToBasie@datingvista.ie
Subject: Good Afternoon
Came across your profile, and I'd love to read more.
Hope to receive a mail soon. I promise I'll respond.
The Jewellery Collector.

EVENING
IRELAND WAS BURIED under an ocean of snow.

Hugh drove through a sea of ice and slush, measuring the journey westwards in heavy metal tracks. Near Streamstown, Ferdia shifted his bulk, yawned, dug an elbow into Hugh's ribs and pointed north. 'There's Ireland for ya. Hear the latest? The government wants to plant two thousand feckin' wind turbines across the Midlands. Stop here, I need smokes. Need anything?'

'No, thanks.' Hugh pulled into the rural shop and post office car park. His phone bleeped; a missed call from Ronan Lambe. He listened to the voice mail: 'Dude, any news yet? Bet you've got interviews lined up. Negatory at this end. I never noticed how often people ask, where are you working, or, what are you doing now? Unemployment is the *pits*. My future is empty in this poxy place. Have you heard of *anything?* If I don't get a break in a week, I'm outta G'town.'

Ferdia ambled back, a pack of antacid tablets and a carton of cigarettes in one ham-sized fist, two twelve-ounce Styrofoam cups in the other, and a large rectangular box tucked under his arm. He handed Hugh the drinks, flittered open the tablet carton, prised half the contents from the blister pack and chewed them like Smarties. He took a cup from Hugh and gulped coffee. 'Dammit, forgot sugar. Bought this yoke for Master David.' Ferdia showed the package to Hugh. 'I'll make a farmer out of him yet.'

At Drumraney, Hugh slowed and indicated right. They passed a school, rounded a sharp left-hand bend, and eased into Ciara's driveway. A mantle of snow framed the garden where six-year-old David was throwing slush at a snowman. He slipped, tumbled face down, rolled over, kicked both legs in the air and laughed. When he saw the car, he scrambled to his feet and ran towards the visitors, screaming with delight.

Ferdia hoisted David skywards. 'Master David, you'll soon be too heavy for me.' Mush fell from the boy's duffle coat.

'Uncle Ferdi, help me build a bigger snowman.'

'I only play with good boys.'

'I *am* a good boy. Grandad said I'm the bestest boy in the world.'

'Here, add this to your collection.'

David's blue eyes sparkled. 'Wow. John Deere. Thanks.'

Ferdia patted the boy's matted brown hair.

Ciara appeared at the gable end, drawn by the commotion. 'David, come here.' She pulled a grey wool jacket around her. 'You've destroyed Ferdia.'

'Sure, let him be. It's not often we get snow.'

'Hi, Hugh. Did you find your keys?'

'Hi, Ciara. What keys?'

'Eilish said you'd...David! Ferdia, you shouldn't bring presents every time you call. Thank Ferdia, David.'

'Did already.' David grabbed Ferdia's hand and yanked him towards the bungalow. Hugh and Ciara followed.

'Did you hear the news?' Ciara asked Hugh. 'A woman in Oak View Lane disappeared.'

'No. Who?'

'Roberta Lord.'

'Don't know her. Do you?'

'Only to see. But it *feels* like I know her. We've lots in common. Her son, Christopher, is David's age. They found the poor lad home alone night before last. Can't imagine anybody would abandon a kid on purpose. There *must* be an explanation.'

'Hope she's located soon,' Hugh said. 'Any word on the boy?'

'Unharmed, but his mental state?' Ciara shook her head. 'I've no idea how the little mite will cope if Roberta's not found soon.' She shuddered, pulled the jacket tighter. 'Imagine what's going through his mind. Why mammy isn't coming to…His father has organised a search party. I'm getting a group of us to help. Not sure what we can do, but at least it's better than idle talk.'

'Need me to take Master David?' Ferdia asked.

'Thanks, Ferdia, but we're sorted for a few hours.'

David tugged a wooden chest into the kitchen. The big man and the small boy sat shoulder to shoulder on the floor, surrounded by Lego and farm machinery.

'You'd wonder which of them is the biggest child,' Ciara said to Hugh. 'I suppose you're knee-deep in appraisals.'

'Nope. I'm jobless.'

'Since when?' Ciara glanced from Hugh to Ferdia. 'Eilish didn't mention—'

'Yesterday. We met Charlie earlier. He's taken me on until I get sorted. I'll begin the job search tonight. Can you do mocks with me when I get called for interviews?'

'Anytime. I'll contact HR colleagues and see if they've any management vacancies.'

'Thanks.'

Ciara spun a ring around her finger. 'How did Dad seem?'

'Okay. He's lost weight.'

'I've noticed. The business is causing massive stress. Was Malcolm there?'

'Around, but we didn't see him.'

Ferdia stretched for the biscuit tin and offered the contents to David.

'No, Ferdia. We haven't had dinner yet.'

'Sure, a biscuit won't do any harm.'

David's red cheeks dimpled, and he dipped in.

Ciara yawned. 'I'm too exhausted to argue.'

'Where did ye eat last night?' Hugh asked.

'We stayed here. Late night.' Ciara tossed her hair back. 'Global Engineering will survive without my presence for a day.'

Hugh nodded at a laptop on the counter. 'The work doesn't end though.' The screensaver displayed multiple coloured balls rebounding off the screen's border.

'Hmm. Paperwork. It's endless.'

Hugh stood. 'Redundant or not, I've paperwork to complete too.'

Ferdia grunted and heaved himself upright.

'One more game, Uncle Ferdi.'

'Gotta go, Master David.'

'*No.*' In frustration, David threw a toy.

The plastic horse hit a cupboard, bounced and struck the computer keyboard. The screensaver dissolved, revealing what Ciara was surfing.

'David! That's bold,' Ciara said. 'Say you're sorry.'

Hugh moved towards the door.

David stamped a foot. 'I'm NOT sorry.' His eyes welled.

Ferdia hoisted the child into the air. 'Sunday, I'll collect you, and we'll…' he whispered into David's ear.

David's features dissolved into a grin. Teary eyes twinkled. 'The Viking Splash tour? Really?'

'And the Zoo.'

'Promise?'

'Yep.'

'Cross your heart.'

'Cross my heart.'

They high-fived.

David and Ciara waved the men goodbye. Ferdia stuck an arm out the window and gave a thumbs-up.

Hugh thought it a shame Ferdia had no children; he'd be a cool dad. Twenty years earlier, he'd married Charlie's sister, but within six months, she'd died from a ruptured aortic aneurysm. Ferdia never remarried.

'Full of devilment,' Ferdia said. 'But he's a great lad.'

'That's for sure.'

'Needs a father figure though,' Ferdia added, 'but lucky to have a first-class mother. She'll meet the right person in time.'

'She will,' Hugh said and smiled to himself. It would embarrass Ciara if she realised he'd seen her access a dating site.

NIGHT

'YOU LOOK RED-CARPET-ready.'

Eilish was applying eye shadow and talking into a mobile perched on the kidney-shaped dressing table. She disconnected when Hugh spoke.

'I'm tired. Didn't sleep well.'

Hugh dropped his keys on the bed. 'Bet I know where you're off to.'

'What?' Eilish twisted and stabbed herself with the eyeliner pen.

'I talked to Ciara.'

Eilish rubbed her eye. 'You checking up on me?'

'Whoa.' Hugh held up a hand. 'Steady on. We called in to see David. Ciara told us about Roberta Lord. You're one of the search volunteers.'

'Yeah.' Eilish's mobile bleeped. Her thumb danced across the keypad, texting a reply.

'God, you read about disappearances, but when it's someone local...' Hugh shivered. 'Mmm, you smell nice.' He reached for a hug. 'New perfume?'

'Had it ages.' Eilish moved half a step back and put infinite space between them. She used a tissue to dab her lipstick, opened the built-in double wardrobe and surveyed its bloated contents, her fingernails tapping a sharp staccato on the door frame. 'So, did you meet Charlie?'

'Yeah. He's given me temporary work in Mullingar. But there may be a position in Ganestown soon. I'll polish up my CV tonight. How's your mum?'

Eilish zipped up a midnight blue gilet. 'She's got the sniffles after yesterday. It pelted snow in Galway.'

A spasm of guilt stabbed Hugh's heart. He hadn't spoken to his own mother since the weekend. 'City busy?'

'Jammers. Mum bought an outfit.' Eilish gestured at the jacket. 'I found this Rachel Zoe—'

'Seriously, we need to keep an eye on expenses 'til I get fixed up with a—'

'Give over, Hugh. It's a jacket. On sale.'

'You call it a jacket. I call it hundreds of euro.' Hugh waved at the wardrobe. 'I'd say you wear ten per cent of those, eighty per cent of the time, and you *still* buy—'

'Dear God.' Eilish rolled her eyes. 'Next, you'll tell me to cancel my hairdressers' appointment—'

'Something to consider,' Hugh muttered.

'Excuse me?' Eilish checked her profile in a mirror. 'Go on. I'm listening.'

'Listening and hearing what I've to say are two different things,' Hugh said. 'But now you've brought it up, could you go to the hairdresser *fortnightly* instead of—?'

'Women *require* regular wash and blow-dries.' Eilish faced Hugh, hands on hips. 'It boosts our self-esteem. *Plus*, I've got a standard to maintain in my job.'

'You're on holidays for the past—'

'Argh, for fu…' Eilish grabbed a coat and moved towards the landing. 'I can't take your practical logic, Hugh. I'm not the one who lost my job. I'll buy whatever I—'

'You think bags and bling. I worry about bills,' Hugh snapped. He stopped, took a breath, hating the tone in his voice, but couldn't stop himself. 'Look,' he said, 'I feel I'm being reasonable. We can't *afford* more debt.' He was talking to Eilish's back. 'Why the hell is everything I say lately turning into a dogfight? Jee-sus.'

Eilish clomped downstairs.

Hugh called after her. 'That's great. Run away. That's bloody great. I've enough shit to handle at the moment without…And speaking of practicalities, if you're gonna roam through gardens, change into something more sensible than suede Uggs—'

'Stop making everything about you,' Eilish shouted back. The front door slammed.

Hugh punched a pillow. It wasn't all Eilish's fault, but he didn't want to end up mired in unmanageable debt. Her attitude wasn't helpful. He'd bought the rundown house near the end of the recession, and over-borrowed to carry out renovations. Now, he wished he hadn't spent a fortune on a state-of-the-art marble, mahogany and steel kitchen they seldom used. Pure madness. He dialled his mother's landline.

'Hugh? Somebody's stolen money from my bank account,' Kathleen said.

'Doubtful.' Hugh was still seething. 'You've said that before.'

'Can you go over my bank statements? There's money missing.'

'I keep telling you, Ma, it's your electricity bills and insurance direct debits. Did you withdraw—?'

'I want to change banks.'

'I'll be there in ten minutes.'

'That doesn't suit. I'm doing night duty at the homeless shelter. Another helper is picking me up.'

'Tomorrow so.'

'Don't forget Peter's anniversary tomorrow.'

Hugh peeked at his father's portrait, smiling from its wall fixture. 'Why do you keep saying that too, Ma? It's not till July.'

'Yes, July. I still miss him.'

'Me too, Ma. Me too.'

MIDNIGHT

HUGH UPDATED his CV.

On the stroke of midnight, his mobile rang. 'Charlie's in hospital,' Ferdia said. 'He got beaten up—'

'What?'

'Yeah.'

'Where?'

'Dublin. A street off Parnell Square. Head split open. Ambulance took him to Beaumont, and gardaí found his car burned out on a back-road near the airport.'

'Jesus. Did he get mugged, or what?'

'Don't know. Yet.'

'Will he be okay?'

'Probably. He's sedated. I'm outside the hospital now. They won't let me feckin' in to him. I'll hang around and see what's happening.'

'Anything I can do to——?'

'Nah. What's your ETA at McGuire's tomorrow?'

'Around nine. Why?'

'Try to get there earlier. They might need an extra hand.'

'Sure. Wonder what Charlie was doing around Parnell Square.'

'That's what I intend to suss out.'

An hour later, Hugh's mobile rang again. He snatched it up, thinking it was Ferdia with an update.

'Hugh? It's Amy at the night shelter.' The voice jabbered. 'Your mother fell. We called the ambulance. They're taking her to Ganestown A&E. I'll go with——'

A surge of adrenalin pushed Hugh from the chair. 'I'll meet you there.'

4

THURSDAY 10 JANUARY

01:15 A.M.

'START. START.' The starter wouldn't crank.

Hugh switched off the heater, lights and radio, gritted his teeth and turned the ignition key again. The motor whirred but didn't engage the flywheel. He rammed the clutch and accelerator pedals into the footwell and made another attempt. The engine turned. A red wrench symbol glowed alongside the orange light on the dashboard. He put the heater on full blast, raced back into the house, got a saucepan of lukewarm tap water, splashed it on the ice-crusted windscreen, then sped into Ganestown, a seven minute drive.

The tepid water froze up. Arctic air pouring from heater vents gave him coin-sized spots to peer through. Snow streamers blew off the bonnet as he took shortcuts, sliding around backstreet corners, snatching precious moments, heart slamming against his ribcage. Thoughts of his mother hurt and in pain made him nauseous. He made the hospital car park in four minutes.

There's seldom a quiet spell in A&E. Ganestown's Accident and Emergency was in a state of organised chaos. Stressed staff struggled to cope with patients lying or sitting on the blockade of trolleys that lined both sides of a corridor. Family or friends accompanied some, whispering words of comfort. Most sufferers were alone. Hugh found his mother, and stared at her in shock.

Tall, thin, with short, permed grey hair, Kathleen Fallon had full lips and the strong jawline Hugh inherited. Hyperactive, cheery and in a constant flap that there weren't enough hours in the day, Kathleen had taken early retirement from her Matron's post, months before husband Peter passed away. Instead of visiting the many cities they'd planned, she filled each day volunteering at Saint Vincent DePaul's Ozanam House, or at the homeless shelter. Now, his tower of strength sat slumped in a wheelchair, ashen-faced, silent, hair dishevelled. Amy pressed an ice pack on Kathleen's eyebrow.

'It was'—Amy clicked her fingers—'just like that. She tripped. Hit her head against the side of a table. I hadn't a second to react.'

'You couldn't do anything, Amy.'

'A nurse said he'd get an admittance form. Haven't seen him since.'

'Okay.'

'I've to get back, Hugh. Sorry.'

'I'll call a taxi.'

'They wouldn't let me into the ambulance; I drove behind.'

'Thanks for staying—'

'God, it's the least…Keep us updated.'

'Sure.'

Hugh held the icepack against the mottled swelling. 'Ma? Are you in pain?'

Kathleen didn't answer.

He dialled Eilish's mobile. It diverted to voicemail and he left a message while watching a nurse assess and reassign critical and non-critical cases to various zones in the emergency department. He'd never witnessed his mother not in control. She was a master at pretending to experience a flutter of helplessness, and always had a cheery smile as she performed the administrative equivalent of the loaves and fishes, stretching inadequate charity funds to breaking point. For years, their home doubled as a mini-dispensary; bandages, plasters, kisses and soothing words got supplied to children who'd hurt themselves. If she noticed bullying or victimisation, there was no hesitation in getting involved. She'd bristle like an irritable hedgehog and ensure everybody made up before moving on, all smiles again. Love and justice got doled out in equal measures.

Kathleen gripped Hugh's arm. 'Peter tried to kill me.'

'You had a fall, Ma. That's all. A doctor will check—'

'Peter pushed me downstairs.'

'Shhh. You tripped in the hostel. We'll—'

'Healthcare details?' A harried nurse materialised, hands on hips, a folder clutched in her left hand. She stooped and studied Kathleen's face. The top half of a dog-eared internal medical handbook protruded from a white coat pocket.

'Pardon? Um, no. Didn't think of it,' Hugh said.

'Has this lady been a patient before?'

'Not that I know of.'

'Have you filled in the admittance form?'

'Not yet.'

'What's your relationship with—?'

'I'm her son.'

The nurse opened the file and fired off more questions: 'Name and address. How did your mother fall? Were you present when it happened?'

Hugh sensed the nurse held him responsible. 'Kathleen Fallon. No, I wasn't there when—'

'Kathleen Fallon?' The nurse straightened and looked at him. 'Hugh?'

'Yes?'

'You don't remember me.'

Hugh's eyes searched for the nurse's name badge. 'I don't...'

'Tsk, tsk. Guess I'm getting old. I see you've still got those baby brown eyes every girl in school wanted. It's Ruth Lamero.'

'Ruth Lamero? Now I recognise your face.'

'At two o'clock in the morning? I don't think so.'

'Your accent put me astray.'

'Must've picked up a twang on my travels. I've worked abroad for a few years.'

'God, it's been, what? Ten, twelve years? I didn't know you'd come back.'

'Since November.' Ruth shut the file with an elasticated snap. 'Right. We'll sort out the details later. Let's get Mrs Fallon examined and admitted. If you wait in the canteen, I'll find you.'

'Thanks, Ruth. Ma's okay, isn't she?'

'Don't worry, she'll get the best care. I've only been here a few months, but staff speak with affection about Matron Fallon. Nursed most of them at one stage or another.' Ruth took the ice pack from Hugh. 'Go get a coffee. Let us do our job.'

Hugh sipped lukewarm coffee and skimmed a newspaper supplement, but couldn't absorb any details.

Ruth found him after an hour that felt like a year. 'Kathleen's calm now, but confused after the fall. She's had an x-ray. A doctor stitched the wound, and she's comfortable. On her way to St Joseph's ward. Room 24.'

'That's a relief, Ruth. I appreciate your help.' Hugh noticed Ruth's green eyes still sparkled and shone like wet grass. She looked even more attractive now with her long-layered brunette hair pulled into a ponytail, and the dusky beauty inherited from Italian ancestors ensured a permanent suntan complexion.

'You haven't changed,' Hugh said. 'Still look terrific.'

'Hmm. Older and wiser. You settled here?'

'Yep, I've kept Ganestown as my base.'

Ruth's pager bleeped.

'You're busy.' Hugh stood.

'Should've left ages ago, but twelve-hour shifts, with no overtime, get stretched to fourteen, even sixteen. Depends on staffing. So, did you become a detective?'

'A detective? No.'

'Priest?'

'God, no. Why?'

'Oh, back in the day we'd write in our diaries what jobs we wanted, who we'd marry, you know, girly stuff, and we'd figure out the guy most likely to become...whatever. We reckoned you'd be a detective or a priest. You were a good listener.'

'I still want to hear both sides of an argument before making a decision,' Hugh said. 'That taught me I'd a flair for dealing with and managing people.'

'I bet you're good at it too. Still hang out with the school gang?'

'Not so much. Recession pushed most of them—'

The pager summoned Ruth again. She checked the flashing number. 'Gotta go, Hugh. Chances are I'll bump into you during the week.'

'Great, but I hope Ma gets discharged later, and—'

'Kathleen is being kept in for observation until Doctor Abbott decides.'

'When will that be?'

'Does his rounds before lunch, but if he's called away to an emergency...'

'I've to go to Mullingar in a few hours. If I hang around—'

'No point waiting. Go home and rest. By lunchtime, they'll have blood test results.'

'Okay. What room did you—?'

'24. Can you bring in some of Kathleen's clothes? Oh, and the health insurance details. No rush. Leave them at the nurse station on the ward.'

MORNING

HUGH TEXTED EILISH another update.

He found the accordion file containing medical records, and then sat in his mother's armchair. He dozed for a few hours and woke with a crick in his neck. After a shower, he finger-combed his hair, bundled a variety of his mother's clothes and toiletries into a suitcase, pocketed the insurance details and grabbed a Starbucks on his way to McGuire's.

Jana Trofimiack chewed a thumbnail and dialled a number once more.

'Cóż?'

At last.

'Tomasz, I *must* return the McKelvey.'

'I can't back out of this deal. Co jest problem?'

'Mrs Ridgeway missed the painting already. I did everything you asked. It's your fault the replacement wasn't prepared. You and Günther…If I'm caught for this, I'll—'

'That a threat, Jana?'

'Now she's bringing in konsultanci.' Jana's voice rose. 'I've heard the old kurwa might phone policja. I won't take the rap. I'll—'

'You'll keep your mouth shut if you know what's good for you. You and your son.'

'Don't you *dare* threaten Lech. He's got nothing to do with…It's Günther you should be threatening. You *know* his work isn't autentyezny. I've *told* you he isn't capturing the detail. You—'

'Shut up Jana.'

'—and Günther are causing this shit mess—'

'Shut up.'

'Günther's forever behind schedule,' Jana babbled. 'Had the replacement been ready last week like you promised, I'd have switched it, even though I know if the old woman puts it up for auction, it'll get spotted as a fake. A *child* could see—'

'I said, shut. The fuck. Up.'

Jana shut up.

'Let me think.' The man's wheeze sounded like static hiss. 'I got your voicemails yesterday. Günther's putting the finishing touches to the replacement. It'll be ready in a few days—'

'A few—?'

'It's up to you to place it in the house. Put it under a bed, or on top of a wardrobe—'

'I *have* to get it sooner. My boss is on the case. I've told you what he's like. He won't let up. And the konsultanci? I don't *have* a few days. You *must* get me the painting today.'

'I'll ask, but tell me my business, Jana. You want it autentyezny. You want it today. You want, you want. You want everything.'

Jana took a deep breath. 'Tomasz, I'm begging you. Send me the real McKelvey and I'll put it back.'

'You don't listen, Jana. It's already sold. Günther will do this one right.'

'Please Tomasz. Mrs Ridgeway—'

'Won't know the difference. You'll bury it, and then, like magic, find it.'

'Well, the house is full of—'

'Günther knows it's a rush job. The price comes out of your end. Where's the Yeats you promised? Günther's already got that replacement ready.'

'I didn't get a chance—'

'Get it. I've a client lined up. Cash deal. Rozumiesz?'

'Tak.'

'Do widzenia. I'll be in touch.'

Jana mopped her forehead. This scam is out of control, she thought. *How can I get away from these people? Play dumb until Günther's reproduction gets me out of trouble, but after that? Perhaps the old suka will die before she puts the painting up for auction, or I'm back in Polska.*

MCGUIRE'S PREMISES was still abandoned at half-eight.

A fresh blanket of snow glistened in the cold sunshine. A Land Cruiser skidded into the parking area, but with no sign of activity, the driver circled and exited. Next, a rigid-bodied truck turned in, gearbox grinding as cogs meshed. It laboured towards the rear of the building. Hugh heard the muffled whump of a bass beat before the next vehicle appeared; an Audi A5 coupé. The high-end sound system pounded out hard rock. The music faded and a man hopped out.

Malcolm McGuire wore khaki jeans and a lavender shirt. Early twenties, standard build, brown hair and a wan, delicate face, he shrugged into a jacket, gave an apologetic hand wave to Hugh's car, and inserted a key into a metal box on the side of the wall. Roller shutters wrapped up underneath an awning. Fluorescents flickered, soaking the interior in silver light. McGuire's was open for business.

The double entrance doors swished, and Hugh walked in. Malcolm was examining a display of electric heaters.

'Malcolm? Haven't seen you for a while.'

'Oh, hi, Hugh. Dad told me you were replacing Jozef. Apologies for the delay.' They shook hands.

'How's Charlie?' Hugh asked. 'I got a call last night—'

'Ferdia, I bet. They wouldn't let him into ICU, and he kicked up hassle.'

'That's Ferdia.'

'Dad was kept in a drug-induced coma overnight. To let the brain settle. His face...' Malcolm looked away. 'All those tubes. When you see hospital scenes in films, you're detached from the pain, but up close, watching your father reliant on a machine to breathe...'

'Has he said what happened?'

'Mugged.'

More employees arrived and piped music carried through the store's hidden speakers.

'He won't be back for a while,' Malcolm added.

'You're in charge so,' Hugh said. 'I'm supposed to meet Brendan.'

'I'll take you.'

They walked half the length of the shop floor in silence.

'Didn't know you're a metal head,' Hugh said. 'Was that Avenged Sevenfold or Alter Bridge you were listening—?'

'Alter Bridge. Cry of Achilles.' Malcolm led Hugh to a storage area door.

'I'm a Myles Kennedy fan too,' Hugh said.

'Yeah?' Hugh felt Malcolm's eyes study him.

A rotund red-faced man, wearing a hard hat, came around a central bay unit, a batch of printouts under an arm.

'Brendan? Hugh Fallon.'

'Oh, right. Van's loaded. Delivery for the Ganestown branch.' Brendan eyeballed Hugh's frame. 'Jozef's boiler suit should fit. I'll find you a Hi-Vis jacket.' He handed Hugh a sheet of dockets. 'Get somebody in the back store to sign these.'

'Okay. I'll grab a suitcase from my car. Have to take it into my mother in Ganestown hospital.'

'Nothing serious, I hope.'

'She fell. They're doing tests. Should be out later today or tomorrow.'

'Well, no panic back. And don't push the Hiace too hard. The engine...she's a bit feeble.'

THE ART DEALER wanted to check if his website profile had lured in BachtoBasie, but wouldn't use his own laptop in case it ever got traced. He'd wait, savouring the expectation until he got to an internet café or a hotel. Switching between news apps, he was disappointed Roberta Lord's disappearance hadn't attracted national media coverage. He rejected the tie Madeline had left out, and picked another. She'd returned to Paris. Just the way he liked it.

When I take control of the company, there'll be significant changes. Changes that don't include the Hattinger clan.

He packed an overnight case for his Belfast trip, and sat into his car, letting the heater clear the rim of frost from around the windows.

His mobile buzzed.

The secretary had forwarded Ambrose's article from Country Life and Garden, and he read through Amanda Curran's treacly prose:

When Oliver Cromwell reached Ireland in 1649, Ainsley Hattinger was a Lieutenant Colonel in the invading army...

Jesus.

As a reward for valour in battle during the Siege of Drogheda, Cromwell granted him a swathe of land in the Shannon Basin that stretched from Lough Owel to the Shannon harbour in County Offaly. Hattinger built a big house outside Kilbeggan and became landlord to seventy thousand confiscated acres of arable land, forcing farmers to become peasants and pay rent to work their own plots. Agitators got evicted or killed...

Read up on your history, Miss Curran. They got driven like cattle to the river Shannon and given two choices: Hell or Connacht. And Ambrose thinks his ancestor standing shoulder to shoulder with Cromwell will win friends and influence people?

For two centuries, the Hattinger reign prospered...

While their tenants starved.

...and in the 1890s William Hattinger and his four sons began manufacturing bespoke furniture from a site in Tullamore...

Only because after the famine Hattinger evicted the tenants who couldn't pay rent, Miss Curran, which caused the oppressed to band together and form a political party that aimed to reduce landlords' power and allow leaseholders to reclaim their properties. When the Irish Land Commission got established, it dismantled the Hattinger estate and reduced it to a hundred acres. Why isn't this included? Hmm? That's why William began the furniture business, to ensure retention of the 'big house,' his physical symbol of prestige.

The art dealer scrolled past three more paragraphs.

By 1900, Hattinger's furniture gained a reputation among the gentry for top quality products. Demand multiplied. When he'd died in 1916, the company's client list read like a Who's Who of Ireland's rich and famous...

Until the rot set in during the 1980s because of internal squabbles. Ambrose's grandfather and father grew fat on the fruits of their ancestors' labour and became complacent. Sales dwindled. Decreased profits intensified infighting. With no consensus on a practical way forward, the board of directors dithered, disagreed and fell out. The minority voices calling for change and investment in external expertise got overruled by the stubborn majority who upheld a laissez-faire policy. For your information, Miss Curran, laissez-faire means minimum interference. Something you should take on board.

By luck, the company's woes turned after Madeline Hattinger married "a commoner…"

Luck? Me? A commoner? I knew it. Bitch wouldn't profile me because I don't have "pedigree."

The art dealer dialled his secretary. 'Cancel Amanda Curran's piece. It won't go to print. Not now. Not ever.'

MID-MORNING

HUGH'S HIACE CHUGGED to Ganestown.

The van's body rattled. Its steering was loose, the suspension worn, and it dipped on its axles when he applied the brakes, which meant the shock absorbers had passed their sell-by date. The odometer read 229,000 kilometres, and neither the heater nor radio worked, but the engine sounded good. He rang Ferdia, held the mobile to his ear and hoped no traffic cops were prowling. 'Did you see Charlie?'

'Won't let me in for fear I'd give him MRSA. If he didn't pick it up stretched out near Parnell Square, there's a fair chance he won't get it off me. They've taken him off the ventilator, so I'll shoot in later. I'm due in a meeting now. Some Health and Safety lark.'

'And I'm on my way to Ganestown with two pallets of timber, cement and copper piping.'

'Good man. Wanna visit Chas tonight?'

'Depends. Ma's in hospital—'

'Aww, Jaysus. Never rains, eh? What happened to Kathleen?'

'Nothing serious. She slipped in the hospice. I'm meeting the doctor around lunchtime. If she's discharged, I won't be able to go.'

'Text me if you can make it, and I'll pick you up at Ganestown Hotel around eight. Give Kathleen my regards.'

Ganestown kept its small-town ambience because it had consistently been by-passed and passed over for structural government funds. The new motorway, decreed as a lifeline, was relegating the town to an exit sign, and the lingering effects of the recent recession, coupled with the epidemic of emigration, threatened to turn Ganestown into a ghost town—something legions of plunderers over centuries couldn't achieve. Main Street was an embarrassment of weathered shop fronts awaiting commercial revival, and patchy Wi-Fi access prevented tourists from lingering. Hugh drove by a derelict factory, its concrete carcass a constant reminder of what once was, the adjoining car park now used by teenagers as a tyre-shredding doughnut practice arena.

The lead up to Christmas had generated a frenzy of activity. Council works that kicked off years earlier, then stalled, were being revived—a ploy to sway floating voters in the upcoming local and European Parliament elections. Side streets were being dug up, repaved and pedestrianised. Enterprise development officers hoped that cable upgrades and a new sewage system would incentivise entrepreneurs to pick Ganestown as a business base, increase consumer confidence and kick-start a renewed lease of life for the area. There was still a way to go before the town caught up with its more politically astute neighbours, but politicians kept repeating the mantra that rural Ireland had weathered recession and was 'open for business'. Time would tell.

In Rossbeg Industrial estate, McGuire's Hardware squatted amid a slew of small businesses. A bookie's office and a petrol station guarded the estate entrance. A wine distributor had taken possession of a pool hall, and a TV satellite company had moved into a unit previously leased to an artisan baker.

Hugh followed the delivery signs and parked alongside a van wrapped in a block of frozen snow up to the wheelbase. The back store full-length shutters were closed. He stamped his feet to aid circulation and pulled open a 'Staff Only' door, cut from the mainframe. A hut constructed from breeze blocks sat in one corner of the warehouse. Inside, a bleached blonde reclined in a high-backed swivel chair and chatted on a landline. She chewed gum, looped strands of hair around a Bic biro, studied Hugh's approach and continued her conversation. Beside her, a portable three-bar electric heater strained to counteract the minus temperature.

The blonde put the receiver to her bosom, slid open a glass window. 'Can I help?' The smile was as fake as her eyelashes, and the tone suggested she hoped she wouldn't have to.

'Stock delivery. Anybody here to unload?'

The blonde spoke into a tannoy, the words indecipherable. An engine growled, and a propane Hyster forklift swerved into the aisle. The machine rattled along the passageway. Forks clanged as the driver fast-tracked over a bump. A teenager hopped off and pressed a switch on the wall. The roller shutter rumbled and wound around itself. The lad caught Hugh's eye and jerked his head at the Hiace. 'That one?'

Hugh nodded and turned to the woman. 'Can you sign these dockets?'

'Milo'll do it. Milo Brady.'

'Is he here?'

'I saw him outside a minute ago.'

'Can you buzz him?'

'Tsk. Wait a sec, Sal.' The blonde stabbed the tannoy button again with a blood-red fingernail. 'Milo. Office.'

'Thanks,' Hugh said. 'Do I need to sign in?'

The blonde flapped an arm like a farmer shooing sheep. 'Chill. He'll be back.' She swiped the window shut.

Hugh strolled around to ward off the cold, wandered back towards the breeze block hut and watched the teen unload the van. A shower of hail pelted the Hyster. He started the circuit again, this time taking a wider circumference. Near a door leading into the shop, he spotted a figure leaning against a wall, checking stock sheets.

The small man held a biro between his teeth and frowned at a sheet of paper littered with red marks. Head tilted, his right index finger explored the inside of his left nostril. Pulling the digit out, the man inspected his catch and pitched the prize over his shoulder.

Hugh walked over. 'Milo?'

'Yeah?'

The reek of cheap cologne assailed Hugh's senses. Scrawny, wearing Mr Mole glasses, Milo had sad, smoky midnight blue eyes, a receding hairline which would leave him bald within a few years, an Irish winter pallor and hollow cheeks that reminded Hugh of Munch's tortured figure in *The Scream*. Age around thirty, Hugh reckoned. A sprinkle of snow covered Milo's jacket, and the brown shoes, slick with melted slush, looked like a dog had chewed them.

'Hugh Fallon.' Hugh held both hands behind his back.

'What's your pitch?' Milo's adenoidal voice resembled a lamb's bleat.

'No pitch.' Hugh pulled out the dockets. 'Delivery from Mullingar.'

Milo clicked his fingers.

Hugh dropped the invoices into Milo's outstretched palm. 'Today's my first day.'

Milo pinched his lower lip. 'Where's the stuff?'

'Over here,' Hugh pointed.

Milo pushed away from the wall.

'How's business?' Hugh asked for something to say.

Milo thumbed through the sheets, checked them against the delivery and scribbled his initials. 'It's shite. But turns out *I'm* doin' okay. He tore off the counterfoils. 'Guess who gets the manager's job that's coming up in a few weeks? You're lookin' at him. Can't wait to get into a nice warm office. Big change from freezing me balls off out here. Gimme your number. Might want more shit delivered.'

Hugh wrote his mobile on a slip of paper and swapped it for the dockets. 'Well, thanks for that. I'll get out of your way.'

Milo grunted.

Some manager, Hugh thought. What an attitude.

The Hiace skidded as he swung the van around. He pressed the wiper switch, and aluminium screeched across the windscreen. The rubber had worn away, the blades useless against frozen snow. Near the main entrance, he spotted Sharona Waters crouching beside her Renault Clio. He parked, and walked over. 'Problem?'

'All done.' Sharona loosened the scissor jack and straightened. 'I only came in for piping to fix a leak, and I get punctured. That's three punctures in two months; twice here, and once at home. I'm jinxed.' She pushed the wrench onto a lug bolt and stood on the handle to tighten the nut.

Hugh lifted the punctured tyre into the boot, pointed out a gash beside the valve. 'Something sharp pierced it. Doesn't look repairable.'

'Great. More expense. Need that like a hole in the head.'

'Want a hand fixing the leak?'

'It's a small job, Hugh. I'll solder on this new bit.' Sharona threw the jack and wrench into the boot. 'Not even worth calling the landlord. Thanks anyway. Oh, will you tell

Ferdia not to arrange any meetings about that premises 'til next week. I'm away tomorrow for a few days.'

'Will do. Enjoy your break.'

'Not a break. It's an art gig in Belfast. A friend of Charlie's needs help.'

'Safe driving. Get a new spare before you head off.'

'Yeah. Are you driving that van?'

'My new company vehicle. I'm redundant—'

'No way.'

'Afraid so. Charlie's given me a...I suppose Malcolm told you 'bout Charlie.'

'Malcolm's told me nothing. We're not together anymore.'

'Aww, God, I'm sorry to hear that.'

'I'm fine with it. What happened to Charlie?'

'He got mugged—'

'What? When?'

'Last night. He was in Dublin, and...'

Milo Brady's eyes tightened, a hunter squinting down the barrel of a gun, gauging distance. What were they talking about? He polished his glasses, replaced them, saved Hugh Fallon's number into his contacts, lit a cigarette and glanced towards them again. 'Keep off my turf, asshole. Your wheels aren't immune to a Stanley knife either.'

AFTERNOON

EILISH WAITED UNTIL lunchtime to contact Ciara. 'Can we talk?'

'What's up?' Ciara asked. 'You didn't show to help search for Roberta Lord. You okay?'

'I'm in an absolute mess. Can we meet?'

'I'm swamped preparing appraisals. Tonight?'

'I *must* talk to you. Now. Meet me in the car park. Ten minutes.'

'Christ, Eilish. Phone me when you arrive. I'm not freezing my ass off out there. Your ten minutes means an hour.'

Eilish redialled Ciara when she had the Global Environmental Engineering Group European headquarters in sight. Ciara crossed the car park, jumped into the Passat and blew into her palms. 'Jesus, it's bitter. Uh-oh. What's the matter?'

Eilish took a breath. 'Jill's revelation? I'm the other woman.'

Ciara stayed silent.

Eilish exhaled. 'Well, say something.'

'Keep talking.'

'God, I want to die. Richard and I…We…clicked.'

'Hmm. I wondered why you disappeared the other night. Hugh never loses keys.'

'No. Sorry. I wanted to tell you, but couldn't find the words. You wouldn't approve, and—'

'Jesus, Eilish. I won't condemn or condone you. Okay, maybe condemn you a little. Let me see, how can I put this? What in *hell* are you doing?'

Eilish swallowed. 'If you were a stranger, it'd be…I know this sounds crazy. I'm friends with Richard and Jill for years. I teach their kids for Christ's sake.'

'How long's it been going on? When did—?'

'September. I was in Ganestown, met Richard on the street, and he asked if I wanted coffee. We chatted about kids, holidays, his haulage business, you know, the usual stuff. He leaned into me and said, "I can't resist you anymore." Anymore? Jesus, I swear I hadn't noticed he'd resisted me in the first place. I laughed it off, and he repeated it, dead serious. The Irish part of my brain popped up to say, don't be an eejit, he's double your age, for God's sake.'

'And a trice married outrageous skirt-chaser,' Ciara added.

'He's not—'

'Ah, give over. Richard never misses an opportunity to brush against me, squeeze my ass or look down my top.'

'That's his way. He's—'

'He's a lech. How'd you get sucked into his bullshit anyway?'

'It was harmless fun. I admit I was willing to let him…remove a few bricks from my defence wall, but I didn't expect him to blast them all away in one fell swoop.'

'So, what I'm hearing is, one flirtation led to another.'

'Yes.'

'What's the attraction?'

'We shared conversations I should have had with Hugh.' Eilish pulled out a tissue. 'You've *got* to believe me. I didn't *ask* for this. I—'

'Well, you *did*. You *said* you were willing—'

'I *allowed* him into my safe zone, and he pushed past my barricades before I realised we'd reached a point beyond friendship. It. Just. Happened.'

'Does Hugh suspect?'

'No. God no. Hugh's…I love him to bits—'

'Funny way of showing it.'

'We…Richard is…We're compatible on so many other levels. He's fed up with Jill dragging him to charity events, putting up a front for the neighbours. It's tearing him—'

'Has he spoken to Jill about this?'

'They don't communicate any more. Well, not about anything important, anyways.'

'Unlike you and him.'

'Yes. No. I mean, I can imagine how that appears, but honest, I, he's…What I'm saying is, I *thought* he was…it *felt* we were perfect for each other.'

'You said the same 'bout Hugh, remember?'

Eilish sniffed and wiped her nose. 'I didn't *consider* consequences down the line. I assumed…We'd such a…*connection*, an affinity. We *never* had a "where-is-this-going?" conversation. I'd no idea he'd planned to tell Jill he'd met somebody else. What'll I do?'

'What do you *want* to do?'

'I don't…I want to live my life for me.'

'Oh, here we go. God almighty, Eilish.'

'I've changed. It's affected…' Eilish leaked tears again, and she wiped them away. 'I'm cranky as hell. And Hugh suspects something's up. It's a struggle to avoid him. I pick rows when he's home. It's rotten, stuck in this mess. Jesus, our friends use me as an agony aunt for their issues.' Tears trickled. 'I'm the rock of sense, the holier-than-thou person who dishes out advice like: "if you're concerned about your relationship, you'd walk away," or, "women who get into those situations—" '

'That's rubbish—'

'It's true. And here I am, slap bang in the middle of an affair.' Eilish twisted the tissue into sodden pulp. 'And the worst…You know what's worse? The way I feel. It hurts. Jesus. Why can't I manage my own fucking life? It's *never* like this in films.'

Ciara pulled more paper hankies from a jacket pocket and handed them over. 'You're mature enough to separate life from fiction. What can I say? You think it's fine to demolish a friend's marriage? Or are you on a mission to sabotage your own relationship? Christ, Eilish, I'd love to shake sense…How many lives will you wreck before—?'

'Right now, Ciara, I don't need a lecture. You know what?'

'What.'

'Never mind. This was a mistake. I shouldn't have bothered to—'

'Forget yourself for a minute.' Ciara counted on her fingers. 'There's Hugh plus Jill and two kids in the immediate circle. Lives ruined. Families destroyed. And why drag me into this? What do you expect *me* to do? Give you a pardon? If you want absolution, try the confessional box. I can't help. You've made your own choices.'

They stared out opposite windows. Eilish sniffled in the silence.

'What's your plan?' Ciara asked. 'You can't unscramble the egg.'

'I've told Richard we're finished.'

'When?'

'What?'

'When did you tell him?'

'Jill…when I saw the hurt we'd…I'd—'

'When. Did. You. Tell. Him?'

'Tuesday. Tuesday night. After I left your house. And I…I informed him face-to-face last night—'

'Informed? Face-to-face? You…*met* him?'

'He phoned. Asked if we could meet, and—'

'Argh, for…sweet baby Jesus.'

'See? I *knew* you'd be—'

'I'd be what?'

'Judgemental.'

'God*dammit*.' Ciara slapped the dashboard with her palm. 'I thought you were *sick* when you were a no show at last night's search. Instead you…Jesus *Christ*, Eilish.'

Eilish snivelled. Words wedged in her throat. 'I was so…caught up, trapped in my own emotions, I didn't consider Jill. What if my name comes out? How—?'

'Did you ask why he picked now to tell Jill?'

'Yes.'

'And?'

'He wants us to be together, and he doesn't care if—'

'Is that your wish?'

'No. God, no. How'll I face Jill? We'll meet at school.' Eilish clutched Ciara's arm. 'How can…? Will you—?'

Ciara held up a hand. 'Let me stop you right there. Whatever you want from me, the answer's no.'

'If the school board finds out, will they ask me to resign?'

'I hope as a society we've moved on from—'

'And the parents. What will they say? They'll see me as a bad example.'

'Hmm. That's a possibility.' Ciara shrugged. 'You know Ganestown runs on gossip.'

'Shit. Should I tell Hugh? It'll break his heart. What'll I say? How do I say it?'

'One issue at a time, Eilish.'

'Hugh's redundant—'

'He'll get another job.'

'Will he? It's made me…I'm not sure what I want anymore.' Eilish condensed tissue paper into corrugated folds. 'Life's a rinse and repeat cycle of eat, sleep, laundry, rubbish bins, bills…and now we've to tighten our belts? I get it; redundancy equals cutbacks. But I didn't sign up for not being able to afford *basic* items—'

'Christ, Eilish.'

'I expected us to maintain a…a certain standard.'

'Maintain? Or be maintained?'

'Both.'

'You're selfish.'

'I seldom see him. If he'd given me more attention, made time for us, this—'

'Oh, please,' Ciara said. 'Hugh's busted his ass to keep you in the style you've become accustomed to. You're spoilt. You've always been spoilt. Stop laying guilt on Hugh. At times, I can't for the *life* of me fathom how he puts up with you. Learn to take responsibility for your own actions.'

'Hey, whose side are you on here?'

'What? Side? I'm not taking sides.'

'Yes, you are. I can hear it in your voice.'

'I'm neutral, Eilish. I like Hugh. Jill's *my* friend too, and I can read you like a book. Sounds like you want to offload your guilt, without doing the penance. Forget it. My advice? Focus on your relationship. Don't tell Hugh or anybody else about Richard. "The truth will set you free" crap only works in romance novels. Why hurt the person you love? You *have* planned to stay with Hugh?'

'I—'

'Haven't you?'

'Yes.'

'Splendid. If you bump into Jill, pray Richard hasn't mentioned your name, or else prepare for a slap across the face. And get yourself checked out, health-wise. Full medical screening. Oh, and if you think counselling will help, go. Alone.'

'Jesus. I don't know if I can take your practical advice right now—'

'You asked for it,' Ciara said. 'You don't have to take it. Look, I've to get back in here. After work, I'm off to Dublin. Dad got mugged last night.'

'God, that's dreadful. But what'll I *do*, Ciara? I can't function.'

'Forget Richard, and I don't ever, *ever* want Hugh or Jill to think I've taken your side in this tangle.'

Eilish drove home. She stopped at the gateway and peered out like a thief, scrutinising the area for signs of Hugh. Reassured, she hurried into the house and crammed clothes into a suitcase. Muddied thoughts swamped her brain. She needed time to think.

A CONFERENCE CALL overrun left the art dealer with a tight timeframe to catch the four p.m. flight to Belfast, but before leaving Tullamore, he visited the internet café and logged onto DatingVista.

Yes. Women can't resist jewellery.

From: BachToBasie@datingvista.ie
Sent: Thurs., 07:11
To: thejewellerycollector@datingvista.ie
Subject: Me
Hi,
Good morning, and thanks for the mail. Can I say, I'm a novice at online dating, and unsure what to write? Let's see; I consider myself a kind, generous person. I'm loyal, dedicated, and seeking somebody who's prepared to share and experience every facet of life, particularly a person who's NOT afraid to commit.
No. I've no plans to walk down the aisle yet! (Lol) I've a good sense of humour—another quality I admire in a man. Hey, we can't be serious ALL the time, right? I enjoy music (all kinds), reading (American classics) and keeping active. (I've joined a gym – New Year's resolution). I'm not much of a drinker, and I don't smoke. I love romance and affection. Staying in, cuddled up on the couch, can be as much fun as going out.
I live outside Ganestown, with my son, who's my world. So, if we're on the same wavelength, and I haven't put you to sleep, keep in touch. Phew, that wasn't so bad!

What plans have you for the rest of the week? I
guess I'll be building (more) snowmen!
I look forward to hearing from you.
BachtoBasie

The art dealer re-read the mail and deliberated how best
to respond.

Construct comparable sentences. Use her own words back.

He looked at his watch and logged out. The timing
didn't matter. Later tonight would suffice.

*Lol? We'll see who'll be laughing when we meet. Like both Bach
and Count Basie, you're already dead.*

A COMBINATION OF traffic snarl-ups and a torrential
squall of sleet conspired to delay Hugh getting to the
hospital. A lorry attempted to turn into the oncoming
traffic flow. Drivers stared ahead, loathe to give way. Hugh
mounted a footpath and steered around the bottleneck. A
hundred metres further, he ground to a halt again. Red and
blue lights flashed in his rear-view mirror. He checked the
time. Half-two.

The ambulance sped by.

Hugh took a risk and slotted the van in behind. When it
turned off into the hospital main entrance, he swerved by,
whizzed into the underground car park, dumped the Hiace
in the first free space he found and raced upstairs to St
Joseph's ward. He handed the health insurance card to a
nurse writing up a report at the nurse station. 'Have I
missed the consultant?'

The nurse shook her head. 'Got delayed. Could be…I
don't know.'

Hugh crammed the suitcase into the small built-in unit,
and sat with his mother and watched hailstones skiing down
the windowpane. Water cascaded from a drainpipe that had

fractured at a connection outside the window. Kathleen watched him. 'You're okay, Ma. The blood test results will be back soon. I'll have you home later, tomorrow at the latest. Rest now.'

Kathleen closed her eyes.

At three p.m., a ward sister bustled in; the advance scout on a reconnaissance mission. Behind her, a big man with a bay-window belly strode into the ward. Doctor Abbott had a craggy face and bushy eyebrows that looked like an eagles' eyrie clinging to a cliff face. He mumbled a curt greeting, positioned glasses on the end of his nose, and glanced through a file clipped to a railing at the foot of the bed.

Hugh took the hint. 'I'll have a word afterwards, doctor.'

Doctor Abbott murmured to his patient.

Hugh waited in the corridor. The nurse reappeared and rushed into the next patient's room, intent on avoiding the doctor's ire by ensuring it met his standards.

When the doctor's bulk darkened the doorway, Hugh stepped into his path. 'Is my mother allowed home today?'

'Not today.' Abbott edged past.

'Is there a problem?' Hugh blocked his path. 'Did she suffer an eye injury?'

'The eye will heal.'

'So, what's—?'

'I've requested a neurologist to carry out tests on Mrs Fallon.'

'Why? Did the x-ray—?'

'I'm querying early stage dementia. I want your mother to undergo further tests.'

'Why? Because Ma misplaces keys and household things from time to time? Happens to me—'

'Until I get my colleague's evaluation, my patient stays put.' The doctor glared over the rim of his spectacles. 'It may be the onset of Alzheimer's.'

'Alz…That's…Old people get that. Ma isn't sixty yet.'

Doctor Abbott removed his glasses, breathed on the lens and polished them with his tie. 'Alzheimer's can occur from forty onwards, and it's a short life sentence. Leads to death between four and eight years, but it can advance quicker. Or slower. There's no cure.'

'No cure?' Hugh blinked and stared.

The doctor exhaled and moderated his tone. 'The neurologist will assess your mother. Talk to me during the week.' He vanished, leaving Hugh slumped against the wall.

JANA TROFIMIACK SNATCHED at the phone. 'Có?'

'It's me.'

'Tomasz? I'm stressed—'

'Fuck your stress. The McKelvey's finished.'

'It couldn't be…Is it—?'

'Jezus, Jana. You wanted it today. Then, when I move mountains to get it for you—'

'But—'

'You want it or not?'

'Yes. Kiedy?'

'Tonight. Or tomorrow morning.'

Jana breathed a sigh. 'Dobry. What time?'

'Jezus Chrystus, how do I know? Answer when he rings and take the replacement to the woman's house. He'll also give you the Yeats copy. Make the switch. I need that Yeats painting soon. Na razie.'

EVENING

THE ART DEALER ditched his BMW in Midland Airport's short-term car park and sprinted to the terminal. The automated check-in machine printed out a boarding pass, and he snaked through the customs queue. In the departure lounge, he bought a newspaper, boarded the plane, buckled up and opened the paper. A passport-size photo of Roberta Lord was on page three:

Lead in Missing Persons Case?

Roberta Lord has been missing for three days. The twenty-nine-year-old disappeared last Monday after returning home to Oak View Lane, Ganestown, with her son Christopher (6), at approx. 5:30 p.m. Christopher's father, Ruben Gardner, discovered the boy alone three hours later.

"There's no way Roberta left of her own free will," Ruben declared. "When I reported her disappearance, the police said they couldn't interfere for forty-eight hours, so, through social media and with the help of locals, I organised search parties to comb through vacant houses within the area. We've plastered fliers across Ganestown. I even hired a psychic to hunt for clues in Roberta's home."

Earlier today, a Garda spokesperson confirmed they were treating the disappearance as "suspicious," and "several people are helping us with our inquiries."

"Gardaí interviewed me last night," Mr Gardner admitted. "I heard one of their suspects got released from prison two weeks ago, after serving a sentence for abduction and assault."

"Detectives face a frustrating challenge when they tackle a missing persons' case," the spokesperson added.

Voluntary or involuntary disappearances have reached unprecedented levels in Ireland – from 3000 in 2001, to 12,000 last year. While the vast majority return, journalist Jessica Ryan reports and remembers a selection of those who vanished, and never came home.

The art dealer turned to a double-page spread of photos and profiles of men, women, teenagers and children, with times, dates and last sighting. Ignoring the cabin crew's safety demonstration, he settled in to read and instantly recognised three pictures sprinkled amid the others. A jolt of adrenalin surged around his body.

Victor and victim. Hunter and hunted.

He looked over the images, eyes flashing past dozens of pictures as his mind placed the seven victims in chronological order. He turned the page. Two photos, side by side at the bottom right-hand corner, caught his attention:

Relatives of Denise Alexander reported the sixty-eight-year-old retired national schoolteacher missing when she didn't return home on Thursday, March 12, 2015. She boarded a bus at Rosses Point, for a night out in Sligo, and CCTV footage placed Denise in the bus depot at 5:35 p.m. A short time after, Denise spoke to an elderly couple on Adelaide Street, near Hawk's Well Theatre. There's been no sighting since.
Slim, with shoulder-length grey-black hair and hazel eyes, Denise is 5' in height and wore a red coat with a matching soft shoulder Guess sling bag.

The first.
Identical...*to mother. Impulse plus opportunity equalled victim number one.*

The art dealer pondered.

Yes, first victim. Mother doesn't count. That was putting a wounded dog out of its misery. An act of mercy.

His eyes shifted to the second head and shoulders photograph.

Elizabeth Carroll.

Detectives are still appealing for help in tracing a Co. Louth woman who vanished on Friday, February 19, 2016.

Elizabeth Carroll, 33, a single mother, disappeared between 9:30 p.m. and 10:30 p.m. while walking through a residential estate in Dundalk, on her way to a colleague's birthday party.

Police used search dogs and quizzed several hundred people during extensive inquiries, but no evidence of abduction ever emerged.

Wrong place for her.

Right place for me.

Friday.

Heavy rain.

His mother's anniversary still a month away. He'd collected a new cattle prod and was stuck at a traffic light on the outskirts of town when a woman tapped on the car window looking for directions. The lift was a "Good Samaritan" gesture. On reflection, he'd never picked up anybody before, so a primitive part of his brain must have homed in on her scent. She'd given him a condensed version of her life story.

Hapless victim. Fate sealed.

He remembered her raised eyebrows, the unspoken question when he reached behind and picked up the eighteen-inch battery operated prod. No time to react when he jabbed the electrodes against her neck, again and again. Awkward. Even in a big car.

Could have got caught. Too exposed. Stupid.

He'd pulled into a lay-by and found it much harder to strangle someone than he'd thought possible. The challenge lay in blocking the carotid artery and jugular due to layers of fat around her throat. Once the woman stopped breathing, he relaxed his grip, and she'd inhaled another gulp of air. The jagged high-pitched wheezes made him yearn for a rope. Or a cord. He tried again. Air rattled in Elizabeth's lungs. She thrashed, struggling to stay alive. He'd zapped her twice more, dug both thumbs on her windpipe, kept them there long after the body became limp, and until the tingling pain of pins and needles forced him to remove his numb digits. Under cover of darkness, he'd transferred her to the boot and wondered what to do with the body.

Killing was easy. Hiding evidence was hard.

He'd crossed the Silver River at Kilcormac and buried her in the peaty soil of Boora bog. Primary settlers from the Mesolithic era wouldn't mind another body.

That was a mistake. If it's ever found, the bog will have preserved her.

The art dealer scratched phantom knuckle pain, remembered how his fingers cramped in agony for days. And then, the wait. For a week he'd anticipated an official inquiry, imagined somebody had glimpsed a number plate...

Nobody ever came.

After that, he'd pressed tennis balls to strengthen his fingers.

Must buy a stun gun in Belfast.

Gardaí are still seeking the public's help in tracing Monica Flynn. On Friday, March 10, 2017, Monica (28), and her three-year-old son left Galway and arrived at Tullamore train station hoping to spend an enjoyable weekend with relatives. That night, Monica and two cousins enjoyed a meal in Chiquita's, a Mexican restaurant on Church Street, before they visited several bars, mingling and chatting with friends.

At 11:53 p.m., a group that included the trio entered Heat Niteclub, attached to Fieldbrook Hotel. After 2 a.m., Monica disappeared. When gardaí examined CCTV footage, they caught her on video entering the nightclub, but there was no footage of her leaving. They identified people Monica spoke with, arrested two, but released both without charge. To date, detectives have no prime suspect.

Number three.

For a year he hadn't felt the urge to kill again. Until that night. He'd entertained clients in Chiquita's restaurant. Conscious of the internal pressure building as he watched three women seated at an adjacent table, his companions continued the conversation while he eavesdropped—easier as the women's chat became more animated. By the time they'd paid for the meal, he'd learned her name, her son's name, Stephen, Monica's relationship status and what they'd planned for afterwards. He'd chauffeured the customers to Fieldbrook Hotel, his brain shrieking: "Danger. Too close to home." But she'd been in the restaurant, on that day, at that moment, at that table, for a reason.

Destiny.

The headache hammered, demanding deliverance, and he'd embraced the familiar pain like an old friend. He'd mooched around the nightclub until Monica appeared. From a distance, he stalked her, slipped close when she stood alone at the bar, swigging another cocktail and shouted over the music: 'Stephen needs you. This way's quicker.'

He hadn't waited for a response or gave a backwards glance, just pushed through the heaving crowd, towards a never used fire exit that opened onto Kelly's Lane. Whether Monica assumed he was one of the management team, or driven by concern for her son, she'd battled to keep up, obedient as a pet dog. He recalled her breathless questions. Recalled slipping on rubber gloves, opening the passenger door and Monica clambering in. Thanked him. Asked if he knew the way and if Stephen was okay…

The cattle prod kept her stunned. Outside Tullamore, he'd driven down a twisty back-road. Her neck, thin as a sapling, was easy to squeeze. A nice one to practise technique. He'd locked his fingers together for extra purchase. A single spastic leg twitch, and…nothing.

The first I buried on the farm. It made sense, with machinery available. Didn't have to traipse across bogs or woods to find a suitable spot. Buried deep, with no chance of accidental exposure by freak weather conditions, or a protruding limb getting spotted by a walker or uncovered by a stray dog. Hattinger's land includes their family cemetery. I've created my own graveyard and maintain control over the dead.

"It could be a runaway or an abduction. We've no evidence regarding Joanne Cranley," a police spokesperson admitted. Joanne, 31, vanished outside her rented apartment in Monaghan town on Sunday night February 18, 2018, after she returned from Belfast. "The search team and forensic investigation uncovered nothing of substance," the source added. "Tracker dogs traced the scent to the road, and the trail ended there. But the file remains open. We're always hopeful people will recall something and come forward with concrete information."

The art dealer studied the photo.

Number four. It's not the image I've got in my mind.

She'd applied for a position in the Belfast office. After reading her CV, he had all the information required. He'd have preferred to take her to the farm, but it was too distant. Instead, he'd crammed the young woman into a heavy duty canvas sack, filled the space with rocks, and dumped the body in a lake outside Donaghcloney.

His gaze shifted, searching for number five.

Isobel Stewart. August 17, 2018...

His ears popped as cabin pressure decreased.

Not enough time now to reminisce on Isobel. Later.

He flipped back the page and skimmed the photos again.

Where was number six? Eileen.

He couldn't remember her surname. Less than two months ago. Newbridge. A quiet bar. He'd spent two weeks looking for a prospect, visiting bars, awaiting the opportunity. The woman, seated alone at a table, expecting somebody who didn't show. Asked him for a light. He'd told her he didn't smoke. That was their conversation. He observed her check a mobile; listened to her talk to a childminder. She went outside to get a better signal, giving him a moment to add a drug to her drink, ready to tip it over if she returned before it dissolved. It took an eternity, fizzing and foaming. He'd sipped coffee and speculated what reaction the Rohypnol would have on her.

She came back, polished off the drink, rechecked the phone, gathered her belongings and stumbled to a silver hatchback. He'd tailed the half-dazed woman home, parked a distance away, waiting for the babysitter to leave.

Eileen answered his knock.

So easy.

Ashen-faced, with traces of vomit on her chin, she'd unchained the lock, maybe thinking the babyminder was returning. It almost made him feel sorry for her.

Almost.

Near the farmhouse, the woman reacted to the drug. She shuddered and choked, froth lathering her mouth and vomiting all over his car's expensive leather upholstery before she died from a seizure. He vowed never to use his car again.

The effort it took to clean up after her.

A half bottle of prescription drugs in Eileen's coat pocket, plus the combined alcohol and Rohypnol had set off the allergic reaction. The art dealer recalled the clothes she'd worn; black coat, mauve skirt, a long-sleeved grey T-shirt. He remembered the tattoo – a Celtic cross – on her left wrist. He glanced through the pictures again. Her photo wasn't there. His gaze returned to Isobel Stewart.

Isobel Stewart. The days spent tracking her, the gambles I took. Careless. The whole house of cards could've tumbled, but it was hours well spent. It challenged me. Made me sharper. Helped me evolve.

The pilot requested the cabin crew to take their seats. The woman beside him stretched. 'Are you in Belfast for business or pleasure?' she asked.

'Business,' the art dealer said. 'You?'

'Same. No rest for the wicked.'

'Indeed.'

I'm attending a convention at the Merchant Hotel,' the woman smiled.

'That's my hotel too.'

The woman nodded. 'Perhaps we'll bump into each other.'

'Perhaps,' the art dealer said.

HUGH LEFT A voicemail for Ferdia, saying he'd meet him at the Ganestown Hotel at eight.

When he got back to McGuire's, tension on the shop floor was palpable. Upstairs, he poked his head into Malcolm's office. Malcolm was slumped across the desk, staring at a computer screen.

Hugh jangled the Hiace keys. 'Returning these. You alright?'

Malcolm straightened and pressed a button on the laptop. 'Yeah.'

'Any word on Charlie?'

'Brain swelling's reduced, so he's off the critical list. Still in intensive care, though.'

'Ferdia and I are calling in later.' Hugh waved the dockets. 'Can I leave these with you? Milo Brady signed them.'

'Leave them on the accountant's desk. The office two doors down.' Malcolm twisted in the chair. 'Um…when Dad told me you were starting here, he said to call you if I needed advice.'

'Did he? Oh, sure.'

'I'm supposed to let Milo go.'

'Really? Okay.'

'Dad took him on a few months ago 'cos he's family.'

'Oh?'

'He's my cousin. But the role isn't working out.'

'Milo told me he's in line for a management role in Ganestown.'

'No chance.'

'So what's the issue?' Hugh asked. 'You've got a problem telling him?'

'No. Well, yes. Milo's got an attitude, but he's family. I think Dad's using this as a test, to see if I'm able to...I dunno.'

'When have you planned to tell him?'

'Today, but...' Malcolm pushed up his jacket to check his watch. The wrist was bare. 'Too late now. He'll have left. Tomorrow. What'll I say to him? How do I start the conversation?'

'That's a face-to-face talk,' Hugh said. 'Say you've reviewed the entire business. Restructures are necessary, and he's surplus to requirements.'

'Sounds frosty.'

'It's purely a business decision, Malcolm, nothing personal. Milo's still on probation. Charlie tried to help him and it didn't work out. Move on.'

'Okay.' Malcolm doodled on a notepad. 'Um, Staff's asking what'll happen, now that Dad's out of commission. What our plans are.'

'Yeah. I sensed the worry when I came in.'

'Word is, you're here to close the place. A hitman.'

'Where'd they get that idea? That's mad. I'm a part-time van driver.'

Malcolm glanced at the laptop screen. 'I suppose they view anybody new as an angel of death. I can't stop rumours.'

'No. I suppose it's only natural that staff want to know. So, did you divulge your plans?'

'Me? What plans? I'm not long out of college. I've no practical experience,' Malcolm rubbed his forehead, 'or plans. There's a massive difference between academic theory and actual business. Caught up in a family concern is the worst thing. Nothing's ever right. More's always expected. Ciara was smart to leave and make her own path. I should get out too.' Malcolm clicked the mouse and studied the screen. 'Jesus.'

'Hmm?'

'Nothing.' Malcolm closed the lid.

'I've to sign on at the dole office in Ganestown tomorrow,' Hugh said. 'If you want me to meet Milo with you, I'll—'

'Thanks. I'll do it.' Malcolm wrote on the notepad. 'So, we've reviewed the business, and he's what?'

'Surplus to requirements. And don't forget restructures are necessary.'

'Oh, yeah. Got it. That's good enough.'

'Good enough is never good enough, Malcolm,' Hugh's tone sharpened. 'Pretend I'm Milo. Go through it again...'

NIGHT

'HOW'D THE HEALTH and Safety meeting go?'

Ferdia burped, perfuming the interior of the jeep with a whiff of curry. His right wrist rested on the apex of the steering wheel, left fist curled around the gear-stick. 'A young lad asked me what steps I'd take if a fire broke out on the premises. Got the impression feckin' quick ones wasn't the right answer. Still, the fat manual he handed out will be handy for killing wasps next summer.'

They listened to the tail end of a news bulletin and the weather forecast: "More snow. Hazardous driving conditions." Ferdia tuned into Radio Nova, and Gary Numan's "Are Friends Electric?" neutralised the snap of hailstones hitting the jeep's roof.

'Hope we'll make it before visiting hours are over,' Hugh said. 'What time do the wards close?'

'No idea.' Ferdia yawned. 'We'll relieve Ciara and Mal of sentry duty. Chas won't want a gang of us 'round the bed.'

They swung into the multi-storey car park, both scanning for a free space. Nothing. Ferdia spun into an area reserved for hospital staff and slotted the jeep between an Insignia and a Jag.

'You'll get a Denver boot if you park here.'

'Nah. Clampers won't risk it. What if it belongs to a consultant who forgot his tag? Consultants raise a feckin' stink if they get clamped.'

'You sure?'

'Positive.'

Inside, a security man pointed them to Saint Anne's ward.

'Least he's out of the Richmond ICU unit,' Ferdia said. 'Must be off the critical list.'

Halfway along the corridor, Hugh spotted Ciara in one of the four-bedded rooms. Curtains enclosed the hospital cots, cocooning patients for the night. She moved aside, waved them forward, trying to smile.

Charlie looked a mess.

Wires protruded like coloured tentacles from under the crepe bandage wrapped around his head. His face, mottled and lacerated, the right eye swollen shut. Stitches crisscrossed a five-centimetre incision over an eyebrow. A bruised lump the size of a golf ball bulged from his forehead. Two splints kept Charlie's nose in place; both nostrils packed with gauze, and the stitched top lip was puffed up to three times its regular size. The total facial area, coated in Betadine, gave the exposed skin an eerie orange glow. A drip-feed hooked into an arm. More tubes snaked out beneath the bed sheets and ran to electronic monitors that beeped in rhythm, counting heartbeats and pulse rates.

Malcolm sat at the head of the bed, scrolling through his smartphone.

'Things people do to get feckin' attention,' Ferdia said.

Charlie's left eye snapped open. He tried to smile, lifted a hand. 'You shouldn't have come in this weather.' The words were a croaked whisper. 'Sorry I couldn't make it in to show you the ropes, Hugh.'

'Malcolm took charge,' Hugh said. 'You concentrate on getting better.'

Ferdia pointed a thumb at the corridor. 'Ye ought to take off. Drive easy. Roads are slippery as a skating rink. We'll hang on for a while.'

Ciara leaned on the bed and kissed Charlie's cheek. 'See you tomorrow, Dad.'

'Don't travel if—'

'I'll bring David in, after…' Ciara waved at Charlie's face.

'Remember I'm taking Master David off your hands Sunday and Monday?' Ferdia said. 'If it's any addition, bounce him over to me earlier.'

Ciara picked up her coat. 'Might take you up on that.'

'Don't worry, Dad.' Malcolm's voice was high-pitched with contrived cheerfulness. 'We'll cope.'

Hugh followed them out. 'Any idea how long he'll be here?'

Ciara sagged against a radiator. 'Doctor says there are no major injuries, well, except for the pounding his brain took. They're concerned the head kicks might trigger an intracranial haematoma. They were monitoring a clot; the neurosurgeon was ready to operate, but it dissolved.' She dabbed her eyes. 'It'll take weeks for the broken nose to heal, and the bruises and puffiness to disappear. They said he could experience blurred vision for months, and it's not unusual to have short-term memory loss. Recovery after post-concussion syndrome varies; anything from three months to a year. And there's a possibility psychological problems could develop.'

Malcolm put a supporting arm on Ciara's shoulder.

'I'll be in Mullingar by lunchtime,' Hugh said. 'Anything I can do to help, just ask.'

'How'd you end up on Temple Street?' Ferdia's voice, low and harsh, rumbled through the ward.

'Two guys mugged me.' A phlegmy cough rattled in Charlie's throat.

'That tells me what happened, not what you were up to.'

'How do I look?'

Ferdia's eyes travelled up Charlie's arms to his face and back again.

'Not bad. George Clooney, except more handsome.'

'Be serious.'

'As if you got smacked with a frying pan. Reminds me of that time I was in a dust-up with a Charolais bull. Still, once the swelling reduces—'

A nurse opened the curtain, studied the IV bag and line. 'You sore, Charlie?'

'Hmm.'

'I'll get something to help you sleep.'

Hugh tiptoed in.

Ferdia browsed through the bedside locker, pushing aside the fruit and soft drinks that Malcolm or Ciara had brought. 'Need clothes?'

'Ciara brought them.' Charlie closed his eyes.

'Grand.'

The men stood in silence until the nurse reappeared, hustled them away and administered an injection. When she returned to the nurse station, Hugh and Ferdia crept back to Charlie's bedside.

Charlie was asleep.

THE ART DEALER ordered room service.

He switched on his laptop and linked into the international edition of RTÉ Player. The nine o'clock news showed graphic images of the aftermath of a bomb blast in the Middle East. Government ministers denounced the assault on innocent civilians. A stern-faced Garda in full uniform filled the screen, with Roberta Lord's headshot in the top right-hand corner. The art dealer turned up the volume:

"I appeal to each resident within a two-kilometre radius of Oak View Lane, Ganestown, to inspect farms, outhouses and adjacent woodlands for tracks or traces of Roberta's disappearance. Roberta is one point five metres tall, with shoulder-length blonde hair. She was wearing blue jeans, a white top and a grey spotted reefer jacket. If you noticed any suspicious person or activity near Oak View on Monday last, or have information that could help us in our inquiries, contact Ganestown Garda Station. We need your assistance in reuniting this family with their gifted daughter."

The camera panned to a sallow-complexioned woman, body stiff as steel, face seamed with worry, sat behind a conference table. She gazed unblinking into the camera lens:

"These have been the bleakest hours of my life. I fear for my daughter. We're at our wits' end. I'm asking you to help us put an end to this heartrending experience. Somebody's *bound* to have information. We're desperate. Roberta's a wonderful daughter; a mother, whose sole focus is to make the…the best life for herself and her son. He loves and misses her. We all do." Mrs Lord clasped a handkerchief, using it as a lifeline. The stress bubbled to the surface. Her voice quivered: "Hope gave me the strength to make this appeal. Hope that *somebody* saw *something*. Hope that Roberta will show up at our door. I'm *appealing*, I'm *pleading* with you. Please help us find Roberta. Please." The woman placed her head in her hands. Sobs shattered the stillness, and cameras zoomed in, capturing her anguish while the corner of the screen flashed contact numbers.

'Dreams die first,' the art dealer murmured. 'And hope dies last. Time to get acquainted with BachtoBasie.'

OUTSIDE THE HOSPITAL, Ferdia lit a cigarette, coughed, foraged in a jacket pocket, found a bottle of Gaviscon and gulped the liquid. He spotted Hugh's frown. 'I'm grand.' He filtered the words through a fog of smoke. 'Smoker's cough.'

'Did you make that doctor's appointment?'

'Yeah. For tomorrow.'

They walked along the footpath leading to the car parks. In the sodium streetlights, Hugh stared at Ferdia's jaw muscles clamp as he sucked nicotine into his lungs. 'What did you detect on the search and find mission?'

'Twigged that, huh? The smell of bullshit, that's what I detected. Mugged me arse. Watch on his wrist. Mobile and wallet in the locker. Muggers grab what they can. Snatch 'n' run. They don't beat a man half to death an' rob his car. An' if they do, they hide it for a week, then use it for a raid down the country. Where's the sense in driving it five miles outside the city to burn it? That's—' Ferdia's head swivelled at the shrill yaps of a dog in agony. 'Here.' He tossed keys to Hugh. 'Wait in the jeep.'

'Leave it, Ferdia. Don't get involved. It isn't your—'

'Be right behind ya.'

'Christ, Ferdia, why can't you—'

Ferdia melted between rows of cars. Hugh held up the fob. The jeep double-beeped, blinkers flashed. He reversed out of the space. On Radio Nova, XTC's "Making plans for Nigel" segued into The Rah Band's "The Crunch."

Hugh tracked Ferdia's advance.

The big man zigzagged between vehicles, zeroing in on the animal whining in pain and fear. Hugh rounded the parked cars, headlights illuminating the area. Two men stood in the driving lane. One, his back against a dirty white van, stabbed at a phone pad and squinted at the screen. A cigarette dangled from his lips, the tip glowing as he inhaled. The other was Hugh's size, but broader, and wearing a V-neck pullover, frayed at the collar. One hand gripped a leash attached to a terrified terrier, and he was taking his temper out on the dog, flaying it with a short stumpy stick. The animal yapped in terror, straining to get free.

Hugh braked, stepped out of the jeep, heart pounding.

Ferdia shadow loomed over the scene. 'All right men?'

'Mind your business.' The man pulled the restraint tighter, dragging the dog closer. Tiny paws scrabbled for a foothold, and the noose tightened, choking off the yelps. The man lashed out at the terrier again.

'Pick someone your own size.'

Dog man looked up, dropped the lead. The dog's paws found purchase, and it scrabbled for safety under the van. 'Thought I said to mind yur fuckin' business. Won't tell you again.' He wielded the stick in a wild roundhouse slash. Ferdia glided inside the swipe, ducked a fraction and let the stick whistle over his head. He bunched his right fist and hooked it out. It travelled less than thirty centimetres, the knuckles thudding into dog man's unprotected floating rib. The man folded, sank and yodelled in agony, sucking air into starved lungs that whistled like a leaky accordion bellows. The second man gawped, reversed and his heel snagged the dog leash entangled under a wheel. His head bounced off the van's side panel.

Ferdia slackened the lead, and enveloped the terrier in a ham-sized fist. 'I'm commandeering this little fella, lads. I'll find a place for him. Safe home.' He held out his free hand to Hugh for the jeep keys. 'What?'

'Nothing. Wondered if you need back-up. Not that I'd be much addition. You okay?'

Ferdia tapped away cigarette ash. 'Spot on. There's a special place in hell reserved for people who're cruel to animals.'

The terrier licked Ferdia's face.

'Way you hit that guy, I thought you'd kill him.'

'Nah. I pulled the punch. No point crippling the man.'

'You'll teach me a few boxing moves, Ferdia.'

'You're too old to start. What age are you now? Thirty? Thirty-two?'

'Twenty-eight.'

'Huh. Anyway, getting into scraps isn't your style. Street fighting rules are simple; there are no rules. Any boxing skills you've got go out the window. If you're ever in trouble, forget the fancy stuff. Kick the other person's knee. Hard. It'll give you a chance to run like hell.'

'Running from physical confrontation is my go-to strategy,' Hugh said. 'I don't aim to *be* a boxer, just want to get in shape.'

'Grand. Meet me at the gym anytime.' Ferdia swung out of the car park. The terrier curled up in his lap, half asleep. Hugh's mobile beeped. A text from Eilish:

Mum's sick. I'm staying over for a nite or 2.

'Your mother's sick,' Hugh said.

'Mustn't be serious or I'd have got word.'

Hugh texted back:

Give her my regards. See you

tomorrow or Saturday.

Nite nite. Xx

He looked across at Ferdia. 'What's on your mind?'

Ferdia scratched the terrier's head. The contented dog's ears twitched, as she chased rabbits in her dreams. 'Funny how they concentrated on Chas's face,' Ferdia said. 'Like 'twas a warning.'

'About what?'

'Good question.' Ferdia's fingertips drummed the dashboard. 'Charlie's a decent skin. But at times, bad things happen to good people.'

THE ART DEALER followed signs pointing to an area off the foyer where residents could browse the web or print boarding passes. He logged into the dating site, re-read BachtoBasie's mail and considered his response. It required a subtle balance between realism and credibility, without revealing his background.

From: thejewellerycollector@datingvista.ie
Sent: Thurs., 21:48
To: BachToBasie@datingvista.ie
Subject: Good Night
Hi, yourself.
I'm delighted you replied, and your photos are amazing. I love your username! Now there's a broad musical taste! Well, I'm stuck in Cork airport (walked its length six times). No idea when we'll take off—I trust I'll make it to Dublin in one piece. Nothing special planned – except take clients to the Gaiety Theatre Saturday night, if I get back! Oh, and loads of domestic chores to organise, if I set my mind to it, and I've got a pile of books to read. Odds are, they'll take precedence. I live in Dublin but often pass through Ganestown. I'm also a novice at this

online dating—took ages to download my picture! I'm cautious at having my personal information for everyone to view, but needs must.

I hope you'll have a relaxed, chilled-out (snowman building) weekend, that doesn't include road trips. More snowfalls predicted, so at least your son will be thrilled. Have you found this site a reliable location to make new friends? Keep in touch.

The Jewellery Collector.

The art dealer changed a few words to match BachtoBasie's tone, added another exclamation mark, pressed 'send', and erased the browser history. Back in his bedroom, he considered how Jana would react to his unscheduled visit. Until now, her expertise in Eastern European ceramics and Russian art, along with an impressive list of contacts, made her a key member of his management team. But other consultants had learned from her and built their own connections. She wasn't needed. No preparation time gave him an advantage in keeping her under pressure.

The element of surprise.

'Victor or victim,' he muttered, taking an Antiques Trade Gazette magazine from his briefcase, 'and I'm the victor. Always.'

5

FRIDAY 11 JANUARY

MORNING

JANA TROFIMIACK GLANCED at her phone on the passenger seat, willing it to ring.

Preoccupied, she stage-laughed as Lech chattered in the back. The paintings hadn't arrived last night.

'Uważaj! Czerwone światło, Maia!'

She jammed the brakes, blocked half the zebra crossing, and tolerated pedestrian's glares.

'Zielone światło, Maia!'

Jana smiled. Lech. Soon a man, she thought. Six in two weeks, and he'd never given her a moment's kłopot. So considerate. They'd had adult conversations for years. Counting herself fortunate, she'd continue to shield her fragile, flawless treasure from this vicious world, as long as breath remained in her body. Yes, she fretted about him. The future. What'll happen if his maia died? Who'd care for him? How could he survive? And how'd *she* live if...? Jana blessed herself, and again for luck. They depended on each other. She double-parked outside the school.

'Kocham moją Maia!'

'Love you too.' Jana watched Lech thread through other children. At the door, he turned, waved and disappeared inside.

Jana had parked on Ann Street when her mobile rang. She answered, listened to a voice grunt a location two streets away. She hurried over, stood shivering in a restaurant doorway, looking left and right. A man rounded a corner, walking fast, a supermarket carrier bag in his hand. He got to Jana, passed her the bag, didn't speak, and kept going.

Jana peeked at the contents, looked up the street. The man had vanished.

Back in the car, she removed the two paintings. Her nose wrinkled at the smell of fresh paint. From a distance, the McKelvey *looked* okay, and at least it was in the original frame. But Günther still hadn't managed to…It'll have to do, Jana thought. She looked at the Jack B. Yeats painting. Again, it wasn't…Shaking her head, she re-wrapped it and dialled Dorothy Ridgeway's house, told a maid to expect her in half an hour, placed the McKelvey in an oversized shoulder bag, and drove to Glenavy.

HUGH TRAWLED ONLINE for sales management positions.

Initial enthusiasm swung to apprehension: no suitable roles available. He'd planned to pick a dozen management roles, get meetings under his belt and be in a position to interview for a dream job within a few weeks, a month tops. Now, that timeline wasn't practical. Plan B. He phoned the recruiter who'd forwarded for the Pharma-Continental role.

'I've one position here, I'll email it to you,' James O'Neill at Midland Recruitment said. 'You're way over-qualified, Hugh, but forward me your updated details. I'll include it in the shortlist.'

Hugh read the field sales management role, spent an hour re-editing his CV to fit the position, and mailed it. Then he completed paperwork for Pharma-Continental. Anything to delay a visit to the dole office.

'WHY SHOULD I spend my money at Hattinger's? What makes *you* different from the other art houses?'

The art dealer smiled. 'I'm glad you asked me that.'

Having breakfast with the nouveau riche, who saw art as a trophy to proclaim their status, was a necessary evil to secure their future business in times of debt, divorce, disaster or death. In a few years, most would become the nouveau pauvres, but meantime, he had to tolerate them. Earlier, he'd used the hotel internet to log onto the dating website. His message to BachtoBasie hadn't received a reply.

He'd checked that he sent the message.

He had.

Clicked on In Box again.

Still blank.

The potential client was staring at him. The art dealer sipped tea and refocused. 'A number of gallerists concentrate on artists,' he said. 'Others place emphasis on customers. We focus on both. I only work with knowledgeable collectors interested in art. Our artists are a mix of well-known, local and new talent.'

Why didn't she answer?

He drew a triangle in the air. 'I build deep, meaningful bonds between ourselves, our clients and our artists. We are a family business, and each new client or artist becomes a cherished extension to our clan. That approach cements our relationships. It makes the business of buying and selling easier.'

'This is a big deal for me,' the client said. 'What guarantees me your full attention?'

The art dealer maintained eye contact. 'I've got wonderful staff who shield me from the hype, the pretentiousness and any petty power plays that occur. That allows me to concentrate on our most important properties, clients and artists. I consider myself fortunate to be among an elite group who meet, associate and—'

'Your clients meet? Each other?'

'Of course. We're family. We help and guide each other in art and in business life.'

'So, if I give you a cheque for five million, will you sell me one painting or a dozen smaller pieces?'

Why hasn't the bitch replied?

'I won't accept your cheque. Won't sell you anything.'

'Why?'

Because you don't have five million, and I'm fed up feigning interest in your petty life.

'That's not how I do business,' the art dealer explained. 'I don't know enough about you on a personal level—your likes, dislikes, tastes. Are you buying as an investment or a lifestyle? And your partner and family? Have *they* a preference? Perhaps it's different from yours. I'm sure it is. I have to know you before making recommendations.'

The man nodded. 'Well then, we'd better talk again.' He raised a hand for the bill.

The art dealer stopped him. 'My treat.'

'Thanks. Appreciate you taking the time to—'

'Pleasure.'

Recheck email.

They shook hands and examined exchanged business cards.

'Get your people to talk to my people,' the man said.

The art dealer placed his hand on the new client's arm and moved him towards the reception area. 'May I suggest…'

The man departed, and the art dealer logged into DatingVista, nerves burning with anticipation.

No response.

He felt the headache throbbing in time with his heartbeat. Jaw muscles clenching, he read over the email again, searching for words or negatives that could've made BachtoBasie wary, and couldn't find anything. Angry, he logged out and walked to Hattinger's premises on Ann Street.

Jana Trofimiack.

The humane way would be to take Jana for lunch and explain that the decline in business, yada, yada, yada, but he preferred to toy with her, a cat with a mouse. He'd use her to vent his frustrations.

Like a matador, I'll dish out the significant strikes in private, and when the bitch is in a weakened state, I'll deliver the coup de grâce in public. It'll teach everyone a lesson. Yes, El Matador. I'm the one that waves the muleta. I'm the one who'll make her surrender before I execute the fatal blow.

When the receptionist paged Jana, she materialised, nervous, dry-washing her hands. 'Welcome.' She had prominent cheekbones, almond-shaped eyes, black hair pinned in a messy top-knot, and a layer of face powder that failed to hide the sheen on her upper lip. Jana almost genuflected, offering a clammy handshake. 'Nobody told us…Had you a nice trip? Can I get you kawa…coffee?'

The art dealer moved away from the piercing voice, persistent as a pneumatic drill. His mouth curled in distaste at the touch of Jana's palm, and the stale garlicky smell that blasted from the woman's mouth made him cough. In the bathroom, he rinsed off Jana's nervous sweat, then followed her to an office.

I'll use the Ridgeway issue as a catalyst.

Jana interrupted his thoughts: 'Did you read the email I sent you—?'

'I seldom read your correspondence, Jana, and to date, I've missed nothing notable. I assume the consultants are on-site today?' The art dealer removed a tennis ball from his pocket and squeezed.

'Yes. We have an in-house meeting scheduled.'

Veins stood out on the art dealer's wrist. Arm muscles screamed with acid. He slackened his grip on the ball and opened the briefcase. 'This shouldn't take long. I don't foresee any polemic disputes today.'

'Sorry?'

'Oh, excuse me. I forgot your English isn't…Let me put it another way; I don't expect any heated debates.'

Jana relaxed.

'Where's Mrs Ridgeway's McKelvey? Why—?'

'The email I sent? I spoke with Mrs Ridgeway. She found her painting behind a settee. It must have slipped between—'

'Good.' That Dorothy had located the McKelvey made the art dealer livid. 'What date have you pencilled in for Ridgeway's auction?'

'No date yet. We've catalogued the collection. I guess—'

'Guess? Is that what I pay you for? Guesswork?'

'No. I—'

'My instructions were explicit. This sale *must* conclude by the end of February. Why haven't you fixed a date?'

'Mrs Ridgeway postponed—'

The art dealer threw a pen on the table. It skidded across the veneered surface and slid over the edge. 'Your capacity for incompetence continues to confound me, Jana. If it's not scheduled now, we won't get another chance until after Easter.'

Jana fidgeted, attempted to bury herself in the seat. 'Mrs Ridgeway wants to wait until after—'

'Dorothy Ridgeway doesn't appreciate the intricacies of the market. January is the opportune time to—'

'She said—'

'*Don't* interrupt me. When I speak, you listen. Every word you say imperils your prospects here. I'm considering if you possess the mandatory skills for this position. Are your talents better suited elsewhere, perchance? Burger King, maybe? Or is that pushing your intelligence? If I get a *hint* that a competitor has secured this sale, I'll...' The man's nostrils flared. 'Where did you study business management? Please, don't answer. Pass me the Ridgeway paperwork. Another consultant can close it. I'm assigning you to other duties. You've lost the commission on this auction.'

If that BachtoBasie bitch doesn't reply by tomorrow, Jana is next, regardless of her closeness. I'll find a way.

'Why? I've worked on this catalogue. The sale will be an *outstanding* success when—'

'Yes, well, let me help you redefine the notion of *outstanding* success, and your expectations will become more realistic.'

'I'm sorry? I don't—'

'Sorry doesn't pay the rent.' The art dealer's stare bullied Jana into silence.

Jana studied the ground.

He took a folder from his briefcase. 'I've received complaints with regard to your hygiene.'

'My hygiene? Complaints? From who?'

'Clients. Staff.'

'I don't—'

'When did you consider the pong of stale garlic as being appropriate in the workplace? Can't you comprehend how repellent it is for customers? Hmm? When are you planning to demonstrate a soupçon of aseptic concepts?'

'Pardon? I—'

'You reek worse than a rancid ewe, Jana. From today, I *forbid* you to engage with clients. And your hair? It's...Do you own a hairbrush?'

'Yes.'

'Use it. Now, shall we begin?'

MID-MORNING

'WHAT THE FECK are ya playing at?'

Ferdia waited until the nurse left the ward before firing a verbal blast at Charlie. His brother-in-law still mirrored someone who'd fought a tiger, but overnight the forehead swelling had reduced. They'd removed the nose splints, and the facial bruises had turned a mustard yellow, with crusts forming on the lacerations. The drip needle remained, and a nasal cannula hung on his nostrils.

'Told you I got mugged. I've made a statement to—'

'Don't care what account you gave our boys in blue. I'm sure they didn't believe you either. A two-year-old could see through your bullshit.'

Charlie groped for a water beaker. Ferdia guided the straw to his mouth. A Filipino nurse stuck her head around the curtain and put a finger to her lips. 'Shhh.'

'So what's the story?' Ferdia's voice dropped an octave.

'I owe a man money.'

'Who?'

'A loan shark.'

'How much?'

'I paid him—'

'How *much*?'

'Five.'

'Feck's sake, Chas. Surely to God you've more sense than getting tangled up—'

Charlie lifted a hand in surrender.

'So now what?' Ferdia asked.

'I've a week to repay them the balance.'

'Them?'

'Yeah.'

'Hah. I feckin' knew 'twas a warning. Where?'

'What?'

'Where'd you meet them?'

'Lidl, beside Temple Street hospital. I hoped they'd listen to reason.'

'Wondered what you were at up there. Who's the loan shark?'

'It doesn't *matter*, Ferdia. We'll...I'll manage.' Charlie twisted the beaker.

'Grand. What's the bottom line?'

'Fifteen thousand.'

'Is that fifteen more, or fifteen minus five?'

'I've paid five. I owe ten.'

'Can you get your hands on that sorta cash?'

'I'll find it. Somehow.'

'Mother of Jaysus, Chas. That's the decade's dumbest deal. You'll never repay them in dribs 'n' drabs. Interest rates go up a thousand feckin' per cent every week. Sharks thrive when everybody else is on the struggle bus. Thievin' bastards. I'll—'

Charlie's mobile rang. He handed the plastic mug to Ferdia and answered the call. 'Ciara? I'm A1. Great.' Charlie had put up his defensive shield. 'Don't worry. You've enough on your plate. Ferdia's here. How's David?' Charlie listened. 'Bet he's all excited. See you both soon. Me too. Hmm? No, no, he wasn't. Not yet. It's not a problem. Malcolm'll drop by, first chance he gets. Okay. Huh-uh. Okay. See you then. Bye.' Charlie disconnected and dropped the mobile on the bed. 'Ciara says David's on countdown to next weekend.'

'Aye, we've a couple of gigs planned.' Ferdia handed the beaker back to Charlie. 'Sure, I'll sort them lads out with cash. You can repay me whenever. What did you say the names were?'

'I didn't. Thanks, but we'll figure'—Charlie coughed, the words stuck in his throat—'it out.'

'Who's "we"?'

'I meant me. It's my mess. I'll work it out.'

Ferdia sensed an opening. 'The rate'll climb. Could be twenty grand by now.'

'No. The balance includes interest.'

'Betcha it doesn't include compound interest, penalty interest, plus any other kinda feckin' interest they can voodoo up.'

'I'll find a way—'

Ferdia grabbed the mobile phone off the bed, turned away from Charlie's grasp, and scrolled through the recent calls list.

'Ferdia—'

The Filipino nurse reappeared, stared hard. Ferdia scowled at Charlie and put a finger to his lips. 'Shhh.'

The nurse shook her head.

'What's the man's name?' Ferdia asked.

Charlie deflated. 'Dessie Dolan.'

'How'd you find him?'

'I didn't. He found me.'

'How?'

'One day, out of the blue—'

Charlie's mobile rang again.

'God almighty.' Ferdia exhaled and tossed the phone to Charlie.

'Ah, Sharona. Thanks for the call.' Charlie had built his wall up again. 'Indeed. Pure bad luck. What? Argh, a bit, but I'm…Of course. Drop by anytime, but I should be out in a few days. Say again? No. Thanks. I've everything I need. I am. Great care and attention. Sorry? The line is…Oh, right, that's good. Where are you now? Ah. You should be there in less than an hour. You'll get on well with Dorothy. Keep in touch. Thanks, Sharona. I will. You too.' Charlie disconnected. 'Where was I?'

'One day, out of the blue,' Ferdia said.

'Oh yeah. A man called me—'

'So you've a mobile—?'

'Number withheld.'

'Dessie Dolan?'

'It was a voice. Could be anybody.'

'You met him on Temple Street and he gave you money?'

'Ahh, yeah.'

'And you go *back* to Temple Street to make repayments?'

'Um, sometimes.'

'So, how'd the arrangement turn sour?'

'I got a call. They…he wanted the balance paid in full. Thought I could negotiate.'

'Huh. When's the balance due?'

'A week.'

'Lemme see.' Ferdia dug a mobile from his pocket. 'A week from…so, that's what? Next Tuesday?'

'Wednesday.'

Ferdia clicked the calendar app. 'Wednesday, the sixteenth. Ten thou. Same spot?'

'Yes.'

'What time?'

'Nine.'

Ferdia yawned. 'Leave it to me.'

'What'll you do?'

'What do ya think I'll do?'

'Not sure, but the way you said that it sounded like a bulldog's snarl.'

'Nonsense. I'll pay the man what he's owed. That's it. I don't want you shelling out shekels for the rest of your life.'

'Ferdia, I—'

'Did the cops ask for descriptions?'

'It happened too fast. I was on the ground before—'

'Snuck up behind you, eh?'

'Yeah. I didn't have a chance. One wore a cowboy hat, a Stetson. I don't remember his involvement. The other guy did the damage. He'd long hair. Darkish.'

'That's as useful as an ashtray on a motorbike, but I've got the gist. How much did you borrow?'

'What?'

'Jesus, Chas, how else can I put it? How much did Dolan loan you? In total?'

'I don't know. Probably…twelve thousand.'

'Why pick Temple Street to collect and deliver cash?'

'That's where he said.'

'Huh. When did this caper start?'

'Beside Lidl.'

'Mother of divine…If I want to pull feckin' teeth, I'll become a dentist. That's telling me *where*. It doesn't tell me *when*.'

'Couple of months ago.'

'Around Halloween so?'

'There or thereabouts.'

'And you met them on your own?'

'What's with the questions, Ferdia? What the hell does it matter? Yes. On my own.'

'Wondered why I wasn't invited along, that's all.'

'Didn't want to get you involved.'

'Ciara or Malcolm clued in on this?'

'No. NO.' Charlie pulled himself up in the bed. 'This isn't their concern. I don't—'

'Grand. I expect you'll get another call. Feckin' loan sharks always have a new balance. Let me know the final tally.'

'Ferdia, I…You've taken a weight off my mind.'

'You'd do the same for me.' Ferdia gave a two-fingered salute. 'It'll all pan out, and I'll get my reward in heaven. Slán.'

In the corridor, Ferdia winked at the Filipino nurse and flipped her a wave. She raised her eyes to the heavens and smiled back. Outside, he joined several smokers grouped outside the main entrance, wrapped in light dressing gowns or heavy bathrobes, prepared to bear the elements for a nicotine fix. A middle-aged man pulling a transportable IV pole stand, sucked in smoke to satisfy cravings. Ferdia borrowed a light from him, wandered towards the car park, searching pockets for coins to feed the ticket payment machine, and wondered why Charlie was still lying.

HUGH WEAVED HIS way through the conga line of people congregating outside the Ganestown Department of Social and Family Affairs building. Inside, a hallway led to a corridor where, he guessed, a hundred people queued. Hugh joined the human train. No one spoke. They shuffled forward, heads downcast, resembling mourners at a funeral lining up to sympathise with the bereaved. The stench of stale cigarette smoke dwarfed the overwhelming sense of resignation and hopelessness. Despair filled the hallway like a dark cloak. This was a place where fun came to die.

'Did ya get a ticket?'

'Pardon?'

The man ahead of Hugh spoke again. 'Did ya get a ticket?'

'No.'

'Ya gotta get one. They'll call your number.'

'Oh. Where do I—?'

The man pointed to a doorway at the top of the queue.

'Thanks.'

Hugh pushed through and entered a room. Seven Plexiglas-partitioned booths divided the government employees from the welfare recipients, with rows of stackable chairs bolted to the floor. People read, texted, knitted, filled out forms or milled around. Official documents covered every centimetre of wall space: job prospects, courses, threats of imprisonment for anybody caught cheating the system. Spotting a machine welded onto a support girder, he pressed a button marked "jobseeker," and a slip of paper spat out.

516.

He stood aside, waited his turn. Numbers flashed in cryptic sequences over hatches, and hapless clients got bawled out if they didn't get to their allotted window quick enough.

'Dude?' A black beanie, hood pulled low, hid most of Ronan Lambe's face. 'This is a prison. I'm inmate number 4-7-9.'

Hugh said: '5-16. I meant to return your call.'

'No worries. Any joy on the jobs front?'

'I scraped up temporary work. Van deliveries. Nine, ten hours a week. You?'

'Zilch. Feels like I'm never gonna catch a break. Unemployment's horrible.'

'It won't be for long.'

'Hope so, dude. Jesus, this place doesn't help. It's as if they—'

A man burst forward and caused commotion at hatch two. 'I was here before her.' He jerked a thumb at an inoffensive woman.

'I called your number five minutes ago, where were you?'

'I went out for a smoke.'

'I'll get to you after I've finished with—'

'Jesus. I'm here scratching my arse for the last two hours.'

'What's the rush? It's not like you've a job to go to. Stand over there and scratch it again.'

Ronan nudged Hugh. 'See? *That's* what I'm talking about. We're second class citizens—'

'I hear you.'

'—shit on a shoe. They resent us, dude. Blights on society. We get free money and they're pissed off pushing paper. You'd think it was *us* who's responsible for this…That we're *happy* to be—'

A voice rose at hatch five. 'Forms. Pfff. You always ask for more forms.' A broad, bearded Eastern European, wearing a beige three-quarter length coat and a wide synthetic smile waved his arms. 'No good. Pliz, is my birthday tomorrow. You fix for me, and I have happy birthday. Big party. Tak? Yes?'

'Nie. No.' The woman behind the glass didn't lift her eyes from the computer screen.

'What?'

'No.'

The man's smile faded. He beat the counter with a clenched fist. 'But why?'

'Because we've received information you're employed. I've confiscated your Social Security Card till our investigations are complete.'

'What? You…How'm I supposed to live? You want me to eat grass? Hmph? Like a cow?' His accent disappeared. 'You're—'

'Four-seventy—'

'—lucky there's a pane of glass thick as you are between us, or I'd—'

'Happy birthday. Four-seventy-nine.'

'You…Aww, fuck.'

'FOUR-SEVENTY-NINE.'

Ronan straightened. 'Get in touch if you—'

'Sure.'

Hugh hoped the doctor had got delayed on his ward rounds; this could take a while. He rang Eilish. Either she'd switched off her phone, or the battery had died. After two o'clock, 5-1-6 flashed over hatch three.

'PPS number?'

Hugh gave the number.

'You available for work?'

'Yes.'

'Job searching?'

'Yes.'

'Interviews lined up?'

'Not yet. I've applied—'

'Fill these out.' A bundle of forms got shoved under the Perspex. 'And these. And sign these here, here and here.'

Hugh gathered the ream of paper.

'Have them back Monday. Signed. Next.'

SHARONA WATERS TOOK the A26 from Lisburn to Glenavy.

Magnificent white oaks lined the way along a curved gradient driveway to Dorothy Ridgeway's house. To her left, a tennis court and basketball hoops. On the right, several horses, protected by winter turnout blankets and tail covers, lifted their heads. The driveway turned, expanded into a forecourt and revealed a sprawling mansion.

Sharona steered around a frozen central fountain, parked beside a Range Rover, and pressed the bell on an arched, double-sized oak door that looked sturdy enough to resist a battalion. The bell's clang resonated deep inside the cavernous house.

A middle-aged Filipina woman welcomed Sharona into a double-height hallway, and ushered her into a sitting-room with cornices and a herringbone teak floor. A turf fire drew Sharona to its heat and peaty smell.

'I'll tell Mrs Ridgeway you've arrived.'

Sharona didn't have time to explore. A short, stout lady breezed in, chatting on a mobile. She wore jodhpurs under a heavy woollen coat. '...you *must* visit. Its *ages* since we've...' The woman's voice, full and low, sounded mezzo-soprano. 'Fantastic, Madeline. And I'm *thrilled* you'll make it to the fundraiser tomorrow. Can't wait to meet you again. We've *so* much to catch up on. Okay. See you there. Au revoir.' The woman disconnected, coughed and pushed glasses up into her white wavy hair. 'Sharona? How about ya? I'm Dorothy. Charlie speaks well of you. I hope—'

Her phone rang again. 'Yes? Oh, hi Edwina. Could you *believe*...? I know. Next time I'll plead a migraine. These cocktail nights have transformed into a bitch-fest about'— she studied Sharona—'what's his name again? I always leave demoralised. I wish she'd give my head peace. Listen, I've a visitor. See you tomorrow night.' Dorothy honked into a tissue, wiped her red nose. 'I hope I don't give you this dose, Sharona. Our daughter Debra arrived home with it last weekend. I ought to be in bed. Now, let's chat over brunch.'

'Hi, Mrs Ridgeway. Coffee would be lov—'

'You'll stay for brunch. I insist. Pia will organise it. You're famished after the long drive. Debra's heading off to London, and I'll be here on my lonesome. And call me Dorothy.' She viewed Sharona with flu-ridden, bloodshot eyes.

'All right, so. Thanks. We can discuss your McKelvey.'

Dorothy slapped a palm against her forehead. 'Duh, you won't believe it. Hattinger's manager found it earlier. Behind a settee, of all places. I can't grasp how it happened; I must've moved it for safekeeping while they catalogued the other pieces, because there's no way on *earth* I'd *ever* sell that painting. *Why* put it behind a settee? For the life of me, I can't remember, but there's no other explanation. I feel terrible, dragging you this distance. In any case, you were well on your way when Jana got here. She helped me feed the horses. Which reminds me, I must contact Ambrose Hattinger and apologise. I'll make sure you get travelling expenses.'

'I enjoyed the drive, Dorothy. Your home is amazing, and I'm delighted you've found the painting.'

In the hallway, they stopped to watch a young woman walk backwards down the helical stairs, hauling an outsized suitcase. A hat perched on straw-coloured, shoulder-length hair, and she wore a fawn jacket over a short skirt.

'Debra! Please tell me you're not leaving dressed as an underwear model? I don't mind titillation darling, but I'm sure nobody at the airport has the slightest interest in a do-it-yourself gynaecology course. No wonder you've got flu.'

Debra winked at Sharona and kissed her mother's cheek. 'I'll phone you tonight, Mum. See you in two weeks.' Debra lugged the suitcase across the hall and dragged it outside the front door.

Dorothy gestured after her. 'Debra. My baby, the investment banker. Away to meet her fiancé. Blake, my husband, used to call him her fiasco. I'm dead set against Debs dating this chap. I've told her: "Debra, we invite those people to tea; we don't *marry* them." Will she heed me? No.'

Sharona wanted to ask, 'What people?' Instead, she said: 'Is he in banking too?'

Dorothy waved an arm and shrugged. 'Some alternative medicine business. Has an office in Harley Street. Very attentive, but he's…well, he doesn't *fit*. I suppose she'll land him here again with us for Easter.' She caught Sharona's arm and guided her into a hallway. 'Let's eat, and I want to hear all about *you*. How'd you meet Charlie? He's a dote, isn't he? He doesn't have the arrogance I associate with most business people. What college did you attend…?'

THE ART DEALER'S interrogation persisted.

El Matador.

He queried Jana's artwork selection, how she'd managed promotions in the run-up to Christmas, and probed progress of an up-to-date client list for the gallery. He questioned her time spent nurturing relationships with local artists, and studied her body language, delving further whenever the woman became defensive. The more Jana hesitated, hedged and fudged her replies with a mix of English and Polish words, the deeper he drilled into granular detail, changing topics randomly. His piercing gaze made Jana wriggle in discomfort as she sought to find explanations.

They worked through lunch.

Jana got quizzed on tiny discounts she'd agreed without receiving authorisation, grilled on expenses and cross-examined on development of the new gallery website. The art dealer ignored Jana's pointed looks at her watch. He rejected suggestions on how to improve customer traffic flow, dismissed her ideas for business growth, and vetoed proposals for price hikes. Instead, he enforced an updated set of unachievable objectives for the first financial quarter, targeted local collectors for VIP treatment, and ruled on Easter gifts for their top dozen clients. Only when Jana dug herself into a hole by assuring him the Belfast branch would meet its quarterly sales target, did the art dealer permit her to leave and prepare the conference room. When the meeting got underway, he joined the group.

UNTIL TODAY, SLUGGISH New Year sales hadn't stressed Jana. The weather was a factor, but she'd remained confident the annual January sale would make up any shortfall. Now, after the three-hour onslaught, she questioned and probed the team, combing the group for anybody who'd arrived unprepared. Her aggression flowed like molten lava, as she strove to show the boss man that Jana could take control, and match his management style. She peeked at him, judging his reaction. He was writing notes but appeared to nod in agreement. Jana took this as a good sign. She ploughed on, interrogating the group, interrupting when they made valid suggestions in an attempt to redeem herself in the art dealer's eyes. Mimicking her bosses' behaviour, she grimaced, scowled, pounded the table and sneered at explanations. Red blotches stood out on her forehead.

The art dealer watched Jana's skin flush as she ripped the consultants' excuses to shreds. He chose a moment when Jana was in full flow. 'May I ask a question?'

Jana wilted.

'What, in your opinion, Jana, are the limitations of the traditional art gallery model?' Every word dropped like a sledgehammer blow. 'What changes have you implemented to align us with other revolutionary galleries?' The art dealer raised an eyebrow.

Jana's eyes darted to the exit. 'I'm the sales, marketing and customer service manager, artist relationship developer, curator, consultant, adviser, researcher, administration manager—'

A fake frown flitted across the art dealer's face. 'Your statement is interesting, but doesn't address the questions I asked. Furthermore, how have you measured the brand position we've executed, and what is your current correlation to collectors and commerce?'

'Co?'

'Can you expound on your supplementary strategies, in particular, the details of your handiwork, which will ensure the gallery remains at the forefront of collector's minds, and indeed, the populace?'

Jana's gaze searched the room. No one returned eye contact. 'I do my praca…work—' her eyes teared.

'Forgive me if I appear agnostic.' The art dealer's shark smile was back. 'I'm interested to learn your medium-term plans for sustaining growth. I've significant queries regarding your creative solutions apropos the maintenance of sustainability of our market, and I want to discuss those in an open forum. In addition, I look forward to hearing and understanding the logic behind the stratagems you've considered, guaranteeing we survive, thrive and emerge more robust at year-end. Would you reveal these conclusions to us please?'

'I don't understand your words.' Jana's bottom lip quivered.

'You can't grasp simple English?' The art dealer let the silence build. Then:

'I'm reassigning you to other duties. Also—'

'Co? What duties? I—'

'Also, I'm issuing you a verbal warning; I'll document it on your personnel file. If I've to address this again, you *will* face dismissal.' The art dealer chiselled the words into Jana's brain. 'Henceforth, you're in the stockroom.'

'But why—?'

'Because your managerial skills have become stultifying.'

'I don't know…'

'Stult…useless. Invest in a dictionary, Jana. You may leave.'

Cowed, humiliated and stripped of dignity, Jana cried.

'Leave,' the art dealer said.

Jana exited the meeting.

'You,' the art dealer snapped his fingers at one of the group. 'Organise and chair a panel, with specific emphasis on exploring novel ways to generate further revenue streams. Let's call it, A New Approach to Business. Create a list of measurable improvement proposals. Begin with membership schemes and mail me your top five recommendations by next Wednesday. Start the brainstorming session now.' The art dealer slid out of the conference room.

'CHECK.' THE DEALER turned the river: seven of clubs. Fatigue dropped like lead from Malcolm McGuire's eyes. He stalled a beat, eyeballed the kitty, totalling it up. 'Bet eight thousand.' Malcolm pushed in all the chips he'd clawed back over the last four hours.

Two of the last three players threw their cards into the dump pile. The third man, the one who'd checked, chewed an unlit cigar, saw the bet and raised eight thousand more. Each chip trickled onto Malcolm's pile. Drawn out, deliberate.

'I don't have enough to call,' Malcolm said.

'Fold 'em so.' The cigar dipped, and the man kept his eyes on Malcolm. Daring him.

Malcolm peeped at his hole cards again. King of hearts, seven of spades. Studied the five community cards: King of diamonds, King of spades, seven, nine and Jack of clubs. His house of Kings was a winner all the way. Except…Three cards made two combinations that could beat him. Six, eight and ten of clubs. Malcolm calculated the odds of that happening. Forty thousand to one. Nought point nought two per cent. He placed the Audi fob key on the chip pile. 'See you.'

The man removed the cigar and pointed it at the fob. 'What's that?'

'Key to an Audi A5.'

'Age?'

'A year.'

'Paperwork?'

'All in order. You won't need it.'

The man separated his hole cards and placed the eight and ten of clubs on either side of the nine. 'Straight flush.' He looked at Malcolm's pale face. 'Beat that?'

'No.'

'Cha-ching.' The man's arms enveloped the kitty, swept the pot to him, the fob bobbling like a boat on the sea of chips.

'I'll have cash by Tuesday,' Malcolm said. 'Wednesday at the latest. I'm good for it.'

The man produced a notebook and a pen. 'Gimme your number.'

Malcolm did. The man picked up the fob, tossed it from one palm to the other. 'Don't know if you're good for it or not. One week. Cash or paperwork. I've no problem lettin' your Audi go for eight grand. Don't give two shites 'bout cars, so call me. Tough luck, kid,' the man said, and stacked the chips into tall towers.

Malcolm walked out.

'Hey, kid.'

Malcolm looked over his shoulder.

The man was holding a phone to his ear. Malcolm's mobile rang. The man nodded. 'Just checkin'. Don't have me come huntin' ya'.

Malcolm moved away.

'Hey, kid.'

Malcolm turned around again.

The man pointed his cigar at him. 'You're not a bad poker player. Not great, but not bad. Some days you'll win. Most times you'll lose. Either way, you'll learn. Want my advice?'

'No.'

'I'll give it anyways.' The man clamped the cigar back in his mouth and talked around it. 'You might *think* you know how to play poker, but it takes a lifetime to learn. This is a hard way to make an easy livin'. We're way outta your league, kid.'

Malcolm roamed the Prince of Wales car park, scrolling through phone contacts, searching for somebody around Athlone he didn't owe money to. His stomach growled. The last food he'd eaten was lunch yesterday. Mobile jammed between ear and shoulder, he searched pockets and counted the change trapped in his cupped palm.

Nine euro, and a week to find eight thousand. He *had* to repay the money before the Audi got missed.

It took a dozen calls to get the loan of a Honda Civic that reeked of beer and damp clothes. Malcolm drove towards Ganestown, fiddled with the radio dial. A wall of tinny noise filled the car interior. The speakers sounded crap; thin, no bass. Horrible, compared to the quality high-end Bang and Olufsen speakers he'd got fitted as an extra in the Audi. He turned into Rossbeg Industrial estate and drove around to the back of the hardware shop.

Milo Brady was in the breeze block office, twisting on the swivel chair and talking on a landline. He'd smeared the desk with fillings from a BLT sandwich. 'The way I see it, you can run with the big dogs, or you can sit in the garden and bark. You've gotta show them what you're made of. I've got this place humming like a happy bee. When I take over the sales manager's—'

'Ahem.'

Milo twisted. He'd nicked his chin while shaving, and a dollop of mayonnaise gummed his jacket. 'Catch ya later, man.' He banged the receiver into its casing and varied a range of facial expressions that ended up a smirk. He scratched his chin. 'What's happening, cousin?'

'Nothing. Passing by. Forgot my wallet. Need cash to tide me over.'

'I'm low on funds too. How much?'

'Five hundred.'

'Five hun…? Not a chance.' Milo dug into a trouser pocket, pulled out crumpled notes. 'Twenty, five, five, five. Thirty-five. That's it.'

Malcolm's knuckles clenched. 'That won't get me to Dublin. What's in petty cash?'

'The cupboard's bare, Mal.'

Malcolm grabbed the money. 'I'll repay you tomorrow.' He checked the wall clock.

13:24.

The four-year-old Bob's Your Aunt was in the 1:30 at Lingfield. 12/1. A racing certainty. His sire was Dunne's Dilemma, its dam The Actress. Milo's monkey would've netted him six thousand. Not enough, but sufficient to stake a big win. Instead, he had…thirty-five euro, plus nine. Malcolm rummaged between the seats, found a two euro coin in the cupholder. Forty-six euro, at 12/1. Worth nothing, he thought, but it was easy winnings.

He spun out of the exit and his mobile buzzed. Ciara. No point pressing 'Decline'. She'd keep calling. 'Hey, what's up?'

'Not much. Wanted to hear a friendly voice. I'm having a crap day. You coping any better?'

Malcolm slid the car nose first into a space outside the bookies. 'So far, so good.' His eyes stayed glued on the dashboard clock.

13:26.

'You at work?'

Malcolm switched off the ignition. 'Yeah. Up to my elbows here.' message

'Did you visit Dad today?'

'Haven't had a chance. I'll go in tonight.'

'I've an idea, Mal. After he's discharged, I'd like to take him to my house for a week or—'

'Whatever works for you.'

'Problem is, I can't imagine he'll agree. Dad prefers his own place. Next option, I thought if we took turns to stay with him, till he recovers? Remember what the nurse said? It's vital we keep him monitored. What do you reckon?'

13:28.

Malcolm squirmed. 'Didn't think about it. Listen, I—'

'We should decide soon. Then I had another idea. We could hire a—'

'I'll buy into—'

'Pay attention, Mal. We could hire a live-in nurse for a month or two. It'll give Dad more independence.'

'If it's okay for you, I'm on board.' Malcolm crunched the money in his fist. 'I've another call on hold. Lemme ring you back.'

'Phone me tonight,' Ciara said.'

'Sure. We'll figure...hello? hello?' Malcolm cut the connection and jumped from the car. The girl behind the counter smiled in recognition. He shot a quick look at the clock; the red hand sweeping off seconds.

'Made it,' he said.

AFTERNOON

THE NURSE STATION was deserted.

Hugh dashed along the corridor and careened into Ruth Lamero.

Ruth sidestepped. 'Easy, tiger. Oh, hi, Hugh. I just popped by to see Kathleen.'

'Hope I didn't miss doctor—'

'He's been and gone.'

'Crap.'

'Kathleen's discharged—'

'Great.'

I helped her dress and pack.' The pager beeped in Ruth's coat pocket. 'The release form has to be signed, and go see Keith Abbott before you leave.'

Hugh said, 'Okay, I'll go check out what's what.'

He found Kathleen up and dressed, peering into the built-in wardrobe. Her coat hung on a doorknob. The suitcase sat on the bed, toilet bag beside it. She raised her eyes. 'Not a stitch to wear.'

Tiny strips of gauze patched the scabbed wound; the bruises camouflaged by foundation. 'I'll put a jacket on over this old dress. Where's my purse? I've to pay the hospital bill. We'll stop off at Ozanam House on our way home. When can you take a day off work? We've parcels to deliver. Can't have people without food, and Christmas 'round the corner.'

'Christmas is…Concentrate on getting better first, Ma. Sure, I'll help. No problem.'

Kathleen searched her toiletry bag for perfume, sprayed Chanel Cristalle in the air and stepped into the mist. 'Well? Let's go.'

'Hang on a minute, Ma. I'll get the release forms.'

On the fifth floor, a nurse pointed him to Keith Abbott's office, and a secretary nodded to a seat. A line of overlapped Vogue magazines and the latest *Ganestown Weekly* lay on a coffee table. The front page depicted a blurry, enlarged passport photo of Roberta Lord.

The receptionist closed her laptop and left.

Hugh flipped the pages of a glossy. Before he'd a chance to read the twenty things women wished men knew, Doctor Abbott appeared from an inner room, overcoat buttoned across his beach-ball belly.

Hugh could see the doctor didn't remember him. 'Hugh Fallon. I missed you on the ward rounds. We spoke yesterday. My mother? Kathleen Fallon? Has the specialist assessed Ma?'

Keith Abbott beckoned, turned back into a cubby-hole office, plonked into a seat behind a desk strewn with folders and files. The chair squeaked in protest as the man bent to unlock a drawer and remove a sheet of paper. 'My suspicions got confirmed. Your mother is in Stage Four Alzheimer's.' The doctor took off his glasses. 'I'm sorry.'

Hugh stared, the blood draining from his face. 'What? It's a mistake. I...There's been a mix-up. Yes, that's it, an error. This *cannot* happen to Ma. She...I don't believe...I want another opinion. I *insist*...' Realising he was shouting, Hugh took a breath and lowered his voice. 'It isn't feasible she's contracted this *thing*. I'll query the results.'

The doctor bit on the glasses' temple, leaned forward, using his elbows to push files aside. 'That's your prerogative. It won't change our findings. We've carried out a glut of tests, PET scans...the works. It is what it is.'

Dark and bright spots swam before Hugh's eyes, and he lost his train of thought, unprepared for this cold, matter-of-fact, definitive prognosis. 'I still—' He felt himself getting dizzy.

'I'm sorry this has arrived at your doorstep.' Doctor Abbott replaced the paper back in the drawer.

'I don't...' Hugh began. 'There haven't been any symptoms of—'

'The signs were there for a while,' the doctor said, 'but when you're close to the person—'

'I'm sure I'd have noticed. What does this mean? How will Ma—?'

'Alzheimer's is comparable to a tsunami let loose inside the brain,' the doctor said. 'I've heard people describe it as a volcanic eruption, but every family have their own descriptions. Whatever words you use, the results are the same: it destroys everything in its path. Everything the patient has learned is forgotten, and thus the extended family's lives change. Everyone adapts to survive the stress Alzheimer's generates. Constant fine-tuning becomes your new normal.'

Too stunned to interrupt, too many emotions to handle, Hugh's mind ran amok for the second time in twenty-four hours. Questions jumbled up his brain. 'So, what now? Where do I...? What do I do?' Realism crashed like breakers. It felt as if he was tumbling in waves, choking, unable to breathe. His head swelled with white noise. The pounding in his ears drowned out most of the doctor's words: '...need time to process...at ease in locations she'll recognise...Your siblings will have to...day-to-day—'

'There's only me. I've cousins. We meet at weddings and funerals. You said Stage...?'

'Four.'

'How many stages in total?'

'Seven.'

'How long before...?'

The doctor shrugged. 'Alzheimer's disease usually worsens slowly, but its advance depends on the person's genetic make-up, age and medical condition.'

'Ma's in good health.'

'There are a plethora of factors that determine its progression. Reaction to medication or vitamin deficiencies, for example. Infections. Hypothyroidism. Autoimmune neurological disorders and paraneoplastic disorders can cause rapid—'

'I never heard Ma say—'

'For now it's best you help Kathleen shop, pay the bills, control her expenditure and so forth, the usual everyday transactions, while she maintains a regular lifestyle.'

'And that's Stage Seven?'

'No. That's stage four. Stage Seven is...' The doctor scratched an eyebrow. 'Going on prior cases, you'll have to stop her driving in, I'd say three to six months, tops. She'll—'

'What's Stage Seven?'

'Severe decline. The patient loses the ability to respond or communicate. More often, the end comes with mini-strokes or pneumonia.'

'Who can I talk to? Other families or associations I can contact? I can't...This can't be right.' Hugh's imagination spun, still in a bubble of denial.

Doctor Abbott nodded. 'My secretary will send you a letter. Alas, we've limited resources. The ward nurse has a prescription you need to fill. Ganestown has a good Alzheimer's support group. I recommend you get in touch. However, all the talk in the world won't prepare you. This'll change your family dynamic. You'll become a carer and learn to live it day-to-day. Soldier on. The medication I've prescribed may help delay the process. And um, you might consider gene-sequencing for yourself.'

'Not sure how I'd handle the results if they were positive.'

'Early intervention could be crucial—'

'I'll consider it.'

Doctor Abbott stood, the impromptu chat concluded.

Hugh stumbled out, a vulnerable sheep sheared of its protective coat.

He bought a box of chocolates for the ward staff and plodded back. At the nurse's station, Ruth sorted through a pile of files stacked on the countertop. 'Hugh? Want to talk?'

'I won't be fantastic company after Abbot's—'

'Listen, consultants don't do bedside therapy, but if I'm ever sick, it's Keith Abbott I want in my corner.'

'Managing directors and consultants have *no* emotional intelligence. No idea—'

'Hugh?'

Hugh waved the chocolate box in the air. '*No* empathy. No clue *how* to deliver—'

'Hugh?'

Hugh stopped talking.

'Maybe you're focusing on the wrong person,' Ruth said.

Hugh's shoulders slumped. 'You're right. His manner is the least of my concerns.' He left the chocolate box on the counter. 'You knew.'

'Thanks for those. Yes, I guessed.'

'I don't know anything about Alzheimer's, or how to manage someone with it. Where do I start? How do—?'

'My father has dementia, too. Parkinson's. So I understand your reaction.'

'Oh. Sorry to hear that.'

'One reason I came back to Ganestown.'

'How is he? I mean…'

'It's heart-breaking to see Dad lose his mobility. He gets around with a stick, but soon he'll need a walker. Still has strength in his arms, but his fingers are getting to the point where he can't hold a knife or a cup.'

'God. Tough to witness.'

'It is.'

'How does Alzheimer's differ from…?'

'Both have to do with parts of the brain dying. Different symptoms though. I'll help, but I'm not a qualified carer,' Ruth said. 'If there's anything you need, any queries I can answer, or you just want to chat—'

'I'll have a ton of questions once I get my head sorted.'

'Write them down. Phone me anytime. But give yourself space to process this—'

'Doctor Abbott said that. To be honest, I can't think beyond the next hour. I'll Google later and learn as much as I can.'

'My advice, Hugh, is talk to people who are at the Alzheimer's coal face. I don't recommend Google. It can induce blind panic.'

They swapped mobile numbers. Hugh walked towards the wards, stopped and turned. 'Thought you worked in A&E?'

'I do. It's quiet at the moment. This weather means patients aren't visiting their doctors, so GPs aren't sending them in for minor ailments, clogging up the system.'

'Was busy the other night.'

'Night-time's always bad. No doctor house calls anymore, so anyone who needs help either rings for an ambulance or walks into casualty. Anyway, I reckoned you'd want to see a friendly face after talking to Keith.' Ruth shrugged, 'I waited around.'

'That's…Thanks a million.'

Hugh strode into room twenty-four, determined to keep a brave face, yet obliquely viewing his mother differently. Earlier, she seemed okay. Now she appeared unsteady. Brittle. Was that normal after a few days in hospital, he wondered? Or was it part of the Alzheimer's symptom? A nurse arrived with the prescription. No wheelchair was available, so a porter helped him link Kathleen out to the Hiace.

At home, she sank into her armchair. 'I could start enjoying this fuss.' There was no mention of Ozanam House. Hugh prepared a meal and phoned Brendan at McGuire's.

'Don't worry 'bout bringing the van back today,' Brendan said. 'But there're a couple of deliveries tomorrow for Kilbeggan.'

'I'll be there before you open,' Hugh promised without thinking, then remembered…He phoned Eilish again. This time the phone kicked into voicemail. He left a message, asking if she was free for a few hours in the morning.

'Free for what?' Kathleen asked.

'Eilish will stay with you tomorrow. I've to go—'

'I don't *need* a babysitter.'

'Just to keep you company, Ma.'

'I've managed on my own since your father died, and I'll—'

'You might feel weak after—'

'For God's *sake*, Hugh. Leave me alone. Stop mooching around like a…I don't know what.'

'Well, I need to get your tablets.'

'I don't want them.'

'Okay, Ma. I'll go collect post at my house.'

Hugh drove to a pharmacy. The quantity of tablets will be problematic, he thought, looking at the array of medication. Kathleen wasn't a pill advocate.

THE ART DEALER strolled around Belfast's city centre, inspected a competitors' gallery and met a solicitor acting on behalf of a deceased client. He hated the bureaucratic hassle that third-parties generated—individuals who were neither intimate with art nor loyal to collectors. Dealing with them reduced his role to that of a glorified shop-floor worker. In a music store, he browsed through the classical and jazz sections, memorised titles from Bach and Count Basie CDs, before waving a taxi.

'Where to?'

'Kennedy Way Industrial Estate.'

The art dealer snubbed the taxi man's chatty attempts at conversation. At the business park, he directed the driver to a warehouse and asked him to wait. Inside, he ignored the latest gadgets on display and walked to the desk.

A rotund, cheery Pakistani man bowed. 'Khush'aamdid. Welcome. I'm Kabir. How can we help? You search for deal on iPhone, Ipod or Ipad?' He gesticulated. 'I give good deal. Come, I show you. If you're in the market for—'

'I'm interested in peace of mind,' the art dealer cut in. 'My wife travels a lot, and I want her to have protection if she ever finds herself in a bad place.'

'Ah, Personal protection and piss of mind. Is priceless. This way. Plis.'

The art dealer followed the man into a back store, stacked floor to ceiling with boxes. Kabir reached for one and opened the cardboard flap. 'If you wish your wife safe trip, my friend, this is good present. A direct contact weapon, disguised as a mobile phone. It delivers five million volts. A one-second zap will stop attacker in his tracks. Two seconds, zap, zap, will drop him and give your wife time to escape from museebat...' Kabir searched for the English word '...trouble. You buy?'

'Too bulky. It must fit in a purse or handbag. I want…hmm, more compact.'

'Yes, but dearer.' Kabir delved into another box. 'This one? We call it The Closer. It fits in your hand. Much lighter. See?'

The silver case fitted snug in the art dealer's palm.

Perfect.

'Can you demonstrate?'

'Yes. I show.' Kabir fitted a battery, explained the function buttons and pressed the control switch. A blue-white current pulsed across the top of the stun gun, creating a buzzing sound.

'What happens if it's held against an attacker for over two seconds?'

'Depends on size of person. Big man? Knock him unconscious. Small man…?' Kabir shrugged. 'Either way, lady safe. You take it today, or I can Fed Ex.'

'I'll take it.'

Kabir waved a finger in the art dealer's face. 'If you travel by plane, plis do not put into hand luggage. Separate this, and unlock this. The parts go through checked baggage like a battery razor. No problem.'

The art dealer paid cash and got back into the taxi. He squeezed a tennis ball, aching to try out the new toy. Jana had given him a migraine. Glenavy was fourteen miles away. His hand tingled. The desire to push the immobiliser into either Dorothy Ridgeway or Jana Trofimiack's necks was a living presence. He yearned to view its effect.

Let's see how much they appreciate The Closer up close and personal. Stupid, blind bitches.

The driver eyed him in the rear-view mirror, engine ticking over.

'City Centre,' the art dealer said.

If BachtoBasie hasn't replied by tomorrow, I'll research Jana's movements outside work hours. What she does. Where she goes. Who she meets. Timelines. Or I could arrange a meeting in Dublin, and take her to join the others. Yes, El Matador. Literal translation, 'the killer'.

CONVERSATIONS CEASED WHEN Jana walked through the office.

She buried her head in files, sensing the sidelong stares of co-workers. Her time at Hattinger's was limited. After today, everyone knew that. Nobody wanted to talk to her, terrified they'd get skażone, tainted. She'd quit rather than let him push her out. How could she not meet customers? Silly job, pushing paper around a desk when she should be...What if she defied the boss man? Jana cringed, as a consultant tried to explain the differences between hard paste Chinese porcelain and soft paste European porcelain to a client. Jana fidgeted, longed to butt in, but if he discovered she'd interfered...Was it possible he had cameras fitted? Her eyes searched the ceiling tiles. Or, what if staff were snitches? It wouldn't surprise her. Thoughts of him made her shiver. And those eyes? Stone cold.

Jana had no idea why he didn't appreciate her work ethics. She'd asked staff. Nobody could answer. At first, she'd ignored it as a culture issue. His manner was vicious, but he hated Jana. It was all his fault, her becoming involved with Tomasz. A spaced-out conversation about the asshole boss. A dare, to defy him for treating her like gówno. On one side, the chance to exploit his company and get revenge was a big incentive. On the other, the pressure Tomasz exerted to switch more paintings, along with the risk of getting caught because Günther didn't take enough attention to reproduce them right, was a recipe for disaster. Günther's sloppiness would catch up on them. Now, the dare was reckless. Tomasz was too greedy. The walls were crashing down. On the positive side, she'd been able to send money home to Rzeszów and provide a quality life for her family. If they knew half of what she had to endure to secure their luxuries.

Starved, because she had no lunch, Jana ducked out for food. She ordered kielbasa—comfort food Maia used to make—and used her phone to log on to a travel site. Scrolling through airline timetables she booked two seats on the cheapest flight to Jasionka airport. She finished her food and dialled a number. 'Tomasz? It's Jana.'

'Co? Wszystko dobrze?'

'The package arrived. I delivered it. It's not the most—'

'You asked for it szybko.'

'Tak, but Günther should've…It's still bzdura. I *told* you his work isn't as—'

'Doesn't matter. Is konsultant cancelled?'

'I think so.'

'Dobry. Tell your boss the McKelvey's found—'

'I've told him.'

'That'll get him off your back. Blame the old suka for forgetting where she left it. I've collected cash for the McKelvey. You'll get your share when you give me the Yeats.'

'I'm picking it up tonight.'

'Good. You happy with *that* replacement?'

'It's better. The owner's half blind. He won't notice. Um, Tomasz?'

'Có?'

'I'll be away for a while. We're going to visit my family. Lech's birthday is next week. He hasn't seen his grandmother for ages. We fly to Polska Monday morning.'

'Which airport?'

'Belfast International.'

'I'll have a man meet you there. Give him the Yeats. He'll have your money, minus Günther's fees.'

'Okay.'

'What time's your flight?'

'Six-twenty a.m.'

'How long will you be away?'

'Two weeks.'

'We've lots to do when you get back.'

Head high, Jana left the restaurant, her step brisk. She'd enough money stashed to open her own gallery in Warszawa or Kraków. Ha! She'd get the last śmiać się.

EVENING

STARVED OF COMPANY, Dorothy Ridgeway grilled Sharona, then spent the afternoon regaling her visitor with anecdotes about life in Belfast. And Blake.

Blake had been a stockbroker with interests in art and property. Dorothy, a theatre sister, 'born, bred and buttered' in Belfast, had met him for the first time on his way into the operating room with a burst appendix. They'd married within six months. For over forty years, they'd bought and sold properties and acquired many pieces of art. Blake died the previous summer, aged sixty-eight.

'I'll show you around,' Dorothy said. 'With your art background, you'll have an interest in the bits and bobs we collected. Now, see this one here…?' She reminisced on paintings, sculptures, prints and drawings, recalling the story behind each treasure, where they'd purchased it and why she'd chosen it. Dorothy quizzed and verified Sharona's expertise, and once satisfied, asked her opinion on various works.

'You sure it's safe to have these on display, Dorothy? Why not keep them in storage?'

'What's the point in that? No sense buying exquisite pieces if you can't enjoy them whenever the mood strikes. That's what insurance is for.'

'But does your insurance company not insist—?'

'Until the auction, *I* insist on keeping them here.'

'Oh, okay.'

'Here's what the fuss was around. Isn't it divine?' Dorothy handed Sharona a small framed canvas.

Sharona gazed at McKelvey's oil on canvas of children feeding a calf. 'God, the sense of light and space…Notice how he captured the wonder and nervousness in the boy's face? And that's also shown in the animal's stance when the calf spots the stick in the child's hand. It's magnificent, Dorothy.'

Dorothy smiled. 'That's the first present Blake ever bought me. His dad and Frank McKelvey grew up together in Glanvale Street, a stone's throw from here. McKelvey died the day we married. June thirtieth, 1974. I've a lot of emotional memories attached to this piece.'

'McKelvey did incredible work with natural light and the sun's rays,' Sharona said. 'And the sky…My lecturer used to speak of him in the same breath as Paul Henry.'

Dorothy nodded. 'Exquisite landscapes. Donegal in particular, and the West of Ireland.'

Sharona inverted the canvas, appraised the back. Looked closer. 'Have you taken it from its frame lately?'

'No. Why?'

'Hmm. The Rodman label appears genuine—'

'And why wouldn't it? What—?'

'Pinholes, as if the brads aren't in their original spots. And these scuff marks? Like someone removed the canvas.'

'Rubbish, girl.' Dorothy removed her spectacles, shielded her eyes and squinted at the picture. 'Something pierced the frame when it fell behind the settee. Thank God the painting's intact.'

Sharona let the chandelier illuminations wash across the figures. 'Seems...I'm not sure. Something's off.'

'It's the light in here.'

'You're probably right, and—'

'I am.'

'—and I don't want to upset you, Dorothy, but Frank McKelvey painted this ninety years ago. It's weathered, as you'd expect for its age, but...There was this guy in college, an art restorer. I picked up some bits off him. I've a notion there should be more hairline cracks.'

'I'm telling you, the light—'

'There's a test experts perform on canvases.' Sharona scrutinised the picture again.

'Why would—?'

'To confirm if it's genuine or—'

'Or what?' Dorothy eyed Sharona, suspicious. 'Genuine or what? Of *course* it's genuine. Full stop. Exactly what test? Hmm?'

'They remove the canvas from the frame and view it from behind. If you can make out the image of the entire scene, chances are it's a reproduction.' Sharona sniffed. 'Can you smell paint?'

Dorothy inhaled and coughed. 'Ach, this cold has blocked my sinuses. Put hydrochloric acid in front of me, and I wouldn't notice. But I don't have flu all the time, and I've never...Anyway, that's impossible. As you say, it's ninety years old. Who in their right mind would take a canvas out of its frame for no reason?'

'Can't imagine, Dorothy.'

'Jana was only in the house for a minute. She didn't have time to...But if somebody *did*, and mind you I'm not *saying* they did, but if you're right, and I'm not saying you are, then it *must* be Hattinger's. But Jana said they didn't come across it, and no one else has been here since, so either *you're* mistaken, Hattinger's are liars or Jana…No, she'd never…She *found*…How can…? Someone's telling me porkies.' Dorothy's narrowed eyes combed Sharona's face, judging her reaction.

'I may be wrong, but…' Sharona brought the canvas closer and inhaled. 'I'm positive it smells fresh. If you twisted my arm, I'd say this is a photograph.'

'Photograph? Now I know you're…That's utter nonsense, girl. I'll *prove* it. I've the validation papers and receipt from Rodman's. Someplace. There's no way Blake bought an item that wasn't a hundred per cent genuine. I'm a feeble old woman, but I've still got eyesight.'

Sharona raised the frame closer to the chandelier. 'It's the only conclusion that makes sense.'

Dorothy stood on tiptoe and looked over Sharona's shoulder. 'You're very sure of yourself, young lady. How can you be certain? It *looks* authentic.'

'It's amazing what they can achieve with Photoshop these days.'

'What makes you even *think* it's a photo?'

Sharona pointed. 'This patch here? The paint should be dense. You can see the *image* of texture, but there's no paint substance.'

'Hmm. Don't stir. I'll be back.' Dorothy left the room.

Sharona examined the painting again, wavering between doubt and belief. Something was wrong.

Dorothy returned and slumped into a Victorian mahogany chair. 'I rang Charlie. Told him what you've said. He swears you're the genuine article. If in *your* judgement there's a problem, then I'm bamboozled. Why put a photo in a frame? When was it switched? And where's the original? Jana and Ambrose…I *know* these people. I've treated them like family. This is awful. The piece Blake bought me? I want it back.'

'Dorothy, I haven't the technical skills to verify this, but I can get in touch with an impartial appraiser. My old lecturer, Tristin Reed, is an art historian at Dublin's National Gallery. We could make an appointment.'

Dorothy cupped her face in her hands. 'God, that's…I can't comprehend why people I've *trusted*…You *sure* I need to do this?'

'Ninety-nine per cent.'

'Where's my mobile? I'll phone Ambrose. Give him a piece of my mind.'

'Mr Hattinger mightn't be aware—'

'Course he's aware. It's his company.' Dorothy took the picture and studied it again from every angle. 'Who does he think…? *Nobody* gave him permission to tamper with my property? How. Very. *Dare*. He. I can't get my head…Tell you what,' Dorothy slapped her thigh, back in control. 'I'm in Dublin tomorrow, preparing a fundraiser. We'll get your expert friend to assess my McKelvey, and—'

'Tomorrow's Saturday,' Sharona said.

'Doesn't matter. Get him on the phone. I'll use my powers of persuasion. I want this painting authenticated *immediately*.'

'Okay.'

'Hattinger's will be at the fundraiser ball. You'll come too.'

'Crikey, I—'

'No excuses. You'll be my guest. To be honest, I'd prefer to muck around in a horse barn than spend a night in a ballroom, but it's our duty to give back to the community.' Dorothy touched the frame again. 'I can't accept…No doubt you believe, but…' She placed the painting on a chair and clapped her hands, back in control. 'Right. You'll help me search for the receipt.'

'I should get on the road—'

'Nonsense, girl. You're staying tonight. Tomorrow, we'll travel south together.' Dorothy caught Sharona's arm. 'If you're wrong, no harm, no foul. If you're correct, I demand an explanation. Wild horses won't stop me uncovering what happened. This picture. I can't describe the significance...Its emotional value is priceless. I bet you want answers too. Hmm?'

'Sure.'

'Good. Now, call your arty friend. We'll set up a meet for tomorrow afternoon and untangle this riddle. Let's find the receipt and uncork a bottle of limoncello. It's from a *fabulous* lemon grove we bought in Capri a few years ago. You like limoncello, don't you?'

'I...Thanks, Dorothy. Maybe a smidgen.'

HUGH'S DRIVEWAY WAS a pristine sheet of snow.

He was brewing coffee when Eilish walked in.

'Hi,' she said. An oversized tote bag lodged between their bodies, preventing Hugh's attempt at a bear hug. Eilish broke the embrace. 'That van looks grotty. It'll destroy suits—'

'I'll be wearing a boiler suit when I'm out on deliveries.'

'Wearing a what?'

'Boiler suit.'

'Charming.' Eilish wrinkled her nose. 'You won't need new clothes so.'

'Clothes are the least of my worries. Coffee?'

'No, thanks.' Eilish looked at her watch.

'We must start pencilling in meetings,' Hugh said. 'Another five minutes, I'd have missed you again.' He gestured at the weekend bag. 'I've collected some clothes. Tried phoning you last night. Your voicemail was full.'

'You know there's no signal at my parents' house. I got your text this morning. Terrible news about Kathleen.'

'Yeah. Rough few days.'

'Sorry I can't babysit tomorrow. I've a hairdresser's appointment.'

'It's okay. Ma feels she can manage on her own. For a while, anyway. It'll be—'

'Yeah. I know.'

'How's your mother?'

'Still stuffed with flu.' Eilish studied her fingernails.

'Eilish?'

'Hmm?'

'What's up?'

'Nothing. Why?'

'We're okay, aren't we? I mean, we don't talk anymore. It's...'

'We're both stressed. You...your unemployment, and I'm supposed to be back to screamers with sugar tantrums on Monday.'

'Unless this weather gives you another week off school.'

'We'll see.' Eilish teased her hair and picked at a split end. How's McGuire's?'

'One minute I'm driving that old rickety Hiace, but to be fair, it's no worse than my car, and the next I'm steering Malcolm in the right direction. Dole, plus the sixteen hours a week I'm allowed to work will—'

'God. Enough to starve on.'

Hugh frowned. 'If we reduce expenses, we'll manage. I'm positive I'll get a permanent job within a month. Max.'

'Tara and I arranged a catch-up tomorrow night in the Ramble Inn. Join us if you want.'

'We need to talk,' Hugh said.

'We'll chat tomorrow.'

'In a crowded pub? Can we talk now?'

'Provided you don't come up with a catalogue of do's and don'ts, or tell me what I can or can't buy. You'd swear I shopped in Milan. If I see a bargain, I'll buy it. I pay my share.'

'Did you buy food this week?'

'No, I—'

'You made me rip out a good kitchen, spend fifteen grand on new units, and we've no food? Or milk.' Hugh's arm-wave encompassed the room. 'What's the point in—?'

'Nobody *made* you—'

The kitchen door opened. 'Knock knock,' Ferdia said. 'Front door's unlocked.' He walked through the kitchen, left slush and cigarette smoke in his wake, tossed car keys on the countertop, opened the patio door and leaned against the frame. 'If you're making coffee, I'll have one.'

Eilish burrowed through her bag, found her phone and left the kitchen, closing the door behind her.

'There's no milk,' Hugh said.

'No problem.' Ferdia batted cigarette smoke away with hand flicks. 'Inhuman Resources booked a slot for you next Wednesday.'

'Time?'

'I dunno. Around lunchtime.'

Hugh handed him the coffee mug. 'Depends on Ma.'

'How's Kathleen?'

'She's home.'

'Good.'

'Doctor diagnosed her with Alzheimer's.'

'Aww, Jaysus. That's feckin'—'

'I'm still not certain. There's no way Ma—'

'Hope you're right. Man, that's a planet I never want to visit. If there's anything I can do—'

'Thanks. She's fine for the moment. Barring another mishap, I'll be in McGuire's, so I can pop across for my slot, whatever the hell that means. Good job I opted to buy my car instead of plumping for a company vehicle, or I'd be rightly screwed now. Cigarettes will kill you, Ferdia.'

'I'll be grand.' Ferdia slurped a hefty gulp of coffee. 'I'm relying on medical advances to save me.'

'How'd your check-up go?' Hugh asked.

'Fit as a butcher's dog. Doc took enough feckin' blood to keep Dracula supplied for a month. Said he'll phone when the results come back.'

'What's the latest at Pharma-Continental?'

'Had a three-hour meeting with Denis this morning that he could've summed up in an email. Sales down. Overheads up. He's decided micromanaging is the only way. He's like a neighbour's feckin' goat; always stuck in someone else's garden, mithering everyone. The problems are piling high. And why wouldn't they, when we've damn all salespeople? Boots on the ground win battles, I say. Sales don't just happen. Pounding pavements is the only way to generate—'

'And what's Denis's solution?'

'Full of technical information and not a gram of feckin' empathy in his body.' Ferdia pawed the air to disperse persistent smoke before he slammed the patio door shut and put his backside against a radiator. 'This thing not on?'

'Need to order oil.'

'Huh. If brains were bird droppings, Denis's cage would be spotless. Companies never learn. I've seen it umpteen times. No loyalty to employees. Numbers on a chart.'

'Higher-ups are telling him what to do.'

'Yeah, two of them arrived yesterday. Seagull managers.'

'What's that?'

'Seagull managers? They fly in, shit on everything and fly off, leaving someone else to clean up the mess.'

Hugh laughed. 'It's written in the rules. Arrange meeting. Set low expectations. Do nothing. Claim success.'

'That's it. Rinse, repeat over and over. White noise.'

'Procedures, Ferdia.'

'Huh. Useless if they don't work. Bureaucratic bullshit. Measure what matters, I say, and ignore the rest.'

Hugh shrugged. 'I think Denis finds it hard to decide. I found him reasonable. He grows on you.'

'So does moss. Hope to Christ that's the end of bad news for this year. It comes in threes, you know.'

'What?'

'Bad news. It comes—'

'Jesus, redundancy is enough.'

Ferdia drew a tin of biscuits closer, inspected the contents, saw nothing he fancied and removed the plastic wrap and delved into the bottom layer. 'Anything new at McGuire's?' He pulled out two chocolate treats, pressed them together, dunked them, shovelled the drippy mess into his mouth, and chomped.

'I've told you, I'm a van driver, not the CEO.'

'Aye, but,' Ferdia pointed two fingers at his eyes, then at Hugh's face, 'you notice things. How's Mal?'

'Spends most of the time on a laptop.'

'You might need to give him a leg up.'

'I'll help if I can. He's in town today meeting Milo Brady. Milo's getting his P60.'

'Good. Haven't seen that lad for a while, but I believe he's a regional version of the village idiot. Hope Malcolm asked Ciara how to say the right lingo, else he could make a dog's dinner out of it.'

'He asked me.'

'Ahh.' Ferdia got another coffee-soaked biscuit halfway to his mouth before it broke, splashed into the mug and spattered his tie. 'Any news on that Lord woman?'

'Haven't heard. How's Charlie?'

'Chatted to him earlier. He's in fine fettle.'

'Anyone arrested yet?'

Ferdia used his tongue to dislodge a biscuit crumb, taking his time answering. 'No. And there won't be. Chas got into debt with dodgy people. They roughed him up.'

'No way.'

'Yes, way. Wouldn't pass up the chance to lay my hands on them. I'd soften their coughs.'

'Whose coughs?'

'Gombeen men. Loan sharks. From the Irish word gaimbín, money grabber. Coined during famine times to describe greedy shopkeepers who jacked up food prices.'

'What, pay up or starve?'

'More or less. Anyhow, I'll meet them and sort out a repayment plan.'

'Isn't your fight Ferdia.'

'I promised Chas.'

'You'll land yourself in trouble.'

'Nah. My wallet an' willy is all that ever gets me in trouble.'

'You're mad.'

'You know me.'

'As a rule, there's method in your madness, Ferdia, but that's pure madness, no method.'

'Ah, sure you've gotta swing leather, bite on the gum shield and plough on.'

'When have you planned to meet them?'

Ferdia scraped a thumbnail on the coffee stain on his tie. 'Chas'll set it up after he gets back on his feet.'

'Tell me when and I'll tag along,' Hugh said.

'Grand.' Ferdia stood, hitched up his trousers and tucked the stained tie into the waistband. 'I'm heading to Dublin for the weekend. Gotta pick up the Merc in the morning. Oh,' he delved into an inside pocket and pulled out an envelope. 'There's a fancy gig tomorrow—'

'Yeah. Herbert Park Hotel. Charlie mentioned—'

'See? You miss nothing.' Ferdia took a ticket from the envelope. 'Here. Person I'd planned to bring can't make it—'

'So I'm your second choice?'

'Third, actually. It'll be good craic. After the week you've had, a little downtime will do you good. Eilish won't mind.'

'Eilish couldn't care less if—'

'You can bunk in my hotel room. Loads of space.'

'Well…okay. I need a night out. What happened to the terrier?'

'Passed him on to a friend. He's got a good home. Oh, wear a dickie bow tomorrow night. I'll get them to leave a room key at reception.' Ferdia scooped up his car keys and pin-wheeled the keyring on his index finger. 'So long, sis,' he shouted.

No answer.

Ferdia jerked his head at the closed door. 'Someone in a mood?'

Hugh made a face. 'I'm in the dog house. I'm pissing everyone off today.'

Ferdia saluted. 'Happens to us all. Pass no heed. 'Slán.'

Eilish came back into the kitchen, coat buttoned, tote bag slung from her shoulder.

'Won't be able to meet you for drinks tomorrow,' Hugh said. 'Ferdia's invited me to—'

'Fine. By the way, nobody *made* you rip out the old kitchen.'

'I pay the mortgage, Eilish, *and* the other domestic bills. When I've got money, I don't ask you to contribute. For now, can we pool our funds? House insurance is due in two weeks. Car tax first week in March. We—'

'I work too hard to scrimp. I didn't expect this scenario. It's—' Eilish's mobile rang, a muffled chirp. She delved into her bag and powered it off.

'What can I say?' Hugh said, hoping for a smile. 'It's called life.'

Eilish's frown deepened. 'Life, not Lough Derg. I don't intend to survive on black tea and dry toast for the rest of my life.'

'Ouch, there's the red-head temper. No one's asked you to go hungry, although I've expanded several inches over Christmas.' Hugh patted his stomach. 'Must start exercising.'

'You implying I'm fat? And stop copying Ferdia's routine of using humour to defuse a situation.'

'I'm not, and you aren't...God almighty, Eilish, don't twist my words. Can we tighten our belts a notch? Wear items out? Make them go further? That's all I'm asking.'

'Well then, stay *here* tomorrow night. Tell Ferdia you can't go. Wrap a blanket around yourself and sit in the cold. That way, you won't have to spend money.'

'That's harsh, Eilish. Life's trials should bond couples, not drive them—'

'Stop, Hugh.' Eilish exhaled and held up her hand. 'I'm sick of your logic.' She spun on her high heels and tramped upstairs.

'And I'm tired of your high maintenance.' Hugh walked out.

NIGHT

STAFF AT THE Chubby Cherub restaurant in Belfast's Arthur Street prepared for the Friday rush.

Office workers socialised, unwinding after their week's slog. A designer-stubbled waiter, dressed in tight black Tom Ford and with the flamboyant, exaggerated mannerisms of a dancer, hustled the art dealer to a table beside a mixed group of suited professionals. Solicitors or bankers, the art dealer thought, listening to their conversations that centred on odious co-workers and abhorrent bosses.

A small thin man and a tanked up, argumentative woman with dyed white-blonde hair, got seated alongside the art dealer. The woman continued to rant, her piercing accent setting the art dealer's teeth on edge. The weak-chinned, gormless male stared at the menu and took the verbal abuse. Halfway through their main course, he knocked over a glass of wine. No apology.

The art dealer dabbed at the wine stain on his jacket sleeve, his lips stretching into a thin line. A waitress wiped up. When the man reeled to the bathroom, the art dealer slid from his seat and followed. Gormless man swayed as he faced the urinal, unzipped his trousers and placed a hand on the wall to brace himself. Another customer dipped his hands into a Dyson dryer. The art dealer rinsed his hands, removed the stun gun, connected the battery and pressed the switch. Moved forward.

The outer door opened.

The art dealer stepped back to the wash-hand basins.

A teenager entered and made a beeline for a cubicle.

Clear.

The art dealer wadded up tissues, threw them into a bin, inched behind the gormless man and touched the immobiliser against the side of his neck. The short, sharp shock, jerked him sideways. He slipped on the wet floor and fell face-first into the porcelain urinal. A flusher gurgled.

The sprinkler drizzled water on the crumpled figure, sluicing blood and urine down the plughole. Satisfied, the art dealer returned to the restaurant, resumed his seat, called for the bill and kept his facial expression neutral, while commotion rained around him. Staff members escorted the woman into a back room.

An ambulance screeched to a halt.

The art dealer stepped aside, let the paramedics pass, and then strolled to his hotel. He picked up his room key from the receptionist, went to the internet room and logged online.

One new mail.

From: BachToBasie@datingvista.ie
Sent: Fri. 16:39
To: thejewellerycollector@datingvista.ie
Subject: Good Evening
Hi, again,
It's nice to get a chatty email! I hope you're home safe, and yes, as predicted, we've built a new, improved snowman. We're in beside the fire now. It's freezing outside! I'd prefer to spend 'til bedtime curled up here, but I'm sure my son has other ideas. If this weather continues, I might qualify for a master's degree in snowman making! Yes, I've had a hectic week, but I enjoy my work too much to whinge. I settled here in Ganestown five years ago. Before that, I travelled.

As I mentioned in my last mail, I'm new to this site, so I haven't made friends with anybody yet. I'm convinced we're here for a reason: to find a person we can connect and enjoy life with. I've got a diverse group of friends, and we inspire each other to be the best we can.

The one absence in my life is a soul mate. As a hopeless romantic, I can dream that there's a special man out there. I'd love to meet someone who isn't afraid to share who they are and is open to learning. Together.

I enjoy a 'balanced' healthy lifestyle, and occasional Spontaneity—dancing the night away! I admire honesty, integrity, intelligence, independence, respect, oh, and compassion. 'Kindness is a language which the deaf can hear and the blind can see.'

But enough of me and my 'wants'. This is a silly question: What does a jewellery collector collect? Oh, not sure if this is appropriate, but my mobile no. is 086-0494919. Feel free to phone, if you'd prefer to chat in person rather than mailing. No pressure!

Hope you enjoy your weekend.

BachtoBasie (Ciara)

The art dealer re-read the second last line. He memorised the phone number, erased his online history, double checked he'd logged out.

In-depth conversations I've no control over are not part of my plan.

'Ciara.' He wrapped his tongue around the name, liked the way it sounded.

Honesty, integrity, intelligence. You've fed me the information I need. This will be easier than I imagined. Oh, where's the challenge, Ciara? Eh?

He walked to his bedroom, thinking.

Is the mobile number a test? An experiment to see if I'll call? If I don't phone, will she assume there's a problem, and break contact? I can't allow that. I'm too close.

He took out his iPhone and punched in:

0860494…

Stopped.

Tracks and traces.

He deleted the number, and another thought struck him.

Is Ciara your name? Did you make it up? You'll expect me to respond in kind. Must create my own pseudonym. I need to be careful, but you're in my sights, Ciara. Hah. Lol to you too.

The art dealer lay back, marinating in expectation.

Let her wait. I'll buy a cheap phone tomorrow and call her then. Jana, you crabby bat, you'll have to wait a little longer.

HUGH WATCHED HIS mother's demeanour change.

The happy-to-be-home-in-familiar-surrounds character became guarded, and Kathleen measured Hugh with wary, distrustful sideways glances.

'You peckish, Ma? Thirsty?'

Kathleen refused to talk, recoiled and pushed him away when he plumped cushions around her. Then, like a lightbulb flash, she reverted to standard. 'I'm fine, Hugh. Go home. Don't take time off work on my behalf. I won't be a burden on anybody.'

'You're not a burden, Ma.'

'I can look after myself.'

'I want to spend time with you.'

'You're under my feet. I prefer to potter around on my own.'

'I won't get in your way, Ma.'

Kathleen snoozed. Hugh disregarded Ruth's advice, logged onto the internet, and gorged on Alzheimer's articles. Absentmindedness, comprehension and interpretation difficulties, items turning up in bizarre places, impaired judgement, analytical issues, mood swings and personality changes could soon be part of everyday life. Ma has none of these symptoms, he thought. It's bullshit. She tripped, banged her head and is confused. That's all. Impossible for a youngish, fit person, full of vitality, to wind up with this disease. It's a mistake. Ma would never surrender to that.

Kathleen seemed uncomfortable now, head lolling as she napped. At eleven o'clock she said she was ready for bed.

'Hold on a second, you need to take tablets.' Hugh passed over the drugs, expecting resistance, but Kathleen took them without comment. He stayed in the hallway, ears tuned until the bed creaked. After, he phoned the Homeless Hostel and told the volunteers about Kathleen's diagnosis, then resumed the internet search, combing for evidence to refute the doctor's medical opinion. He read dozens of cases, scrolled through articles and skimmed discussion posts, determined to validate his rationale and disprove Doctor Abbott. Nothing seemed to agree entirely with the doctor or gave clear proof to support his own theory. Yes, there were signs, but…Boggle-eyed and bleary, Hugh continued to seek holes in the doctor's assessment, gorging on information. No concrete validation emerged. Maybe she's a *little* senile, he supposed. But Alzheimer's? No way.

Before going to sleep, Hugh pressed Eilish's number, remembered they'd had a row and punched 'End Call'. Old habits die hard.

6

SATURDAY 12 JANUARY

MORNING

'GOT A CALL last night. They've added another five thousand,' Charlie told Ferdia.

When he talked, a row of black stitches moved in unison across his swollen top lip. The lump on his forehead had reduced.

'Told ya.' Ferdia sat back. The armchair creaked under his weight. 'So, fifteen K?'

'Yes. I—'

'Still on for nine o'clock Wednesday?'

'Yeah.'

'Grand. How long 'til you get out?'

'Doctor said midweek.' Charlie gestured at a newspaper. 'If I stay here for a month or two, the economy might improve. Business okay?'

'Doors are open, but this weather…' Ferdia shrugged. 'Was Malcolm in last night?'

'He rang from the office. He's had a talk with Milo. Told him the role wasn't working out as we'd hoped, that we have to let him go. Tricky conversation, but the fact Mal's prepared to take on those discussions gives me confidence. I told him to develop a thicker skin, so that's a good start. I'm convinced he's on track.'

'Huh. Still, I'd say it was a tough chat,' Ferdia said. 'Always an added complication when you're having it with relatives.'

'He's taking Milo to the ball tonight,' Charlie said. 'As a gesture.'

'Hmm-hmm.'

'See? Life pans out in the end, Ferdia. Ciara and Mal will soon take over the business. Will you keep an eye on the boys tonight? You know what lads are like. If you see a row brewing—'

'That won't happen, but if there's an issue, I'll separate them.' Ferdia scratched behind his ear. 'I was thinking. Has Malcolm got involved in stock assessments, invoice pricing, suppliers, margins, that end of things yet?'

'That's Philip's side of the business.'

'Yeah. I bet he'd welcome another pair of hands, to, you know yourself, ease the workload. And it'd benefit Malcolm to get experience in the accounts department; even for a few days a week. Keep him out of mischief. He needs to learn the drill, especially if you've got plans for him, in time.'

Charlie considered that. 'I'll ask him to take Mal under his wing for the next round of trade appointments. You're right. He has to learn.'

'If you want, I'll mention it to Philip tonight, if he turns up.'

'Nice if he did. He's the financial director of the fundraiser trust too. I think he attended once in ten years. He hates social events. Bet he'll be crunching numbers when you've gone to bed. No, I'll do it. It's best coming from me. Philip can be touchy—'

'Huh. I heard the way he talked to you the day you met Hugh Fallon.'

'It's his way. He's got the good of the company at heart.' Charlie gazed out the window. 'I'll miss being there tonight. I love the chance to chat with people I seldom get to meet.'

'Don't worry, we'll have a party when you're outta here. You can invite them all.' Ferdia stood and stretched.

'Sure you're okay for Wednesday?' Charlie asked.

'Course I'm sure. Don't worry, I've got it sussed. Nothing else to tell me?'

Charlie repositioned a pillow. 'That's it.'

They stared at each other.

'Grand,' Ferdia said. 'I'll head off, so. Gotta pick up my car.'

'What's wrong with it?'

'Argh, got a bit dented. What've you done about your motor?'

'I've asked the guards to pass their report onto my insurance—'

'What room did you say?' A tap of high heels in the corridor.

'Oh, God.' Charlie pulled the bedspread up to his chin. 'Dorothy Ridgeway.'

Dorothy sailed into the ward. The voluminous multi-coloured Paisley shawl that billowed around her shoulders made her appear like a ship in full sail. 'Charlie. And Ferdia. How lucky am I? My two favourite men in one place. I'd give you a hug Ferdia, but I don't want you to get this flu.'

Ferdia enveloped her in his arms. 'For you, I'll risk it, Dorothy.'

Sharona followed, carrying fruit, soft drinks and sugary snacks.

'Howaya Sharona.'

'Morning, Ferdia, Hi Charlie.'

Dorothy's eyes swept Charlie's face. 'Oh my God. What mess did you get yourself into?'

'It's—'

'I hope you're getting the *best* treatment and medication. If not, tell me now. I'm on first-name terms with the consultants here. Are you hungry? We got you—'

'I'm fine, Dorothy. Morning, Sharona.'

Ferdia stepped aside to give Dorothy the armchair and plucked out a handful of black grapes.

'I'll sit here.' Dorothy squeezed by and plopped onto a stool. 'I prefer hard seats; soft ones spread the hips. Now then, Charlie, have they arrested anybody?'

'Not yet.'

'Have you *any* idea—?'

'Just bad luck, Dorothy. Wrong place—'

'But what were you *doing*—'

'Ah, come in Mal.' Charlie beckoned at Malcolm, standing in the doorway.

Ferdia chewed a grape and shook his head. 'God almighty. This place is like feckin' Grafton Street on Christmas Eve.'

'Um, I'll come back,' Malcolm said.

'No, no. Come in,' Charlie beckoned. 'You haven't seen Dorothy in an age.'

'Hi, Dorothy.'

'Hello, dear.' Dorothy's eyes flashed between Sharona and Malcolm.

'Morning, Malcolm,' Sharona smiled.

'Hi.' Malcolm looked away.

'Well, I'm off.' Ferdia squeezed Dorothy's shoulder. 'See you tonight.'

'Remember, first dance with me, Ferdia.'

'There'll be dozens of men camped around you, but never fear, I'll beat my way through them to get you.'

'Oh, stop.' Dorothy patted Ferdia's arm. 'It's me that'll have to do the running as usual. You attract women like butterflies to a buddleia bush. Who are you bringing as your date?'

'Hugh Fallon. Friend of ours. He's going through a rough patch. Needs a night out.'

'You'll make a nice couple,' Sharona said.

Ferdia slapped Malcolm's back and pushed him towards the corridor. 'Let's go for coffee and leave these good people to chat.' He turned back and pointed at Sharona. 'I haven't forgotten 'bout those premises. Gimme another few days.'

'No rush.'

'Slán.'

Malcolm's hunched figure was waiting at the lift.

'Buck up, lad. Chas will be right as rain in a week or two.'

'It's my fault. It's all my fault.'

'Huh.'

On the ground floor, Ferdia caught Malcolm's jacket and bundled him to a corner table in the cafeteria. 'Don't move.'

Malcolm stared at a wall.

Ferdia plonked down mugs of coffee and two plates with slabs of pie smothered with artificial cream. He transferred a dollop of cream into his coffee, stirred and let the silence build.

'Dad told you.' Malcolm focused on the mug.

'Aye.' Ferdia said.

'What'll I do, Ferdia?'

'I'll take care of it.'

'God, Ferdia, that's...' Malcolm leaned across the table. 'I'd have paid them if they'd given me another week. I wouldn't dodge a debt.'

'I know.' Ferdia scooped pie into his mouth and chewed.

'I swear, never again,' Malcolm said. 'Ever. I'm done. They almost killed him.'

'How much did what's-his-name lend you?'

'Dessie Dolan?'

'Yeah.'

'Five G.'

Ferdia devoured another chunk of the pie. 'Chas didn't mention how you and Dolan met.'

'A casino on Fitzwilliam Square. I played in a poker tournament and ran out of cash.' Malcolm's eyes lit up. 'Got two aces as hole cards—'

'So you needed a float?'

'Hmm. This guy said he'd give me a loan. I'd seen him around the circuit.'

'Dolan?'

'Yeah.'

'What did he get from the deal?'

'Twenty per cent.'

'Huh. You gonna eat that pie?'

'No. The third ace got turned on the flop, along with a pair of tens, and I got beaten by a straight flush. Four to eight of diamonds. Flushes are my bogey. I mean, the chances are what?'

'How the feck do I know.' Ferdia tucked into the second slice of pie. 'You said six months ago you'd—'

'This was a once-off. Honest.'

'When did it happen?'

'Before Christmas.'

'Why get Chas involved? He's under enough strain. You should've told me.'

'Dolan forced me to give him Dad's number. I'll pay you back, Ferdia. You won't regret this.'

'Regret taking you into that feckin' bookies years ago. Shouldn't have let you talk me into—'

'Oh yeah. 2013 Grand National. April sixth. Auroras Encore, Remember?'

'No I don't. Wish to Christ you'd lost.'

'66/1. I fancied him. Didn't I say it? Class horse. Trained by Katie Walsh and ridden by Ryan Mania—'

'Shape up, Mal.' Ferdia lumbered to his feet. 'Don't make Chas disappointed he's given you a chance to—'

'I've a hundred questions for him. I'm—'

'You're in charge while he's out. Delegate. You mention this to Ciara?'

'I was gonna—'

'That's the same as you didn't.'

'I told her about the poker game, not that Dad—'

'Keep it between us so. No point telling either of them 'bout our chat. Least said, and all that. If you need guidance on work issues, ask Hugh Fallon or me. And for Christ's sake cop on, Mal. No. More. Gambling. It's time you quit the expecting-everyone-to-mollycoddle-you lark. Take off the trainer wheels and knuckle down. Why can't you play feckin' cards or bet on a horse in moderation like the rest of us? If you can't do that, then for feck's sake man, go and get help.'

Malcolm chewed his bottom lip. 'I'm done gambling, Ferdia. I don't want help. Thanks for doing this. I'm in a different place now. I've learned my lesson. It's over. I'll never again get trapped in debt I can't repay. Ev...ver. I swear.'

'Good man. Now you're talkin'.'

Malcolm's mobile bleeped. He checked the screen, thumb spooling through text.

Ferdia watched him. 'Got change for the car park?'

'I'll use a credit card.'

'I've got coins. C'mon.'

Malcolm hummed his way along the pathway. He used the phone as a guitar bridge, the fingers on his left hand sliding over and back on an invisible fingerboard.

Ferdia said, 'You're in good humour all of a sudden.'

Malcolm stopped strumming. 'Got good news for a change.' At the car park entrance, he wheeled left. 'Thanks again, Ferdia.'

'Hang on. I'm parked over there too. Heard you gave Milo his walking papers.'

'Milo? Oh, yeah.'

'How'd that go?'

'Okay.'

'All in order?'

'Yep. Listen, I gotta—'

'You could've brought Ciara with you. Listen 'n' learn from her experience.'

'I handled it.'

'Wouldn't kill you to bring her along. You don't know everything, and if you think you do you'll never improve. Don't be an amadán. Ask for help.'

'I need to do things my way, Ferdia. Dad wants me to act like a boss.'

Ferdia stared at him. 'Good man.' He watched Malcolm unlock a red '97 Honda Civic. 'Where's the Audi?'

'In for service. I'm picking it up Monday. See ya tonight.'

CIARA CONSUMED THE art dealer's thoughts.

On the flight home, it felt as if colours had become more vivid, senses sharper. Sound was amplified, concentration enhanced. In his mind's eye, he could see every word of her last mail, and he deliberated over words and sentences he'd use in their first phone conversation.

Earnestness and humour. Now, an alias.

He searched the roiling clouds for inspiration. Company names. Client names. Shop names. Teacher's names...

The art dealer's thoughts regressed twenty-seven years.

The teacher, Mr Moran, called him 'potato head'. Moran had always been vicious: he loved to run fingernails across the blackboard and watch children shiver at the grating screech. Moron, they'd whispered behind his back.

The 'potato head' label stuck, and he'd tolerated classmate's vicious taunts for the rest of the year. His surname had generated pig noises, oinks and grunts, but this nickname, endorsed by a grown-up, became acceptable. The constant jeers made him defenceless. Vulnerable. Powerless. The taunts carried into Secondary school. Teachers smiled whenever 'potato head' echoed around the schoolyard. By distancing himself from classmates, he avoided further hurt and he sought, even welcomed, seclusion. Solitude gave him time to heal, regroup and plan.

Challenging everybody wasn't an option, but payback got delivered by stealth. That was more rewarding. One tormentor reported a bike stolen. Months passed before it was found dumped in a ditch. A girl's cat strangled itself; its head caught between two gates. The replacement kitten vanished. The principal antagonist discovered his years of class exercises had disappeared. Mr Moran left a bar one night to find his car paintwork destroyed by either a nail or a screwdriver. The high-achieving quiet boy who never instigated trouble was never suspected.

Potato head. Maris Piper. Maurice Piper. That's my name for this adventure.

Potato head. Should be Golden Wonder.

In the arrivals area, he paid cash for a pay-as-you-go phone, topped it up with credit, discarded the wrapping and drove home. Once settled in his study, he dialled Ciara.

The phone rang. 'Hello?'

'Could I speak to Ciara, please?'

'Speaking.'

'Good morning, Ciara. I'm Maurice. We've been in contact through the dating site.'

'Oh. Hi.'

'Is this a bad time?'

'No, no. Not at all.'

'Thanks for the emails, and for your safe home message. I…'

'Did you manage to get a flight?'

'Eventually. There was a huge backlog at Belfast airport earlier, but I made it, a few hours behind schedule.'

'And home is…?'

'Dublin.'

'Oh, yes. You mentioned that in your email.'

'I *loved* your Mark Twain quote,' the art dealer said. 'So, by now, I guess you're a master craftsperson in the art of snowmen construction.'

Ciara laughed. 'Another week of this weather and I'll be giving igloo building lessons to Eskimos.'

The art dealer laughed too. 'DIY is not one of my strengths. Three words that strike fear in my heart are "easy to assemble." I've got a pile of do-it-yourself tasks I should start, but…I'll work on them next week. For definite. "The secret to getting ahead is getting started." I believe that's a Mark Twain quote too.'

Ciara laughed again. 'When I came back to Ganestown, I bought a rundown cottage, and after countless backbreaking hours, I've managed to get ahead and change the old house into a home. I've enjoyed the task, but it's one I wouldn't repeat.'

The art dealer relaxed. 'I'm so glad you trusted me your number. It's nice to hear your voice.'

'I debated whether to pass it on or not, there are so many weirdos out there, but anyone who can write a nice chatty email, with proper spelling and grammar, can't be a stalker or a bunny boiler.'

'Well, thank you for—'

'Your accent? You're not originally from Dublin, are you?'

'Tipperary, outside Thurles. I settled in Dublin back in 2010. I was in a relationship for four years, but it came to an end last year,' the art dealer lied.

You're giving her too much, too soon. Ask questions.

'Sorry to hear that.'

'C'est la vie. Where did your travels take you before returning to Ganestown?'

'The U.S. West Coast.'

'Ahh. San Fran—?'

'Yes. So, what exactly does a jewellery collector collect?'

'Confession time,' the art dealer said. 'My username is a little deceptive. I don't collect jewellery. I work within the gemstone industry.'

'Wow.'

'And no, it isn't as glamorous as you think. In the same way I'm sure chocolatiers get fed up with the taste of chocolate, gems lose their sheen after a while. However, I love work, and I get to travel. At the moment, we're eying 2020 trends, and here's a heads up: coloured gems will be on shelves in a few months, and opals are—'

'I *love* opals. I love to wear them and watch them shimmer. The colours remind me of an Australian holiday, and sunset at Ayers Rock.'

'Shakespeare called opals the Queen of Gems in Twelfth Night,' the art dealer said. 'If my username misled you, I'm sorry.'

'No need to apologise, Maurice. I assumed from your username…My fault. What are your plans for next week?' Ciara asked.

'Oh, the usual. Paperwork and meetings. You?'

'Same. It's annual appraisals time for me—'

'A necessary evil.'

'Indeed. I'll spend the next week conjuring up related, yet different phrases for each of my team.'

'Ouch.'

'Yes. After all,' Ciara said, 'I can only write "satisfactory," or "exceeds," or "needs improvement," so many times before the words get tedious. Anyway, rant over. My job's great. Not as glitzy as yours, but it pays the bills.'

'How about "demonstrates ability to…" the art dealer suggested. Or, "establishes," "makes excellent use of," "delivers valuable," "displays considerable—" '

'Let me jot those down.'

'I'm sure you're a fabulous employer,' the art dealer said. 'I've found you can't go wrong if you treat employees with honesty and sincerity. If it suits, could we meet for coffee tomorrow? Or lunch?'

Silence.

Too soon. Stupid, stupid, stupid.

'Can I let you know later?' Ciara's tone changed.

'Of course.'

'I've got to go, Maurice. There's another call waiting.'

'Looking forward to hearing from you anytime, Ciara.'

'Okay, then. Bye.'

The art dealer stared at the phone.

I've blown it.

The study seemed to close in. He needed space to think. Seething, he drove to Portlaoise, bought a coffee in a café on Lyster Square, and spied on a pair of teenage mothers slurping lattes and sharing dull details of their lives. They rocked designer buggies with the soles of Toms shoes in a futile attempt to keep their chic-clad litter quiet. One pushed globs of grey goo into her child's mouth, moaning that the dole officer rejected a rent allowance increase. 'And he didn't believe me when I told him Jack's father had absconded. Imagine that?'

'I know. Didn't trust me either,' the second said. 'Acts as if he's judge and jury. I still haven't worked out how I'm gonna keep drawing single mother's allowance after me 'n' Barron get married in June.'

'Mightn't happen. The last wedding date you set, you were visiting Barron in prison, remember?'

'Oh, yeah.'

The art dealer couldn't bear to listen any longer.

Wish I'd brought the stun gun. Dole bitches. Pitiful excuses for women. A perpetual strain on the country's assets, dragging down per capita income. They're identical. Same as Mother.

He drove out to Emo court, parked, and tramped along the curved avenue of towering redwood trees.

Whatever happens, number eight is within my grasp. Ciara or Jana. I'll find a way. In a matter of days, one of you'll be rotting in clay.

The art dealer relished that image.

Either will be much easier than Isobel Stewart. Do you want to know about Isobel Stewart, Jana? Ciara? She'll be remembered as number five.

You see, I got obsessed by Isobel Stewart the moment I saw her posed photo on the front cover of a Trinity magazine, with a child perched on her knee. In a Q&A interview, she'd answered questions on a day in the life of a final year law student. Parents and childminder babysat her two-year-old son at home in Waterford during the week, while she attended college. The piece gave me the area Isobel stayed in. Facebook narrowed the search further. Bus routes and patient tracking brought me through Ranelagh's leafy apartment land. The hunt is easy once you've got a starting point. On and off, I spent eleven days on old-fashioned footwork, but it paid off. Then I shadowed and studied

Isobel's habits. Witnessed how she acted around friends; she was sociable, funny, reserved. I moved closer, listened to her voice. Liked her musical laugh. I deliberately bumped into her one night and inhaled her perfume. Sandalwood. I remember her smile sent shivers up my spine. Occasionally Isobel would walk, other times she travelled by bus or taxi. She'd spend days in college, then disappear to Waterford. With no set routine, the woman posed me a major challenge.

Midnight, August seventeenth last. Lovely night. I watched her leave Good World Chinese restaurant on Georges Street, and wait at a bus stop. I drove ahead, parked outside her three-story red-bricked building, listened for her heel tap, and timed my walk to the building. I stopped, dug in my pocket for keys. Isobel passed me by, stuck a key in the lock, and I stepped inside with her. I got that smile again before she'd spotted the cloth and gloves, her nose twitching at the sweet scent. I saw the panic in her eyes as she inhaled. I learned it takes chloroform a few minutes to work. That lack of knowledge could have cost me, but I was lucky. Once I got her in the car, the rest was easy. I kept her semi-conscious, and by Monday morning, she'd given up hope. Her look of resignation at the inevitability of death was a powerful drug.

Seven weeks to snag Isobel.

Seven strikes to shatter her skull.

Seven minutes to die.

I bludgeoned her in a shed, but, Jana and Ciara, the good news is, I'm getting better. It only took me one, two, three, four strikes to kill Roberta Lord. Sixty per cent improvement. Another fact I learned is that blows from a wooden mallet are more interesting to study regarding its effect on human skulls. The metal hammer makes a more...decisive impact.

Isobel was also my first observation of blood splatters and how far they travel. Not from the blows, because Jana, you probably don't know that the brain has no major arteries, but off the metal surface as I battered Isobel's skull. I studied the effect of each blow, how they dimmed, clouded and quenched the life in her eyes. As a final measure, I forced both her eyelids open, to make sure my face was the final image she'd see, my scent would be on her last breath. I savoured each detail of Isobel's pulpy flesh and the seeping brain matter that resembled uncooked shrimp, floating in yellow fluid. You see, I enjoy analysing blood. I'm enthralled by its composition, but don't like to touch it. Can I tell you a secret, ladies? The thought of blood staining my skin revolts me. I was seven. Fascination compelled me to view a neighbour stun, truss and hoist a pig onto a cantilevered girder, ready for slaughter. I can still see the man cutting the pig's neck, and hear him laugh when the blood gush plastered my clothes and face. I couldn't move with fear, but I opened my mouth to cry. The revulsion I felt when the pig's warm sticky blood filled my mouth has never left.

I sat and scrutinised Isobel's body, spent hours inhaling the coppery smell. Her skin went dirty grey, before it sagged, lost its elasticity and changed to a waxy purple colour. When I tired of the transformation, I doused the corpse with concentrated Paraquat and waited for a reaction. And waited. And waited. After three hours, the herbicide had made no noticeable effect, so when my sense of curiosity subsided, I dumped the body into a new grave close to Monica Flynn. As I was covering the tomb, I remembered a chemistry lesson: when lime—that's calcium hydroxide—and skin come in contact, the reaction with tissue is fast and furious. Lime speeds up decomposition, destroys traceable DNA, so I sprinkled a bag of builder's lime on the body. From my vantage point in the field, I'd a three-sixty degree vista. There was no rush.

It took eighty-six minutes for the two compounds to eat through the outer layers of skin on Isobel's stomach and thighs, and to burn and boil their way across the fatty hypodermis underneath. When I splashed more lime and corrosive liquid on her face, the nose shrank and lips peeled, exposing teeth. Once satisfied I'd destroyed the physical evidence, I closed the grave. Didn't bother waiting to observe the effects of the Paraquat on her bones. Afterwards, I scrubbed, hosed, sluiced and burned all traces, then repeated the whole process twice more. Wonder how long it'll take to boil off your skin Jana and Ciara. Eh?

MID-AFTERNOON

EILISH'S STOMACH CHURNED. She turned, twisted an arm, blinked and peered at her watch face.

1:20.

She dialled Ciara. 'Busy?'

'Harried. Is that a word? God, I'm catching up on emails, my phone's hopping, and I'm supposed to relieve Malcolm at the hospital. Last week's been a crazy muddle. Where are you? I rang you a thousand times. Why didn't you return my calls?'

'God,' Eilish groaned. 'I'm hungover. Didn't get back 'til all hours.'

'Back from where.'

'Pardon? This signal's…'

'I said, back from where?'

'Oh. Nowhere special. Just out.'

'Was Hugh with you?'

'He's with his mum. She's home from hospital.'

'Didn't know she was…Anything serious?'

'Don't think so.'

'Where are you now?'

'Going for a shower.'

'At home?' Ciara asked.

'Hmm-mm.' Eilish felt queasy again.

'But ye're okay?'

'Sure. Fancy a drink tonight? I'm meeting Tara—'

'I'd love it, but count me out, I'll be in Dublin with Dad. You and Hugh…It's all good, isn't it?'

'Yeah. Maybe.' Eilish switched the mobile to her other ear. 'It's the paradox of I love you, I'm leaving.'

'What? Will you *listen* to yourself? I thought you'd got…*that* out of your system.'

'So did I. It's not that simple.' Eilish's free hand crumpled the duvet.

'Chrissake, Eilish, grow up. Cop yourself on. You're still in touch with Richard, aren't you?'

'I…No. We're—'

'Liar! You're full of crap. I *know* you've met him. Jill's been on the phone, bawling her eyes out. Richard isn't answering his mobile either. Weird how you were both incommunicado last night. Jesus, why the *hell* do I even *bother*? Hah. You were with him, weren't you? And now you want to meet Tara and me for a night out *without* Richard, so you can dispel rumours from any gossipmongers. I bet you're not home. I'd stake my house you're with him now.'

Eilish heard the shower turn off. 'I've gotta go—'

'God, Eilish, you're so transparent. I can read you—'

'Tara asked *me*—'

'Handy alibi, and so bloody *obvious*, Eilish. You're a great one to twist things around and put yourself in a favourable light to justify your selfish behaviour.'

'I never…When did I ever—?'

'Gimme a break, willya? Where do you want me to begin?'

Eilish's voice dropped. 'I think I'm—'

'And I think you're self-centred. Spoilt rotten. No consideration for anybody except yourself.'

'You don't appreciate the—'

'Appreciate? Appreciate *what*?'

'My *pain*. The *stress*—'

'Aww, dear Jesus, Eilish. That's enough. I'm up to my neck in stress too.'

'Fine. I'll call you.' The hotel en suite door opened.

'Fine. Cheers for asking 'bout Dad. He's well improved, by the way.'

'Oh, how's Char—?'

Ciara hung up.

TRISTIN REED USHERED his visitors to the National Gallery's private viewing rooms. Distinguished, flowing silver hair parted in the middle, he wore glasses, a pin-striped suit and a polka-dot bow tie. Dorothy passed him the painting.

'Ah, yes. Exquisite piece. 1920s.' Tristin inspected the canvas. 'I believe the setting was a farm that belonged to McKelvey's in-laws, near Bessbrook in County Armagh. The two children were relatives.'

'Well?' Dorothy had the nervous anticipation of a child in Disney World. She coughed, exhaling eucalyptus flavoured vapour.

'It will take a few moments to confirm its genuineness, Madam.' Tristin laid the frame on a desk. 'At first sight, the brushwork in the sky is…mmm, curious.'

'Curious how?'

'These even strokes in a pattern?' Tristin pointed out an area. 'And here? There's evidence someone touched up the canvas. The pattern of the strokes doesn't follow the image of the painting. Typical of a reproduction. I'm looking for the confident marks, the swoops, if you will, of an artist with the picture in mind before committing it to canvas, and, I'm afraid they're not here. Arthur Conan Doyle called it "the sweep of a master's brush." May I have your permission to remove the frame?'

'Yes.'

Tristin levered out the brads lose and examined them. 'Hmm. These aren't original—'

'Is the *painting* original? I've got William Rodman's receipt.' Dorothy delved into a shoulder bag and showed an envelope to the art historian. 'What else do you need?'

Tristin smiled. 'My experience, Madam. Just my experience. Art owners, who acquaint themselves only with artists' names, often get fooled. It's imperative that buyers consider the artist's brush strokes, their favourite subject matters, location of signatures, the sizes and formats they work in, and so on. Likewise, mediums and materials should get due consideration, plus, how it's mounted, titled, numbered, framed and displayed. Also, what gallery the artist uses, supplier tags and labels the painting is liable to include.'

The women crowded closer.

Tristin put the frame aside. 'Once we examine any piece in this comprehensive manner, they're unique, similar to fingerprints. For forgers, there's an unfeasible amount to duplicate. It's not conceivable to deceive experts with experience of art analysis. Doesn't stop the crooks trying though. Nowadays, with photography advances…' He shrugged, opened a drawer, produced a portable ultraviolet fluorescent cylinder, and studied the canvas. 'McKelvey painted this piece between 1916 and 1920.' The art historian frowned, touched the painting, hummed and murmured to himself, absorbed in his world. 'The original would contain a network of spider-web surface cracks…Hmm.' He straightened, expression resigned. 'I'm sorry, Madam, this is a photo. Printed on tea-stained canvas to give it an aged appearance.'

'Sharona said that too.'

'Sharona must have had an excellent tutor.' Tristin winked at Sharona, then turned back to the painting. 'Somebody *daubed* paint on the photo to give the surface depth. The paint has a rubbery texture, consistent with acrylic, which only came onto the market in the 1940s. Popular nowadays because it's quick drying. This area,' Tristin gestured at the children in the painting, 'almost faultless. And here?' He rubbed a thumb across the top of the canvas. 'There's hesitation in the paint application; not the confident sweep I mentioned.' Tristin picked up a lighted magnifying glass and inspected the picture once more. 'Madam, I'm certain it's a photograph, with traces of paint applied to make it appear genuine. Commissioned, I'd say, within the last few days. Acrylic influences the *appearance* of paintings and makes it easier to achieve an exact cleanness, but it doesn't have the same *richness* that McKelvey...Yes, it's a fake. A complete and utter banger.'

Dorothy turned to Sharona. 'Shouldn't have doubted you.' She stood in a boxer's stance; shoulders tucked in, fists clenched. 'My beautiful McKelvey...stolen. Robbed. They've defrauded me. Burgled by those—'

Tristin removed his spectacles. 'I can give you a written assessment.'

'Yes, please. I'll pass it onto the PSNI. Then I'll sue Hattinger's. I'll tell you this: they won't know what hit them.'

'In that case, Madam, may I suggest you take my letter to the PSNI Art and Antique section? I'll give you names. Now, I need background information. Where you stored it, who handled it, who found it...'

Dorothy dictated. Tristin wrote in longhand and signed the letter with a flourish.

'I can't believe this happened right under my nose,' Dorothy said. 'If it weren't for Sharona, I'd be none the wiser.'

'Oh, no doubt Madam, you'd have found—'

'Yes, but by then I mightn't remember who was...Does this occur often?'

'Genuine art and fakes have coexisted for a thousand years,' Tristin said. 'Impeccable duplications get uncovered every week. Allegedly even Michelangelo had a dark past as a forger before becoming one of our greatest artists. So, yes, for centuries, replicas have hung in galleries, either by ignorance or in full awareness of them being forgeries.'

Sharona said: 'You called it "infecting the market," I remember.'

Tristin smiled. 'Art fascinates me. Auctioned pieces can sell from a few euro to a few hundred million, or get bought in charity shops for fifty cent. At times, the charity shop unveils a priceless original, and the expensive auction piece turns out to be rubbish. Nobody wants to be the dunce with a dud, so, if the owner can sell it on without a fuss…'

'Another fool's landed with the flop,' Dorothy said.

Tristin squinted at her. 'Correct, Madam.'

'How much is my McKelvey worth in today's market?'

'At an auction? A hundred thousand euro. If it's stolen on demand? Maybe forty.'

'It isn't for sale. Never will be. I'd slice my arm off before…Memories are worth more than money. Those blackguards—'

'Is McKelvey a popular artist for forgers?' Sharona asked Tristin.

'This is the second I've handled. McKelvey poses a challenge. Claude Monet, on the other hand, is a particular favourite with copiers,' Tristin explained. 'He applied loose brush strokes, and later in life when he developed cataracts, the paintings became opaque. Quite straightforward to copy.'

'Who's the most difficult to forge, if I want to be *sure* of buying a genuine article?' Dorothy asked.

'You'd need deep pockets, Madam. DaVinci perhaps. There are only fifteen known completed works in existence, so anything pertaining to him gets deemed a forgery until categorically proven otherwise. But in my opinion? Rembrandt. Not those painted by his students. Genuine Rembrandts are the most challenging to forgers.'

'Why?'

'There's much more to a Rembrandt than what we see on the surface. He painted scenes back-to-front, adding layers of colour and texture as he progressed. For example, if he worked on a landscape, let's say a mountain shrouded in mist, he'd paint the whole mountain first, and incorporate the mist later. Layer on layer. With people, he'd begin with underclothes and then outer garments. Nowadays, we use imaging methods to scan under the various levels of paint and pencil, to decipher how artists produced masterpieces. So, yes, that level of detail is exceedingly intricate, and impossible to replicate because a photograph can't layer...'

They promised to keep in touch, and the women walked to a coffee shop on Nassau Street.

'Now what?' Sharona asked.

'Now,' Dorothy rooted for her mobile. 'I'll ring Herbert Park to make sure Ewan Plenderleith is directing the final touches for tonight's fundraiser. I'm sorry now I twisted Ambrose Hattinger's arm into buying tickets. Then tomorrow, I can't wait to see the blue skies of Ulster again and involve the PSNI in this despicable scam. They'll want your statement too. To think I trusted those *villains* for years and they repay my generosity by taking me for a senile old sucker who wouldn't notice a forgery. How *dare* they even *consider* fooling me? We'll see 'bout that. When I get Ambrose, I'll...I won't be responsible for what I'll do to him. And you must oversee the revaluing of all my artwork. It's possible they've planted other fakes. Hattinger's will pay dearly.'

'I wouldn't mention anything for the moment, Dorothy. What if he's innocent? After all, it was Jana who catalogued your collection and managed to "find" the forgery. She could say she went out of her way to help you and didn't *know* it was a copy.'

'Hmm.' Dorothy popped a cough lozenge. 'Tristin said that fake was less than a week old. Apart from Hattinger's people, no one else has been around. She knew, and as Ambrose Hattinger is a director, ignorance of facts is no defence. Don't worry, in the cold light of day, I'll keep my gob shut 'til the time's right.'

'I'll go home and pick up clothes for tonight,' Sharona scrolled through her mobile. 'There's a train to Athlone—'

'You'll do no such thing, dear. I'm a friend of Louise Kennedy. Her boutique's around the corner in Merrion Square. Have you visited it?'

'God, no. That's way beyond my price range.'

'Oh, stop. Quality beats price. Besides, it's all about cost per wear, and I need a handbag. The bigger the bag, the thinner you look. Don't worry, Louise will tog you out like a princess.'

'I couldn't—'

'Ach, give my head peace, girl. God knows when I'd have noticed my McKelvey was a dud. As I've said, I'll never sell it, so only for you…When this hits the headlines, and mark my words I'll make sure it does, you'll stand beside me and take full credit for spotting it. Now, dear, let me make a few calls. Then we'll shop.'

EVENING

KATHLEEN FALLON HELD a single wheel tin opener in one hand, a can of tomatoes in the other. When Hugh came in, her frown changed to a smile. 'For the life of me, I can't figure out how this works.'

'Here, let me.'

'Have you time to drive me to the shelter? I can't find my car keys, and we have to organise food for the poor souls.'

'Are you sure you're able—?'

'I'm sure. Can you take me, or will I call a taxi?'

'I'll go with you, Ma. Remember I'm going to Dublin later? Are you okay on your own tonight?'

'You never mentioned Dublin, but I'm fine. Now, let's go. And I need to do some shopping.'

'No problem.'

'And if you've got time, I want you to look at my bank statements. Someone's stealing money from my account.'

'I don't…yes, Ma. We'll do that.'

'Where did you say you were going?'

'Dublin.'

'What's in Dublin?'

'I'll visit Charlie McGuire, then I'm going to a party with Ferdia.'

'Oh.'

At a corner shop, Hugh bought three packs of cigarettes to distribute later.

A dozen homeless people shuffled in circles outside the hostel, stooped and hunched against the freezing fog.

'There but for the grace of God, Hugh. Any of us could end up in their shoes.'

Kathleen instructed Hugh to prepare food while she helped the group select clothes donated by the public. She was back in her element, helping the less well off. Once the men got food, they picked a corner or table for themselves, except for a cluster of five who chatted, heads bent in secret conspiracy.

Hugh divided out the cigarettes. Each smoker stripped the tobacco, pulled out packs of Rizla papers and fashioned four smokes from each original single. Most disappeared outside to satisfy their nicotine cravings, the rest sat staring into space, thinking their own thoughts. Hugh prepared emergency-use dormitory beds, and when other volunteers took over for night duty, Kathleen and Hugh drove across town to a supermarket. The soupy fog had dissipated, but squalls of sleety rain made people scurry for shelter. Hugh found a space in Meadow's supermarket car park and linked his mother into the centre.

January sales were in full flow.

The December credit card bills hadn't arrived yet—time enough to panic at the end of the month. Men clutched an assortment of bags, fingers swollen from lugging bulky bargains, and trailed three steps behind their partners. A rabble of teenage rebels, driven indoors by the chill, pushed and jostled each other as they clustered and converged in the walkways—a hostile zone for anyone not in their age bracket.

'What do you need, Ma?'

'Carrots.'

Hugh grabbed a basket and moved towards the vegetable section. Kathleen caught his arm and pointed. 'That lady. She's robbed our vegetables. Wait here.'

Kathleen marched across the aisle, plucked the carrots out of the woman's trolley and held her prize aloft. 'Now, what else?' She placed the carrots in Hugh's basket. 'Oh yes, marmalade.' Kathleen moved away.

Hugh transferred the vegetables back to the woman's trolley. 'I apologise. My mother...' He shook his head. 'She thought you were—'

The woman patted his arm. 'Take care of her.'

'I will. Thanks for understanding.'

What the hell brought that on? Hugh wondered. He snatched up another bag of carrots and dashed by shoppers, distracted by his mother's actions. Swerving round an aisle, he could see the anxiety in Kathleen's eyes as she scrutinised shoppers' faces. When she glimpsed Hugh, the smile reappeared. 'What did I say I needed?'

'Marmalade.'

Kathleen reached for a jar, brushed against another. Glass exploded in the aisle. An assistant rushed to mop up the mess. 'How clumsy of me, Mrs Furlong.' Kathleen said to a shopper who guided her away from the broken glass. 'Sorry,' she called over her shoulder to the shop assistant. 'That's Mrs Furlong.' Kathleen stage-whispered to Hugh. 'Poor woman. She has Alzheimer's, you know.'

At the checkout, children wailed as they were tugged away from the confectionery section. Kathleen's bill came to under fifteen euro. She handed in a hundred euro note.

'Ma, you've two tens in your purse, don't break the hundred.'

'I need change.'

At home, Hugh examined the bank statements again. 'See?' he pointed. 'That's your pension in, and your debits out. It's all in order.'

'Hmm. I still think there's something wrong.'

After, he combed the house for the car keys, eventually finding them in a bathroom cabinet.

'MAURICE?'

'Ciara? Nice to hear from you again. How has your day been?' The art dealer discarded the bow tie he was knotting and sat at the desk in his Herbert Park Hotel bedroom.

'Hectic. I've built *another* snowman. Not any old one this time. David's so exact. Hah, guess where he gets that from? He's put two pieces of coal for the eyes, wedged branches into the body for arms and sellotaped sticks onto them for fingers. Perhaps he'll be an engineer.'

'No doubt he'd be a success. I've a seven-year-old nephew, and boy, can he tire me out. It's non-stop whenever he visits, or when we go on zoo trips. No idea where he finds the energy. On the plus side, if I want to record a TV programme, I ask him. Technology holds no fear when you're seven. I believe it's vital we spend quality time with children. How else will they learn?'

You're talking too much again. Let her talk.

The art dealer waited.

'About tomorrow,' Ciara said.

'Yes?'

'If the offer still stands, I'll take you up on lunch.'

The art dealer relaxed. 'Excellent. Where suits you? I don't mind meeting in Ganestown. Gambadini's, perhaps?'

'Gambadini's is nice.'

'One o'clock? One-thirty?'

'Maybe a bit earlier? David's planned a¡...Twelve-thirty?'

'Twelve-thirty it is. I look forward—'

'Can I ask you a question?'

The art dealer's eye twitched. 'Sure.'

'When we spoke earlier, you said you left Belfast, but in your last mail, on Thursday, you wrote that you were in Cork?'

The art dealer frowned, stood, and paced the bedroom.

'Which was it?' Ciara asked. 'Or were you in both? I'm not trying to catch you out, Maurice, just curious, in the interest of candidness and candour.'

The art dealer stared out the window.

Bitch.

He gave a short laugh. 'And there's a classic example of why men can't multi-task, Ciara. I was in Cork last Thursday and Friday. Got a flight back to Dublin this morning, and I'm travelling to Belfast on Monday. I was booking my flight when I phoned you, and Belfast was in my head.'

'Oh? I didn't know you could still fly direct from...never mind.'

'Sorry for the confusion,' the art dealer said.

'No big deal,' Ciara said. 'Happens to me all the time. So, twelve-thirty tomorrow?'

'Great. Hope I recognise you. If I appear anxious, it's because I haven't used this modern way of meeting people before.'

'I'll be in a similar boat, but I keep telling myself it's normal for two people to have lunch together. Any plans for tonight?'

'I'm attending—'

'Oh, I remember. You're taking clients to the theatre. Right?'

'…Y-es.'

'Well, have a great night. I'll see you tomorrow.'

'See you then, Ciara, and thank you for the call.'

'Bye.'

The art dealer stared at his phone. The darting pain behind his eye warned of an oncoming migraine.

How could I muddle up two cities? Trying too hard to be clever with the patronising bitch. I wanted this to be a challenge. Have to be careful. Don't get overconfident.

He took a tennis ball from the bedside locker and squeezed.

What clues has she given me? Athletic. Uses gym. Lives in a cottage. Isn't afraid to attempt new projects. Listens and remembers things. Asks questions. Besotted with her son, David. I can make that work for me. If I knew her address, I'd skip this crummy ball and grab her now. But all in good time, Ciara, you candid, condescending whore.

NIGHT

WAITERS, HOISTING TRAYS of cocktails shoulder high, dotted the packed foyer of the Herbert Park Hotel.

A pianist tinkled old favourites to indifferent partygoers. Hugh threaded his way through masses of alpha males harnessed into dress suits, tuxes fastened tight as nooses. Starched collars dug into bulging necks, and shirt buttons strained to retain rolls of flesh. Women, outnumbered three to one, swished and swayed between the men, oozing glamour in floor-sweeping silk and satin ball gowns.

In the bedroom, Hugh changed into formal wear. The last event he'd worn the dress suit was to a Halloween party with Eilish. He rang Kathleen.

'Where are you, Hugh?'

'Dublin. I told you—'

'Oh, yes. Go enjoy the night.'

'See you in the morning, Ma.'

At the bar, Ferdia raised a whiskey glass, said 'sláinte,' tilted, swallowed the amber liquid and gestured at the barman. 'Repeat the dose.' His booming voice and hearty laugh drew a crowd like pins to a magnet.

'Hello, stranger.' Sharona tapped Hugh's shoulder. She wore a black sleeveless dress, hair sculpted into an urbane style.

'Hi, yourself. Didn't expect to see you here, thought you were in Belfast. Drink?' Hugh scooped cocktails from a waiter's tray.

Sharona sipped. 'Just what I need. You won't believe my life over the last thirty-six hours.'

'Art gig finished?' Hugh asked.

'Umm, yes and no.'

'Oh?'

'See, Charlie's friend, Dorothy Ridgeway, realised one of her paintings was missing. We found it, but guess what, it's not her original. Somebody from Hattinger's Art House swapped the genuine piece for—'

'Jesus. Fraud?'

'Big time.'

'You sure it wasn't a copy all along? And Dorothy never knew the difference?'

'Positive. It was forged in the last week. I could still *smell* the paint. I'd say Dorothy didn't inspect it when Hattinger's manager "found" it. Why would she? She trusts, err, *trusted* the staff, and is delighted to see her canvas back. Dorothy's sharp as a razor, but when people you *rely* on break trust…' Sharona shook her head. 'In time she'd have spotted it as a plant, but it happened I was there and noticed something wrong first. When you meet her, you'll see what I mean. Nobody builds up the quality and quantity of art and antiques that Dorothy's acquired by not having a tough interior hidden under layers of designer clothes. And her house? Oh my God, don't get me started on the house. We're heading back in the morning to give the PSNI our statements, and an art detective from Dublin will sit in on the meeting. Dorothy chartered this trip down on a private plane. Cool, or what?'

'Classy. So, is it an inside scam?'

'Brief version: Dorothy had Hattinger's value her art collection, and we think one of the appraisers switched an expensive original for a doctored photograph. Earlier, a detective suggested that Dorothy tells Hattinger's people she's thrilled the painting's found.'

'Sounds like a sting. Trap bait. Wonder if it was a once-off, or an ongoing con. Could this turn out to be more than one swapped painting?'

'God, I haven't the energy to reason it out, but yeah, doubtful if this is the first con job.'

'Looks as if you're at the coal face of unearthing a major swindle,' Hugh said. 'That'll be…' he nudged Sharona. 'To your left. Friends of yours.'

'Who?' Sharona turned.

'Malcolm and—'

'Oh, for Christ's sake. Milo bloody Brady.'

Milo bloody Brady came over. 'How'd *you* get in?' he moved into Sharona's personal space, his back to Hugh.

'None of your business.' Sharona stepped back. 'How'd *you* get by security?'

'Official invite. See?' Milo pulled a crumpled ticket from his pocket.

'Pity whoever gave you the ticket forgot to mention it's a Black Tie ball. You seem a tad out of place in jeans, T-shirt and blazer.'

'Who cares? Heard you and Mal split up. Err, you staying here tonight? What room—?'

'Drop dead, Milo, but do it outside so we won't have to clean up the mess.'

'Don't be like that.' Milo caught Sharona's arm. 'Let's go to the bar.'

'Let's not.' Sharona shook his hand away.

A bell clanged.

The crowd surge ferried the trio forward, then pushed them apart at the bottleneck around the ballroom entrance. Inside the banquet hall, a whiteboard showed the guest's names and table numbers. 'Six and seven,' Hugh read. 'For tonight, Ridgeway and McGuire have amalgamated.'

'Aww, crap.' Sharona aimed her drink glass at the board. 'Are Milo and Malcolm seated with us?'

Hugh pointed further down the list. 'Yep.'

'Double crap. This could get real awkward, fast. Milo's a dickhead.'

'What's with ye two? That was an interesting conversation. You went through him like a dose of salts. I didn't even know he existed till a few days ago.'

'Can't stand the creep,' Sharona said. 'Lately, no matter where I turn, he seems to be there.'

'Milo a stalker? I don't think—'

'Haven't a clue what makes him tick, but I know how to make him explode. What room am I in? Cheek of him. Floating 'round the place like a bad pong. And them clothes? I've seen better dressed wounds. Odious little man.'

'Ignore both of them.'

The room filled up. Four chairs remained unoccupied when the waiters served appetisers.

Dorothy appeared and monopolised the conversation. 'I *love* this hotel. The food is always magnificent, and the service...Ferdia! Come here. I couldn't get near you in the bar.'

Ferdia rammed his bulk between tables and grabbed Dorothy. 'Told you I'd have the first dance.' They managed an awkward pas de deux around the table, toppling a few wine glasses in the process, then Ferdia jammed into a spare chair between Sharona and Dorothy. 'My Sharona, he said.'

'Great tune, Ferdia.'

Ferdia hummed the song's bass intro and grabbed a bread roll. 'Did I ever tell you 'bout the time I met Doug Fieger, the man who wrote it? Sharona's an actual person. Sharona Alperin. Doug penned the song for her, and they became a couple. Heard he died a while back...'

Thrums of conversation reverberated around the room as circling waiters swirled and swooped to top up wine glasses, clear plates and proffer the next course with theatrical flourishes, under the general manager's watchful gaze.

Malcolm and Milo's seats remained free.

Afterwards, the guests mingled and Hugh escaped for fresh air. In the foyer, Ferdia pulled away from a group and swerved into Hugh's path. 'Glad you made it. What diya reckon 'bout this shindig?' Ferdia was well on the way to getting drunk.

'Great meal. And you crammed into the suit.'

Ferdia patted his gut. 'No problem. Dumped two bottles of rubbing alcohol and a bag of Epson salts into a boiling hot bath, lathered meself in a moisturising cleanser and jumped in.'

'That's it?'

'Aye. An old boxer's trick. Couple hours in the tub slashed off half a stone.'

'And then you go eat a feast.'

Ferdia's long burp sounded similar to a trumpet blast. 'Twas a nice bit of beef. Too much feckin' cutlery though. I'd several spare knives and a fork left over. See Malcolm yet?'

'Saw him at the bar earlier. With Milo.'

'Wonder they didn't appear for the grub.'

'Mustn't be hungry. You okay? You seem—'

'Argh, it's been a rough day. I'm whacked after the weight cut. Should've done it during the week. I've rallied now, after a scoop or five of Arthur's finest. It boils down to pacing yourself. I'm gonna shoot across to Ambrose Hattinger in a minute, for a chat.' Ferdia winked. 'Hear the latest? Dorothy was telling me 'bout the doctored photograph?' Ferdia tapped his nose.

'Jesus, Ferdia. Say nothing. You—'

'I'll introduce you.'

'I don't *want* an introduction. They've got damn all to do with me. Or you.'

'It'll be grand.' Ferdia winked again, zipped his lips with a thumb. 'Mum's the word.'

A woman in a low-cut red dress caught Ferdia's arm. 'Jim wants to talk with you.'

Ferdia put an arm around her shoulder. 'Let him wait. First, we'll have a drink.' He pushed nearer the bar. 'What's your poison?'

'Oh, Corona with a slice of lime. Thanks.'

Ferdia called for the beer and nodded to his own glass. The bartender slid drinks across the counter. The woman removed the sliver of lime wedged in the bottle neck and wrapped it in a napkin. 'I save the limes,' she said, 'so I can keep count of my drinks.'

'Me too,' Ferdia said, ' 'cept I use ice cubes. Tell me, did you hear the one 'bout an Englishman, a Frenchman, and a Russian oligarch…?'

Hugh eyed Malcolm McGuire approach the counter, hemmed in by half-a-dozen jostling pals. Milo hung on the periphery. He spotted Hugh staring at him, did an abrupt about-face, dodging and twisting between the bodies pouring towards the bar. Hugh watched Malcolm peeled fifty euro notes off a bulky wad, gave them to the barman and waved his arm to the circle of hangers-on, demonstrating the drinks were on him.

Back in the ballroom, a magician amused guests in the interval between dinner and dessert. On stage, an Elvis impersonator wriggled through 'All Shook Up'. Milo mooched towards McGuire's table. Sharona saw him coming, got up and stood beside Hugh. Milo veered away.

'Why doesn't he want to talk to me?' Hugh asked Sharona.

'Because he's a dickhead.'

'And a drunk asshole. Tell me if he pisses you off.'

'He was an asshole long before he got drunk.'

'Why did you say earlier he was a creep?'

'Milo—'

Dorothy appeared on stage, and fiddled with the mic. Audio feedback screeched. 'Is this on, Ewan? I can't…testing, testing. That's better. Good evening, ladies and gentlemen. A warm welcome on this cold night to our annual fundraiser. My co-founder, Charlie McGuire, can't be with us, but we wish him a speedy recovery. It's ten years since he and I set up this cross-community, cross-border trust that identifies talented young people, and supports them during their university years. More than ever, the continued development and education of our youth is critical…'

'What were you asking me?' Sharona asked Hugh.

'Why you said Milo's a creep?'

'Milo's got no personality,' Sharona swirled her wine, 'and zero people management skills. Treats everyone like dirt. When Malcolm and I started going out, Milo pushed into our group. I made an effort; he's Malcolm's cousin, after all. I friended him on Facebook, and he must've taken that as a thumbs-up, 'cos he asked me out, *knowing* that we were together? Weird, jealous little man. In Milo's world, everything's hilarious when it happens to somebody else.' Sharona sipped her drink.

Dorothy wound up her speech: '…*your* investment in them will ensure strong, sustained economic growth. Please be as generous as you can. Thank you.'

An emcee announced that a jazz band would commence in ten minutes, and the auction for 'exceptional items' would begin at midnight. He urged patrons to dig deep and bid.

Hugh said, 'Malcolm told me he's letting Milo go.'

'Believe it when you see it.'

The ballroom filled up again.

'Has Malcolm spoken to you since…?' Hugh asked.

'I met him this morning when we went to visit Charlie,' Sharona said. 'Couldn't wait to get away. Must've seen my name on the list tonight and vanished.'

'He's at the bar. Nice guy,' Hugh said.

'He is. Though he has issues.'

'Has? Or had?'

'Has. Current.'

'Oh?'

'Yeah. Charlie's convinced it's ended, but any addiction's a serious problem.'

'Huh.'

'Impossible to stop without professional help. And when you've got pond life like Dessie Dolan on hand—'

'Who's Dessie Dolan?'

'Friend of Malcolm's. I was with Malcolm a couple of times, well, I observed from the wings when they met. Dolan's a merciless vulture who preys on the weak and vulnerable. God, him and his ilk should be—'

Across the room, Ferdia called Sharona's name, waved to get her attention. 'You too, Hugh,' he shouted.

Hugh hesitated, then trailed Sharona.

Ferdia swayed. His companion, another middle-aged, fleshy, dark-haired man, gripping a whiskey tumbler, rocked backwards on shiny black shoes. Sweat shone on the man's face, his nose ruddy with burst capillaries. A bespoke suit couldn't hide a protruding belly, and he sported the self-satisfied smirk of a person with a winning lottery ticket. Glasses hung from a lanyard, and he'd skipped the traditional tux, opting instead for a red silk tie, knotted in a flawless double Windsor. Four fat cigar tips jutted like missile warheads from a breast pocket.

'Ambrose, meet Hugh Fallon and Sharona...' Ferdia hiccupped. 'Waters.'

Ambrose Hattinger's eyes drilled through Sharona's clothes, and he sucked in his belly. 'So you're the art consultant. Hell-lo. I'm Ambrose Hattinger. Chairman of Hattinger Furniture, Fine Art, Antiques and Auction Houses.'

'Did I pass my physical?' Sharona's smile did nothing to reduce the sting.

Ambrose leered. 'I'd have been *happy* to work around this…' he flipped a dismissive hand wave '…little matter with yourself. Glad it's resolved. Dorothy's a dear, *dear* friend. It so happens we're in the process of procuring another company; we're at the due diligence stage, that sort of thing.' Ambrose's bombastic baritone, spoken with the assurance of a man accustomed to respect, his swelled chest portraying an air of intellectual arrogance. 'No venture, no gain, eh? It'll be in the public arena in due course. Could be consultancy work for an attractive young girlie after the…' hand wave again '…technicalities get finalised. Men's work.' Ambrose gestured to a cluster of tables. 'That's Adam's end of the business. He's here someplace. Adam? Adam?'

A tall, lean, broad-shouldered man stood, straightened and fastened the bottom button on a tailored charcoal-coloured dress suit jacket. He had a high forehead, piercing Dresden-blue eyes and blond hair slicked into a businessman's cut.

'Ferdia Hardiman, Hugh Fallon and Serena—'

'Sharona. Sharona Waters.'

'Adam, this is the delightful young lady who helped Dorothy sort out the, eh…matter.'

'Good evening. I'm Adam Styne. I understand you solved the mystery. Much ado about nought. So easy to misplace items.'

'Do you find that happens often?' Hugh asked.

Styne stared. 'Every other week. Collectors forget they've locked pieces away for protection, and the initial reaction is: "stolen." In reality, that's rare. Nowadays, even ordinary houses have too much security for criminals.'

'Unless it's an inside job,' Sharona said. 'No quantity of high-tech security can hold out against that.'

'Indeed.'

'Your surname,' Hugh broke the silence. 'Is that the German spelling S-T-E-I—?'

'No. S-T-Y-N-E.'

'What county does it originate—?'

'I have neither the time nor inclination to spend climbing up branches of my extended family tree.'

'Oh.' Hugh tried again. 'Hattinger's are a well-established company.'

'Yes.'

'Are you involved in the business long?'

'Sixteen years.'

'Any advice for a novice?' Ferdia reeled forward, slapped Adam's shoulder, then grasped his arm and shook hands with his wrought-iron grip.

Hugh watched Adam wipe his palm on a trouser leg. 'It depends,' Adam said, 'If you're in the market to buy, and you find a piece that fills a void in your life, grab it. Drop in to one of our galleries and talk to a consultant.'

'Argh, to you, it's another day, another Dali,' Ferdia staggered back a step. 'Me? I'm not great around the whole arty lark.'

'Our consultants will be happy to guide you.'

'A fool and his Monet, eh? Still, might take you up on that offer. Chances are I'll need a birthday present sooner or later. But none of this modern shi…stuff, though. It's gotta be…recognisable. Can I tell you a secret?' Ferdia leaned closer and belched. 'The few galleries I've been in, half the time I don't know what the feck I'm lookin' at.'

'I see. Well, galleries aren't for everyone. As I said, our consultants—'

'Gotta business card handy?'

Adam paused. 'Of course.' He drew out an engraved Burberry leather card holder and handed Ferdia a gold-embossed card.

Ferdia searched pockets, hadn't one of his own to exchange, but found a dog-eared envelope and he tore off a piece. 'Anyone got a pen?' He asked Hugh to write the mobile number.

'You live in Dublin?' Adam asked Sharona.

'No. Ganestown.'

'Ahh.' Styne frowned. 'Ganestown. In the news regarding the disappearance of...' he snapped his fingers.

Sharona nodded. 'Roberta Lord. Yes.'

'Hmm. Stressful on her family. I hope she's found safe and well. Where did you study art?'

'Trinity.'

Adam smiled. 'My alma mater. Do you collect as well as consult?'

'Strict amateur.'

Hugh handed across Ferdia's number. Adam doubled the square of paper and folded it again. 'Nice to meet you.' His smile was as brief as the nod. He moved away and Hugh watched him flick the wadded-up phone number into a corner.

'Seems a decent skin,' Ferdia nudged Ambrose. 'Don't remember him on the golf course. When the weather improves, I'll take him for a game. We'll hack our way through eighteen holes.'

'He isn't a member. No interest in golf.' Ambrose pointed the whiskey glass at Adam's departing shoulders. 'Total focus on business. Knows what he wants and goes after it. He's—'

'For the company or for himself?' Sharona asked.

'—a stupendous ambassador for the company. Rock-solid. He hitched up with my sister, Madeline. More Hattinger than ourselves. They've got a decent enough spread on the Kinnitty road, outside Kilcormac.'

'Madeline Hattinger?' Ferdia said. 'Haven't seen hide nor hair of her in years.'

'She's supposed to be here tonight. Flying in from Paris. Depends on the weather. I'm sure we'll meet again, Serena.'

'Sharona.'

'The night's young.' Ambrose winked. 'I'll get in touch vis-à-vis that consultancy work when we get to the nice fluffy bits.' His eyes raked her body once more and brushed past.

Ferdia gazed after him. 'Madeline Hattinger. Now, there's a waddle down memory lane. Top-notch woman. Best of the feckin' bunch, she was. Often wondered what became of her. Now, what time is it? Let me guess. Time to make a fool of myself. C'mon, if you aren't pissed by midnight, you're not making an effort.'

'Relax, Ferdia,' Hugh said.

'I'm grand. Is this a wake or a party?'

'Sometimes in Ireland, you can't tell the difference.'

Ferdia grinned. 'When was the last time we got fluthered together? I've feckin' spilt more tonight than you've drunk.'

'You don't need more—'

'Why? Who'll stop me?' Ferdia lurched against Hugh. 'A bird never flew on one wing. Feck the Croke Park agreement; we'll drink the country outta recession. It's our duty. Look, see that?'

'What?'

Ferdia dug an elbow into Hugh's side, 'Those two women. We'll get their blood pumping with the Siege of Ennis. Show these young fellas how to do it.' He pointed a thumb at the dance area. 'You'd swear they were shadowboxing.' He swung back to the seating area. 'C'mon, follow my lead.' He propelled Hugh towards with a drunk's determination.

'Give over, Ferdia.'

'Hang on a second willya. Stand still.' Ferdia, now a belligerent colossus, grabbed Hugh's bow tie and pulled it askew.

'What the hell—?'

'It's for your own good, lad. Any woman who fancies you will want to straighten your dicky bow. I'm giving you an edge. You can thank me later.'

'I don't *want*—'

'Narrow the feckin' focus, Hughie. It's the only way to increase the chance of success.'

'Will. You. Gimme a break?' Hugh dug in his heels and straightened the bow. 'You'll get a heart attack.'

'Heart's grand.' Ferdia said. 'It's got broken, battered, bruised, stabbed an' cheated on, but it works. Howaya ladies. We're here, so we've already granted your first wish. Now, what were the other two?'

'Hi, Ferdia.' The women moved apart, and Ferdia sprawled between them. 'Did I ever tell you the one about...?'

Hugh stepped aside and bumped into Dorothy. 'Mrs Ridgeway? Hugh Fallon. Didn't have a chance to introduce myself at the table. I'm a friend of Sharona—'

'Oh, yes. She told me about you.' They shook hands. 'You're best friends with her brother.'

'That's right.'

'You're not in the art business?'

'No. I've worked with Ferdia for a few years, and before—'

'That Ferdia! I *told* him to keep away. He can't resist poking the fire...My God, there she is. Madeline?' Dorothy enveloped a tall, thin woman in an embrace. 'My goodness, Madeline Hattinger. You look...It's been what? Three, four years? I was *so* delighted you rang. Can't *wait* to catch up.'

Madeline's genuine smile didn't shift the worried frown between her eyebrows. 'Six years, Dorothy. I can't believe it. And you haven't changed.' Her voice was soft, controlled, dark hair braided and tied in a simple up-do bun. Diamond earrings complimented a floor-length, black tulle, short-sleeved, high-neck ball gown.

'Let's find a quiet spot to chat.' Dorothy grasped Madeline's hand. 'Out here. Oh, I want you to meet Sharona…'

The three-piece jazz band struck up a toe-tapping eight-bar boogie riff.

Ferdia led one of the women around the dance floor. For a big, inebriated man, he was agile on foot.

Too hoarse to talk, and the crowd too sloshed to listen, Hugh headed for the lifts. In the foyer, he spotted Sharona, Dorothy and Madeline search for a quiet space. Malcolm was at the bar, still fanning a fistful of fifties at the barman. A wristwatch flashed. Milo plucked notes from Malcolm's hand and drifted away, his head bobbed out of sync with the drumbeat. Hugh angled towards him. He'd cut him off and ask if he'd a problem being in the same room as him. Then he stopped. Why bother, he thought. *I don't care either way*. From the corner of his eye, he spied Eilish. She was moving towards the residents' lounge. Hugh ran after her, kept her long red hair in sight as she weaved through the crush. 'Eilish?'

The woman turned. 'Yes?'

'Um, sorry. I thought you were my Eilish. Sorry.'

Hugh turned away, crossed the lobby and forgot Milo Brady.

'Madeline ran her own art gallery before turning her hand to painting,' Dorothy told Sharona. The women had found a half-hidden nook for their chat.

Sharona smiled and shook Madeline's hand. Dorothy has told me lots about you, Mrs Styne.'

'Hattinger. I kept my maiden name. But please, call me Madeline.'

'This is the person who'll run Hattinger's someday,' Dorothy said.

'Oh, I don't—'

'You're more than capable, dear. You two need to talk.' Dorothy turned to Madeline. 'Sharona is opening her own gallery in Ganestown, once she's secured a lease. You could advise her.'

'Be delighted to.'

'Where was your gallery?' Sharona asked Madeline.

'Tullamore. I loved the business, but it's rare for an artist to make a good dealer. To be honest, I was happy when it folded into the parent company. Still, it was a learning curve. I was lucky to encounter great people along the way. Dorothy, for instance.'

'I saw one of your paintings in Dorothy's house,' Sharona said. 'Your Trinity College courtyard takes pride of place in her hallway.'

'Oh, that one was part of my first exhibition. You were so kind, Dorothy. I'll never forget your generosity and thoughtful words.'

'Ach, nonsense, dear. You've a great talent. Why haven't I noticed your work in Hattinger's galleries? Hmm? Excuse me? Excuse me?' Dorothy waved an arm. 'Can we get drinks here?'

A passing waitress altered course and took their order.

'No. No, you haven't.' Madeline shifted in her seat. 'Whatever I produce, I sell abroad. I've a studio in Paris. That's my happy place.'

'Why France?' Dorothy asked, 'and the house you've got outside Tullamore.' She caught Sharona's arm. 'You should see the fabulous mansion and gardens—'

'Fabulous mansion does not make a fabulous...Anyway, I need to challenge myself more...' Madeline glanced at the ballroom entrance, '...and push my work into new territories, but at present, I'm content. I love Paris. It's awash with inspiration. A few galleries represent me, and I host one-woman art shows at their facilities. Forces me to complete a number of canvases regularly.'

'What galleries?' Dorothy coughed and blew her nose.

'Fondation Cartier pour l'Art Contemporain on Boulevard Raspail, and Galerie Xippas—'

'I dropped in on Xippas a few months ago. That's on Vieille Temple?'

'Yes. I—'

'Madeline! I've searched for you everywhere.' Adam Styne caught his wife's arm, jerked her upright. 'Mrs Ridgeway. How nice to see you again.' Adam released Madeline's arm and shook hands with Dorothy. Madeline's flesh turned blotchy, where her husband's fingers had squeezed.

'Hello, Adam.'

'Sorry, Adam.' Madeline rubbed her arm. 'I was—'

Adam smiled at Sharona. 'We meet again, Miss Waters.'

'Hi.'

Styne homed in on Dorothy. 'I've meant to visit. We both have. Isn't that right, Madeline? I told Ambrose to keep in touch with you. Must be difficult since Blake—'

'It's an ordeal—'

'It is. It is. If there's *anything* we can do, please don't hesitate. However, with your drive and commitment, there's no doubt Blake's legacy will continue to live on in the *excellent* work you do. We're delighted to support.'

Adam's eyes flashed to Madeline. 'Aren't we? Madeline and I had this conversation recently. At the end of the day, our youth are the entrepreneurs and business leaders of tomorrow. Hmm?'

'That's the point I was—'

'I hate to break up your...trialogue, but I need Madeline for a moment.' Adam's fingers circled Madeline's upper arm again and pulled her to him, controlling rather than connecting. 'We'll continue this chat later. And your dress, Dorothy. Not just elegant, it's...recherché. Isn't it Madeline?'

The waitress returned with their drinks order.

'Have your coffee first, Madeline.' Dorothy poured tonic into her gin, eyes on Adam Styne propelling Madeline away. 'Recherché. Is that a compliment or an insult, dear?'

7

SUNDAY 13 JANUARY

MORNING

BREAKFAST IN THE Pavilion restaurant was a restrained affair.

Diners accepted they'd already squandered the day ahead. They shuffled forward for juice in a vain attempt to quench raging thirsts. Hugh glanced at the paper: record-breaking heatwaves in South Australia, record low temperature gripping America's Midwest. Overnight, a tropical storm had battered Thailand. A double murder in Dublin West dominated domestic headlines. The Roberta Lord article was reduced to a single inch below-the-fold column on page twelve.

Outside, Ferdia strolled around the hotel gardens. Smoke circled from the cigarette clamped to his lips and hung above his head in the shape of a cartoon bubble. He was still wearing last night's clothes, crumpled now, and minus the bow tie. Hugh joined him.

'Did I insult anybody last night?' Ferdia asked.

'I'd bet you did. You didn't come back to the room.'

'Nah. Stayed up—'

'Rock star lifestyle.'

'—chatting people I haven't seen in a while.' Ferdia rubbed his forehead. 'Christ, I've a headache and a hangover. Must've drunk my body weight in whiskey and beer, plus spent three month's wages on a feckin' vase at the auction. Haven't a clue where I left it. Think I've something for thirst in the car. I'm parked over here.' Ferdia searched underneath the seats, found a mineral can, yanked off the tab, chugged the contents in long glugs, and burped. 'Ahh, nothing beats full-fat Coke to cure the after-effects of a rake of pints. Riddle me this: How come no matter how much drink I consume, I always start the next morning parched?'

'Because,' Hugh said, 'alcohol decreases the body's production of anti-diuretic…never mind.'

'Thanks, professor. You've replaced the brain cells I drowned last night.' Ferdia pushed the cigarette butt into the can and crunched the aluminium container into a ball. 'Ended up chatting up a Kerry woman. Killarney. Melinda, Miranda, something like that. She's either a meteorologist or a gynaecologist. Couldn't figure out half what she said, the racket that band made. 'Twas loud enough to loosen teeth. She wanted me to…whoa, step outta this fella's way.' Ferdia pulled Hugh onto the grass verge as a dark blue 530d roared by. 'Feck sake, take it easy,' Ferdia shouted. He pointed an elbow at the departing car. 'Wasn't that yer man? The art dealer?'

'Yeah. Styne. Adam Styne.'

Brake lights flashed, and the car swerved by a taxi on its way in.

'Nice car,' Ferdia said. 'Span new. Won't have it long if he keeps driving that way. Business must be good in the art world. That's what you need.'

'What?'

'A new car. Get rid of that auld banger. Someday when you need it most, it'll—'

'Yeah, yeah. What were we saying?'

'No idea. I'll head across to Charlie for a while, then pick up Master David. Give Ciara a break.'

'I'm going home. Oh, has Charlie said any more about the loan shark?'

'Not a word,' Ferdia lied.

The taxi pulled up at the main entrance. A porter wheeled out luggage. Sharona and Dorothy followed. Ferdia and Hugh helped load the garment bags and cases.

'Wasn't that a gas gig?' Sharona whispered to Hugh. 'What'd you make of Dorothy?'

'Only met her for a second. Wouldn't want to cross swords with her, though. She rushed off when Madeline Hattinger appeared.'

'Don't take it personal,' Sharona said. 'Dorothy suspects everybody at the moment. Her faith in human nature has taken a deep dive. Still, glad I got to see Hattinger's up close. Wonder what Adam Styne classes as "ordinary houses with too much security." He reminded me of my neighbour's cat, the way she scrutinises and surveys everyone. What'd you make of Ambrose?'

'A licentious—'

'Lewd—'

'Louche—'

'Self-opinionated boor,' Sharona finished. 'A coarse man in an expensive suit. Consultancy work for "an attractive young girlie". Yuk.'

'Who'll be in touch when they get to the nice fluffy bits.' Hugh watched Ferdia hug Dorothy.

'Fluffed up with his own importance. And Adam Styne?'

'Hmm. Cold.'

'Yeah and callous. His eyes pierce through you,' Sharona said, picking at a smudge of mascara. 'Hope I get home tomorrow.'

'Keep me updated.'

'Sure.'

'Slán,' Ferdia waved. He threw the soft drink can into a litter bin. 'If we don't talk in the next couple of days, Hugh, I'll chat to you Wednesday in Mullingar.'

'Exit interview. Yeah. See you then.'

'Tell Kathleen I'll drop in for a mug of tea during the week...'

Halfway home, Hugh's phone rang. He didn't recognise the number.

'Hello?'

'Can I speak to Anthony?'

'Sorry, wrong number.'

'Is that 0865312...?'

'Yes?'

'Anthony Harte?' the voice asked.

'Anthony Harte? He's...*was* my grandfather. He's dead. What's this about?'

'Garda Flanagan, here. Ganestown Garda Station. Sorry to bother you. Kathleen Fallon gave us your number as next of kin. Anthony Harte's—'

Hugh's blood froze. He rolled the car onto the hard shoulder, wheels crunching through packed slush, and slammed on the brakes. 'I missed that. Say again? Kathleen Fallon's my mother. Where—?'

'It's all right, sir. Mrs Fallon's fine. An hour ago she parked her car in the middle of Main Street, locked her vehicle and walked off. Caused a minor traffic disruption. Took us a while to locate her in Meadow's supermarket. Appeared disorientated, so we brought her to the hospital as a precaution.'

'My grandfather was Anthony Harte. Her father...I don't remember him; he passed away, God, twenty-five years ago.'

'Has this happened to your mother before?'

'Not to my knowledge. But she's,' Hugh hesitated, 'got Alzheimer's, and—'

'Well, I'd say that's the end of her driving. We towed the vehicle here. Can you pick it up?'

'I'll organise it after I've visited the hospital.'

'Take your time. No rush.'

Hugh's head swam. Guilty feelings burrowed into his brain. His throat tightened, making it difficult to breathe. He'd made a massive error of judgement. The doctor was right. He should have listened to and heeded the professionals, instead of railing against them. His mother could have crashed or caused a fatal accident. Hugh gunned the Lexus back on the motorway, the car fishtailing. He powered out of the skid and rocketed on to Ganestown.

MID-MORNING

ADAM STYNE DROVE through Ganestown and checked out the jewellery shop.

He'd allowed himself extra time to inspect potential restaurants for a follow-up date with Ciara. Two fitted the criteria: the Malaya and Via Leoni Ristorante, both located on the outskirts of town and neither had CCTV. He guessed she'd pick the Malaya.

Styne parked on a side street, fed a parking meter, wrapped a cashmere scarf around his lower face and walked to Gambadini's. Inside, he kept the scarf around his face and asked for a seat near the entrance. His phone bleeped an incoming text. His heart sank. *Texting to say she can't make it.*

Adam, Paris flight cancelled.

Next one's scheduled for Wed.

I'll stay in Kilcormac until then.

M.

He deleted Madeline's text, switched the phone to silent mode, and waited.

He recognised Ciara when she walked in. Refined. Much better looking than her profile shot. Her walk was brisk and confident. Pushed back shoulders exaggerated her breast size. The gym workouts were effective, he noted, his sweeping glance taking in the designer jacket, a capacious bucket bag and...were they Marni earrings? The total package suggested a liberated woman. He'd met dozens identical to her over the years: slags, who dressed in the latest fashion and worked their bodies to manipulate and distract male counterparts if they weren't getting their way. He stood, lowered the scarf and smiled. 'Ciara?'

'Maurice?' Ciara's cheeks flushed. 'Nice to meet you at last.'

'Pleasure's mine. It feels as though we've crossed paths before. What's your surname?'

'McGuire.'

'McGuire? I heard that name recently. Mmm, doesn't matter. Mine's Piper.' Adam pulled back Ciara's chair, paused the conversation while she removed a jacket.

'Ta.'

Adam was aware of Ciara's covert appraisal. He spotted the waitress moving towards them, and used a handkerchief to hide his features while the waitress filled water glasses and rhymed off lunch specials.

First impression.

Vigilant after last night's phone call, he made a conscious effort to relax his features and let the smile reach his eyes. He adjusted the shirt cuffs a fraction, let Ciara glimpse the Patek Philippe watch. She recognised it. Adam noticed the tension seep away, as his date moved the dial on her intuitive radar to "low." He drank in the woman's facial features, smelled her perfume—a combination of the gingery sweetness found in wildflowers, with a trace of coconut. Her self-conscious smile showed vulnerability, and the familiar trickle of expectancy swirled at the base of his spine. He waited, gave Ciara space to decide how she wanted to begin. The flush in her cheeks diminished. The waitress stood, pen poised.

Ciara said: 'Quiche and salad, please.'

'Salmon, please,' Adam added and coughed into his handkerchief.

Ciara sipped water.

Adam copied.

'Do you have business in this area?' Ciara asked.

'Yes, one of my people meets with the jeweller a few times a year.'

'I didn't mean you to drive especially—'

'Dublin's no distance now with the motorway. I'm glad to be here. Appraisals completed?'

Ciara laughed. 'The groundwork's done, but I've lots more paperwork.'

'Ah, the dreaded paperwork.' Adam's eyes crinkled. 'What area do you work in?'

'Human Resources.'

'So you're involved in every evaluation?'

'Yes. Bi-annually, for my sins. Those appraisal phrases you gave me will be useful next week.'

'You're welcome.'

'Now'—Ciara smiled—'I've to come up with suitable terminology for the not-so-notable performers.'

'Hmm, how about: failed to, needs to demonstrate, has not made use of, must establish, unwilling to, avoids—'

'Wow, that's good from the top of your head.'

'Result of a Trinity education.'

'I'm impressed. I've made a mental note,' Ciara said. 'But you enjoy the work?'

'It has its moments. I've excellent staff.'

'So you're the manager. A Head of Function.'

'With the salary of a temp.' Ciara tossed her hair back and leaned forward, inhaling the rich woody scent of Adam's aftershave. 'Do you find the constant travel draining?'

'It's part and parcel of my job.' Adam topped up water and mimicked her pose. 'Trips include an airport, a conference room and return to airport. It can become monotonous.'

Ciara rubbed the milky-greenish opal on her finger. 'Travel, they say, broadens the mind.'

'Indeed. I admire your ring, Ciara. Opals are most effective in contact with air and skin humidity.'

'Oh?' Ciara moved her hand, highlighting the stone's colours. 'I wear it because I love how it shimmers. Also, it gives me a sense of security.'

Adam reached out, touched the gemstone. His finger grazed Ciara's skin. 'Opals contain water, so they get brittle over time, and the colour fades. It's normal.'

'I'm so used to looking at it, I don't know if it's lost sheen.'

'If you're not wearing it, I suggest you place it in an airtight container with a damp piece of cotton. That prevents it from drying out. Or a jeweller can revitalise it if the stone gets dull or scratched.'

'What's the most expensive opal you've handled?'

'I saw a black one in Antwerp last year. The price could have purchased a medium-sized island in the Indian Ocean. Sorry, Ciara, I promised myself not to mention work.'

The waitress arrived with food.

Adam sensed Ciara relax. The aftershave helped caress and lull her senses.

She wants to believe and trust. This'll be easy.

'Can I offer you a glass of wine?' he asked.

'No, thanks.'

'You wrote in one of the mails that you've travelled extensively,' Adam said.

Ciara nodded. 'America. Hmm, this is delicious. I wanted to spend my life in San Francisco, but when I got pregnant, I moved back to my roots. My employer advertised for an HR manager in Ganestown, so it was a painless decision. I told you about the old cottage I bought?'

'Yes.'

'Twelve kilometres from here. Two minutes to school. Fifteen-minute drive to work. No traffic jams. Perfect.'

'Was it easy to adapt after the frenzy of San—?'

'I miss some things. However, Ireland has its advantages. I've got amazing friends and a fantastic family that's prepared to help out. After the initial upheaval, it was an easy adjustment.'

'Yes. It's essential we have a support hub to fall back on. A contingency.' Adam sipped water, waiting for the personal questions.

Ciara put her knife and fork on the plate, patted her lips with a napkin and placed a hand under her chin. 'So, Maurice, when did you get married?'

He leaned back, stared at her, unblinking. 'I've never married.'

'Just testing. Where were you born?'

'Tipperary. Between Cashel and Thurles.'

'Brothers or sisters?'

'I'm an only child.'

Ciara frowned. 'Oh? What does your father do?'

'He owned a jeweller's shop in Thurles. He's dead.'

'You didn't take over?'

'Too slow for me.'

'How long since your relationship broke up?'

'Over a year.'

Ciara sipped water and looked over the glass rim. 'How long were you together?'

'Four years.'

'Children?'

'No.'

'You didn't want children?'

'I did.'

'She?'

'No.'

'Was that the reason you broke up?'

'Somewhat, but not…well, why do any couple separate? Incompatibility, I guess. We grew apart. She went her way.'

'What was her way?'

Adam remembered to flash a grin. 'You're very personal.'

'You don't have to answer.'

'I can see you are good at your job.'

'Yes.' Ciara waited, eyebrows raised.

Adam leaned forward, made sure his hands stayed away from his face, and his eyes remained above Ciara's neckline. 'After our relationship broke up, she moved to Paris and, I presume, got on with her life. There's no contact between us.'

'What caused the breakup?'

Adam made a face. 'People change. Not to suggest that I'm faultless. Nobody is. But work pressure…'

Ciara listened. Said nothing. Wanted more.

'It takes two to cement a relationship,' Adam added. 'There was a lack of communication on both sides. I'm convinced my soul mate's out there, but I'd prefer to be alone and content…' he gazed into Ciara's eyes, '…than be in a relationship and miserable. It's difficult to form a connection when I'm away so much, but I believe in integrity and commitment, and the business trips won't last forever. I joined the site two weeks ago, so I've just dipped my toe. You're the first person I've met. I enjoyed the directness in your emails and our chats.'

Ciara nodded.

I can tell by the positive vibes and body language I'm getting through.

He wondered how many dates it would take to replicate Isobel Stewart's demise.

Must buy lime. Need gloves too.

The waitress approached with dessert menus.

Ciara checked the time on her mobile. 'Goodness, I'm sorry, Maurice. I've to pick up my boy.'

'Oh? Are you sure—?'

'I'd love to continue this chat.' Ciara pushed back her chair. 'Apologies for the rush. I enjoyed lunch, but I've got to go. Thank you.'

Adam paid and held Ciara's jacket while she slipped her arms into the sleeves. 'Will you say yes to a dinner invitation? The Malaya, or Via Leoni Ristorante? During the week if it suits? Or next weekend? Friday or Saturday?'

'Ooh, a man of taste. I'll get back to you.'

They walked outside.

'Friday, perhaps?' Adam asked again.

'It's been ages since I'd a night out.'

'Or would Saturday suit better?'

'I can understand why you're involved in sales. You don't give up, do you?'

'Only when it's something I want.'

'Next weekend sounds great, Maurice, barring any unforeseen circumstances on the home front. I haven't eaten Malaysian in ages.'

Knew it.

'If you wish, I can collect you. That way, you can enjoy a drink and not worry about getting breathalysed.'

Must buy a Bach CD. It'll help lower her reserve.

Ciara pursed her lips. 'Or I could call a taxi.'

Too pushy.

Adam reined in. 'Of course. You decide what works.'

'I will.' Ciara halted beside a red Nissan. 'Oh, one other question.'

'Yes?'

'What play did you see last night?'

'Pardon?'

'Gaiety Theatre? You took clients, remember?'

Styne hesitated, forced a laugh. 'You have me there, Ciara. It's slipped my mind. I have the booklet...' He fished through an inside coat pocket. 'No. Must be in the car. I can't remember the name...'

Ciara cocked her head. 'Really?'

'It was one of those...' Styne shrugged, palms upwards, open, non-threatening. 'My mind's gone blank.'

Ciara nodded. 'As a Christmas present, my son and I got tickets for The Snow Queen. It's running in the Gaiety since November. Great show. For kids. I knew we were going mid-January and your email reminded me to check the ticket date. I thought we'd missed it. It closes next week. I wondered why a group of business people wanted to see a children's pantomime. Hmm?'

Styne frowned.

'I suppose you meant the *Gate* Theatre.' Ciara waited for clarification.

Styne's scowl deepened, suspecting a trap.

Ciara shivered and used the bucket bag as a barrier. 'Or maybe not. Why am I getting the sense you're holding back, Maurice? You sure you're not married? In our phone conversation yesterday evening you said you have a nephew. Now, you say you're an only child. Which is it? Or has your mind gone blank on that too? Did you take your wife and son to The Snow Queen last night?'

Styne stayed silent.

'Was there a smidgen of truth in *anything* you said over lunch? Are you still in a relationship?'

Styne shook his head, at a loss how to retrieve the situation.

Ciara moved aside, pressed the car remote. 'You know, I *wanted* to believe the Gaiety Theatre was a genuine slip. Like the Cork-Belfast airport mix-up? Now that I think about it, the idea of a high flying executive booking his own flight sounds implausible. Maybe I'm wide of the mark, and if I've misjudged you...well, I'll cut to the chase: Thanks for lunch, Maurice, if that's your name. Don't *ever* contact me again. I haven't got time for silly games, and I *won't* be in touch regarding next weekend. Goodbye.'

Ciara slid into the seat, slammed the car door, started the engine and roared off.

Blindsided, Adam Styne glared in disbelief at a cloud of exhaust fumes.

HUGH RACED INTO Ganestown hospital's reception area.

The switchboard operator checked a computer screen. 'St John's ward. Second floor.'

'Thanks.' Hugh sprinted away.

'Her room number isn't on the system yet,' the receptionist called after him. 'Ask a nurse.'

Upstairs, an old man stood forlorn by the unoccupied nurse workstation, desperate to catch someone's attention. The brrring-brrring of an office phone pealed, no sooner answered than it rang again. A visitor rushed by. Her rich top note of oriental fragrance diluted amid the excess of pungent hospital smells; iodine, Savlon, floor polish, alcohol swabs, burned toast and bleach. An intercom crackled, and a voice called a doctor to ICU. A child cried. The old man shuffled away. Hugh took his spot, pressed the buzzer and stared at the unblinking red eye of a security camera monitoring the corridor from its anchored sentry perch high on a wall.

Giving up, he dashed along the corridor, ducking into rooms on either side until he found Kathleen. A nurse counted tablets from a dispensing trolley, took her blood pressure and made notations on a chart.

Kathleen reached out, gripped Hugh's hand. 'Why aren't you at work?'

'It's Sunday, Ma. From now on, we're spending our weekends together.'

'Wonderful. Or as young people say, WTF.'

'Ma, please tell me you don't know what that means.'

'Course I do. I'm well able to keep up to text speak. It means, wow, that's fantastic. What did you think it meant?'

'Um, Welcome to Facebook?'

'Where's Facebook?'

'It's not a place Ma, it's—'

'Will you change the bulb in the bathroom at home?'

'Sure.'

'And when will you paint the kitchen? You promised.'

'I'll start it tonight.'

'Don't forget the hall.'

'Yep.'

'And replace the lightbulb in—'

'I'm on it, Ma.'

'And paint the hall.'

'Yes, I'm on that too.'

'And the bulb—'

'Yep.'

'Why am I here, Hugh?'

'You lost your bearings, Ma. No big deal.'

'What's happening to me?'

'You'll be fine.' The words caught in his throat and he coughed, silently cursing his traitor voice.

'Can you bring in nightclothes?' the nurse murmured. 'And Ruth Lamero asked me to page her if you dropped in. She wants a word. Hang around for a minute.'

'Okay.'

The nurse wheeled the trolley out.

'Thank God you're alive,' Kathleen said. 'Go. Quick. They're hurting me. They'll *kill* you. Don't let them catch—'

'Nobody'll hurt you, Ma. I need to see a nurse.'

'Don't leave me alone, Peter.'

'Peter's…I'm Hugh, Ma. I'll be back in a second.'

'I'm telling you—'

'Everything's fine.' Hugh patted his mother's arm. 'Everything's fine.'

Ruth was leafing through a file on the nurse station counter.

She pushed the health insurance card towards him. 'Meant to return this.'

'Thanks. Didn't expect to be back so soon. It's bloody difficult to prepare for specific scenarios when you don't know if they'll take place, or even when they might occur. It's so…' Hugh wrestled for the right word, '…vague. Ma insisted I leave her alone last night. I thought she was okay. Genuinely figured the doctor's prognosis was wrong. So stupid.'

'Not stupid, Hugh. Nobody likes to receive bad news. It takes time to accept.'

'If I'd stayed with her, this wouldn't have happened. How long will she be here this time?'

'There's nothing we can do. Tests will be back tomorrow. Probably let home on Tuesday.' Ruth tucked a strand of hair behind her ear. 'And it's not your fault. If it weren't this, it'd be something else. Prone to disorientation is another symptom.'

'God.' Hugh paced the length of the counter. 'Another factor I can't control.'

'Alzheimer patients can potter around at night, Hugh. They put on fires, or wander outside, or drive into town. It's a challenge to keep—'

'How'll I curb that? I *can't* stand guard twenty-four seven. Wish I'd relations nearby to share the burden.'

'One day at a time, Hugh. Stay positive.'

'Actually, I'm scared out of my wits. It's easier to pretend there's nothing wrong than accept reality. I know I have to man up, but I've no idea how to handle the situation. Am I delusional in assuming I can make a difference? I'd convinced myself this would work out, but since I got the phone call from the Garda station, everything's changed.'

'Someone said: "We're born, we die, and in between, we try to understand," ' Ruth murmured.

'Rod Steiger, I think,' Hugh said.

'That's where you are now,' Ruth said. 'Figuring-out-the-best-option stage.'

'I'm asking myself: Why Ma? Why now? Am I duty-bound to tell her? I'm so accustomed to my safety net: nice to know it's there, even if you don't require it. Now I'm sliding, with nothing to grab onto. Does she realise she's got Alzheimer's? A minute ago she said she doesn't know what's happening to her.'

'Alzheimer's is a horrible disease,' Ruth dodged answering the question. 'Your mother expects you to support her independence. Easy to say, but it's a big ask.'

'Doctor Abbott said that too. And he was right about the symptoms. They were there for months, a year and a half, actually. Since my father died. I didn't recognise—'

'So far, you've dealt with the fallout brilliantly.'

'Have I? Muddled more than managed, if I'm honest. Don't consider myself brilliant. It feels like I'm running through a minefield, waiting for the next explosion. I need a project. Something that'll help Ma long-term.'

Ruth reached across and tapped Hugh's jacket sleeve. 'Keep positive. Focus on what you *can* do today, instead of worrying about tomorrow.'

'What I *want* to do is bury my head in the sand. How can I get beyond this hurdle? Will I be able to cope? It'll put a block on my career. The compromises...God, that makes me sound mercenary, but I *am* concerned. My security, interests, work...That mantle of invincibility has vanished.'

'That's honest,' Ruth said. 'Alzheimer's controls everybody it comes in contact with, not only the patient.'

'I should get involved in practical stuff, like converting a downstairs room into a bedroom. Make Ma's life more manageable.'

'Good carers know there's more they could and should do,' Ruth said. 'I'd love for the public to rally round and share the load.'

'I should talk to one of those carers.'

'I've a cousin, Sarah, who's a geriatric nurse. She's emigrating in a few weeks, the whole family are; her husband can't get work. She'll be happy to advise you or offer short-term support. Might provide you with the headspace to come up with a plan.'

'I'd appreciate any guidance.'

Ruth wrote on a pad and tore off the sheet. 'Here's her number. Even if you want to talk to a nurse who understands and cares for Alzheimer's patients, ring her.

'I will. Thanks. I…' Hugh studied the phone number. 'I've tried to visualise what my wishes for Ma are. I haven't got a clear vision yet, but I want her to enjoy a quality life, and provide a gold standard comfort service.'

Ruth nodded, said nothing, letting Hugh reason through his deliberation process.

'There's a quality to dying,' he continued. 'And whenever her time comes, she'll want to pass away peacefully and with dignity. I don't believe she's afraid of death, but Ma hates being a burden. Depending on anyone is her worst nightmare.'

Ruth squeezed Hugh's hand. 'Your presence and support are all that matters. Although Kathleen might lose her past, she deserves the present. And future.'

'Should I tell Ma she has Alzheimer's?'

'I'd say Kathleen's well aware of becoming more forgetful and won't thank you for the reminder. You *could* tell her she may have a memory disease.'

'Hmm. I'll leave that conversation for another day,' Hugh said. 'It seems like one step forward, two steps—'

His's mobile buzzed. 'Eilish?'

'Hugh? I—'

'Eilish? God, I hadn't a chance to…You won't believe what happened. I'm back in—'

'Hugh, listen. It's taken me hours to build up the nerve to call you. It's over.'

'What?'

'Our relationship. It's finished. I've…met somebody else.'

'What?'

'I've picked up my clothes. I swear, I never once imagined we'd…Sorry. We weren't supposed to end this way.'

'Eilish? Eilish? Can you hear me? I'll be home in…Hello? Hello? Shit.' Hugh checked the phone signal. Four bars. He redialled. Eilish's number diverted to voicemail. 'Who's somebody else? This. Cannot. Be happening.'

Hugh sprinted away, skidding on the parquet floor.

Ruth called after him, 'Kathleen's insurance—'

'Hold onto it,' Hugh shouted over his shoulder. 'I've gotta see Eilish.'

PUCE WITH RAGE, Styne strode to his car, murder on his mind.

A headache replaced the low burn of expectancy.

My plans. The time I've wasted. I knew the bitch would be a challenge.

He grabbed a tennis ball, squeezed, and pounded a fist against the steering column.

Can't ask anybody where she lives. People remember conversations, especially when she'll be reported missing. How to proceed? How to advance the search? How to get her?

'She didn't see my car,' he muttered. 'Should've asked the company name and track her from work.'

Too risky. What did she say about the house? An old cottage twelve kilometres from here. Two minutes to school, and a fifteen-minute drive to work.

'You won't beat me, bitch.'

Blood boiled in Styne's head and he tapped Ciara McGuire into a search engine and almost hit the enter key. Almost. He drove into Ganestown and used the hotel Wi-Fi to search the web for Ciara again.

Two hits. Drumraney and Glencara townlands. He clicked onto Google maps. Either could be twenty minutes' drive to Ganestown.

Stupid. Stupid. Stupid. Why didn't I ask where your cottage was? National schools.

He inputted a search request and got a hit on eight sites. None near Glencara. Naomh Clar National School was beside Drumraney.

Styne wrote the information and erased his search tracks. Back at the car, he fed the school address into the sat-nav. Twelve point two kilometres.

Worth a visit.

AFTERNOON
EILISH HAD LEFT the house keys on the kitchen worktop.

Hugh added voice messages to her mailbox until it filled up again. He dialled Ciara McGuire. She'll know, he thought. They told each other everything.

No answer there either.

He roamed the house, dazed, searching for clues that didn't exist, pulled out drawers usually jam-packed with clothes, and stared at the blank space. The double wardrobe in the bedroom was bare. Clothes rails, wedged with designer gear yesterday, were empty, except for a few wooden hangers. Eilish's perfume scent clung to the bed. The lavender aroma hit Hugh like a slap, and he lay on the sheets, breathing in her fragrance. Grief, layered with a sense of anger and rejection poured out in torrents. Shattered sobs shook his body, aching for the person he loved, and the dreams he'd lost. Tears soaked the pillowcase. After, he sat under the shower and let hot water relieve the numb pain. Images of Eilish, with flashbacks of their three years together, ran in his mind like looped film reels. He dressed and redialled Ciara McGuire.

'Hugh?'

'Give me answers, Ciara.'

'About what?'

'Eilish. She's gone. She must've told you. Why didn't you say?'

'Say what? Gone where?'

'Gone. Left. Broke up.'

'Jesus. I'd no idea she'd planned to—'

'I won't go away. You can't avoid me indefinitely,' Hugh said.

'I'm just home. Ferdia's calling to collect David—'

'I'll be there in fifteen minutes.'

Ciara met him at her front door.

'I'm so sorry, Hugh. This sounds stupid, but are you okay?'

'As if I'd got kicked in the guts with a steel-toed boot. Eilish won't answer my calls.'

'Come in. Coffee?'

'No.'

'David? Go tidy up your room. Ferdia will be here soon. How did Eilish—'

'She phoned. Said, "We're done. I've moved out." That's it.'

Ciara winced.

'They planned this,' Hugh said. 'Eilish knew I wouldn't be around last night. Did she tell you? You know who it is, don't you?'

'I'm not comfortable getting caught in the middle—'

'Don't you?'

'Yes.'

'Who?'

'Richard West.'

'Richard...? Jill's husband? That guy's ancient. Old enough to...How long's it going on?'

'Not sure. Eilish hasn't been herself for a few months. I assumed ye had a domestic. She told me last week, how...um, I'd to drag it out of her. Far as I was aware,

Eilish had sorted her issues out, between you two, I mean. We spoke yesterday, ended up in a row. Haven't heard from her since. I've no idea where she is, or what's going on inside her head.'

'Richard West knows,' Hugh said. 'I'll call round.'

'No. Jesus, Hugh. That's the worst idea ever.'

'Why?'

'Why? Because...it is.'

'But we were content. How can the person you live with tell you they're—?'

'Eilish *was* happy. Is. I mean—'

'I can't believe she couldn't talk to me.' Hugh rubbed his eyes.

'Maybe she didn't want to hurt you.'

'Well, see how that worked out? I'd rather she hurt me with honesty than destroy me with lies. Wish we'd never met.'

'Who's hurting who?' Ferdia spoke from the doorway.

'Nobody,' Hugh said.

Ciara gazed out the kitchen window.

'What's going on?' Ferdia asked.

'Eilish called quits on our relationship.'

'What? Argh, for feck...Where's she now?'

'No idea.'

'Aww Jaysus, I'm sorry to hear that. But sure, these things happen, and—'

'Yeah. Relationships have their ups and downs, right?'

'Exactly. This'll blow over—'

'I can't remember when we disagreed or argued about *anything*, 'til a while back. Since then, she's acted strange. You saw it yourself last Friday. It's been on my mind to push for answers, but I *knew* deep down I wouldn't want to hear them, so I let it go. I'm kicking myself now. Should've made time to talk. Wish I could say I don't give a damn, but I do.'

'Can't feckin' fault yourself for—'

'I *do* blame myself.'

'David? Ferdia's here. Are you ready? Get your coat. Hugh, listen—'

'We spoke about our *engagement* for Christ's sake.' Hugh pushed back his hair. 'I was…we'd planned a future together. I'm…' His shoulders slumped. 'I don't know which way to turn.'

'Don't blame yourself, Hugh,' Ciara said. 'You didn't cause it, can't control—'

'Don't worry. Eilish'll be back. It'll be…Howaya Master David?' Ferdia ruffled David's hair.'

David high-fived Ferdia and Hugh.

'Nothing's worse than getting hurt by the one person you trust never to hurt you.' Hugh turned away.

'I'm not choosing sides here,' Ciara caught his arm, 'but people change, and they forget to tell each other. Eilish should've—'

'Yeah, right. Should've. Could've. Didn't.' Hugh moved to the door. 'I've gotta go. Ma's back in hospital.'

'God. Is she—?'

'Disorientation. Another part of Alzheimer's.'

'Aww, feck. Let me know if there's—'

'Thanks.'

'We'll get moving too; I'm parked in your way. You right, Master David?' Ferdia turned to Hugh. 'Willya meet with Eilish? Try to work it out, like?'

Ciara frowned at Ferdia.

'Work what out?' Hugh asked.

'Ye're *bond*, man. Your relationship.'

'What's the point?'

'I'll have a word with her.'

'Keep out of it, Ferdia.' Hugh turned up his coat collar. 'Eilish has made up her mind. I hope *he* can provide the style and luxury she's aspired to. I thought we'd be together forever. Didn't think forever was this short.'

STYNE SET THE mileage counter to zero and followed the directions intoned by the robotic computer voice. Eleven kilometres out, he saw the school. The sat-nav instructed him to turn left. There was no turn. Irritated, he switched off the GPS and inched along the unfamiliar road. Thick blankets of snow made any landmark undistinguishable. He passed a cluster of houses; three on his left, two on the right. Checked the counter again. Thirteen kilometres.

Turn around. Could be in the other direction from the school.

Rounded a sharp bend.

A detached cottage sat fifteen metres off the road, flanked on three sides by mature Leylandii. The driveway curved towards the front entrance, and a dark Mercedes had parked halfway up. The red Nissan and a light blue car sat side by side near the hall door.

Styne drove on.

At a crossroads, he reversed and backtracked for another inspection, slowing as he approached the house. Ciara and two men stood by the door. A small figure scooped snow in the garden.

Styne's heart thumped. He pressed the accelerator.

I know those faces.

It took a second.

The blitzed culchie from last night. Ferdia...somebody. Muck savage. And...Fallon. Why are they here? Whatever the connection, it doesn't matter. I've seen enough.

Near Tullamore, he phoned the home number of a garage owner. When he answered, Styne said, 'A taillight broke on my wife's Q7. I need it fixed immediately. And I want a car.'

'It's Sunday. That's not an emergency.'

'If we're involved in an accident tonight, be it on your head.'

'Of course, Mr Styne.'

'I'll pick the replacement car in an hour.'

'I won't get a chance to look at the Q7 until Tuesday or Wed—'

'Have it ready Tuesday.'

Remember to delete the sat-nav details later.

He hummed and piloted homewards. 'The opal might have given you a sense of security today, bitch, but it loses its power at night.' He ripped up the paper he'd written Ciara's details and let the pieces flutter out the window.

'Victor and victim. And to the victor come the spoils.'

EVENING

JANA TROFIMIACK CRAMMED the last of her possessions into a suitcase. Lech bounced on the lid, and Jana tugged the zip. He had packed his knapsack yesterday. She stacked the case beside the front door with the rest of their luggage and inspected the apartment, her home for ten years. From the hallway, through the kitchen and into the lounge, her steps sounded hollow in the bare rooms. Already, the apartment gave off an air of abandonment.

'Co czas wyjeżdżamy?'

'You've asked that a hundred times,' Jana smiled. 'The taxi will collect us at four-thirty.'

'In the morning?'

'Tak.'

The Jack B. Yeats oil on board of The Boat Builder, lay on her bed, the switch unnoticed by the half-blind owner. Remove brads. Swap canvas. Replace brads. Forty seconds.

Jana slipped it into a Sainsbury's bag, ready for Tomasz, then doubled back the quilt and gazed at three other pieces. Two more by Yates, already out of their frames. The watercolour and pencil on paper, she estimated was worth fifteen thousand. Sterling. The second, a charcoal and gouache: twenty-five thousand. The third piece was still in its original frame. A twenty-five by thirty-centimetre oil on canvas, she couldn't resist. Jana studied Paul Henry's The Turf Gatherer; a woman dressed in a red skirt bowed under a weighty turf creel. Quarter million. Minimum. Lech's college fund. Her art gallery. Too precious to take on a plane.

Jana took the painting from its frame, rolled it loose, painting on the outside and popped it into a postal tube. She wrote a Polish address on the cylinder and added stamps. The other two pieces got placed in separate cylinders. Same address. She broke the three frames and shoved the pieces into a rubbish bag. On the walk to the post office, she tapped out a resignation letter to Adam Styne's secretary:

Dear Mr Styne,
I'm resigning. Effective immediately.
Jana Trofimiack.

I'll be fourteen hundred miles away when they get the email on Monday morning, Jana thought. She speculated what his reaction would be when he found out she'd quit. Worried? No. Angry? Yes. Jana frowned, wondering if she'd forgotten anything, and watched Lech running ahead. The rubbish got buried in a builder's skip, and Lech helped push the postal tubes into a post box. She'd made up her mind. Jana and Lech were never coming back.

Concentrating on her son, Jana didn't notice the unmarked police car tailing them.

HUGH COLLECTED HIS mother's nightclothes, returned to the hospital and, after the nurses had changed her, kept vigil.

A tea trolley trundled along the corridor. Kathleen picked at food. A nurse gave her a thimbleful of tablets and she got drowsy. We assume we're organised, getting to grips with life, Hugh thought. Until chance intervenes and makes a mockery of our plans. Ferdia's comment that problems come in threes sprang to his mind. Job. Eilish. Ma. What else can happen?

He squirmed in the hard chair and watched Kathleen drift in and out of sleep. In the hallway, occasional tap-taps of visitors' heels offset the swish of nurses' sandals on the parquet floor. Muffled morsels of conversations soared and faded like shuttlecocks; a tranquil hour ahead of the frenetic evening bustle that kick-starts the night shift.

Ruth peeped in. 'How's Kathleen since?'

'I'm out of my depth here,' Hugh whispered.

Ruth beckoned him out of the room. 'I'm off duty. Let's grab a coffee.'

'Thought I'd got a handle on life,' Hugh said. 'Then, bang, bang. Earlier, Ma said the nurse wants to kill her, then there are snatches of lucidity, where she dishes out orders like a drill sergeant.'

'Such as?' Ruth linked Hugh towards the lift.

'Argh, I promised I'd paint the kitchen. A sugar rush. Too many Ferrero Rocher over Christmas. Amazing how Ma couldn't remember how to park a car, but she didn't forget the painting? Worst time of the year for paintwork, but the garden shed's jammed with bloody paint tins, so I've got to do it. I think Ma's being deliberately confrontational, but I'm putting it down to annoyance at not being able to do as much as she wants. It would be easy to react, but I don't want to upset her either.'

'I understand.'

'Wish I could paint.'

'Wish I could play a musical instrument…'

Hugh got the coffees. Ruth cleared a canteen table, pulled up two chairs and sat across from him. 'Talk to me. How are you?'

'I'm good.'

'Liar. But congrats. That's a brave front you've put up.'

'You're right. It's an act.' Hugh picked up a sugar sachet. His mobile hummed and shimmied along the laminated tabletop. They both peeked at the screen. Ferdia.

'Take the call,' Ruth said.

Hugh pressed the 'Off' button, sipped coffee and said, 'Since we've met, I've spent the time talking about me, Ma, my needs, her wants. What happened to you? Where'd you disappear to after the Leaving Cert?'

Ruth sat back. 'Booked my spot on a nursing degree course in Galway—'

'I studied in UCG,' Hugh said. 'Can't believe we didn't bump into each other.'

'I went on a gap year. Hiked across Europe and enjoyed that so much I spent another six nomadic months roving between Australia and Alaska—'

'And I'd moved on when you took up the college offer.'

'Yep. We slipped by like ships in the night. I finished my degree and applied for a job in Manchester. I've a sister there. Lives in Didsbury. I met a guy, got engaged—'

'Congratulations.'

'Didn't work out. He'd…issues I assumed were due to a stressful job, plus a two-hour commute each way to work, until I realised he'd met someone else in a nightclub, while

I worked double shifts to keep a roof over our heads. Stranger, friend, boyfriend, fiancé, back to zero.'

'Sorry.'

'That's six months ago. Water under the bridge. I'm well past it. You can waste days, weeks, dissecting a situation; women are great at that. We try to put the pieces back together and justify what could've happened, if only...Or, you can leave the pieces where they fall, and move on. That's what I did. At present, I'm enjoying life while the search for Mr Right continues. What've you been up to for ten years?'

'After college, I got a job in Bower's bakery. Didn't enjoy desk work, so they put me on the road as a sales rep, and I found my forte. Studied for an MBA at night. Four years ago, I became a manager with Pharma-Continental—'

'Their reps call here.'

'That was my team.'

'Was?'

'A third of the workforce got made redundant last Tuesday week.'

'Ouch.'

'Hmm. So, in under a week, let me see, I lost my job. Ma's diagnosed with Alzheimer's, and I got dumped.'

'Eilish?'

'Yeah.'

'I got your side of the phone call earlier. Sorry. Sounded...terrible. God, it's so unfair. You get into a rough patch, and life kicks you when you're down.'

'Mmm. Lulls us into a false sense of complacency. Makes me realise we're not in control of our destiny as much as we'd hope.'

'What happened with Eilish?'

'Same as your guy. She met someone else. To an extent, I'm at fault too. When you work flat out, come home tired, eat, she watches soaps, I fall asleep. Conversation falls off the page. It's hard to strike a happy medium.'

They reached for sugar sachets together, fingers touching for an instant.

'You'd imagine it should be easier to talk when you live together, but it seldom is,' Ruth said.

'On the plus side,' Hugh added sugar to his coffee, 'I've a temporary position that could become permanent in a few weeks, and I intend to enjoy life as my search for Miss Right goes on.'

'Touché.' Ruth tilted her head. 'A man of action, eh?'

'Success is inevitable once you believe it's possible. Are you glad to be back here?' Hugh asked.

'After my engagement broke up, I came home to lick my wounds and help with Dad. I fell in love with the place again. I suppose we don't value what we have; the grass is greener, etcetera.' Ruth twisted a napkin. 'All the places I've visited, I never considered settling long-term in any of them. And I didn't realise how much I missed my family. The Midlands has lots going for it, and Ireland has a *charm* you get nowhere else. You get a new perspective and appreciation of home, having been away from it for a while. So, I applied for a post, and here I am. I've learned Ganestown isn't a place to use as a pit stop while planning to head off again. It's taken me years to figure out I'm content here.'

'You've got the wanderlust out of your system.'

'Could be. I've my own higgledy-piggledy modest abode, and work is…an eternal struggle, but it pays the bills, even if it leaves little for the latest fashion.'

'You look—'

'Terrific?'

They laughed.

'Great,' Hugh said.

'Ta.'

Hugh drained his coffee. 'You're wrecked after a long day. Thanks for the chat. It's been great catching up.'

'No need to thank me. I've done—'

'You've listened. Having your ear is a huge help.

'Call anytime.'

'Okay. I'll walk you to your car.'

'Aww…'

Outside, soft snowflakes spun. The crackling cold exploded against their faces like an icy slap. Hugh caught Ruth's arm, steadied her on the glassy footpath. Frosty patterns on car windows resembled intricate designs of lace.

Ruth pointed. 'I'm parked over here.'

'Sorry for being a pessimist every time we meet, Hugh said. 'The last few days a lot of issues have whirled 'round my brain.'

'I reckon you've got it well under control.'

They lingered beside Ruth's car.

Hugh drew Ruth closer, curled his arm around her. His heart pounded.

Ruth chained both arms around Hugh's waist, smiled and angled her head upwards. A vein pulsed at the side of her neck. The kiss hovered between them.

The moment passed.

'Um, I'll go back and sit with Ma for a while, and I'll contact Sarah—'

'Great idea.'

'Well…'

'Well…' Ruth squeezed his arm, smiled and opened the car door. 'My offer stands.'

'I'm sure I'll have more questions in a week or so.'

'I'm off tomorrow and Tuesday. Back on duty Wednesday night. If you want me, call.'

'I will. Thanks for letting me use you as a sounding board.'

'Remember what your mother still has, Hugh. Her mind is forgetting, but she has spirit and the capacity to love, to appreciate life.'

'I'll keep that in mind. Sleep well.'

'I wish. Because of Dad's condition, I've got involved in a local support group—'

'Doctor Abbott mentioned that.'

'We're meeting tonight at half-eight in Ganestown Hotel.'

'Oh? Should I be involved in that?'

'Well, no pressure. If you can make it—'

'Anything to delay this painting job.'

'Then, come along. It's only for a few hours, but it'll help to know others are going through a similar process. There are carers with relatives at the same stage as Kathleen. If you've got questions on long or short-term supervision—'

'Great, but I'll still phone Sarah.'

'I recommend you do. More options, the better. See you later.'

Hugh watched the car taillights disappear. Ruth's touch was a soothing salve that helped quench inner turmoil. He checked his mobile; Ferdia hadn't left a message. He dialled Sarah. Her voice was soft and warm. 'Sorry about your mother,' she said when he told her his name. 'Ruth contacted me earlier. Said you might call.'

'It's now beginning to dawn how tied up I'll be,' Hugh said, and filled Sarah in on Kathleen's condition. 'I need cover next week, and I'm minus any help.'

'I'm available 'til mid-February.'

'What's your hourly rate? I—'

'Let's discuss that when Kathleen gets home. Text me the directions. I'll be there whenever.'

'That's a huge relief. Thanks.'

'I've seen this before. I'm sure your mum will remain healthy for years, but you have to face reality and plan for the future. The sooner you build a care network around her, getting support systems in place, the less hard decisions you'll have to make later.'

'And the time to organise that is now,' Hugh said, 'not when I'm in the middle of a crisis, right?'

'Exactly.'

'What do I *need* to do, as opposed to what do I *have* to do? I'm thinking...support, understanding and reassurance, but that's not enough—'

'It's wonderful,' Sarah said. 'But keep monitoring. Needs will change. Be ready to act when they do. The most important thing is to make sure Kathleen knows she's loved. Look, it's only been a few days. You need time to get your head around—'

'Yeah. Too many emotions to process. I want to delay the inevitable. Forever.'

'It takes most people months to get to the stage you're at, Hugh. You've accepted where you are and started to consider options. That's all you can do.'

AT HIS HOUSE, Adam Styne cleared the sat-nav data and grunted at Madeline when she asked him how long he needed the jeep for.

He picked up her key fob and drove fast to Tullamore. A kilometre from the town, he got out, smashed one of the back taillights, then continued to the garage, swapped the 4x4 for a nondescript Mazda 6, and cruised to the farm.

The rigger brush transformed 16 D 17035 to 18 D 47888, and he lined the boot with used silage wrap. After, in the farmhouse, he changed into a pair of work boots, found plastic gloves under the sink, then sat at the kitchen table and considered, rejected and refined his preferred options. Preparation to the nth degree was impossible; specific issues that could arise, he'd resolve on the fly. That's the enjoyable part, he thought. Reliant on my wits.

He opened presses, rummaged around and found two plastic cable ties.

I'll need them later.

He glanced at a wall clock.

19:05.

Still too soon.

'The challenge,' he muttered. 'Boy meets girl. Boy kills girl.'

Check the room.

In the hallway, Styne stood at the foot of the stairs and studied the spot where he'd broken his mother's neck.

EILISH SAT ON the toilet seat, stomach churning, and rang Ciara's mobile.

Her mind raced through a gamut of emotions; concern, trepidation, panic. The phone cut into voicemail. She cancelled the connection, hunched forward, hugged her stomach and studied the digital pregnancy kit test, measuring a two-minute countdown by the plink-plink drip from a leaking tap.

Same result.

Eilish counted backwards, hoping she'd mixed up the dates. Stress, she thought. That's it. A build-up of stress. Tried Ciara's mobile again. 'Pick up. Pick up. Answer your bloody phone. Please, God, make her answer the phone.' She swallowed, blocked the copper taste rising in her throat, but couldn't stop the queasiness.

I'm getting sick again.

Eilish twisted, embraced the toilet bowl and waited for the nausea to pass.

A week. Sweet dreams to shit reality in seven days.

'Eilish? Tea's on the table.'

Eilish's stomach convulsed at the notion of food. 'Be there in a jiffy, Mum.' She got to her feet. The bathroom spun, and she fell back. When the woozy spell eased, she groped for her mobile and typed a text:

> Ciara.
> Call me back.
> I need you.

ADAM STYNE'S MIND drifted back to Monday, June second, 1997.

The day his life changed. Revision mode for the Leaving Certificate exam. Seated near the rear of a classroom, reading a magazine article about a killer who'd terrorised early morning joggers in New York's Central Park, and paying little attention to a classmate's query to the biology teacher, Mr O'Sullivan: "Sir, can you clarify how genetics...?"

The journalist had made comparisons between these murders, and the Zodiac killer in San Francisco over twenty-five years earlier.

It's not Zodiac; Zodiac sent cryptic messages. This is a sniper, shooting people in the back. Zodiac never did that. The modus operandi is different. Not a copycat.

The class discussion on genetics didn't click until the following Friday night, sitting across from both parents at the dinner table. The television flashed pictures of people entering and exiting polling stations. His father, taciturn unless he'd swigged poitín, grumbled and criticised all politicians contesting the general election, and said it was a foregone conclusion Bertie Ahern would replace John Bruton as Taoiseach. Bored, his mother used the remote to switch channels, watching nothing. Flick, flick, flick.

Adam recalled O'Sullivan's words: *"...that's the science of genetics. For example, earlobe attachments are an inherited trait. If both parents have attached earlobes, you'll show the same characteristics. Parents with attached earlobes cannot give birth to offspring with the dominant unattached earlobe trait."*

Adam touched his unattached lobes. Why hadn't he noticed before? How come it never registered? That implied...No, impossible. Somebody would've commented before now.

For three weeks, he'd fought to concentrate on exams while his imagination ran riot, torn between a belief that the teacher was mistaken, or else they'd adopted him. A search produced no documented evidence. He became surlier, defied his father and, for the first time, hit him back. He'd got his hair cut skinhead short and awaited a response. His father, cautious as a bully now, ignored him. His mother noticed but said nothing, wary of her son's latent ire. Then Adam's mind swayed to the other extreme. Styne senior would never agree to an adoption. Any child he raised, had to come from his own loins.

O'Sullivan was wrong.

June twenty-first, the day after his parent's wedding anniversary. He'd taken a break from studying and was watching a film. His mother stormed in. They'd arranged to go for an anniversary meal, but some incident on the mud bowl they called a farm forced a change in plan, prompting a transformation in her temperament.

'Adam. What exam have you tomorrow?'

'Don't have any. It's—'

'Upstairs. Now! Go. That's enough rubbish.' She unplugged the television.

'It's—'

'Films won't help you pass exams.'

'I said I don't have—'

'We haven't sacrificed everything for you to drool over half-dressed actresses. If you've got spare time, there's lots of work outside. Move. Or I'll call your father.'

'Yeah? Go on then. Call him. You can both tell me who my actual parents are.'

'What?'

Adam stared his mother down. 'You aren't my parents.'

The words triggered a stinging backhand across his face. 'How. Dare you.' Spittle flew from Mrs Styne's mouth. A ring gashed his lip, and the taste of blood almost made him sick, but her expression told him he'd hit a nerve.

O'Sullivan was correct.

'You're my son,' she said.

'Your son?'

'Our son.'

'You're a liar.'

His mother looked away. 'What brought this on? You *must* believe—'

'A two-faced, deceitful bitch.'

Mrs Styne's body sagged. Tears rolled.

Sudden as Adam's fury rose, it abated into a silent rage. Aloof, he waited for his mother to regain composure before the interrogation began.

'Who're my real parents? Why'd they let you adopt me? Where are they? How—?'

'I…it wasn't…Calm down. You're hysterical, Adam. I'd…everybody has relationship problems. We got engaged. Planned to marry in June but broke up after St Patrick's Day…Too much drink. We were together again within a few weeks, and our marriage went ahead. John…I…I was afraid to tell him the…terrified he'd leave.

What could I do? It was a different era, for God's sake. Decades ago. It was a *fling.*'

Adam's heart flipped. 'You…got pregnant? And all these years you've *pretended* I was—?'

'It was a once-off. I wasn't sure if—'

'He's beaten me black and blue. Treats me like *shit*—'

'Everything we do is for your good.'

Enraged, he'd leapt up. 'You're a whore.'

Shaken by the sudden, brutal way her son had exposed her past, Mrs Styne tried to pacify and plead with Adam not to divulge the secret she'd concealed for two decades. 'I'd no one, nobody to talk to, or confide in. No parents, relatives or close friends nearby to call on for advice. I wanted to tell John. Umpteen times. I drove myself crazy with worry. After a while, it became easier to forget…no, I don't mean forget, that's impossible. It became *simpler* over the years to leave bad memories behind. Please, Adam, let this rest.'

He couldn't.

Instead, he'd pumped his mother for more information, showing neither sympathy nor mercy. 'So you've lived a lie? Forced him to rear your bastard?'

'I wanted you to have the best. A child requires both parents, Adam. I *had* to keep the…it to myself. I convinced myself you were John's son.'

'Liar. You *knew.*'

'Of *course*, I…Adam, can't you understand? I'm a mother. I chose to give *you* the best opportunities—'

'For *yourself*, you mean. You've destroyed two lives—'

'I couldn't bear for John to work himself into a state every time he'd look at you and see another man's image in your features.'

Her words propelled Adam into a frenzy. A blinding headache pierced his skull. He'd grabbed his mother and throttled her. She'd clawed the air, and he'd squeezed until her eyes bulged. As her struggles abated, realisation dawned that his mother was more useful alive. Adam relaxed his grip, watched her fight for breath. He was back in control. These people were dead to him. First, though, they'd pay. Then he'd get out.

From that day, Adam ensured a gauze of guilt shrouded his mother. He'd confronted, criticised and condemned, dangled the secret like the sword of Damocles, not satisfied till he'd crushed Mrs Styne's will. The more fear she displayed, the more bullish and unrelenting her son became, weaving a tapestry of terror, and threatening to expose the closet skeletons if she didn't satisfy his demands. He didn't ask about his real father.

Didn't care.

He demanded nicer accommodation. Holidays. He'd no idea how she'd swayed John to hand over the money.

Didn't care.

His mother's lifelong concern of too much body fat became a non-issue. She lost weight and became stooped, round-shouldered in defeat. Some weekends, he worked alongside John, and this calculated action left Mrs Styne in a state of frantic ambiguity, making her more receptive to requests.

She'd started drinking.

Adam monitored the steady increase in alcohol consumption, unconcerned. His relentless barrage persisted, despite his mother telling him she wished for death. When she'd nothing more to give, Adam told John the truth. Two days later, John smashed his car into a tree. Authorities deemed it a drunk-driving accident, but Adam knew. He secured the farm in his own name.

Mrs Styne suffered prolonged bouts of depression, abetted by an enlarged appetite for whiskey and painkillers.

The weight of the guilty conscience she carried for a quarter-century, and exacerbated by her son's censure, inflicted irreparable emotional damage. Mrs Styne lived each day in a drink-induced stupor. Drugs and mental torture kept her compliant—a virtual house prisoner. She became a submissive victim.

A month before his wedding, Adam decided it could have a grave effect on his long-term plans if the Hattingers met his drunken embarrassment of a mother.

No alternative.

He'd called her upstairs. Pissed, as usual, Mrs Styne huffed her way to the landing, and a push sent her backwards. Brittle bones broke as she crashed thirteen steps. Unlucky for some. One little thrust for a greater good.

Adam stared as her mouth opened and closed; a fish out of water. Blood pulsed from a gash on her arm, and he stepped across the body, ached to kick her twisted neck, but slipped outside, abandoning his mother at her hour of death. He'd delayed his return until he was confident she'd died. Sniffed her piss and blood when he'd returned, bracing himself for an Oscar winner's performance. Thoughts of her gore-stained clothes and skin repulsed him, but he'd have to handle her; that's what a devoted son was apt to do upon discovering his mother's dead body. He'd left the overcoat on, called the ambulance, positioned himself in a way to contact the least amount of contamination, and cried. Could have wept all night, but calculated police may interpret anything over three hours as artificial. Gardaí tiptoed around as he cradled his mother. A post-mortem uncovered the years of alcohol and painkiller abuse, and the verdict of accidental death was a formality. Adam wasn't questioned or asked for a statement. At the funeral, people shook their heads at the heartbreak of losing both parents in horrific accidents.

For years he continued to nurse a deep repulsion for his mother, and by default, all single mothers. He trained himself to compartmentalise and control these emotions, dedicating the next decade to building a stellar business reputation. Until Thursday, March twelfth, 2015, his mother's anniversary.

The conference in Sligo dragged; his blinding headache, unbearable. He'd called into a pharmacy to buy painkillers, and his mother walked by. Identical shuffle. Same mulled wine-coloured coat with matching handbag. The woman stayed on Adelaide Street, paused to chat with two pensioners. Adam strolled on by Hawk's Well Theatre. A quick glimpse behind him. The woman had disappeared. A flood of resentment bubbled in his brain. Now he knew why he was doing this.

He wanted to kill his mother again.

Doubled back to John Street. Passed a church. Glimpsed a red blur inside before the heavy door closed. He'd followed. Into the narthex, through another entrance into the nave, and looked around. A single aisle, with pews on either side.

Nothing changes in churches.

Dim. The warm smell of candle wax and incense. The woman in the red coat stood at a Regal Votive candle stand, positioned under an alabaster statue. She lit half-a-dozen candles, and the flickering light made Our Lady's crown glow. He watched the woman genuflect and kneel in a pew, the rosary beads yo-yoing in her hand, each bead the size of a hazelnut shell. Her lips moved in silent prayer as she ticked off Hail Mary's with a thumbnail.

Styne slipped into the seat behind the penitent in the pew, checked no one else was in the church. He'd reached forward, encircled an arm around her neck and pulled the woman back. Propped his knees for leverage, locked both arms and cranked. Right. Left. Right again. The woman's back arched, fingernails tore and scraped skin from his wrists. The beads broke and slipped from her grasp. On the third twist, the cervical vertebrae dislodged. A loud crack, similar to the sound his mother's neck made. The resonance rang around the cavernous church. He let go. The woman slumped forward, her forehead resting on the back crest of the bench in front.

A door slammed.

Styne's heart stopped.

An old man, stiff with age, hobbled from the sacristy to the altar. Styne moved away from the woman and watched from behind a concrete column. The man moved around the chancel, stepped onto a ladder and draped a statue in an emerald green cloak.

Heart palpitating, hands slick with sweat, Adam darted for the exit. Stopped. Wavered. What if he'd left traces?

Should I hide the body? No, run.

Our Lady's eyes seemed to glare in the candlelight.

He ran.

Drive around and collect the body. No. Too dangerous. Leave the body. No. Potential exposure. DNA. Forensics will pick up my traces from the woman's clothes or skin. So what? My DNA isn't on file. Better chance it, rather than risk getting caught. Or, if I park at the church gate and carry her out? Drape a coat around her? Fifteen seconds. Less. Ten seconds. No, too risky. Leave her.

Soaked with sweat, mind in a tizzy, he'd driven blind, lost in the one-way street system. Stopped at a pedestrian crossing on O'Connell Street. Gazed at a suitcase in a shop window.

Bag shop.

Destiny.

He'd parked on a double yellow line and run inside. The biggest suitcase, an eighty-two-centimetre aluminium Samsonite with a hard shell and frame, cost three hundred euro. Had to use a credit card, even though the transaction could get traced.

No choice.

Two left turns brought him to a side road beside the church. Adam wheeled the suitcase up the path, the rumble of the wheels smothered by the high-pitched whine of a hoover. The sexton vacuumed the altar steps, and along the side aisle, dragging the equipment after him. Adam crossed to the other aisle, blessed himself at the first Station of the Cross, and pretended to pray, prepared to kill the sexton too, if necessary.

The dust-catcher knocked against a confessional box. The sexton turned off the motor, squirted liquid polish on seats, gave them a vigorous rub, and nodded to the woman who appeared deep in prayer, or asleep. He glided the chamois leather along the confessional stall, struck out at, and missed, a cobweb that waved from an upper corner of the wood frame. Then, the man shambled back to the altar, unplugged the electric cord and reconnected it in a socket at the rear of the church, tugged the vacuum behind him, yanked the tube when it caught the side of the suitcase, crossed the aisle, repeated the process and cloth flick. Halfway up the aisle, he limped back, removed the plug from the socket, reconnected again near the altar…

Styne wanted to strangle him.

…then unfurled a green altar cloth in preparation for St Patrick's Day.

Bang. A door closed. The noise, gunfire loud, made Adam jump. The sexton went into the sacristy.

Clear. Styne unlocked the suitcase, hauled the woman's body into the aisle, doubled up her legs, packed her in and knelt on the lid. Zipped it shut. Done.

A middle-aged couple stepped aside at the church entrance to let him pass. Adam dipped his finger into a holy water font, blessed himself, and wheeled the corpse out.

The couple smiled.

With the suitcase in the car boot, his thoughts centred on getting rid of the body.

Where? Woods offer the best choice. More camouflage.

In a garden centre, he bought a spade, torch, canvas sack and a pickaxe, before driving in ever-increasing circles, seeking a suitable site. It took hours to find a well-trodden track at the foothill of Knocknarea. He strayed off-trail and started to dig in the fading light. An hour's grunt work hardly dented the undergrowth. Friction tore skin off his hands when the pickaxe blade stuck in tree roots. He'd abandoned that site. Found another. Same result. He'd driven through Collooney and Castlebaldwin, wondering what to say if he got stopped at a checkpoint. His guilty face would give him away.

What possible explanation would work?

Lough Key shimmered in the moonbeam.

Too exposed, but another of the lakes? Feasible.

He'd taken the N4 east from Boyle, aimed for Knockvicar. Spotted a dry sandstone wall, and prised several rocks loose, hefted them in next to the suitcase, and travelled another two kilometres to gain access to the water.

Isolated, this time of night.

A concrete platform, built for anglers, had several rowboats moored along its length. He unfolded the body, rolled it into the canvas sack, filled the remaining space with stones, and searched the car for twine or a piece of rope to seal the bag.

Nothing.

Panic.

Until the thin strip from a wire-bound notebook solved that problem. Tried, and botched an attempt to pitch the sack; knew he hadn't the strength or momentum to heave it far enough. Rowing into deep water was his only choice. More heart-stopping moments when the extended water weeds hindered the half-submerged body, but it found a pathway, and its disappearance in a rush of air bubbles was a relief. Whatever length of time it took the sack to disintegrate and the fish to feed on her flesh, the weeds would keep the evidence submerged.

A week later, he'd read about Denise Alexander's disappearance. A retired teacher. He'd burned the suitcase and handbag and felt inner peace once the fear of getting caught subsided. The demons were sated, but only until the next anniversary. Then he'd got the urge to kill again.

Styne opened the door and turned on the dimmer switch.

The single low-watt filament bulb bathed the windowless space in orange light. Cold and dank seeped from a bare cement floor, the room barren except for a chair and a rug. The air stank of mildew. He hadn't been in here since the Isobel Stewart sanitation session. He threw the plastic ties in a corner, changed into farm clothes and left his phone on the kitchen table. Wouldn't need it till afterwards. Now, manual labour was necessary to release pent-up energy.

Otherwise, I'll get over-enthusiastic and kill Ciara McGuire too fast.

NIGHT

'WERE YOU IN to see Dad today? Or even phone him?'

Malcolm cringed, sorry he'd answered Ciara's call. 'Didn't get a chance.' This had been the worst day he'd ever had at Fairyhouse. One win from a seven-card race meeting. The Gaffer, a 25/1 winner in the first, delivered a result. After that, he'd spent the day chasing losses. Tyson missed out to The Harbour Master by three-quarters of a length. 'Hmm? What? I Missed that?' He tapped the laptop keyboard, and circled the mouse around tomorrow's UK meetings, still smarting that And Here's The Kicker, at 20/1 got beaten into third place.

'I said, are you working?'

'Yeah, still in the office.' Only three race meetings in the UK tomorrow. This weather was killing his opportunities.

'You're in the office? On Sunday?'

'Yeah. Working on a presentation.'

'I'm almost speechless.'

'Yeah, well…' Earlier, in Fairyhouse, he'd picked the 12/1 second favourite, Granny Smith, in the fourth, Conquistador at 66/1 in the fifth, because he was getting edgy, and punted on Ben Bulbin in the sixth, hoping for a 33/1 pay-out. He'd torn up his ticket when the horses were halfway around the course; Ben Bulbin was fourth, and fading fast. He knew the Willie Mullins trained horse would win the last, but at 1/3 favourite, the odds were useless. Instead, he'd placed his last hundred euro on 50/1 outsider, Mystic Mac, and prayed for a miracle. The miracle didn't happen. Fairyhouse was a washout. The next meeting there was in two weeks; his luck would've changed by then, and he'd regain today's losses, plus interest. But that was then. This was now, and he needed money.

'What's that? The line's breaking up.' Malcolm skimmed through the runners for Monday's first race in Fakenham. Couldn't decide. He scrolled through the card.

'I said you should get out more. Socialise. Find another girlfriend. All work and no play makes—'

'Makes two of us.'

'For your information, I'd a lunch date today.'

'Yeah?'

'Yep.'

'How'd it go?' Malcolm's glance brushed through the starting prices. Mrs McGinty at 16/1 looked a decent punt.

'I got a bad vibe.'

'Someone local?'

'Tipperary, I think. Or maybe Dublin.'

'Oh, like that, was it?'

'Hmm.'

'Trust your instincts.'

'Always. That's why there won't be another date with him.'

'You're too cynical. That's your punishment for the shit you do in HR.' Malcolm exited that screen, clicked on the Plumpton meeting, analysed the card. The favourites should win. Useless prices. He clicked again. Wolverhampton. Scrolled down.

'My purgatory. You okay, Mal?'

'Fine.' Hard Times and Hobson's Choice, 18/1 and 14/1, respectively. If either of them, plus Crystal Gaze in the January Maiden Hurdle at Fakenham, came home first, it would net…

'You seem distracted,' Ciara said.

'Sorry. I'm ah, kinda sore. Audi skidded on the way in here.'

'Oh my God. Are you hurt? Have you been to—?'

'Bruised, that's all.'

'Have you painkillers?'

'Yeah. Um, the car's more smashed up than me.'

'So that's the reason you couldn't get to Dad.'

'Hmm-hmm.'

'Why didn't you say?'

'Didn't want to worry you. I'll find a way to visit tomorrow.'

'Much damage?'

Malcolm thought for a beat. 'I reckon four grand's worth.'

'But the insurance company will—'

'Not worth losing my no claims bonus for something small.'

'Oh, damn. That's a pain. How long will it take to—?'

'A week, once I get the dosh together. It's the whole left wing and door, plus labour costs, car hire—'

'Malcolm?'

'Yeah?'

'If I loan you the money, swear you won't gamble it.'

'I swear. If you can give, I mean lend me cash, I'll be on the road inside a week.' Malcolm held his breath.

'Okay. If I transfer money to your account now—'

'I'll repay you Friday. Monday at the latest. You know I'm good for it.'

'Hmm. Make sure you visit Dad tomorrow.'

'First chance.'

'He'll be discharged midweek. I want to take him home, but we haven't discussed—'

'Let's chat with Dad tomorrow night,' Malcolm said. 'He might've already decided what he wants. No point in us making decisions for him 'til we find out.'

'Yes, he's told me he's going to his own place, but I'm not sure that's the...You're right. I'll sleep on it. Goodnight, Mal. Chat tomorrow.'

'Yeah. Night.'

GANESTOWN CAREGIVERS ASSOCIATION acted as a crutch for families at the end of their tether. Ruth introduced Hugh to a man who spelt out how life with Alzheimer's evolves.

'AD,' the caregiver said, 'is a faceless, shapeless, thieving bastard. It begins as a seed and spreads like a chestnut tree. A person can move through the stages in months, or it mightn't become full-blown for years. It's a brewing storm. At the outset, you'll notice no major changes. There's no sign of the destruction that's occurring; it's so gradual, you doubt yourself. The worst is when our relatives can't recognise or remember us,' the man added. 'The loss of shared experiences is…' He shrugged his shoulders. 'You lose so much of the person. Alzheimer's recognises no boundaries.'

'Ma's doctor described it as a tsunami in the brain,' Hugh said.

'That's accurate.'

'How did you find out? What were the first signs?'

'She phoned me in the middle of the night,' the carer said. 'A burglar had broken in. Caused a major panic, I can tell you. Of course, there was no break-in, but I changed the locks to give her peace of mind. Within a week, the calls began again. More robbers. One night, mother rang my sister. This time the intruders were playing music. My sister dashed across, but too late. Mother had slipped on the stairs. Ambulance. Hospital. Broken hip. They gave us the results of a PET scan, and our Alzheimer's nightmare began.'

'How did it advance from normal chat to memory loss?' Hugh asked.

'I'd ask her a question, and she'd repeat what she heard back to me. See, her brain couldn't find an answer, so she'd echo the last words she heard. Other times, she'd recite the sentence a dozen times. Ad nauseam. We're at the stage now where she can't follow any conversation.'

'God. That's twenty-four-seven care,' Hugh said. 'Have you got home help? How do you cope?'

'There are days I'm detached and numb,' the caregiver shrugged, 'as if it's happening to somebody else, and I'm here to lighten the person's load, but the sense of helplessness is crushing. You know it won't get any better, and that makes you want to scream in rage. Yes, at times I *do* scream, but only when no one's around.'

'Is your mother at home or in a care facility?'

'Home. I've three sisters, and we've worked out a rota system. We're lucky. A lot of families don't have that well of support. Government cutbacks have played havoc with carer assistance. We're reliant on community generosity for funds. But money's tight, and time's short. Sorry for being blunt, but better you know up-front what's involved.'

'Feels like my mooring's untied and I'm adrift,' Hugh said.

'We all experience that,' the man nodded, 'but when there's no other choice, you'll find the strength to handle it. It's up to the primary caregiver to adjust their reactions and expectations as each phase kicks in. There's also a whole new language to learn. The symptoms are similar for each Alzheimer patient, but the journey depends on their life experiences.'

Before he left the meeting, Hugh thanked Ruth for inviting him along.

'I learned a lot,' he said, 'and that carer I met?'

'Yes?'

'He freaked me out.' Hugh gulped a deep breath. 'But, it was vital to get his perspective. They're a rare breed. I mean, "we". I've to count myself part of that group now, learning to live with indecision. That should be the title of an Alzheimer's conference: "Living with Uncertainty." Oh, I spoke to Sarah. Thanks for the contact.'

'Glad to help. So, you off painting now?'

'Think I'll give it a miss. Too much on my mind. Hope you sleep well. Text me when you're home safe.'

'Aww. That's sweet. I will. You look after yourself too.'

Hugh's house was cold as an icebox.

Letters splattered on the hallway floor. Doctor Abbott's plain envelope stood out, a stark contrast against the colourful excess of junk mail.

He fretted about his mother and his own future, made notes of questions he'd ask at Wednesday's exit interview, brooded over Eilish, scribbled out what he'd written, began again, changed his mind and tossed the crumpled paper into a bin.

His phone hummed. He read the text:

Hiya. Home safe n sound. Glad u found meeting useful. Tks for coffee and chat. Ring if there's anything u want to talk about/discuss.
See u soon. R.

Upstairs, Hugh sat on the bed and looked at the space filled with memories. He rubbed the sheets as if Eilish's body might magically appear. The residue of her perfume teased his senses. He wished there was a way to switch off, but there was no release button. Emptying a bedside locker, he poked through photos, mind gliding between chats they'd shared, jokes they'd laughed at, places they'd visited, and betrayal. That's what festered and swelled, dragging him further into depression. He tried to pull himself together, but it was a losing battle. Grief knifed through him and he couldn't stay home alone any longer.

Weary with worry, brain shutting down from exhaustion and emotional strain yet too wound up to sleep, Hugh trudged into Ganestown and roved the streets in an effort to outrun a hurt that wouldn't cease. Frozen and wet through, he found himself across town, near his mother's home. Rather than return to his own houseful of memories, and needing something, anything, to blank out Eilish, he opted to paint.

ADAM STYNE WAITED until after ten.

His headache hammered, and he didn't bother to change out of farm clothes.

A whiff of cow manure and silage will be the least of your worries, Ciara.

Sub-zero airstreams from Scandinavia had brought in another wave of dense fog and snow. Earlier, the journey from Ciara's house to Ganestown's ring-road took twenty-five minutes. The drive back was taking twice that.

After all this, you'd better be at home waiting for me, Ciara.

He tried to pick out landscapes he'd memorised earlier, but the fog and darkness hampered his vision. He guessed bedtime would be the same as Roberta Lord; around eleven p.m. The dashboard dial read 22:50.

At the National School, the fog unfurled, revealing a full moon. Styne slowed, looking for the knot of houses near a road bend.

There.

A light still burned behind a curtained window in Ciara's home, her car in the driveway. He extinguished the headlights, cut the engine, freewheeled in the gateway and coasted into the drive.

Armed and ready. Last chance. Turn back? No way. Hunter and hunted. I'll be the final voice she hears, the last face she sees.

The Mazda rolled to a stop. Styne inspected the house perimeter, waiting to see if the car movement triggered a sensor light.

Nothing.

He turned off the dome light, snapped on latex gloves, picked up the stun gun and eased out, senses fine-tuned. Moonlight glittered on the glazed snow. He studied the garden boundaries, primed for escape if a dog or human appeared. In the murk, a snowman resembled a headstone. The scent of timber smoke filled his lungs.

Styne stepped nearer the house.

Stopped.

Ears honed, absorbing the night sounds. Another two paces. Raised his head, strained to listen.

No sound.

He spun, checked the road.

No traffic.

He thumbed off the immobiliser's safety catch, trod another step, testing each one before letting his boots sink into snow. Frost sheathed the windows of the Nissan. Crouched at the side of the car, he peeked around, studying the doorway...

Stay in the open. Footprints will get erased.

...Moved closer to the front door with its frosted glass panel. He pressed the bell, tensed his body, ready to bulldoze through a security chain. A light cascaded the hallway, and the door opened.

Stupid woman. No door guard.

Ciara hadn't time to react or register the syrupy stench of silage. Styne pushed in and touched the stun gun against her neck. The voltage propelled her backwards. Her head walloped off a wall, and she crumpled, unconscious before she hit the floor. Styne used his heel to close the door, immobiliser ready for attack. The jacket Ciara wore earlier hung on a coat-stand. Another door, ajar, at the end of the passage, had a Santa Claus sketch stuck to it.

Boy's room. What's his name? David.

He stuck his head inside the room Ciara had vacated.

Sitting-room.

A laptop sat open on a desk.

Styne listened for a footstep, a voice, a question.

No movement.

Just the hiss of silence.

He stood outside the child's room, inched one foot across the wooden threshold and whispered, 'David?' The hall light bathed the bedroom in a ginger hue. Other cute cartoon sketches adorned the wall; a tractor with disproportionately sized wheels, a house with four crooked windows and a pencil line of smoke that curled into clouds. He stepped inside. 'Da...vid?' A superman figurine crunched underfoot. An A4 sheet, pinned to a built-in press, showed a stick figure drawing of a red-haired man. On the single bed, a teddy-bear sat propped against the pillow. Rows of farm machinery toys lined against a wall, alongside an empty Nintendo Switch box. A pile of folded clothes sat on top of a wooden trunk. Styne moved back to the hallway, poked into rooms; a kitchen-cum-living room, another bedroom, and sniffed the air.

Coconut.

Back in the hallway, he checked on Ciara. She was wearing a short-sleeved Nike T-shirt and black skirt. Still inert. In the sitting-room, a mobile lay on a typist desk shelf beside the laptop. He traced the power lead, unplugged it, wrapped the cord around the computer, powered off the phone and stuck it in a pocket. Then he caught Ciara in a fireman's grip.

Styne's legs strained.

Fat bitch.

Had to bend again for the laptop, secured it under an arm, and groped for the light switch. Clicked it off, unlatched the door and staggered outside, past Ciara's car. Her floppy body was causing a weight imbalance. His knees buckled.

Should have reversed in.

His breath blew in ragged gasps. The laptop fell when he opened the boot and dumped Ciara in. Her head thwacked off the side, legs refused to bend. He pushed in the limbs and slammed the lid. The metal lip banged against bone and sprang open.

This isn't working.

Winded, he leaned against the Mazda, wiped sweat from his brow, and steadied his breathing.

Ciara whimpered.

Styne jabbed the stun gun to her neck. Her body jerked, shuddered and went limp.

No idea how long she'll stay knocked out. Remember chloroform for Jana.

He unlocked the passenger door, muscled Ciara into the front seat, closed the boot lid, retrieved the computer and reversed out as another blustery snow shower descended.

'So, Ciara. How wrong you were that we'd never meet again. Here we are. And oh so soon.' The window steamed up, and Styne switched on the heater. 'How was your day since?' The belt alarm pinged. He stopped and strapped in the comatose woman. 'Don't want you to get hurt. Or as you might say, lol. And look? See that? More beautiful snow. What's that? My day? Well, a little frustrating, actually, because you didn't allow me enough time to organise a proper welcome for you. Besides that, it's been good, oh, except for a tiny hiccup at lunchtime, which again you were accountable for. Yes, yes, I admit I was at fault too. I hadn't prepared enough. But, to quote another of your lines, let me cut to the chase: the majority of the blame lies with you, Ciara, you obstinate bitch.'

Ciara groaned.

Styne pressed the Taser to her neck.

No buzz.

What? Why—?

Ciara mumbled, fingers grasping at air. Her arms shook.

Styne turned on the interior light. He was holding her mobile.

Christ.

He swapped the mobile for the stun gun, and zapped Ciara into oblivion again. 'Relax.' He stroked her leg, wiped his brow on a sleeve. 'We've got all night to enjoy each other's company. And you're wearing the opal ring. Well, guess what? Your security shield's got holes. Your bastion of protection. Poof.'

Adam prised Ciara's phone apart and thumbed out the battery and SIM card. 'It's quite annoying that your prying and asinine attempt to trip me up made me lose control, forcing me to bump up my timeline. Well, you'll pay for that. *I'm* the one in control now. I doubt there'll be any checkpoints tonight. Fortune favours the fearless, what say you? Yes, sleep now while you can. Over the last twelve hours, I can't tell you how I've anticipated our night together. I'm particularly interested in seeing what resistance you'll put up. How much control *you'll* muster when I hold the aces, you bitch. You'll learn *I'm* the winner. Winners control the game. Perhaps I'll send photos of your last moments to David. I imagine he'd treasure a memento. Hmm?'

The snow shower eased as they crossed the Tullamore River. Clouds cleared and revealed the full moon and the million galaxies that glistened from the heavens. Styne glanced at Ciara, still conked out. At Blueball, he pitched the phone battery out, broke the SIM in two and threw a segment after it. Two kilometres further, he tossed the other half. Then the gloves. Nearing Kilcormac, he stopped, got out, ground the mobile underfoot and lobbed the pieces into a ditch.

'Perhaps your ghost can reassemble all the bits and send a text from Nirvana.'

Must get rid of my pay-as-you-go phone.

00:09.

'It's Monday, Ciara. You'll be home shortly.'

Styne indicated left and turned in the pot-holed by-road. Ciara moaned and got Tasered again. He opened a window to dispel the odour of burned flesh and steered up the farmhouse driveway. Halfway in, it divided. The right-angled split gave access to the front, the left led to the rear. He steered left and parked near the back door. 'Welcome.'

The belt buckle had twisted under Ciara. When he got it open, Styne caught the unconscious woman underarm, pulled her across the kitchen and along the tiled hallway. A T-Strap high heel screeched in protest, gouging a furrow in the laminated wood floor.

Styne stopped.

Where's her other shoe? Must have fallen off in the boot.

He hauled Ciara inside the windowless room.

MALCOLM'S FINGERS TAPPED the keyboard symbols.

Ciara had kept her promise. This money would change his losing streak. Crystal Gaze at Fakenham was a dead cert. He studied the other horses and riders in the 17:20 at Wolverhampton. Early Riser, the 20/1 shot caused him to hesitate; definitely an improver, but his eyes kept returning to Hobson's Choice. Trained by Gary Lyndon, and the jockey was Tommy Doyle from County Leitrim. Good omen, Malcolm thought. 16/1. It would work out. It *had* to.

He placed his bets, pressed "send," and Ciara's four thousand euro transferred electronically to a bookie's bank account.

STYNE DUMPED CIARA on the rug.

He turned the dimmer switch high, dragged the chair closer, and contemplated her features; a scientist studying a specimen in a Petri-dish. Her skin was pale as a moonbeam, breath ragged, arm muscles twitching.

'Wakey, wakey.' Styne slapped Ciara's face. 'I want to study your reaction, the moment of despair when you realised all's lost. How gratifying it will be to hear you beg.'

I'll dangle a literal lifeline, several, in fact, before yanking them out of her reach.

Styne rearranged her hair. His eyes drifted downwards. A necklace of freckles spread around Ciara's neck, her arms a blanket of stippled flesh. He leaned closer, inhaled her scent. Dropped to his knees and nipped her jaw. Waited for a reaction.

Nothing.

He burrowed his head in Ciara's neck, hand closing around a breast. Pinched a nipple as he slathered a snail trail of saliva from her chin to ear. His lips locked on an earlobe, right hand tracing a path along Ciara's stomach, down her leg, avoided the crusted blood that congealed on the wound below her knee. He watched her face for any change in expression, as his fingers slithered under the skirt, along the inside of a thigh, groping their way higher.

No response.

'I'll tie you up in a minute. First, let's have fun.' Styne's left thumb prised open Ciara's jaws, and he forced his tongue in.

Ciara stirred. Drool dribbled from her mouth.

'Wake up, bitch. I've begun without you.'

He sucked on Ciara's tongue, explored molars, bit her inner lip, while the right hand continued to worm. Fingertips touched cotton. Pulled it aside.

Wet.

'You've started too.' Styne shoved his tongue deeper into her mouth.

Ciara choked, swallowed, and her teeth clamped vice-like around the intrusion.

A sliver of pain jetted along Styne's trigeminal nerve. He rolled away, the high-pitched squeal similar to a stuck pig. His mouth was on fire, full of red-hot embers. Teeth spun in their sockets, and flames lapped at his facial nerve ends. He gobbed, showering Ciara with saliva and blood clots. Noticed his fingers, and Styne's lips curled in disgust.

Bitch. Bitch. Filthy bitch.

He used the rug to wipe off menstrual blood.

Ciara groaned.

Incensed, Styne grabbed the immobiliser and rammed it into her neck, dumping its power into her nervous system. Ciara juddered, a puppet on a string, as the continuous high-volt, low-amp electrical charge ripped through her, hijacking and scrambling neurological impulses, depleting energy reserves, and converting blood sugar to lactic acid. Styne's blood, sweat and sputum sprayed Ciara's neck, acting as a conduit. Her body jerked, shook and spasmed. He watched the convulsions, and kept the stun gun against her skin until it ran out of charge.

Ciara's sightless eyes gazed up at him.

Styne hawked and spat on the body. In the downstairs bathroom, he searched presses for analgesics, but could only find a bottle of mouthwash. He inspected his tongue in the small mirror over the washbasin. It was split, swollen, bleeding, and it throbbed in torrents of piercing pain. He swigged the liquid, closed his eyes against the burn, gargled, spat, swilled again, scrubbed his hands, inspecting each fingernail, then cleaned them a second time.

Foul bitch. Mucky, scruffy, filthy whore. Must find the shoe.

Styne searched the Mazda boot, the dim bulb forcing him to scrabble around.

Where is it?

He pulled out the silage cover, explored each corner, and rooted under the front seats.

Nothing.

His fingers found Ciara's laptop. He opened the lid, pressed the "off" button and watched the screen blink, flare and die. Still rattled, he combed the area between car and house. Repeated the process in reverse, ignoring the pounding pain.

Must have slipped off when I moved the bitch into the front seat.

He tried to imagine the consequences, weighed up his options.

Was it worth a return trip?

No.

Did I leave anything behind that could incriminate me?

No.

Did anyone see me?

No.

Does the shoe matter?

No.

What did I handle or take that could convict me?

Only the bitch, but she's easy to get rid of.

Styne turned on the immersion heater, then used the plastic wrap to cover Ciara's body, holding his face away from the smell of fresh urine. He carted the corpse out, jammed it into the boot, banged the lid and stood thinking.

Her clothes. My blood is on them.

He hunted in a cupboard underneath the kitchen sink, found scissors and a five-litre container of liquid sodium hydroxide. He shook it. More than half-full.

The cattle, settled for the night, rushed forward and stuck their heads between feed bars.

Styne started the Hitachi and operated levers. He cocked his head, listened harder.

What's that noise? Bearings rubbing together. Not as smooth as they should be. Sounds clunky.

In the silage shed, he positioned the bucket underneath a bale and scooped. The engine strained, whining in protest, and refused to hoist the wrapped feed. He pushed and pulled the joysticks, willing the mechanical arm to lift, but the machine didn't respond.

Too heavy. Not enough pressure. Pinched tube. Oil leak. No midnight snack for cattle tonight.

He made a mental note:

Phone mechanic.

Styne threw the oven cleaner drum into the cab, guided the machine across the farmyard, halted beside the Mazda and manhandled Ciara's body into the loading bucket. Then he inched the digger into a field. Near a corner, Styne juggled pedals and controls. A boom arm arched and Ciara's corpse tumbled into a snowbank. The mud bucket blade sliced into soil, curled and lifted, the digger swivelled on its turntable with the grace of a ballet dancer and dumped its load. Styne jockeyed the bucket into the grave for another measure of clay. The engine revved and whined, hydraulic tubes hissed, striving to lift and complete the action. Failed.

Won't be able to bury you any deeper.

'Wide and shallow. Same as yourself, Miss McGuire.'

Styne jumped from the cab, unrolled Ciara's body and used the scissors to shear her clothes. Then he rolled her face up into the shallow grave. He twisted open the oven cleaner lid, upended the container and let the sodium hydroxide glug onto Ciara's body and face.

'Bye, Ciara, you bitch.'

He threw the empty container into the cab and bundled up the clothes and silage wrap. Then he backfilled the grave and compacted the clay into a neat mound.

The next snow shower will cover it. Once the machine's repaired, I'll flatten the earth out.

The Hitachi clanked its way back, passed by the sheds. At the roadside gateway, he powered off the engine, locked up the digger...

The grease monkey can work on it here.

...then walked back to the shed and scrubbed the paint from the Mazda's number plates.

At the farmhouse, Styne checked his iPhone. No missed calls. He chucked the laptop into a large refuse sack, stripped and added his clothes, work boots and Ciara's shoe to the junk. Upstairs, under the shower, the tepid water didn't relieve his headache. The night hadn't played out as he'd envisaged. The magic never happened. He stumbled to his old bedroom and lay in the darkness. His raw, inflamed tongue kept clicking against teeth, causing nerve endings to vibrate in pain.

Bitch died too quick. Should've suffered more, after the stress she caused me.

He wrestled with the pillow, couldn't find a soft spot. Jagged thoughts crisscrossed his mind. The lost shoe bothered him. He hated to leave traces.

I should go search for it. Did I leave any evidence in her house? Lime. I ought to have marinated her in lime. To make sure. Should've burned the body. Fire destroys DNA. Dammit. Damn her. Damn them all. My mouth. Have to cancel next week's appointments.

Adam Styne writhed and twisted.

03:47.

Propelled by pain, he dressed and used bathroom bleach and out of date Vanish Oxi Action to remove traces of Ciara McGuire from the farmhouse. Every crack and crevice got scoured – he'd learned of the unlikely places body secretions ended up from the scrubbing spree needed after Isobel Stewart. He rolled up the stained mat, scrubbed and vacuumed the Mazda twice, tipped the hoover contents into the refuse sack, shoved the rug on top, and chucked the bag in the car boot. He drove out, stopped at the digger, collected Ciara's clothes, the old silage cover and oven cleaner container and added them to the rubbish.

In Birr town centre, Styne offloaded some of the rubbish in an industrial bin. On the Roscrea road, he came upon a builder's skip, near full with debris, and rammed the mat, Ciara's shoe and a pile of clothes into a corner. In a housing estate, he split and divided the remainder between several residential bins. He then dismantled his pay-as-you-go phone and used a jagged piece of masonry to mince the pieces into unrecognisable bits of plastic, discarding them at intervals on the drive home. The laptop got hurled into a stream. At the farmhouse, he vacuumed the garage car again.

Get rid of hoover tomorrow.

The headache, an octopus around his brain, squeezed tight, turning his world into a red and black blur, demanding a release.

Three hours rest, then I'll go to Tullamore Court Hotel. Need to get noticed.

Styne couldn't sleep.

Dark dreams and adrenaline kept him awake; dissatisfied, frustrated, unfulfilled.

8

MONDAY 14 JANUARY

4:45 A.M.

JANA TROFIMIACK PULLED two suitcases, nudged Lech ahead into Belfast International airport terminal and studied the flight information display. The flight was on time. An automated voice barked unintelligibly. To her right, a train of people waiting to get through security, tail-backed down the escalator and into the arrival's hall. On her left, another line of travellers queued for bag drop. Lech yawned and rubbed his eyes. A man and two women brushed by. Jana looked around for her contact, saw no one she recognised, and joined the line. She checked the passports and tapped the icon on her mobile where she'd saved their boarding passes. *If the contact doesn't get here before we go through security, I'm not waiting,* Jana thought. *I'll sell the Yeats painting, and Tomasz can keep the money he owes me.* She listened to the low hum of conversations around her. An electronic ping-pong over the loudspeakers preceded a flight departure announcement. The trio that had hurried by, were now directly ahead.

A finger tapped her shoulder.

Jana turned.

'Tomasz sent me.' A man unzipped a rucksack, took out an envelope and handed it to her. 'For you. You have something for me?'

Jana bent to open a suitcase, and with no drama and minimum fuss, Jana, Lech and the contact got hemmed in and removed from the line.

'Police.' A woman, one of the trio, caught Jana's arm. 'I'm arresting you on suspicion of art fraud, theft, conspiracy to commit crimes, extortion, money laundering and involvement in running a criminal organisation.'

'What?'

'Do you understand?'

'Co? I—Lech?'

Lech, half asleep, barely realised that the second female officer separated him from his mother.

'Lech!' Jana was screaming now. 'Let go. Let me go. Let him go. Where are you taking my son?' She wrenched her arm away. 'What are you doing with Lech?'

'Don't resist, Ms Trofimiack. You're surrounded by police.' The female officer snapped a handcuff around Jana's wrist. 'I'm taking you to a police station for questioning. We'll take care of your son. Now, please step with me towards the door.'

Jana's dreams of a new life nose-dived when she saw the confusion and fear in Lech's eyes. She wanted to reach out, tell him everything was okay, but handcuffed, she'd no choice but comply with the officer's request.

MORNING

HUGH SPENT THE night painting.

Once he'd completed the kitchen, it made the hallway seem anaemic, so he tackled that. Then, the upstairs landing. Outside, the fog lifted and shadowy rays of diluted sunshine picked their way across the walls.

He rambled outdoors and let the crisp air flush paint fumes from his lungs. Kathleen's demands had a cathartic effect; the monotonous brush strokes helped ease internal turmoil. Mothers must have an intuitive perception when their offspring's conflicted, he thought, and what's necessary to begin the healing process.

Robins and chaffinches sang a strident disharmony of whistles and tweets, in their celebration of a new day. Except for a single cirrus cloud that scarred the sky, the world was pristine. After sprinkling breadcrumbs on bird tables, Hugh showered and vowed to tidy up his own home later. No point in delaying the inevitable; staying mired in the past wasn't helping his mentality. He needed to remove Eilish's presence from the house.

'Why aren't you at work, Hugh?'

'You keep asking me that, Ma. I came to see you first.'

'I'm ashamed to have given everybody so much trouble.' Kathleen frowned. 'Why're you mooching around like a broody hen?'

'I want to spend a while with you.'

'Leave. Go home to Eilish.'

'Hmm?'

'Eilish hasn't visited in ages.'

'We've parted ways, Ma.'

'Oh? I need to get out of here. Take me to the hostel. Nobody should be without food on Christmas day.'

'Doctor hasn't given permission yet, Ma. He'll call around later. Don't worry about the hostel. Amy and the other volunteers will make sure everyone's fed.'

'Christmas day is always hectic. They'll—'

'It's not Christmas day, Ma. Christmas was weeks ago. Today is January fourteenth.'

'What?' Kathleen gaped at Hugh.

'Yep. Christmas is done and dusted for another year.'

Kathleen cried.

'Ma? What's the matter?' Hugh sat on the bed and hugged her. 'Ma?'

'*Get away* from me. You left me here, locked up, and those souls starving on the streets? I *hate* you.'

'No one's hungry, Ma.'

'I don't believe you anymore. You've kept me here throughout Christmas. Never visited once. Leave. I want to die in peace.'

'I'm staying.' Hugh used a tissue to dry his mother's tears.

'Go. How's Eilish? I haven't talked to her since Christmas.'

'See? Now you remember being with us for Christmas.'

'Course I do. What's the matter with you?'

'Nothing, Ma.'

Hugh's mobile buzzed. Sharona Waters. 'Top o' the morning from Glenavy. Quick call. You said to keep in touch, but I haven't had a chance 'til now. Yesterday was mental, and already today the poo has hit the fan. I've only got a sec, so here's the lowdown: Two detectives from the art and antiques fraud squad are here with Dorothy. They've arrested Hattinger's manager, Jana Trofimiack, at Belfast International, on her way to Poland. Caught her passing another painting to an accomplice. Jack B. Yeats this time; that's the artist, not the accomplice.'

'I've heard of him.'

'They charged her with theft and forgery. Story's gonna hit the headlines over the next few hours.'

'So it's confirmed. This person swapped fakes for genuine articles?'

'Yep.'

'Jesus, when this breaks, art appraisers will be in demand.'

'Depends,' Sharona said. 'Anyhow, Dorothy's going for the jugular. She wants to push this into the public domain as a warning to other collectors. An hour ago, reporters and

TV crews arrived in convoy and set up Lowel Pro Lighting Kits and Sony camcorders. And before you ask, no, I haven't a clue either. I'm just reading off the equipment boxes. There's a guy beside me with a boompole—'

'A what?'

'Boompole. A microphone with a furry thingy on the end.'

'Oh, yeah.'

'Dorothy wants me involved. She's telling everybody I'm a saint.'

'Saint Sharona. Has a nice ring to it.'

'First foray in front of the media.'

'You'll adapt.'

'Crikey, I'm jumpy as a spring lamb. Any advice?'

'Enjoy the attention. Let me know how you get on. Oh, don't wear white...'

Kathleen dozed. Hugh dialled Ferdia and filled him in on Sharona's news. David chattered and sang to himself in the background.

'That's the ripple effect,' Ferdia said. 'You drop a pebble in the middle of a pond, and the ripples shake up whatever's in its path.'

'Sounds like Alzheimer's.'

'Huh. Wonder where this'll end?'

'We'll know more in a few days.'

'Any word from Eil—?'

'No. And before you ask, I haven't phoned her either.'

'Aye. Best leave it for a spell. Cool heads an' all that.'

'Yeah. Where are you now?'

'Dublin. David's school is still closed. We stayed at Niamh's place last night. We're—'

'Who's Niamh?'

Ferdia coughed. 'A friend. I met her, I don't know, a few weeks back. Next time she's in Ganestown, I'll introduce you.'

'Is that the friend you gave the terrier—?'

'God bless your memory. Yeah. Anyway, me an' Master David—'

'Stall a sec. Why didn't you take Niamh to the ball last Saturday?'

'She was busy, and sure, you needed a night out. David 'n' me are off to visit my relations in the Zoo. Then we'll check in on Grandad Chas. I'll—'

'So, Niamh is…significant?'

'Argh, you know yourself. We're getting on grand. That's all I'm saying. I've put you on speaker. Say hello to Master David…'

AFTER SIPPING TEPID coffee in the Tullamore Court Hotel, Adam Styne bought painkillers in a pharmacy, and continued up Church Street to the internet café. His dating website mailbox contained four new messages.

One from a Russian dating agency.

Delete.

Three Ghanaians wanted to deposit twelve million euro into his bank account, once he'd forwarded bank details, plus an administration fee.

Delete. Delete. Delete.

He erased Ciara's correspondence and declined DatingVista's invitation to upgrade his account status. The site had served his purpose.

No contact, no comeback. Won't need it for Jana.

Later, he rambled around the hotel foyer, conspicuous, before settling in with a newspaper. His life unravelled at ten a.m., when Hattinger's company solicitor rang and told him about Jana Trofimiack's arrest, the quantity of cash and the stolen Jack B. Yates piece.

'Impossible,' Styne lisped. 'Jana hasn't the brainpower of a…' His tongue knocked against teeth and a stream of pain blinded him.

'Unfortunately, it's true, Adam.'

'Is this connected to Dorothy Ridgeway's valuation?' Styne rubbed the pain from his forehead.

'Yes. Forgery implication as well. Ms Trofimiack got nabbed before she boarded a flight to Warsaw. I advised the lady not to make a statement, to no avail. She admitted swapping Mrs Ridgeway's McKelvey for a reproduction.'

'God damn the stupid—'

'Quite. You and I better meet tonight to begin preparatory work on a defence strategy. We need to leak our story to the media in advance and control the message.'

'Yes, yes. I'm aware—'

'It's *essential* we frame answers for the inevitable police and journalist's questions, Adam. My sources tell me the PSNI have queried dozens of thefts and switches.'

'Ridiculous. The woman isn't capable of, or smart enough to even—'

'Three years, Adam. Ms Trofimiack admitted it's gone on for three years. That's a lifetime for management not to suspect. It doesn't bode well that this con got plotted, prepared and executed under your guard.'

'How could I suspect if collectors didn't?'

'It's obvious the victims were chosen with care, Adam. But—'

What else did she say?'

'Ms Trofimiack requested another solicitor to represent her, so I'm not privy to her latest statements…'

Styne dumped the vacuum cleaner into an industrial bin at the side of a restaurant and drove to Kilcormac. Time to involve Madeline. Agitated, he called the solicitor back. 'What's happened since? I want more details.'

The details weren't pleasant. Two more arrests in London, and one at Hattinger's Manchester branch. 'Jana's taken my advice, albeit too late, and refused to speak until her new brief shows up,' the solicitor added. 'The others have underplayed their involvement, in return for reduced sentences. At present, the score stands at forty-three.'

'Forty-three what?'

'Pieces of art. Police have procured confessions for either exchanged or stolen property amounting to—'

'Forty-three?'

'Yes. And as they've accrued that much information within a few hours, Adam, who can foresee where it'll end?'

'What's your guess?' Styne asked. 'How extensive will it get?'

'Colossal, I'd say. On average, at fifty, sixty grand a pop, well, you do the math. Oh, and we're awaiting detectives from Harcourt Square. Rumours abound the gang was targeting collectors from the Republic too, and there's speculation you're intertwined in the mix.'

'That's ludicrous—'

'I know Adam, I know. It's an unwarranted, unfounded, unsubstantiated fishing expedition. But in these matters, the cui bono question is always asked.'

'How could I benefit? What possible—?'

They'll sling everything at you to see what sticks. Your business dealings will get scrutinised. Even simple things, goodwill gestures, every little…will be perceived as a bribe. Have you considered what to salvage from this rubble?'

'How could I? That's what I pay you for.'

'In my opinion, this caper's too vast to stay under wraps.'

'Then *find* a way to convince clients—'

'I don't see any walk-away position here, Adam. There'll be no winners. No amount of spin can mask the gravity of this debacle.'

'Well, better start earning your wages. Update me in an hour.'

A STEEL CLANG reverberated around the prison.

Jana Trofimiack sat on the thin mattress and eyed the graffiti-riddled, foul-smelling cell. Her feet were numb. They'd taken her shoes and replaced them with extra-large paper slippers that were no barrier to the bakterie crawling on the cement floor.

Her toes curled.

The shame she'd brought on her family. Images of Lech's face as the police led him away, haunted her mind. Her stomach rumbled, but she ignored the food tray with its hash browns and rasher, swimming in globules of grease. She's made an error asking for Hattinger's solicitors. They'd no interest in her. Their concern was Adam Styne. How to zwolniony, absolve his name. And how could she think straight? She'd thought someone was stealing her luggage. The alarm, panic. Arrest. Lech ripped from her arms. Jana rubbed her hands together, smearing the fingerprint ink further, and glad Lech hadn't witnessed *that* procedure. Processed, they'd called it. Treated her with the same concern as a dead sheep. She'd hate him to see his maia powerless and defenceless. Where had they taken him? Nobody talked to her. Nobody cared. She wondered what went through Lech's mind when he saw the policjant handcuff his maia. Had he forgotten her already? Was he imagining she'd abandoned him? Hadn't she always said Maia would look after him? Lech understood she'd never desert him. Didn't he? Where was his imagination now? Was the new solicitor interested in her case? Bah! Not enough to visit before his breakfast. It felt like she'd been a month in this wiocha. Jana bowed her head and whispered: 'I'll be with you tomorrow, Lech. I promise.' She tried to blank his teary-faced image, as her brain whirled and plotted. What deal would get Lech back?

The imperceptible click of a lock sounded loud as thunder. The cell door opened. A prison guard looked in and pointed at the hallway. 'Interview room. Your solicitor's here.'

The solicitor looked young. Too niedoświadczony, inexperienced.

'What's going to happen?' Jana asked him.

'A judge will decide your detention pending a trial date. Or you might get bail.'

'Kiedy?'

'Pardon?'

'When?'

'Two, three days.'

'Why detain me? My son—'

'The judge *may* grant bail *if* he's certain you'll appear whenever the date's set. Possession of stolen property is a bailable offence.'

'How much is bail?'

'Depends on how critical the court deems the crime.'

'When is court date?'

'Six, nine months.'

'Six...? What'll happen—?'

'Police will object to bail on the grounds you're a flight risk. You'd purchased a one-way ticket to—'

'If they object, where will I go?'

'Nowhere. You stay here.'

'I *can't*...How can I namawiać...persuade the police not to...object to bail?'

'Show the judge you've got ties within the community. Get character references from your employer.'

Jana considered this as two police officers joined them. Character references? From Adam Styne? Hah! Fat chance. If she paid bail, she'd lose the pieniądze squirrelled away for her art gallery.

The woman officer smiled. Jana took that as a positive sign.

'Are you taking any prescribed medicines, Jana?'

'No medicine. Where's my son?'

'If you're hungry or thirsty, tell us. We're not savages.'

'I know my rights.'

'Have you got family nearby?'

'Where've you taken my son? I want—'

The male officer pulled out a chair and sat across the table. 'Should've considered that before you thought up this scam.' His cold stare and loud voice setting the tone of the interview. 'We have you now.' He leaned forward and spoke with exaggerated glee. 'Tomasz snitched. Grassed you out to save himself, he did. Sang like a blackbird. You're the brains. Lech will be a grown man next time you walk the street together, in, oh, I'd say twenty years.'

'Co? No. That's untrue. I'm not...you don't understand how much my son misses me. He *needs* me.'

The policeman snorted. 'The boy doesn't give you a get-out-of-jail-free card. After your conviction, Social Services will decide where he goes. Wales. Or maybe Scotland.'

Jana's idea of manipulating the legal system vanished like water down a plughole. She glanced at the lawyer. He didn't return eye contact.

The reasonable female officer spoke. 'The Public Prosecution Service Office will need convincing you're guilty of a crime. They'll decide.'

'Decide what?'

'Whether there's enough evidence to convict—'

Her colleague sniffed. 'That'll take two minutes with the proof we've collected.' His pitiless eyes gave Jana no hope.

The woman scowled at her colleague. '—to convict, *and* if a trial is the best option in the public interest.'

'How do I get bail? I *must* see Lech. He—'

'Cooperate. Answer our questions. Plead guilty to handling stolen property. Throw yourself at the mercy of the court. I'll put a word in for you.'

The man grunted, threw a biro on the table and strode out.

The woman smiled. 'Don't mind him. We can appeal for a monetary penalty if you give us information that will lead us—'

Jana looked at the lawyer, seeking approval or encouragement. He thumbed through a notebook and didn't look up.

'Get my son,' Jana said. 'Then I'll tell you wszystko. Everything.'

HUGH WAS PARKING at McGuire's when his phone rang.

He looked at the number, and his blood pumped, primed for a positive response from Midland Recruitment. 'Hello?'

'Hugh? It's James. Quick call about that position. The company has shortlisted the candidates for interview—'

'And?'

'Didn't include you in the mix. Sorry. They're concerned you're over-qualified, that you'd see this job as a fill-in until your preferred position arises. I expect other management roles will pop up before the end of the month. I'll be in touch.'

Hugh's heart plummeted. He'd hoped he wouldn't have to revisit the social welfare office or drive the rickety old

Hiace again. Brendan Enright waved from the warehouse entrance. Hugh walked towards him and called, 'I'll start deliveries.'

'There's an order for a builder in Edgeworthstown, but no stock,' Brendan shouted back. 'I expected a delivery last Friday, but the supplier couldn't deliver.' He shrugged. 'This weather.'

'God. A wasted trip.'

'Should've rung you. Sorry. I'll let you know when it's ready.'

Hugh U-turned, frustrated. 'I'll check in with Malcolm.'

'He's not here. Could've gone to visit Charlie...'

MID-MORNING

'DID JANA GIVE you any inkling?' Madeline asked Adam when he furnished her with bare details. 'I'm sure you're not involved—'

'Of *course* I'm not.' Waves of anger radiated off Adam Styne. 'Why would I place my life's work in jeopardy? For a paltry...On a shitty...' His voice sizzled like lightning hitting a power cable.

'Don't worry. This too will pass.'

'Pass? Pass? Have you taken leave of your senses, woman? You're delusional if you think this issue will disappear. Media will tar me with the same brush. I built the business on customer loyalty, trust and confidence. My company's *dead*; no one will have faith. We're destroyed. Everything I've accomplished...' Styne's tongue hit a loose tooth, and a dart of pain exploded in his brain. 'Ruined. Kaput. My reputation is junk bond status. I'm a pariah. All because of that Polish...'

Styne withdrew into the study, seeking ways to infuse a positive twist, rejecting each idea as unworkable. How did his precise, controlled life turn disastrous in the space of twenty-four hours?

Madeline interrupted her husband's thought stream, called him to watch a news bulletin. RTÉ's sombre crime correspondent described how a joint cross-border Garda and PSNI operation foiled an art theft scam. Four people were in custody, with more arrests imminent. A police spokesperson said that although the crime ring was international in scope, it centred in London. Several addresses in Northern Ireland and the UK were being searched.

Styne flicked onto BBC and Sky. They showed similar versions of the same story.

Pain and pressure pounded his brain. He wanted to smash the television, but the ticker tape rolling the Hattinger news story across the bottom of the screen lured him to stay, and an on-screen strap highlighted updated breaking news regarding arrests and searches. This was ruination. He massaged both temples. It didn't ease the pain. 'I'm wiped out. Annihilated,' he said. 'The business has collapsed around my ears, and there's nobody, *nobody* I can get on board to solve this nightmare.'

Madeline bit a nail. 'This stress is frazzling me, Adam. I'll go help Ambrose draft media responses—'

'I *forbid* you to let Ambrose *near* the media. His dressing up meaningless prattle and extraneous guff to mask the stench of his ineptitude won't help. I don't understand how the Hattinger gene pool got so diluted, but your waddling imbecile of a brother hasn't the brains of a dodo.'

'Reporters will be all over the story before we get—'

'Go. Help him prepare a statement. Your jeep's in the garage. Take the replacement car. I've a meeting here with our solicitors this evening.' Styne's attention sharpened when a TV camera zoomed in on two women.

'This is Sharona Waters, the person who detected the forgery,' Dorothy Ridgeway gushed.

Sharona Waters? Fundraiser Ball. Last Saturday night she said...

'Without Sharona, those scammers would've duped and cheated me out of my most prized possession,' Dorothy continued. 'God knows how often they've swindled other defenceless senior citizens. Sharona's a fantastic—'

...she said "unless it's an inside job. No quantity of high-tech security can hold out against that." She'd known in advance. The cunt toyed with me. WITH ME? I'll swat her. Same as I would a flea.

Styne stalked across the hallway, rage vibrating from every sinew. 'There *must* be a way to turn this disaster into a triumph,' he muttered. 'I'll hire a PR team. Go on a deep-drill, damage limitation exercise.' He prowled lapping the study in search of solutions.

*Create a crisis management plan, but even that could prove fruitless if...*Styne halted, mid-stride. *I've lost Hattinger's, but this may be a chance for a fresh start. A new departure.*

He patrolled the room again. 'I'll dodge any conjecture associated with the scam. There'll be no permanent stain on me or *my* record, once I can answer the question, "How could you allow this to happen under your nose"?' He considered ways around that query, pacing faster. 'I'll get the solicitors to create well-crafted, measured responses. When the hullabaloo blows over, I'll launch modern showrooms. Styne Art Showrooms.' He visualised the words in his mind's eye. SAS. 'No, too Germanic. Styne Auctioneering and Art Showrooms. That's better. What font? Something creative, functional, trustworthy. Monotype Corsiva, perhaps.'

He pictured that.

'Yes,' he muttered. 'My innovative new establishment will emerge, phoenix-like from the rubble. I have the contacts.'

Survive and thrive.

'No more being answerable to any Hattinger. Ambrose will demonstrate his usual incompetence. The rest of the vultures will squabble over whatever pieces remain. I'll be the winner. Back in control.'

I'm entitled.

Styne inhaled. 'Devil's in the details.' He felt his heart rate slacken off. 'When you focus on the problem, stumbling blocks turn into stepping stones. I owe you an apology, Miss Waters. You've helped me more than you realise, you dark-haired bitch. No, no, please don't thank me. It's no trouble. It will be a genuine pleasure to take care of you. To thank you *personally*. A thrill kill. And then, it's that northern shrew, Dorothy Ridgeway's turn. Jana, wherever you are, I'll find you, but for the moment, you must wait.' Styne stabbed at the iPhone screen, typed in 118.ie, hit people search, tapped out **SHARONA WATERS GANESTOWN**, and pressed "find."

AFTERNOON

HUGH LISTENED TO Radio Nova's 'battle of the bands' on the journey back to Ganestown. Greenday versus Blink 182. Greenday won the phone-in vote by a ten to one majority.

A strong wind had risen by the time he reached the outskirts of the town. Despite the sleety squall, children roamed the slushy ground in Ganestown Park, using their bodies to anchor kites. Hugh circled the square and found a parking spot. Dozens of people milled inside the social welfare office. Different faces, but the stench of subdued hopelessness prevailed. Two staff, barricaded behind their pexiglassed partitions, fought to deal with the job seekers and keep the queue winding forward. Hugh punched out a ticket and glanced at Ronan Lambe hunched over a hatch. When Ronan moved away, Hugh caught his eye and waved.

Ronan held up a single pamphlet. 'Research, dude, for courses I can enrol in.'

Hugh lifted his envelope. 'Dole forms.'

'Yeah. I've given in mine. Any news on the jobs front?'

'Got turned down for a job interview.'

'Bummer, dude. I feel your pain.'

'507,' a voice roared behind them.

'That's me,' Hugh said. 'If you get wind of any vacant sales management positions...'

'Ditto, dude.'

'5.0.7.' Annoyed now.

'God, we never get a break. You've got the sour one, dude.'

'Thanks. See ya.'

The sour one glared. 'This isn't a club. If you wanna socialise, find a bar.'

'Sorry.' Hugh fed the documents into a bowl-shaped space at the bottom of the glass partition and tried to ignore the conversation at the next hatch. People lifted their heads; a reprieve from their own misery.

'Where do I go now?' The man's voice grew in volume. 'I'm blue in the face askin' what 'n' hell I've to do next. Dear God, is there no one who'll tell me where I am in the system? Six weeks ago, I came in an' asked 'bout money for courses. You said you didn't know, go to FÁS. I went to FÁS. They told me to come back here an' get a form to show them I'm eligible. I came back here. No forms; you were waitin' for a new batch. In the end, I got it an' brought it to FÁS. "Bring it back to the dole office," they said, "an' get it stamped." I brought it back here. "Take it back to

FÁS," you said. They stamped it as well. Now they've sent me back to you. I'm *mithered* from all this over and back. Me head's meltin'. I need dizziness tablets after all this up and down like a…a—'

'Language.'

'—fucken yo-yo.'

'Tsk. It isn't FÁS anymore, it's Solas. Anyhow,' the administrator smiled with the professional insincerity of a politician, 'you don't qualify.'

'What?'

'You don't qualify.'

'Why?'

'You're between Jobseekers Benefit and Jobseekers Allowance.'

'What the fu…? You. Can*not*. Be serious. You mean, all that weeks of shite? Jezz…sus.'

'You'll hafta fill out this form, and sign…'

The man howled at the injustice of the system.

Hugh watched the woman pore over his signed forms and key the information into a mainframe computer. She typed with her left forefinger and saved the data by banging the heel of her right hand on the "Enter" key.

'What's next in the process?' he asked.

'Dunno. Depends if they need more information.'

'What information?'

'Dunno,' the woman said.

'Any idea when—?'

'Dunno.'

Hugh gave up.

'And turn up on your sign-on days. Or else.'

'When are sign-on days?'

'Dunno.'

'Is it the same day each week?'

'Dunno. Take this to the post office, Wednesday.' The woman pushed out a postcard-sized sheet. 'You'll get your money there. This's a provisional form. We'll post you out another.'

'I hope this is a short-term solution,' Hugh said.

The woman snorted. 'Next.'

INVALID PERSON SEARCH. Please search again.

Adam Styne growled in frustration.

Bitch. You won't beat me. Facebook. Are you on Facebook, Miss Waters?

Sharona's Facebook page showed her leaning against a red door. He zoomed in. House number 29.

Where is that in Ganestown?

His eyes skimmed photos for clues.

None.

Have you registered to vote, Miss Waters?

Styne typed "**register of elections,**" and got directed to "**CHECK THE ELECTORAL REGISTER.**" He tapped on **Province** and **County Council** and typed in **Sharona Waters.** In the box marked **Town/Street** he inputted **Ganestown,** and in **House Number** he added **29.** The drop-down menu gave him a list of nine locations.

Selected the first.

Your details could not be found...

Reasons your details could not be located...

Click here to fill in form RFA2...

He pressed "undo" and clicked the next location.

And the next.

And the next.

Three-quarter ways along the list, the screen revealed: **Sharona Waters.**

Click on name to view details.

29 Mountain View...

'See? There are always choices, Miss Waters. All one has to do, is search until you find the most appropriate.'

Styne rang the solicitor. 'I've another matter to deal with tonight. We'll meet tomorrow afternoon to discuss tactics.'

'I've already left, Adam. As I said earlier, we should build defence walls. I've cleared my diary to make myself available—'

'Good. Book yourself into Tullamore Court Hotel and start work. I'll meet you tomorrow afternoon.' Styne disconnected and phoned a local mechanic. 'Adam Styne here. A tube has burst on my Hitachi. It's *essential* my machine gets fixed today. Cattle need feeding.'

'It'll work if you split the bale—'

'Today.'

The migraine was a force ten, but Styne embraced the pain, relishing the release later. Unable to concentrate on business, he withdrew to the farm. Gusts of northerly winds buffeted the barns. He plugged the stun gun into a socket and toiled for three hours. The strenuous manual work exhausted him, made arm and shoulder muscles weak as water. He checked the Taser was working by pressing it against a cow's rump. The docile bovine bellowed in surprise as the current flooded her system. She lashed out and galloped across the shed, lowing in pain.

Styne's smiled.

Preparation complete. I'll go to the farmhouse and rest, before revisiting Ganestown.

EVENING

AFTER SPENDING AN hour at the hospital, Hugh returned to his own home, switched on the heating, and remembered the oil was low.

Another bill.

He cranked up the volume on Rammstein's VOLKERbALL and let the Teutonic titans dislodge lingering money concerns, while he gathered Eilish's leftover clothes and placed them in boxes for donation to a charity shop. He thought her scent was still on the bedsheets but knew it was more a memory than an actual presence. The only physical reminders were a shallow dent in her pillow and a single strand of red hair. He swallowed the thickness in his throat, bundling bed linen into the washing machine; the simple action more a challenge than he'd thought possible. The dream had disappeared. Banished forever. Finis.

He made a coffee and strolled outside. Till Lindemann's guttural vocals, along with the band's blend of industrial keyboards, synthesisers and grinding guitar sounds, followed him. January's sun sank low over the horizon, while long shadows fought to retain their grip on the carpet of snow. A shower of hailstones signalling hard frost later sent him indoors, and he sorted through photo albums that evoked memories of their time together. Sharona rang and broke the trance. 'Did you watch me on telly? How'd I sound?'

'Didn't get any news today, Sharona. I'll tune in at nine o'clock and give you my verdict.'

'Hope I came across okay. God, what a crazy day, but in a good way. I'm heading home. Past the Boyne Valley Bridge now.'

'I'd say you're exhausted.'

'Wrecked. My kingdom for a long soak in a hot bath. Haven't slept since last Thursday. Dorothy's a *dynamo*. She's generating massive publicity for her art auction. Woman's a born marketeer. Oh, the media circus has decamped, and moved their tents to Hattinger's headquarters on Belfast's Ann Street. Tomorrow is their turn in the spotlight. Let *them* cope with being the focus of interest.' Sharona yawned. 'Can't wait for my own bed and a twenty-four-hour deep sleep.'

'Me too. Safe journey.'

'Phone me after the news. I want your feedback on how I came across.'

'Will do.'

Hugh browsed, threw most of the photos into a box for disposal, but kept a few dozen, and a flash drive with GIF's and JPEG's. Some memories he couldn't consign to a rubbish bin. Part of Eilish would always remain.

After the nine o'clock news, Hugh rang Sharona.

'You home yet?'

'An hour ago. Checked my emails. Listen, can we meet tomorrow? I've noticed something weird in my email account.'

'Sure.'

'Great. How'd I come across?'

'In a word? Professional. As if you'd been in front of a camera forever. Your face is everywhere. An all-channel global launch because of Hattinger's international reputation, and Dorothy's praise. You're the heroine of the hour.'

'Still hasn't sunk in,' Sharona said. 'Everything that's happened in the past few days, I mean. It's—'

Through the phone, Hugh heard a door buzzer peal.

'Oh, dammit,' Sharona said. 'Who's that?'

'Probably an early election canvasser. Or Jehovah's Witnesses'.'

'God. One sec, Hugh. I'll get rid of them.'

Hugh rinsed his empty coffee mug, half-listening to Sharona's steps on the stairs, the tinny rattle of a safety chain unlatching. 'Mr Sty—?'

Her surprised tone made him straighten. 'Sharona? You okay? Sharona?' Hugh grabbed car keys. 'Sharona?' He was outside when Sharona's mobile clattered, and the call disconnected. He turned the ignition key. Symbols that routinely lit up the dashboard remained blank.

'Start. Start this one time. Start.'

Hugh pumped the clutch, twisted the key again. The engine coughed once and died. He gritted his teeth, tried again, ramming the clutch pedal. Nothing.

'Fuck.'

He leapt from the car and kicked the front tyre, forgetting he was wearing tennis shoes. An arrow of pain pierced his toe.

'Fuck.'

Hugh limped down the driveway, stared through trees at his neighbour's house. Dark. Nobody home. He pressed Sharona's number. Went straight to message minder. Punched Ferdia's speed dial button. Engaged. Dialled Ganestown Garda Station. No answer. He scrolled through P. Q. R...

Ruth.

He stabbed her number and shambled along the road, hopping on the heel of his sore foot. The tennis shoes slipped and slid on the icy surface. Ruth's phone rang. He prayed she'd answer.

'Hugh?'

'Ruth. I've an emergency—'

'Is it Kathleen? How can I help?'

'She's fine. Can you collect me?'

'Where are you?'

Battling for breath, Hugh gasped the quickest route. Each red-hot rasp burned as if a blunt blade had carved his chest. He'd covered a kilometre before Ruth caught up. Winded, panting, soaked with sweat, lungs burning, leg muscles searing, foot throbbing, he buckled himself into Ruth's Corsa and pointed towards Ganestown. 'Totally…out of shape. Head for Mountain View. Trouble, I think. Need to join a gym.'

'I knew you wouldn't wait a week to contact me,' Ruth teased. 'What's happening?'

'Problem at Sharona Waters' house.'

Ruth zipped through an orange traffic light.

Hugh dialled Ganestown Garda Station.

The desk sergeant remembered Hugh. 'We spoke yesterday. Garda Flanagan. Your mother—'

Hugh cut in: 'I've another problem now in Mountain View. 29. Sharona Waters. A friend of mine. Someone's broken into her house—'

'Mountain View you said? There's a cruiser on patrol out that direction. A meet 'n' greet for the boyos doing doughnuts on icy roads. I'll get the lads to swing by and see what the story is.'

Hugh directed Ruth into Mountain View estate.

Oncoming full headlights blinded them. Ruth braked and pulled in to let the car pass, then swung by the parked vehicles and stopped at 29.

Hugh jumped out, groaned in pain when his foot hit the ground.

Sharona's car was in her driveway, the house in darkness. His eyes skimmed the area, saw where a vehicle had reversed in, and driven out, its tyre tracks preserved in crusted ice. He rang Sharona's mobile again.

Nothing.

Hugh hobbled to the front door, the streetlight picking up footprints in the snow. He avoided a scuffed area that looked as if something had got dragged from the house, and banged on the door. 'Sharona?'

No answer.

He peered in the letterbox, eyes searching the dark hallway. He pounded the door again.

'There's no one there,' Ruth said. 'Are you sure she was at home?'

'She was here five minutes ago, checking emails, and…that car…'

'Which car?'

'The car we met. The lights that nearly blinded us?'

'Yeah?'

'An Offaly reg Beemer.'

'Was it? I didn't notice. So?'

'I *know* that car. Adam Styne.'

'Who's Adam Styne?'

'An art dealer. I heard Sharona say a name, "Mr Sty", before…Let's go.' Hugh hopped back into Ruth's Corsa.

'Wait. Go where?'

'We need to follow that Beemer and stall him.'

'What?'

'I'll fill you in on the way.'

Ruth reversed and sped out of the estate. 'What in hell's happening? Where are we going? That car's miles away by now.'

In the side mirror, Hugh glimpsed a squad car, blue lights spinning, turn into Mountain View.

'Phone the cops again,' Ruth said.

Hugh did. No signal. 'Shit. I was on the phone to Sharona. Her doorbell rang. I'm *sure* she said Mr Styne, or was trying to.'

'Where now?' Ruth slowed coming up to a roundabout.

'Motorway,' Hugh said. 'No, take the Tullamore exit.'

The car see-sawed over a speed bump and onto the ramp.

'Styne lives outside Tullamore. Kilcormac. That's our best shot.'

'God, that's…ring the Garda station again.'

Hugh dialled. Engaged. 'I'm almost positive I heard her say Styne's name.'

'You were *sure* a second ago.'

'Sty. Styne. I know only one person with the surname Styne. S-T-Y-N-E. I met him briefly Saturday night. Adam Styne. Detectives are investigating the company he works with, for art fraud. Sharona Waters helped break the case.'

'Hattinger's.' Ruth snapped her fingers. '*That's* where I recognised her name from. I got the tail end of her interview on RTÉ—'

'If it's the same Styne. It *must* be. Hasn't it? It's an unusual surname. And the car—'

'She might know fifty people with a similar sounding name, but how'd she disappear so fast? Did she go with him?'

'Not willingly.'

'How do you know?'

'That, I'm positive of.'

'Well then, he must've taken her. Kidnapped her. God. Why?'

'Maybe it's to do with the art racket.' Hugh massaged the pain from his leg.

'How—?'

'Two, two something.' Hugh said. 'That car number plate was two, two…God, it won't come to me.'

'How'd you manage to spot that?' Ruth passed an artic lorry; Richard West International Haulage.

'I saw it leaving a hotel car park yesterday morning. Two, two…Jesus.' Hugh redialled the Garda station. 'If we don't catch up with him between here and Kilcormac—'

'*If* he's gone that direction. He could be—'

'It's the only lead we've…It's ringing. Why won't somebody answer?' Hugh strained to see beyond the headlights burning through the darkness. 'There.' He pointed at distant fog lights. 'That's him.'

The phone rang out.

Desperate now, Hugh pressed Ferdia's number. "The customer you are calling is not reachable at present. Please try again later." Aww, Jesus wept.'

Ruth changed into fourth gear. The speedometer gauge climbed to seventy.

A kilometre further.

The gauge hit eighty.

Another kilometre closed the distance.

An Audi A4.

'Shit.'

Ruth sped on, odometer needle now in the red. 'So, at least we can *assume* this Styne guy can tell us where Sharona is. *If* he was at the house, he's the last person with her.'

'He was. He abducted her.' Hugh nodded, convincing himself.

'You can't be certain,' Ruth said. She held the steering wheel in a death grip, concentrating with the intensity of an F1 driver. 'God, I hate that word, abducted. Anybody you know who'd have his address? Street? House number?'

'Styne's brother-in-law told us he lives in Kilcormac,' Hugh said. 'A house on the Kinnitty road. His wife is Madeline. Madeline Hattinger.'

'Anything else?'

'Two, two...shit, why can't I remember? Two, two, five...I think. That's all I've got.'

'I could call a colleague in Tullamore hospital and get the Records department to find his details.'

'Can you do that?'

'Not sure it's legal, but yeah. This's an emergency. Here.' Ruth tossed Hugh her mobile. 'Zero-five-zero—'

'You've no reception.' Hugh checked his phone screen. 'Jesus, I've no signal either.'

'Crap.' Ruth slapped the wheel.

Four more kilometres.

They tore through a bend. The Corsa's frame juddered, and Tullamore lit up the horizon.

'You'll come off the motorway in a minute,' Hugh said. 'There's no way he'd risk going through the town with a kidnapped person. What if he got caught in traffic and—?'

'What if she's unconscious?' Ruth said. 'Maybe in the car boot, and he doesn't give a damn—'

'But at any stage, she could scream, or kick...*If* we're on the right track, I reckon he'll take the ring-road. Follow the signs for Birr. There'll be gardaí and a squad car in Kilcormac.'

The car careened by the IDA Business Park, got stuck behind a bus that tilted on its left axle, and proceeded at a glacial pace towards the N52 junction. The bus jerked to a halt at a traffic signal, blocking two lanes. Air brakes hissed, and it bounced on broken suspension springs. Puffs of noxious gases belched from exhaust pipes, like smoke from bellows.

Sixty slow seconds slipped past.

The lights changed to green. The bus crawled a few metres. Stalled. Ruth squeezed the Corsa alongside. The light sequence changed to red again.

Ruth braked.

Hugh fumed.

Ruth kept the Opel in gear and the rev count high, staring at the traffic lights, moved her foot from brake to accelerator before the filter arrow turned green. She spun right onto the N52 and the car hydroplaned on the icy surface. Hugh braced, anticipating a spin-out. Ruth changed gear, mashed the accelerator, worked through the controlled skid and forced the Corsa into obeying her touch. 'Phew.'

The outside temperature gauge read minus six degrees. They passed the fifty-kilometre speed sign, and Ruth accelerated again. A wobble forced her to slow…slightly. A hazy red neon sign glowed in the distance, looking like an alien spacecraft hovering in the frosty air.

Hugh pointed. 'If that petrol station's open…'

Closed.

They barrelled past Blueball service station.

Ruth chewed her lip, downshifted, powered around an Insignia and eased by a Land Rover. The full beams picked out taillights. 'Ahoy, captain,' she said. 'Car ahead.'

'We're nearly in Kilcormac, Ruth. I hope we've made the correct guess. If not, we're—'

'Beemer. 530d,' Ruth said. 'What's that reg number again?'

'Two, two—'

'Three-two-five?' Ruth finished.

Hugh leaned forward. '*Yes*. That's it.' He touched Ruth's arm. 'Pull back.'

Ruth slackened off. The BMW gained a hundred metres and drove into Kilcormac.

'The station is…' Hugh pointed. 'Jesus. I don't believe it. The bloody cop station's closed.'

'Cutbacks,' Ruth said.

Hugh glanced out the passenger window. 'The Kinnitty road's here on the left.'

The BMW maintained its steady speed and stayed on the N52.

'Shit, we're following the wrong car.'

'I'm not sure, Hugh. It's too much of a coincidence to have the make and model, along with half the reg number in your head…Anyway, he's not likely to bring a body *home*. We'll go another bit. See what happens.'

'Give him space so.'

'Try the phone again.'

Hugh did. 'Still no signal.'

They listened to the wheels whish, eyes glued on the car in front. Hugh shifted in the seat, impatient. 'Where the hell's he going? We're way beyond Kilcormac.'

Ruth didn't answer.

A white van overtook, and the trio travelled in convoy. After a kilometre, white van man swung off the main road.

A forest outline loomed in the moonlight.

Six kilometres.

Past Fivealley.

On their right, an LED streetlight lit up a church in its ghost-grey beam. Hugh fidgeted. 'We'll be in Birr soon. Should we overtake? Make him stop?'

'And then what? It might be an innocent person out for a drive. Or, if it *is* the kidnapper, we don't want him to know we're following him. What if he's got a gun? Birr's only a few kilometres away. We'll let the gardaí there—'

The BMW indicated left.

'We can't follow off the main road, Ruth. When he turns, pull over.'

Ruth skidded to a halt.

Hugh shuffled back to the side road, more a laneway, a boreen. He watched the BMW's taillights bounce a few hundred metres ahead. Brake lights glowed, and the car vanished.

Hugh limped back to Ruth, darts of pain slicing his foot. 'We're here. Wherever that is.'

Ruth peered out at him. 'Now what?'

'I'll check where he's gone. If there's a house, I'll—'

'You'll what? Ask him to come out and play? Forget it. Let's go to Birr.'

'Gimme a minute. I'll find out if we're right.'

'What happens if we *are* right?'

'Then we'll drive to Birr.'

'Let's go there now.'

'We've no proof of anything. I'll go check.'

Ruth shivered. 'I'm not thrilled with this idea.'

'If I'm not back in ten minutes, drive to Birr. Garda station's on the Square.'

'Five,' Ruth said. 'I'll give you five minutes.'

Wispy clouds clothed the moon.

Hugh shuffled along the lane, struggling to walk in the tyre track groove. Above him, a canopy of sagging tree branches arched and joined. The timber creaked and groaned under the weight of snow and ice. Slivers of moonbeams filtered between the gaps, giving faint shape to objects. Underfoot, frozen snow and rough ice crunched like crisp cornflakes. Hugh craned his neck, forcing his eyes to adjust. Except for the distant growl of a Harley with its modified pipes and kamikaze rider puttering along the main road, the night was still. The cold penetrated his bones. He shuddered. What had seemed bright from the comfort and warmth of Ruth's car, now became dingy and menacing.

Something rustled in a hedge.

A fox howled. An owl hooted a rejoinder. Icicles dripped from naked branches, their plops, eerie whispers. The hair on Hugh's head bristled with tension, as mangled nerves and stress ramped up his heartbeats. Eyes wide open, searching the tree-line, a snow pellet dripped on his face, making him jump. He didn't see the pothole. Ice splintered, a gunshot in the stillness. His left ankle twisted and bolts of pain rippled up his leg. The runner acted as a sponge, soaking in weeks of slush.

Hugh shuffled on, each step producing a paroxysm of agony. He'd lost all feeling in his toes. To his right, through the trees, he made out the shape of a large structure. On the left, a machine sat hunched in a gateway. The invasive, cloying stench of silage hung in the air. It clung to clothes and stuck in his throat. The tree-line ended. A two-story house materialised out of the gloom, a grim and cheerless dark silhouette. The muted glow of an artificial light shone from the rear of the building and bounced off the tyre tracks.

Every fibre in Hugh's body hummed with fear. His heart rattled against ribs, thumping trip-hammer fast, and nerves jangled, screaming at him to turn and run. The thin light beam hindered rather than helped lessen the intimidating atmosphere. He crouched and crab-walked to the house, inched around the gable end, and sensed movement behind him. He straightened, spun, and raised his arms for protection. A faint buzz. The side of Hugh's neck burned and he got hurled backwards by an invisible force. His skull drummed against the concrete wall. A ball of white pain flashed. Then, like a blown fuse, everything faded to black.

Hugh had no idea how long he'd been unconscious.

He blinked.

A light appeared, disappeared and reappeared in a wavy haze.

He blinked again.

The light got brighter, triggering an intense migrainous pain that made his head feel big as an inflated ball one second, and as if a compactor had crushed it the next. Dazed and disorientated, slumped on a chair in a small room, legs numb, arms locked at his wrists, his brain worked in slow motion. Through blurred vision, he saw Sharona's outline lying on the floor. A man towered above her, growling. '…in blood, *bitch*. You'll pay in *blood*.'

Hugh wrestled with the plastic restraint, trying to force slack. Pulled muscle agony shot up his arms. He tugged harder. The yellow tie dug into his wrists.

His vision cleared.

Sharona was gagged with duct tape, ankles crossed and tied, arms twisted behind her back. Tears trickled, but she stared at her nemesis, defying him.

'You've. Ruined me. You, the Polish bitch, and that interfering northern *cunt*. You've no idea the sacrifices, the years of...My achievements. My business. You've destroyed my life. Court cases. Compensation. MY COMPANY. You'll pay. You toyed with me at the ball last Saturday, you and this...hop-along Fallon. Forget about anyone coming to your rescue. The *stress* you've brought on me. The *anxiety* you've caused. You'll pay in blood, both of you, after I find his transport. To the victor comes the spoils.' The man pressed a mobile unit to Sharona's neck. A surge of current flowed across the top of the device and her body jerked. The hair on the side of her neck singed. The coppery, charcoal odour of fried flesh fused with the stench of sulphur and filled the room with its repulsive reek. Her body slumped, skin turning greyish-white.

Hugh realised he could move his legs, but chronic pins and needles made both feet heavy as cement blocks.

The man pivoted.

Adam Styne.

A bulging-eyed madman, face suffused with rage, had replaced the suave businessman. Flecks of froth foamed at the sides of Styne's mouth. His piercing blue eyes blazed with malice, teeth bared in a feral snarl.

Hugh moved a fraction in the chair, struggling to generate feeling. His heart galloped, body awash with adrenalin, shoulder muscles knotted, on fire with the battle to free his arms.

Styne stepped towards him.

Sharona groaned.

Styne twisted his head.

Hugh tugged at the ties again. Thunderbolts of pulsing pain drilled into his skull.

I'm dead, he thought. We're both goners. There's no way I can save us.

Ferdia's voice swam in his consciousness:

"If you're ever in trouble, forget the fancy stuff. Kick the other person's knee. Hard. It'll give you a chance to run like hell."

Styne bent…

Five.

…transferred the stun gun to his left hand…

Four.

…tested the tie around Sharona's ankles. Hugh clinched and unclenched his toes, squeezing circulation back into his legs, forcing blood into trapped nerves. He breathed deep, filling his lungs. Styne's malign energy seemed to suck oxygen from the room.

Three.

Styne turned Sharona on her side, checked the wrist binds. Hugh tensed calf muscles, and the agony reduced to a cold burn.

Two.

Sharona coughed, choked on the gag. Styne caught a corner of the grey duct tape and ripped it free. 'Breathe, bitch. I don't want you to die. Yet.' Gulps of air rattled in Sharona's throat, rushing into starved lungs.

One.

Styne stood.

Go.

Adrenaline levels spiking, Hugh exploded from the chair like a gusher. Pain surged when his feet rammed against the floor. He powered across the room, eyes riveted on Styne's right leg, his mind streaking from Alzheimer's and redundancy, to rows and relationship break-ups. He channelled every ounce of rage, frustration and anger he'd stomached over the last week, into this front leg kick.

The right heel caught Adam Styne flush on the kneecap. The audible crack as Styne's patella broke and relocated, sounded like a twig breaking. Pads of cartilage snapped and shifted. Muscles and tendons controlling leg motion were torn asunder. Styne's leg twisted inwards, the kneecap shattered, forced out of its groove. His arms thrashed, the mobile fell and he face-planted the floor. Hugh whipped his foot forward and smashed the runner into Styne's jaw. The psychopath's condyle fractured, and the impact snapped the temporal crest.

Face muscles tight with pain, breath sawing his lungs, Hugh's eyes searched for something sharp to cut the ties. Each step blasted lightning rods of agony around his body.

'Hu...Hugh.' Sharona coughed.

He whirled. 'Sharona. Hang on. I'll get a knife. One second.' Hugh checked Adam Styne, unconscious, marinated in a pool of blood. 'You're safe,' he said to Sharona. 'Styne can't hurt you now.'

Sharona gaze focused over Hugh's shoulder. Her eyes widened, an unspoken warning. In his peripheral vision, Hugh spotted movement in the doorway, and he spun to face this new threat.

'When you get to the part where you call the nurse, she's here,' Ruth said, holding a tyre iron, chest high.

'Can you find anything to cut these ties, Ruth?'

Ruth produced nail scissors from a coat pocket. 'Girl Scouts,' she said. 'Always be prepared.' She cut Hugh's ties, moved to Sharona and sniffed. 'Get me water, Hugh.'

'He knocked us out with that.' Hugh pointed at the stun gun and rubbed his neck.

'Hugh, get me water. Now.'

'Okay.' Ruth's face swam out of focus.

Someone shook him and screamed. 'HUGH!'

It cleared the fuzziness. 'Water. Right. I'll get water.'

Hugh lurched through the hallway, spotted a green push-button landline telephone on a Victorian-style chaise longue. His stomach cramped, tightened and stretched. He gagged, swallowed the bile and dry-heaved, hunting for a toilet. Sweat beads clung in patches to his skin. He changed direction, made the kitchen sink and retched.

When his breath steadied, he filled glasses with water.

'I *knew* you'd find me, Hugh.' Sharona's voice was a croaky whisper. 'You're caked in blood.'

Hugh rubbed his dishevelled hair. 'So much for that good night's sleep.' He wiped sticky palms on a trouser leg. 'There's a landline here. I'll call 112.'

Ruth examined Hugh's head. 'Use the church as a landmark. Both of you look as if you're auditioning as extras in a vampire film. And you might have a concussion, Hugh. That cut needs stitching. This is Mr Styne, I presume.'

They studied the back of Adam Styne's head and neck, matted with blood and perspiration. Hugh gripped his shoulder and flipped him face up. A mottled, swollen bruise, the shape of Australia, had formed across Styne's forehead; his face ballooned up to twice its size. Rivulets of mucus and blood oozed from a broken nose and blended with sweat, the mix branching out resembling tributaries across his pain-lined face. His right leg flopped. Clouds of doubt flitted across Styne's eyes as realisation set in. The mask of invincibility now shattered, his confidence leached away with the gore that soaked the cement floor. An acrid oniony stink emanated from him; the smell of fear. Styne used elbows and left leg in a bid to back crawl. Shoes slipped on the bloody floor. He coughed, spat out a tooth, and bubbles of blood popped when he gurgled words: 'Mphffff.'

'Shush,' Ruth said. She picked up the Taser and pressed it to Styne's neck. 'Go to sleep.'

9

TUESDAY 15 JANUARY

12:01 A.M.

SIRENS HERALDED THE arrival of a squad car.

An ambulance crew followed and moved Sharona to Tullamore General. A guard patrolled the external house perimeter, preserving the scene. Two more supervised the interior. Another separated Hugh and Ruth and questioned them.

A second ambulance pulled in. A male nurse sedated Styne, started an IV line and swaddled his head, face and leg in bandages. Hugh overheard him whisper to a detective that "they should get this man on the operating table while the wounds were fresh."

Someone draped a blanket around Hugh. The nurse examined his wrenched, swollen left ankle, and said the big toe on his right foot was fractured. He cleaned and daubed antiseptic on the facial lacerations and head wound, and gave him an anti-tetanus injection before accompanying the stretchered Adam Styne out. The ambulance departed, siren screaming.

In contrast to the squad car's flashy entrance, two vans crunched quietly into the driveway. Men from the first vehicle erected half-a-dozen dazzling solar light towers, and three people from the second van stepped into white Tyvek hooded overalls, boot covers and face masks. The forensic team had arrived.

Still woozy, Hugh watched the Technical Bureau squad and the forensic crew work side by side, a well-oiled machine, putting chains of evidence together. The tech guys dropped aluminium stepping plates throughout the room and hall, creating pathways and concentrated on mapping and photography. One used dark cloths as backdrops, drew diagrams, took notes and captured observations on tape. His colleague circled items with yellow chalk and placed toothpicks with flags on objects of interest.

The forensic team used kit from their murder bags to collect material evidence, sealing fibres in Ziplocs and paint samples in screw-capped plastic containers. A woman used a Spectrum 9000 light source to search for trace evidence under skirting boards and in corners. Another swabbed Hugh's footwear. Gardaí came, went, and revisited the scene again.

'Hugh, is it?' The speaker looked around Hugh's age. Muscular, with just-out-of-bed tousled crew cut hair, a hawkish nose and a ruddy weather-beaten appearance. His eyes projected an air of alertness, and the authoritative voice sounded accustomed to giving orders and getting results.

'Yes.'

'Detective Mulryan. Call me Marcus.'

'Hi.'

'We'll move you out of here and let Dusty get working on fingerprints. Only step on the tread plates. We'll take you for an x-ray soon. May I borrow your phone?'

It wasn't a polite request.

Marcus passed the confiscated mobile to a colleague and then took Hugh through his version of events. The detective maintained eye contact while he jotted down information, and also kept track on the forensic team. When he'd finished, he reverted to earlier questions, seeking further clarification. Once satisfied, Marcus disappeared to quiz Ruth. Another Garda sat beside Hugh, and the interrogation began again.

Hours passed. Pre-dawn crept in like a silent assassin. A Garda returned the phone and assisted Hugh to a patrol car. Even with illuminated brilliant white lights, the house appeared bleak. Ruth drove behind them and assisted Hugh into Tullamore hospital. The Garda presence meant normal A&E protocol got scrapped. Hugh was whisked past people in a far worse condition and propelled to the top of the triage train. The radio repeater on the guard's shoulder squawked. He listened, gave a 'sorry-gotta-go' shrug, and left.

Hugh said: 'You should've gone for help, Ruth.'

'Same applies to you.'

'I only planned to see if we were in the right place. You'd no idea what you were walking into.'

'When you didn't come back, God, I was never more terrified. I thought, if you're in trouble, I'll belt him.'

'If you'd gotten close enough.'

'Didn't figure that far ahead.'

While Hugh was in x-ray, Ruth found Sharona, sat with her for a while and added her phone number to Sharona's contacts. 'Ring me if you need anything,' she said, and watched Sharona doze. When she got back to A&E, Hugh confirmed he'd a fractured toe. Marcus, the detective, arrived with a list of follow-up questions. When he'd finished, Ruth asked: 'Have you arrested Styne?'

'He's on the operating table.'

'Handcuffed, I hope.'

'Of course.'

'You'll charge him.' A statement, not a question.

'Lots more forensics before we reach a conclusion,' the detective said and rubbed his hands together. 'I'll be in touch, Hugh.'

A doctor stitched and wrapped Hugh's head, bandaged his left ankle and fitted a short leg walking cast on his right foot. It looked like a ski boot.

'How long will I have to…?'

'Four to six weeks.'

Hugh hung onto the forearm crutches, collected painkillers and a prescription, and said he was leaving. The doctor reluctantly discharged him. 'With the bang your head got, I'd prefer to keep you under observation for twenty-four hours.'

'I'm fine. I'll rest at home.'

'Remember, get yourself to a hospital if you suffer *any* pain, dizziness, or—'

'Yeah, yeah…'

'You look identical to that guy in The Mummy,' Ruth said to Hugh on the drive home.

'Brendan Fraser?'

'No, Arnold Vosloo, *before* he turns into a human—'

'Thanks. Will Sharona be okay?'

'She's asleep. We'll visit later. Styne used chloroform to knock her out. I got a sweet taste and burning sensation at the back of my throat when I cut Sharona's ties. Chloroform inhalation also causes tremors and shortness of breath. That's why she needed water.'

'Oh.'

'Shortness of breath reminds me, where's your car?'

'Wouldn't start. It's overdue a service.'

Ruth turned into Hugh's drive, inched by his car and parked near the door. 'Remember what the doctor said. If you get blurred vision or find you're sensitive to noise, or if you find you're slurring words or…no matter what, call an ambulance. Straight away.'

'Sure.'

'That means at once.'

'Okay.' Hugh hobbled to his car and left his car key on the dashboard.

Ruth promised to collect him before teatime, and they'd visit Sharona.

The crutches were clumsy and awkward.

Hugh discarded one, used the other as a cane, and staggered upstairs for a shower. His skin still stank from the smell of stale silage. After, he powered up the mobile. Three bars. He rang his local garage. They promised to collect his car and bring a replacement.

'Key's on the dashboard,' Hugh said.

Next, he dialled Ferdia. 'I tried phoning you last night. Couldn't get through. Boy, I needed your brawn—'

'Weather caused a power outage. Half the Midlands had no reception. What did ya need muscle for?'

Hugh filled him in.

'God all feckin' mighty. That's ten degrees more stupid than anything I've ever done. Styne, eh? Goes to show, you never can tell with people. Bit of a drastic reaction over a feckin' picture, all the same. How's Sharona?'

'Bruised. In shock. She'll be okay.'

'Man, it'll take me a week to get my head around you breaking a fella's jaw.'

'And knee. You told me. Remember?'

'Didn't tell you to use a soggy shoe. Still, better to give than receive. 'Bout time you heed what I say.'

'A once-off episode. Don't want a repeat.'

'You'll be grand. If you're not living on the edge, you're taking up too much space.'

'Thanks. You in Dublin?'

'Aye. We're—'

'With Niamh?'

'Huh. The clip on your head didn't cause memory loss. Yeah. We're on the way to McDonald's. Master David wants a Happy Meal. Don't tell Ciara. Then we'll head for home. I've left messages, but her phone's turned off.'

'Maybe she's stuck in a meeting.'

'Yeah. Funny, though, she usually calls to say hello to Master...argh, you're right, I forgot, she's in the middle of feckin' appraisals. I'll try again in a while.'

MID-MORNING

RUMOURS TRAVEL AT breakneck speed in rural communities.

The activity on Styne's farm caused locals to gawk and tongues to wag. A sheep farmer watched strangers move around his neighbouring fields. He observed them use hand tools to dig through snow and assemble a tent in one area, blocking further attempts to mine juicy details. But it didn't stop the gossip. By midday, the farmer's tales had got recapped, rehashed, inflated and enlarged, spreading across the hinterland quicker than an internet virus. Conjecture increased a hundredfold when the forensic team mounted the Hitachi on a flatbed lorry and towed it away.

THE GARAGE MEN unloaded the replacement car and were winching Hugh's Lexus onto a tow truck when a hospital secretary called: They were discharging Kathleen. "Should I call a taxi, or...?"

'I'll be there in an hour.' Hugh hoped for a day's grace to organise himself. He phoned Sarah. 'If you're still free—'

'Kathleen's discharged?'

'Yeah.'

'I can make it after three.'

'Great. You've taken a load off my mind.'

'See you then,' Sarah said.

Hugh stared at the garage man securing his car onto the truck. A searing pain pierced the back of his eyes. Through blurred vision, he stumbled to the bathroom and lay over the toilet bowl, gasping. He heard the replacement car key dropping through the letterbox, but wasn't able to move. After his stomach settled, he texted Ruth the directions to his mother's house, then he pulled on a wool knit cap and went to the hospital.

KATHLEEN WAS IN the nurse's station, chatting with the staff.

She clapped her hands. 'I *told* you. I said, Hugh will be here to bring me home, didn't I? I *knew* he'd come.' Kathleen inspected the bandage and touched Hugh's face. 'What happened?'

'It's nothing, Ma.'

'Did you crash? Are—?'

'I'm okay. Honest.'

'Tsk. Who put on that dressing? I'll dress it right. Sorry for making you drive this distance. I should've called a taxi. Hope I'm not too much of a disappointment.'

'It's no distance, Ma, and you're not a disappointment. Don't say that.'

'I keep forgetting to tell you, Hugh, somebody's stolen money out of my bank account. Can you...?'

Here we go again, Hugh thought. 'I'll check into it, Ma.'

'You're the best son. Where are we going?'

'Home.'

'Good. Remind me to get you to check my bank statements. Someone's stolen money from my bank account...'

EVENING

GLOBS OF OINTMENT coated Sharona's neck.

She was half-propped up in bed, eyes inflamed, jaw bruised and swollen. Hugh sank into an armchair and stretched out. He'd forgotten the painkillers.

'Hope they'll discharge me in the morning,' Sharona said. 'Dorothy rang earlier, she's on the way.'

'I'm off duty till tomorrow night,' Ruth fluffed up the pillows. 'Call me if you want a lift.'

'Thanks. Thank you both. Again.' Sharona shuddered. 'Those eyes? I'll never forget Styne's laser eyes. No emotion. Robotic. As if the human pieces of him had…disappeared. Made my skin crawl. I kept thinking: Why me? Because of a forgery? And that room? Christ.'

'Push it out of your mind.'

'Tell that to my brain. It keeps planting images in front of me. Styne would've killed us. I thought *you* were dead, Hugh. All that blood and…you looked like something that escaped from Francis Bacon's studio. Then you blinked. Crikey. What an experience. And you tearing across the floor—'

'More a clumsy clomp,' Hugh said.'

'Oh, and the sound of you coming up the driveway? If I could, I'd have ploughed through a wall. You know in nightmares where you can't escape the boogie man? That kinda panic.'

'Must book into a gym.'

'Your leg,' Sharona said. 'You were dragging it along like Quasimodo.'

'I'm no James Bond or Jonathan Creek.'

'Stay the way you are,' Ruth said.

'When I came to,' Sharona said. 'I remembered the shock of seeing him at my door. Then I thought, had I disconnected? Or, did you catch what I was saying before Styne knocked me out? Reception is crap in parts of the house. Then I wondered if I'd even *mentioned* his name or not. Reckoned I was dead for sure.'

'Our minds play tricks to save us when we're under pressure,' Ruth said.

'So, I did say his name, and you managed to catch up with him before we got to the farmhouse?'

'Yep.'

'Why didn't you phone the cops?'

'We tried. There was no signal. The weather caused a transmitter failure. But you were in our sights all the way,' Hugh said. Ruth drove like a—'

'Dear, I came the *minute* I found out. This is *horrendous*.' Dorothy Ridgeway floated in and enveloped Sharona in a hug. 'I'll never forgive myself for getting you involved in this scandal. I can't *believe* it. Mark my words, whatever about my painting, Hattinger's will pay for this...*atrocity*. Now, tell me, have you considered a solicitor yet?'

'Err—'

'Silly me. How could you? Now listen, I'm a friend of Victor Attwood. You've heard of Victor?'

'I don't—'

'Ach, you *must've* read his cases. Finest barrister in Northern Ireland. Let me assure you, Hattinger's haven't a *clue* what'll hit them. Victor isn't nicknamed "The Rottweiler" for nowt. I'm staying in Tullamore tonight. He'll be here by lunchtime tomorrow. We'll set up a meeting with Ambrose Hattinger.'

'God, I don't—'

'Leave it to me, dear. I'm taking this as a personal affront. Hi, Hugh. Nice to see you again. I appreciated your presence last Saturday night. Who's this lady?'

'Ruth Lamero,' Hugh said. 'Ruth? Dorothy Ridgeway.'

They shook hands. 'You're a nurse,' Dorothy said.

'That's right.'

'Hah, knew it. Years as a theatre sister means I can spot good nurses a mile away.' Dorothy glanced from Ruth to Hugh and back again. 'Are ye a couple?'

'No, we're—'

'Old friends,' Ruth added.

'What does that mean?' Dorothy asked. 'You *should* be a couple. You've got the look. Go work on it.' Dorothy swished to the other side of the bed, plopped onto a chair and patted Sharona's arm. 'Now dear, sleep and don't worry, I'm here. Bye, Ruth. Bye, Hugh,' Dorothy said and turned her attention back to Sharona.

Hugh and Ruth tiptoed out.

'Who's that...*tornado*?' Ruth asked.

'The lady who had her painting stolen.'

'Wow, stupid people to pick on her,' Ruth said. 'That's the type of nurse we need to cut through red tape and put the skids under consultants.'

'Yep. Hungry?'

'I'd love a coffee.'

'Starbucks in Ganestown?'

'Great.' Ruth drove away from the hospital. 'You know what Dorothy said, us being a couple?'

'Huh-uh.'

'I thought that about you and Sharona.'

Hugh glanced across. 'You serious? Why?'

'You seem...close.'

'You're right. Close as family. One of my best friends is James Waters, Sharona's brother. A similar taste in music brought us together years ago. We've hung around ever since. I've known Sharona for nine, ten years now. Whenever she was home from college, she'd tag along to gigs with us. I see her and treat her as the little sister I never had.'

'Oh.'

In Starbucks, Hugh reached across and squeezed Ruth's hand. 'I dread to imagine the consequences if you hadn't answered your mobile.'

Ruth responded to his grip. 'I'm glad the Ganestown transmitter still worked when you rang.'

'Jesus, yeah. Me too.'

'But you'd have figured out another—'

'I was out of ideas.'

'So I was the last option, huh?'

'You were my only—'

'You'd no idea what you were getting into.' Ruth hugged herself. 'What you did? Rash. Lucky you don't have an ACL or meniscal tear.'

'I acted on reflex. You can't pick all your battles.'

'Don't remember you involved in fights at school,' Ruth said.

'I've never lifted a finger to another person until last night. And it's scary knowing I'm capable of violence, if provoked.'

'Any domesticated animal will fight in a life-or-death situation, Hugh. Was that the scariest moment in your life?'

'God, yeah, but we didn't have time to consider options. Sharona was in trouble. There's no way I'd leave her in danger.'

'One of your strengths, eh?'

'What?'

'Not backing away.'

'I'll fight my corner in the boardroom, with words and reasonable logic. I'm neither a softy nor a hardass. At different times, standing firm or conceding is the correct decision. The trick is to recognise the right instance.'

'Like with break-ups,' Ruth said.

'Exactly.'

'How are you dealing with…? I mean, it can be—'

'It wasn't a breakup. Call it what it is. I got dumped. Big difference.'

'But still, it's tough, especially with everything that's happening around you.'

'Yeah, it hurt. I thought I was an important chunk of Eilish's life. Seemed we were well-suited in most things and it's bloody painful to realise I'm not. After my initial I-don't-believe-this blowout, I expected…grief, but all I feel is relief. I know that makes me seem cold. I *want* it to be more painful. I should have a…an *incensed* reaction, but—'

'Everyone's different,' Ruth said.

'—but in hindsight, the relationship ended long before Eilish left,' Hugh added, 'and I was too close to notice. When I look back, oh, six months, even longer, there hadn't been any emotional progression. I dunno, it's possible I've been subconsciously building mental blocks. Sounds harsh, but that's how I feel. I heard what you said about leaving the pieces where they fall. I agree. If we aren't compatible, then better it ends now.'

'At times, break-ups are meant as wake-ups,' Ruth said.

'Exactly. Why hold on if it's not meant to be? Life's short. My ego got badly dented. Move on. Let go.'

'Hmm. Sometimes being strong means letting go,' Ruth said. 'You've great patience too; I've noticed you with Kathleen.'

'I'll need it.' Hugh gave a short laugh. 'At times, my patience wears thin. Ma's great. Has been, I mean, *still* is great. She's my most prized treasure. Dad died eighteen months ago. Heart attack. So we've only got each other for support. There's lots of love between us.'

'I know.' Ruth sipped the coffee. 'If your mother is your prized treasure, what's your most precious possession?'

'Material wise?' Hugh asked.

'Yeah. Stuff you can't live without. Objects of sentimental value.'

Hugh thought for a beat. 'Valued possessions? My house. Crap car. This chain my parents bought for my eighteenth birthday.' Hugh touched the gold chain he wore around his neck. 'After Dad died, I put his wedding ring on it. Haven't taken it off since.'

'That's nice.'

'And sentimental value? A lot of my belongings are valueless, but I cherish the memories and emotional attachments behind them. A concert ticket, for example, that I've kept—'

'What band?'

'Metallica,' Hugh said. 'Reading Festival, August bank holiday weekend, 2003. I was twelve. Dad brought me. We were deaf for a month afterwards. That was my first big rock concert. A weekend to remember. Several birthdays and Christmas presents rolled into one. What's important to you?'

'My family,' Ruth said. 'Health. Photos of a trip to Disneyland, and my sister's wedding for memories. Everything else is replaceable.'

'Go back ten years,' Hugh said. 'Did you imagine then how your life would be a decade later?'

'Hmm, mid-teens, the world was my oyster. I'd planned to cure all ills, save the world, travel, have a zillion friends—'

'Did you succeed?'

'I learned to lower my vision. Nowadays, I help to improve and prolong the quality of lives by easing pain. My zillion friends are a handful, stirred among hundreds of acquaintances.'

'What's the difference?'

'I've a friend who works in maternity; we call her the catcher. She says: "A friend will never lie to you and will always serve as an alibi for you." Acquaintances are people you meet in passing. Ships in the night.'

'That line came up before.'

'When we were talking about college,' Ruth said. 'You'd left by the time I—'

'Oh yeah. Hope we'll be more than passing ships this time around.'

'Why didn't we date in school?' Ruth used the spoon to gathered coffee foam from the mug.

Hugh scratched his jaw. 'Too nervous to ask. I was awkward around girls. Naïve. Didn't know what to say.'

'Didn't stop you dating that posh one, though, what was her name? Daphne? Darlene…?'

'Danielle? Danielle Mitchell?' Hugh said.

Ruth pointed a finger at him. 'That's her. Whatever happened to Danielle?'

'We were kids, friends. After Leaving Cert, she studied medicine in UCD. Haven't heard of her in years.'

'So why not me?' Ruth pressed again.

'You took off with Ray.'

'Who?'

'Ray.'

'Ray? Oh, Ray Brennan. God, I'd forgotten him. Wonder what happened to old Ray.'

'He won the lottery.'

'No way? How much?'

'Fourteen million.'

'Good God.'

'Rollover jackpot for weeks and weeks. One winner.'

'You. Are joking.'

'Yeah, I'm teasing. Ray's a carpenter, part of the diaspora. I've no idea where he is. Haven't seen him for a while.'

'Snooker,' Ruth said. 'Ray used to mitch and play snooker.'

'And got away with it, 'cos he was teacher's pet.'

'Hmm, he was a favourite all right. What're your favourite things?'

'Fighting neighbours,' Hugh said, 'pushing old-aged pensioners under buses—'

'Be serious.'

'Okay. The aroma of fresh bread and homemade pie. Birds singing. Satisfaction of a job well done. You?'

'Crisp clean sheets and pillowcases when you get home from holidays. Hmm, luxury. Who do you admire most?'

'That's easy. Nameless people like the Chernobyl clean-up workers who saved Europe from becoming a wasteland. They're the modern-day superheroes. And Red Cross volunteers who risk their lives when they go into godforsaken war-torn countries, to tend the wounded. That takes real courage.'

'Good answer. That's enough questions for one day,' Ruth yawned. "You need sleep, and I'm exhausted even before starting night duty tomorrow. Need a lift anyplace in the morning?'

'Have to go to Mullingar. Exit interview. I'll be fine.'

'Are you insured if anything happens?'

'I'll take it easy.' Sleet drummed against the café window. 'Damn this weather. Can you drop me off at the Garda barracks? I've to collect Ma's car.'

Ruth linked Hugh to the Garda station entrance.

The icy chill pressed them together. Hugh left the crutch against the wall and drew Ruth closer, curling his arms around her. His heart pounded. Ruth's arms circled Hugh's waist. She smiled and angled her head upwards. A vein pulsed at the side of her neck. The kiss hovered between them. 'Déjà vu,' she said.

'No way,' Hugh said. Their lips met for a long moment until the cold air pushed them apart.

'Can't wait for the encore.' Hugh inhaled Ruth's strawberry and vanilla essence scent.

Ruth's lips brushed his ear. 'Me too. But someplace warmer.'

'Text me when you get home,' Hugh said.

'I will. Keep safe.'

They kissed again.

Hugh shivered in the sleet. Although wet and freezing on the outside, Ruth had warmed his heart.

NIGHT

SARAH LEFT, AND Hugh settled in to watch the news. His mobile bleeped. Ruth's goodnight text. Then it rang. Malcolm McGuire's voice pierced like a soprano's high G note.

'Slow down, Malcolm. Say again?'

'Ciara's disappeared.'

'What?'

'Ferdia brought David home,' Malcolm's voice cracked, 'and they found a shoe in her driveway and the hall door unlocked.'

'Christ. That's not like—'

'I phoned her office manager. Said Ciara didn't show today. Assumed she was sick. We're…Dad's…and the other missing woman. Ferdia's contacted the police.'

'Had Ciara visitors? Maybe she's—?'

'Her car hasn't moved. I chatted to her Saturday night, a—'

'Did she give any hint—?'

'Nothing.'

'Jesus. Did she visit Charlie? Is she—?'

'No.' Malcolm blubbered. 'Dad keeps telling her not to drive in the snow. I'm wanted in Ganestown. We're at our wit's end.'

'Where's David?'

'At Ferdia's place. Can you call into Mullingar and—?'

'Of course. I'd planned to—'

'And pick up my laptop? I'll meet up and collect it off you.'

'Sure.'

'I'll be in touch. This'll destroy Dad.' Malcolm wept into the phone and cut the call.

Hugh jabbed in Ferdia's mobile number. Voicemail. Rang Eilish, then cancelled the call; she'd have got word. Tried Ferdia once more. No answer. Changed his mind about Eilish, pressed her number. Engaged. Still busy when he rang five minutes later. He wanted to assist, but he'd be useless in his present condition. And he was reluctant to leave his mother alone again.

After Kathleen settled, Hugh took painkillers, removed the head bandage and had a shower. The water helped ease pain. He redialled Eilish's mobile, left a message and went to bed. It had been a long day. The combination of tiredness and sedatives knocked him out. Later, a noise woke him. The phone hummed and vibrated on the bedside locker: A text:

Dad transferred 2 Mater Private. Suspect heart attack. No word on Ciara. Guards say disappearance is suspicious.

10

WEDNESDAY 16 JANUARY

MORNING

'LOOKS LIKE THE food's overrated.'

Adam Styne moved the nebulous mess that stuck to a blunt plastic fork like glue. He twisted his head, tried to pull himself into a comfortable position, and eyed the speaker who'd slipped around the railed curtain encircling the hospital bed. The thin mattress and hard pillows negated any relief. The cast on his leg weighed a ton.

The speaker placed a folder on the bed, settled into a chair, removed a scarf and leather gloves, pinched the sharp crease in his trouser leg and brushed away an imaginary speck. He looked at the plate of gruel and made a moue with his lips. 'Mushed up on account of...' he gestured at Styne's face.

'Who are you?' Styne stiffened in agony. Any mouth movement sent darts of pain crashing through his wired jaw and skull. Fatigued and groggy, his voice sounded slurred and slow. He stopped moving and let the wave of pain pass.

'Allister O'Brien. Your barrister.'

'I know you.' Styne attempted to avoid letting his tongue hit teeth. 'That court case with—'

'Yes. Opposite sides of the fence on that occasion. Now we're allies.'

'I asked for—'

'I'm his colleague. My experience will be more relevant if the State takes a criminal action against you.'

'I'm innocent,' Styne said. 'What experience?'

'I'm a psychiatrist *and* a barrister. I've worked in mental institutions, plus I'm qualified in forensic evaluations.'

'Mental—?'

'Yes. I represented you at your court hearing yesterday. They're transferring you to a psychiatric unit. Judge ordered you to be medically assessed.'

'What?' Styne attempted to sit up and was sorry he made the effort. 'Psychiatric unit? Where?'

'Haven't told me yet. The powers that be aren't obliged to disclose where they're *planning* to send you. They'll tell me once it's decided.'

'God damn—'

'Easy, Adam. Are you hurting? Shall I call a nurse?'

'Yes, I'm in pain. They're deliberately keeping pain medication from me.'

The barrister looked at Styne from over the top of his glasses. 'I doubt that, Adam. The rule is: first, do no harm. You're being pumped with pain breakers, and—'

'This place is…' Styne tried to talk without moving his tongue. He pointed a finger. 'I want you to sue Hugh Fallon for causing this damage. Physical and mental torture, pain, distress.'

O'Brien opened the folder, took out a pad and scribbled a note. 'All in good time. He'll be a hero for a week, while this story gets splashed across the front pages. Let him have his fifteen minutes in the spotlight. After the initial news dump and rush to judgement, other tragedies will catch the headlines. While all that plays out, we've got pressing matters to address and—'

'When will they move me?'

'Soon. Tomorrow. Or the day after.'

'What day's today?'

'Wednesday.'

'What'll happen after I'm—?'

'Assessments.'

'For what? I've done nothing wrong.'

'The State will evaluate to see if you're competent to stand trial for abduction.'

'I can explain.'

'So can I,' the barrister said. 'For now, we'll call it a trigger moment brought on by stress, and compounded by, um, activities of a staff member across the border. Temporary insanity, right?'

'I'm not insane. I—'

'Adam, insanity isn't bad. It's a protection, understand? For the moment, we'll go with temporary insanity. And you feel terrible. Right?'

The men stared at each other.

'Right,' Styne said.

'Excellent,' O'Brien smiled. 'Now, in other news, gardaí are looking into the possibility you've a connection with the disappearance of two people from the Ganestown area. They've triangulated phone grids in an attempt to determine your movements on the evenings of...' the barrister flicked back through pages of notes, 'Monday, January seventh, and Monday, January fourteenth last. They haven't found any record you were in that vicinity on the dates in question, which is good news. However, if they find a *scintilla* of DNA—'

'They won't. They can't. I wasn't there. I'm not going to a mental hos—'

'That's out of our hands, Adam. The State's entitled to assess your mentality. Detention in accordance with provisions of the Mental Health Act, is a detailed and time-consuming process. It's never done flippantly. Stringent procedures follow strict guidelines. Everybody's story, every word and document gets dissected. Once your physical wellbeing is under control, the next stage is your mental health.'

'My mental health is fine. What use are you if—?'

O'Brien held up his hand. 'Adam, you *abducted* a person.' He leaned forward. 'Entered her *home* and...' He settled back. 'It's not my job to decide if you're guilty or innocent. My task is to safeguard your rights while the State collects evidence, considers its case, and if they decide to prosecute, that you receive a fair trial and an impartial jury. My other—'

'This is a setup. Let's go to court. Let the truth come out.'

'Trials aren't about truth, Adam. My other duty is to ensure minimal custodial sentence *if* a guilty verdict is—'

'Jail? I can't—'

'*If* you're found guilty. Let's not dwell on morbid thoughts.'

'What will this assessment entail?'

'Lots of questions, starting from the year you were born. Verbal and written tests; nothing you can't handle. Like psychometric assessments for senior management positions.'

Adam hadn't time to reflect before a small, smiling, middle-aged Asian man stuck his head through the curtain gap. 'Good morning, Mr Styne. Good news. Today you learn to walk again.' He held up a pair of axillary crutches and tapped them together. 'Now, no weight bearing on your right leg for six weeks. When you come back for check-up, if I find any sign of wear on the cast, I'll be furious.'

The barrister introduced the doctor. 'Adam, Doctor Anasi. He worked in Belfast during the eighties, has a lot of experience with ah...pinning and stapling bones. He's pleased how well the operations went, and with your overall progress.'

'I am.' The surgeon pointed at Styne's face. 'They wired your upper and lower teeth, and implanted plates to bone, to give you normal eating motions in a week or so.' He snapped his teeth together to show Styne how they'd work. 'The leg, now, that was interesting. You can thank God the shattered tibia—'

The barrister held up his hand. 'I think at this juncture, medical attention might outweigh the efficacy of prayer, Doctor, hmm?'

The doctor got the message. 'Six months, you'll be almost perfect.'

Allister O'Brien stood, fixed the cashmere scarf around his neck. 'Looks like you've a busy morning ahead, Adam, and so have I. Oh, I've been in contact with Madeline—'

Styne's eyes reduced to slits. 'What's Madeline got to do—?'

The doctor left the crutches aside and stepped outside the curtain.

'She'll be a witness to your mental health. Like it or not, she gets questioned too.'

'Why?'

'About living with you for fifteen, sixteen years. Going forward, it'll be useful to learn what Mrs Styne will say, so I suggested either a visit—'

'She didn't. I don't expect her to.'

'—or write. She chose to write.' The barrister took an envelope from his pocket and placed it on the bedside locker. 'Read and fill me in. It's important we ascertain your wife's um, emotional state. Whether she's a friend or foe.'

'She won't have anything good to say. Are the galleries open?'

'Closed for the moment.'

'Make sure they stay that way until I get back.'

'Again, that's out of my hands, Adam. But...' O'Brien shrugged, 'it's feasible somebody may buy them out.'

'What do you mean? Who'd—?'

'Someone might make a generous cash settlement. Oh, I don't know, I'm plucking a name from the air here, Dorothy Ridgeway perhaps?'

'What are you saying?'

'Just that if a saviour offered a cash deal, I'd say Hattinger's might take it. After the last few days, it would help cushion the shock, and all that.'

'But—'

'Adam, I'm speculating. I'm hearing rumours. At the moment, I can neither substantiate nor refute factoids. If you wish, I'll ask on your behalf.'

'Get me into court. Put me in the witness box. I'll show—'

The barrister frowned. 'No.'

'What?'

O'Brien played with his shirt cuff. 'I'd consider that reckless, Adam.'

'Why?'

'Three reasons. One, you don't need to. At present, there's no forensic evidence pointing at you for the disappearances of...'

'Don't know anything about those two women,' Styne said.

The barrister stared at his client. 'Who mentioned two women?'

Styne broke eye contact.

'Perhaps you read some reports,' the barrister continued. 'Whatever. As I was saying, there's no indication of your involvement in either Lord or McGuire's

disappearances. Suspicion isn't proof, and without proof…'
he shrugged. 'No evidence usually equals acquittal.'

'Usually? What do you—?'

'Circumstantial evidence generally means nothing in a
trial, Adam; it's a tiny speck on one side, stacked up against
the presumption of innocence on the other. Until opposing
council starts throwing little chunks onto their side of the
scale. Fibres, blood specks, body fluids, a fingerprint…all
these pieces acts as a counterbalance against our story. Add
enough of them together and they can metaphorically tip
the scales.'

'There's nothing to tip.'

'Excellent. Yet people *have* got convicted solely on the
weight of circumstantial evidence, Adam. For instance, if
work and home computers revealed—'

'I said, there's nothing to reveal.' What's the second
reason?'

'Let me finish my first reason, Adam. We've no idea
what evidence will be found on the bodies. We'll have to
wait for those results, but sometimes, the best clues come
from the victims. Now, my second point. If there *is* a court
case, it'll be twelve, eighteen months away. By then, the
emotional heat will have abated, and it's *my* job to ensure
certain facts get suppressed. Eighteen months is a long
time. Memories fade and thankfully the public have a short
recollection span. Witnesses become unreliable, evidence
becomes stale and victims get lost in the shuffle.'

'And the third?'

'The third's to do with perception. You're innocent so
far in the eyes of the law, but in the court of public opinion
most jurors make up their minds after the opening
statements. In this case, you'd be deemed guilty even before
a trial starts. After all, why would our *State* spend a fortune
building a case against an innocent man? Hmm?'

'Let them—'

'It's Miss Waters' *abduction*, Adam.' The barrister leaned over the bed again. 'You'd get crucified on cross-examination. And your manner…well, jurors would pick up on your resistance and reluctance to engage. Those that haven't already made up their minds, won't listen to the *man* on trial, they'd see a predator.'

'So, I'm—'

'Innocent until proven guilty. And it's *my* job to create doubt. Obfuscate. Leave the jury psychology to me.'

Styne glared at O'Brien. 'I want to go on the stand and refute all the lies—'

'No.' O'Brien stared back. 'There's no such thing as lies, Adam, only greater or lesser degrees of interpretation and misunderstanding.'

'Ahem.' The surgeon peeked around the curtain.

O'Brien straightened. 'Well, I'm off. Defence counsel never rests. Meantime, good luck with your physio.'

'I need my phone. Newspapers. Television—'

O'Brien buttoned his coat. 'Gardaí are withholding your mobile as evidence, Adam, and the media is full of bad news. Trust me, you don't want to see, hear or read it. Concentrate on getting well.' He picked up the folder.

'Wait.' Styne pasted a phoney smile. Beads of sweat shone on his forehead. 'This assessment? What can I expect?'

O'Brien held up a finger to the doctor. 'One moment, please,' and turned towards Styne. 'Whoever killed those women must be angry, Adam. Angry with himself. Angry with…everyone. Whatever his motives were for doing this, be it revenge or retribution, it's um…traumatic. Imagine that *tension*, that *weight*. Impossible to suppress. *Especially* difficult to conceal from professional psychiatrists. So, when gardaí apprehend that person, if I were his barrister,

I'd be telling him it's important, nay, *vital*, to show the authorities how cool, calm and collected he is. Nothing is stressing him, aside from finding himself locked up for no reason. And amenable too; every word calibrated to convey an *eagerness* to help get this mess sorted, and resume his life. I'd suggest submissive, even. Yes sir, yes sir, three bags full, sir. Less defiance, more compliance. Get it?'

'Yes. But I want more morphine. I'll telling you the doctors are deliberately—'

'Adam, I don't mean to trivialise your picayunish bias, but staff are doing everything to alleviate your pain. As I said, everything is documented. We're at their mercy at present,' O'Brien tucked the folder under his arm, 'but when you get to your next destination, a little soft-pedalling on your part won't do any harm. I appreciate answering questions you consider irrelevant is not your natural...metier, but this is not a business environment, so no heroics. Understand?'

'Yes. What are you going to do?'

O'Brien's mouth twisted into a lob-sided grin and he slipped on his gloves. 'What I do when I'm dealing from a position of weakness. Feign strength. Thank you for the questions, Adam. I welcome them as a base for further discussions. We'll talk again soon.'

MID-MORNING

HUGH COLLECTED DOLE money at Ganestown's post office, bought a smartphone, transferred the contact numbers from his company mobile, and drove to Mullingar.

McGuire's customers and staff huddled in groups, debating in subdued murmurs how they'd react if a family member went missing, thankful they could express their views from a distance and didn't have to go through McGuire's ordeal.

Hugh shuffled upstairs to collect Malcolm's laptop.

'Hugh?'

He spun around. Brendan Enright stood behind him. 'Awful news 'bout Ciara.'

'Terrible. I can't believe it either.'

'What happened to your foot?'

'Aw, got into a fight.'

'You? Hah. Good one. I bet you fell. Um, the accountant, Philip Waldron, told me yesterday...' Brendan used air quotes '...to "inform you" that you've been, err, let go. We can't afford...I'm on the van now.'

'Isn't he man enough to tell me himself? I haven't even met him. Who's filling your current role?'

'That'll be me too. Sorry.'

'Not your fault.'

'Don't know how I'll get time to do deliveries as well as everything else.' Brendan held out his hand and touched his thumb and forefinger together. 'Yesterday, I was this close to resigning. I've let customers down. I *hate* when logistics...' His voice dropped. 'We all want the store to do well, but Philip's fanning the flames, telling people we're gonna get sold.'

'I hope you'll stick with it,' Hugh said. 'Charlie's spent a lifetime in this business. He needs loyal staff around him now more than ever. He'd hate you to leave.'

'Thanks for the vote of confidence. We'll see what pans out.'

ACROSS TOWN AT Pharma-Continental, Hugh watched a former colleague walk away from the building, dragging her feet through the snow, labouring to propel herself forward, the weight of unemployment heavy on bowed shoulders.

Ferdia's Merc wasn't in the car park.

Hugh left a box of folders, the company laptop and mobile phone at reception. Before he got to the canteen, a discord of voices flooded out, ricocheting around the corridor. Staff strove to adjust, with the inevitability of their situation slowly sinking in. Each person wanted to express their frustration with people who understood their predicament.

'I got pissed last weekend. That's how much I've planned *my* future.'

'Me too. Unemployment was less scary from the bottom of my third wine bottle.'

'Why am I finding it so hard to tell people I'm out on my ear?' a third asked. 'I've paid a *fortune* in tax, so why do I get the sense I'm a blight on society?'

'Yeah. I'm avoiding friends. I *hate* the effect *my* redundancy has on *them*. And sympathy? Being unemployed makes people see you in a different light; you're targeted as a failure.'

'Is it just me or have you noticed how they talk strange too? Like, *at* you. And louder, as if you've become a lesser person. Dumber.'

Hugh asked the group, 'You job hunting?'

'Yeah, I applied for a job as a shelf packer in Tesco,' a middle-aged man said. 'And I'd an interview at McDonald's last Monday. Got placed on a panel. If I get the job, I've to smile and say "would you like fries with that?" '

'I'm getting involved in the agribusiness,' a woman spoke up. 'Imagine that? No, me neither. My husband's a farmer. From power suits to a piggery. How 'bout you, Hugh?'

'I got a temporary van-driving stroke delivery gig.'

'You've lots of management experience. You'll pick up work, easy. And Eilish has a good job.'

Hugh shifted in the seat.

'I've fixed stuff in my apartment and painted walls,' Ronan Lambe said. 'Another week I'll be climbing them. I've scratched Sky sports. Could sell a kidney, I suppose. In the welfare office, a woman told me that if she gets peckish at night, she can't make a sandwich for herself, 'cos her children would go hungry. When you have to count slices of bread, dude, that's rough. Can't wait to see Ganestown in the rear-view mirror on my way outta this poxy place. This town is dead to me.'

'Me too,' another voice chimed in. 'I've cancelled my gym membership. Read someplace that if you walk up and down standard stairs eighty times, you lose three hundred calories.'

'Huh. How many calories will I lose if I plant my foot eighty times in Wiseman's backside, dude?'

Hugh fiddled with car keys. If HR stall me much longer, I'll leave, he thought. This exit interview is minor compared to Ma. If they'd give me the redundancy cheque, I'd go now.

After one o'clock, an HR person came to collect Hugh. 'Files? Laptop? Mobile?' she asked.

'At reception,' Hugh said.

She checked, then walked ahead of him to the boardroom. The sharp clip-clop of heels on tiles acted as a conversation blocker.

Denis Wiseman and another man had entrenched themselves in the boardroom, barricaded behind a laager of manuals and files.

Denis waved to a chair. He gripped a coffee mug in both hands, manufactured a concerned frown, and read from a typed sheet. 'I want you to understand we *do* recognise the impact this streamline will have on employees, their families and the region. I take full responsibility…'

No, you don't, Hugh felt like saying.

'...but the unthinkable has become the inevitable. Demand for our products hasn't grown in line with expectations, due to the competitive market in which we operate, making our existing business model unsustainable. Therefore, in response to tough trade conditions...'

Here comes the hand-waving speech, Hugh thought, and tuned out, letting the words, gestures and bland business balderdash wash over him.

'...faced with significant financial challenges...management team has developed a plan...restore efficiency...job losses...no option...'

After he'd delivered the same weasel words to dozens of staff, Denis had tweaked the script into a well-rehearsed routine he should have been able to rattle off by rote, but still needed to have the words written. When he placed the mug back on the desk, Hugh refocused.

'...hard to let traditional attitudes go. We spent years building beliefs, developing habits that are *comfortable*. Similar to a person who has'—Denis scratched his chin— 'worn glasses for so long, they forget they're on.'

This was Hugh's opportunity to say his piece, but he let the silence build.

The second man kept his face buried in an iPad screen. The woman who'd collected him, scribbled an illegible scrawl on an A4 notepad, underlining and circling key words as if her life depended on it. Not one of the troika had made eye contact with Hugh or called him by his name.

'Well, ahem, I'm confident that displaced workers will secure new jobs,' Denis continued. 'Despite the discomfort downscaling evokes, I expect workers with your skillset will have no problem finding employment.' He ran out of breath.

Hugh weighed up options. Will I cut the crap, he thought, and tell him I accept and understand the reasons for redundancy, but reduced headcounts across the board in a stagnant economy is restrictive. Should I tell him cost cuts need balancing with progressive strategies and investment, to gain momentum on the upswing? That there'll be an efficiency backlash, because his slash-and-cut policy is too severe, and will diminish the company's capacity for growth when rural Ireland finally recovers from the worst economic crunch in a century. Should I give him short-term answers? Medium-term solutions? Long-term remedies? Would he listen? Did he care? Does my opinion matter? Hugh studied Wiseman's face and said nothing.

Wiseman harrumphed again. 'With these changes, indications are we'll be on the road to recovery by end of the next quarter—'

'I'm sure you've considered all options and courses of action.' Hugh stood and fastened his jacket.

Wiseman handed him an envelope. 'You'll find the, ahh, relevant documents, plus your redundancy...Ferdia and HR will triangulate with you next week regarding any questions you have. Oh, and we're allowing you to keep your mobile number, so your contacts and friends can get hold of you.'

'Thanks.'

'No. Thank *you*. I'm confident if you stay liquid, you'll find a similar position—'

'The expression is "stay fluid", Denis.' Hugh moved, and the Human Resources duo jostled to thrust business cards at him.

Four years of hard work erased, just like that. Hugh said goodbye to everyone in the canteen. They promised to meet up, knowing they wouldn't. At least, he had money now to pay for car repairs and his mother's carer.

AFTERNOON

ADAM,

Forty-eight hours since the guards knocked on the door, and now your barrister wants to know if I'm on your side?

Yes, I know you think I haven't got the level of introspective awareness or confidence to gather my thoughts, and the shock of this will send me to therapy. Well, I've news for you: I'm stronger than you realise. This is easy to write because I've carved the words in my brain for years. My one regret is that I never had the courage to tell you face-to-face. Now, I don't need to.

Remember Trinity College, Thursday, May 13, 1999? Probably not. The day you lifted a weight from my shoulders. Me, insecure, low self-image, no self-esteem and overweight, panicking about exams. I couldn't believe you'd even bother talking to me. Oh, I'd noticed you around, we all did; the girls had a crush on you. Imagine my surprise when you asked me to go to the cinema. You asked me what I wanted to see, but we went to a movie *you* picked, and I was happy being with you.

Why'd you choose me, Adam? Out of all the other girls? I'm sure I didn't represent the most fun. Did I have a mark saying: 'Pick me?' Did I seem that desperate? Insecure? Lonely? Did you size me up and think, 'this is her. This is the one I can bend and manipulate'? Thinking back, I know you didn't home in on the more attractive girls because I fitted whatever profile you'd visualised. I was the patsy. You zeroed in on my weak spots, my vulnerabilities, and exploited them. You invaded my world. Yes, invaded. I'm from planet earth, you're from planet Adam, and everything revolves around you. And I let it happen because I desperately needed your approval. When did you decide what kind of magic spell to weave? You know, the spell you cast around, asking advice, making it appear you were getting to know my family and forming a bond? Was it after

I disclosed my innermost thoughts and dreams to you? Did we inadvertently tell you what to become, so you could hide who you are while erecting this new persona of being our saviour? Congratulations, Adam, you fooled us all, and influenced my every waking thought. You learned to mimic the emotions I expected in certain situations, figured out what I was looking for, and morphed into a perfect being.

I never knew the real you until the day we got married. Within hours of saying 'I do', I witnessed your grooming by seduction change to ensnaring by menace and threat. Overnight, the weight you'd lifted off my shoulders got replaced by an iceberg of anxiety. You turned my faith for the future, into fear, and our home into a prison. I spent my days trying to maintain a smile, and my nights alone, crying. I stopped laughing.

Oh, the signs were there, but I wanted to believe everything would be fine. God, I was so wrong. You've no idea how often I contemplated suicide. I spent years going through the trauma of self-doubt and introspection until I realised I wasn't responsible for your mental abuse. Paris was a blessed relief. Of course, I knew the idea was to prevent me from building family opposition to a number of your business decisions, but actually, it suited me to be out from under your control, and not have to live in the constant spotlight of intimidation. It gave me space, freedom to do what I wanted, and it helped quell my fear of ending up useless.

On the positive side, I can now come home, knowing the house will be empty. I won't have to endure being criticised under your guise of being supportive or undergo further erosion to any sense of worth you've left me. My cooking, for example, which you said you loved, suddenly became garbage. Then, my dress style, which you'd complimented me on, became 'you look like a whore'. I'm ashamed to say I let you dictate how I presented myself at functions, wearing clothes you'd picked out. God, just typing this makes me cringe; how could I have let you decide what I *wore*? Then, your criticism of my paintings, my family, my life. Why'd you marry me if you hated us so much? It's taken a long time to get into my brain that you <u>Just. Don't. Like. Us.</u> Your words were sharp weapons, countering, discounting, blaming, judging and condemning. You undermined, threatened, commanded and denied. Everyone was wrong. Except you.

How did the man I couldn't resist become the monster who wouldn't let me go? You used your social image as a skin to hide behind. Ambrose was in awe of your business acumen, but he didn't have to live with you. I genuinely thought I was going crazy. You'd say something, and when I'd question it, you'd deny ever saying it. I've often asked myself 'did I hear those words, or imagine them?'

I stood by you when you needed me because I loved and feared you in equal measures. You recognised that flaw and used it to break me even more, attacking everything that meant anything to me. You were quick to pick up on patterns of behaviour, anything that gave you an edge, a toehold into my mind, and used it against me. You do it with everyone. You trapped me with your plausible reasonableness and brow furrowing fake concern, feeding me promises I craved to believe. You'd an ability to speak sentences with two meanings: one for me and one for everyone else in the room, and it's taken me nearly two decades to understand what you were doing. Controlling. You were right. I was wrong. *Your* sense of humour was normal. *You* weren't emotionally abusing me, it was *my* doing because I was too sensitive. *My* concerns never got dealt with, because yours were foremost.

You're such a bastard, Adam.

Living with you has been comparable to tiptoeing through landmines, awaiting the inevitable explosion. And wow, could you ignite. Over stupid things. I got blamed, and you'd argue nonstop until I'd apologise for things that weren't my doing to begin with. Again, bigger fool me for giving in, but your emotional blackmail and intimidation drained me. You told me I was incompetent, helpless and would be useless without you. You made me feel worthless. I wasn't capable of running an art showroom in Tullamore and my paintings were terrible.

We'll see.

I'm so angry at having to change my life, even though you're no longer, and never again will be part of it. Angry at what you've put us through, and we're hearing from strangers what you've done. Angry with myself that I took so long to realise we were all accessories in your life. I must be a glutton for punishment. Most people who get involved with a malignant narcissist, eventually break away, because to survive, they must. Why didn't I? That's the question I keep asking myself, and I've no answer. Fear? Maybe. Acceptance? Probably. Terror of your reprisals? Absolutely. Everyone should have freedom of choice, however, you removed my ability to make any. I'll never be the person I once was because you made me a victim. Right now, I feel like a shattered mirror that's glued back together. It'll never portray a perfect image, but someday it'll turn into a beautiful mosaic stained glass; flawed and distorted—yes, thanks to you—yet sparkling and unique.

I've spent my life with you saying 'yes' when I meant 'no'. From today, that changes. Whatever splinters of me remain intact, I'm taking back control of the life you sabotaged. #MeToo. I'll heal, once I don't have to put up with you shoving your manipulative opinions down my throat.

Whatever my feelings for you are, Adam, I can't get my head around the fact you're now branded a kidnapper. I've been guilty of naivety, and I know you're an egotistical, controlling asshole, but I couldn't be so gullible to live with somebody for that length of time, and not know they're capable of abduction? Could I? Surely your charismatic camouflage hasn't slipped that far? I hope and pray there's an explanation, or is that saying more about my mental state than yours? For what it's worth, part of me can't imagine any human could be capable of doing the things you're charged with, but if what the media says is true, then I'm glad you're caught, and I hope you burn in hell. Either way, guilty or innocent, we're finished.

Madeline

EVENING

HUGH LODGED THE redundancy cheque and spent the drive back to Ganestown making phone calls.

'Detectives aren't treating Ciara as a missing person.' Malcolm's voice sounded cowed. 'Gardaí keep saying it's suspicious, but—'

'What? Why? That's...It's *more* than suspicious. She's—'

'I know, and they're listening to me, but they won't interfere in case there's an innocent explanation, and she shows up.'

'And how long's that going to—?'

'Forty-eight hours.'

'Dear Christ. What can I do to help?'

'Were you in Mullingar?'

'Yeah. I have your laptop.'

'Can I pick it up? I'll meet you in Ganestown Hotel.'

'Half an hour.' Hugh dialled Ruth next.

'I'm here with Sharona,' Ruth said. 'She'd forgotten her house keys got locked inside when Styne pulled the door closed, so we contacted a locksmith. Took *ages* to replace the locks. Her mobile was under the stairs. Still worked once she put the bits back together. Then we cooked. I'm fed for the night shift.'

'Can we organise dinner too when you're off night duty?' Hugh asked

'Ooh, lovely. I'm on nights up to and including Friday.'

'So Saturday's okay?'

'Saturday night's excellent.'

'What time?'

'Eight?'

'Great,' Hugh said. 'Why don't I cook? I've a family recipe, handed down for generations...Jesus, what have I said? 'Me' and 'cook' shouldn't be in the same sentence. That was a rush of blood.'

'Too late. You've committed. I accept. No pressure, but I'm—your favourite word—a terrific cook.'

'And modest,' Hugh said.

Ruth laughed. 'Better believe it. I'll bring wine. How'd your day go?'

'Busy tying up loose ends.'

'Any vertigo?'

'No. How's Sharona?'

'Well on the mend, but the news on Ciara McGuire has upset her.'

'We both know Ciara. Can't understand how or why she'd disappear. It's not like her to go AWOL without letting—'

'When I get into work, I'll check if she got admitted to any of the Midland hospitals. Perhaps there was an accident. A car crash. This weather...'

'Car's still at home, unless she borrowed one,' Hugh said. 'I don't want to hear she's hurt, but it would be a relief to know she's safe.'

'I've gotta go, Hugh. See you Saturday. Meantime, phone, if you want.'

'I want. I'll call tomorrow.'

'Good. Hold on. Sharona wants a word.'

Hugh overheard the women murmur, then Sharona took the mobile. 'It's all over social media about Ciara. Jesus. It *can't* be true. Is it? Why would...? I mean...God. Where could...? How? It's...Aw, Jesus.'

'I can't understand either. Hope it's—'

'I met her a couple of times when I was with Malcolm. She went out of her way to be nice and make me feel at ease. And poor David? I can't imagine the agony Charlie and Malcolm are facing. I want to phone them, but I feel...helpless.'

'Me too,' Hugh said. 'I phoned Malcolm a few minutes ago. There's no update. All we can do is wait. And pray for good news. I expect Ciara met friends, and they've taken off, on impulse. She'll appear in a few days, laughing at us for causing a fuss.'

'Ciara never struck me as...yeah, hope you're right.'

'Hmm. Ruth said you're well improved.'

'Bit shaky. Like after a week with flu. Dorothy arrived back to the hospital before breakfast. Gave me a list of friends who want their artwork appraised. Imagine that? Me? An appraiser?'

'Nice work.'

'I'm not in an *academic* position to evaluate other people's art. There's a world of difference between a lucky break and getting hyped as an appraiser. I'd have to enrol in refresher courses, get back into study and research.'

'That shouldn't be an issue.'

'Part of me wants to leave everything associated with this episode behind, but…Oh, remember the chat we were having before Styne called?'

'No.'

'I'd started to tell you something weird is happening with my emails—'

'Oh, yeah.'

'I think I was hacked.'

'What? How? By Who?'

'No idea. And I could be wrong, but—'

'I'll pop over in a while and we'll figure it out. Is it possible you've made—?'

'Don't think so.'

'Okay. See you in a bit.' Hugh pressed Ferdia's number.

'Rough day,' Ferdia said, 'Where're you?'

'On the outskirts of Ganestown.'

'Did you have the exit interview?'

'Yeah.'

'I'm home now, but I've to go out later. Drop in for a chat.'

Malcolm snatched the laptop case from Hugh's hand. 'Thanks. This waiting's the worst thing ever.'

'How's Charlie?'

'He's kept in. Minor stroke. Stress can cause awful harm. Doctor's hopeful he'll have no long-term effects. Listen, I've to head out to Ciara's place. I need to organise a search. Err, I forgot my wallet. Can I borrow cash?'

'Sure. How much?'

'Three, four hundred?'

'Four hun—?'

'I've no idea when I'll get home.'

Hugh frowned. 'I don't carry cash. I'll go to the ATM and see what it'll let me withdraw.'

'I'll go with you. Save you coming back here…'

Ferdia looked worn-out.

Raw emotion showed on his gaunt, unshaven face, eyes underlined with black circles, shoulders slumped in grief. 'You missed Master David's bedtime story,' he said to Hugh. A timber fire blazed in the hearth; the flickering flames casting shadows over the drowsy, curled figure on the couch. Ferdia stroked David's cheek, his touch light as a snowflake's kiss. 'Say night-night to Hugh, Master David.'

'One more story, Uncle Ferdi.'

'It's way beyond bedtime.' Ferdia lifted David onto his shoulder. 'We'll read tomorrow.'

'Will Mammy be home tomorrow?'

A coughing bout gave Ferdia a few seconds. 'I'd say she'll be home by the time you wake.'

'Why did she leave and not tell me?' Tear tracks glistened on David's cheeks. 'Mammy *always* tells me where she's going.'

'I'll be heading out soon to bring her back.'

'Promise?' David tugged Ferdia's sleeve, pulling the pledge from him.

'I promise.'

'If you know where she is—'

'Mammy got delayed, that's all. She thought she'd get home in time to tuck you in. Hold tight now.' Ferdia tramped upstairs.

'Is she stuck in snow? What if—'

'Nah. She'll be fine.'

'Uncle Ferdi?'

'Hmm?'

'I'll go too. I'll call her. I can shout really, really loud.'

'I know. But its best you get sleep, Master David.'

'Does she know I'm here with you? Mammy might…might be at home now, calling me, and…'

Hugh gazed into the flames.

Ferdia's heavy footsteps stomped downstairs, and he threw more logs on the fire. 'Feckin' madness that cops don't want to get involved in a search before forty-eight hours.'

'Especially when they're saying it's suspicious,' Hugh said.

'They say that about every case. Lots of gardaí around earlier, not too many an hour ago. Feckin' cutbacks.'

'Malcolm's gone out to Drumraney. He'll organise it,' Hugh said.

Ferdia cracked his knuckles. 'I'm guessing Ciara's nowhere local.' Ferdia handed Hugh a box full of loose photos. 'Master David wanted to see himself as a baby.'

Hugh fanned the snaps. David's baptism; the baby doll-sized in Ferdia's big hands. Ciara, laughing at the camera. Charlie, proud as a peacock, smiling in the background. Older, dog-eared black and white pictures: Ciara at Eilish's tenth birthday party. On holidays together in Tenerife. A weekend in London.

'How'd the meeting go? Sorry I wasn't there for you.'

'Director Wiseman couldn't wait to get rid of me.'

'Director, huh. A title given, not always earned. Fella's all box and no biscuits. Light on people skills, but heavy on connections. That's what counts.'

'Dished out business cards like—'

'Holy water in Lourdes?'

'—confetti at a wedding, but yeah. Glad I didn't bother preparing a speech from the dock.'

'Anything else I missed?'

'Denis said you'd "triangulate" with me.'

'Jaysus. That's his word of the week. Said it half-a-dozen times over the last few days. Any word from Eil—?'

'No.'

'Huh. Talked to her earlier, but she said nothing 'bout, you know…'

'Good.'

'Aye. Anyhow, I've a bit of business to sort out in Dublin. Babysitter should be here in a few minutes.'

Ferdia reclined like a cat in sleep mode; relaxed but ready to explode at the slightest sound. Waves of energy, similar to heat haze, radiated off him. His arm sinews writhed, biceps jumped and bulged, threatening to rip his shirt. Hugh tried to draw him into conversation, but the glum giant withdrew into his own private limbo, bottling grief, face hard as teak. They sat in silence, staring at silhouettes the flames threw on the walls and ceiling, loath to break vigil, hoping for the best, fearing the worst, and powerless to act in the interim. The doorbell chimed. Ferdia propelled himself from the armchair and grabbed a briefcase. 'There's the babysitter. We'll have news on Ciara's whereabouts soon.'

RUTH HAD LEFT when Hugh reached Sharona's house.

A tawny tabby stepped into the hallway, swishing her tail in the air.

'Say hi to Cleopatra,' Sharona said. 'She belongs to a neighbour, but calls in for titbits.'

The cat inspected Hugh and ambled off.

'Come in and have a taste of what we cooked earlier, to demonstrate the standard that's expected Saturday night.'

'God, word travels fast.'

Sharona grinned. 'Ruth left floating on air. You've made an impression.' The smile waned. 'She told me about your mother. And Eilish.'

'Yeah, she's going through a similar process with her dad.'

'Anything further on Ciara?'

'No news.'

They moved to the kitchen. A dish with lavender oil and spiced berries sat on a warm radiator, infusing the area with its fragrant scent.

'I can't fathom it out,' Sharona shook her head. 'Dear Jesus, why—?'

'No idea. There's a good possibility it's all a crazy mix-up. Ferdia believes she'll be back tonight.'

'Hope and pray he's right.' Sharona withdrew a casserole dish from the oven.

'What's the problem with your emails?' Hugh asked.

'Eat first. I'd imagined it was an error, a glitch. I assumed…The thing is, I didn't take my laptop to Belfast, and when I got home and logged on, I noticed the emails I'd received since last Friday weren't in "bold." Somebody read my mails and didn't bother, or forgot to click the "mark as unread" button.'

'You didn't check your emails anyplace while you were away?' Hugh tucked into the leftovers.

'Didn't have time.'

'How could somebody get your password?'

'I've different passwords. I don't keep them under lock and key. They're in my purse, written on a scrap of paper.'

'But if you got hacked, it means—'

'Malcolm maybe? He had loads of opportunities.'

Hugh blinked at her. 'I can't imagine him rummaging through your handbag for passwords. That's criminal.'

'I can't see it either. Wouldn't put it past Milo Brady, though.'

'Milo? Yeah.'

'Remember, I said it's as if he's stalking me? Lately, no matter where I am, he turns up. Feels like I'm in a locked cage, chased by a dog.'

'Two different things, Sharona. Even if your email…it might be a random hack. Change the password.'

'Right. More than likely I'm over emotional after the last few days. But…No, that's too weird.'

'What?'

'I got punctured twice outside McGuire's. I mean, could it have been on purpose?'

'Yeah, too weird.' Hugh polished off the food and sat back.

'But, see, the thing is, Milo—'

'I don't like him either, Sharona, but I'd say you're judging the man wrong.'

'You reckon?' Sharona said.

'It may be a glitch, or else you're spot on, and your laptop's breached. A guy I know, Ronan Lambe, is a computer whiz. He'll know if your account has been accessed. Or not. I'll make a call.' Hugh left a message on Ronan's voicemail.

'And meantime?' Sharona asked.

'Check your bank account and credit card activity. Leave this computer idle 'til Ronan calls. If it's hacked, best not let the person cop on he or she's got rumbled.'

'Jesus, I've just remembered something else.'

'Go on.'

'A few weeks ago, Malcolm and me were in a pub. I went to the loo, and when I came back, Malcolm was at the bar buying a drink for Milo, who, as usual, leeched onto us. I'd left my handbag on the bench, and I swear he was rifling through it, but I wasn't sure and you can't accuse—'

'No.'

'I asked him what he was doing, and he said the bag had fallen and he'd picked it up. No big deal, right?'

'Right.'

'But…'

'Hmm.'

'Except, with Milo…'

'Yeah. See what Ronan says,' Hugh said. 'A day or two. Patience is a virtue.'

'And a vice. So, I wait?'

'Yep. You'll get your chance.'

'If I'm right, I want my pound of flesh. Then I'll decide what to do with my life. Have to get back to reality.'

Hugh's mobile beeped, and he read Malcolm's text:

> Detectives are questioning a man
> named Adam Styne about Ciara's
> disappearance.

'What the…?' Hugh showed Sharona the message.

They read the text together.

Sharona's face turned pasty. 'Jesus! How can that be? Oh. My. God. That's crazy. Ohmygod.' She put a hand to her mouth. 'I'm gonna get sick. Why the…? He kidnapped me for, I don't know, some weird revenge thing 'cos I hurt his business reputation. But Ciara? I don't get this. Crikey. They must've found evidence, or…Jesus.'

'Makes sense,' Hugh said. 'Styne abducted you. It's logical that he's interrogated on other missing persons. Doesn't mean he has anything to do with their disappearances, but detectives need to eliminate him as a suspect. Also means so long as Styne's name is in the spotlight, you're linked to him. What'd you say about getting back to reality? Whatever happens from here on, your life has changed.'

'Then we're both connected because you rescued me. *Both* our lives will change. Forever.'

NIGHT

THE LONGER FERDIA thought, the more sense it made. Dessie Dolan snatched Ciara and was using her as a bargaining chip to ensure Charlie didn't renege on Malcolm's debt.

Fuelled by conviction, Ferdia turned onto O'Connell Street, eyes glued for breaks in the stop-start traffic. Nobody on planet earth would stop him taking Ciara home to Master David. He willed himself to stay objective, but it wasn't working. Cold fury made his blood boil. He circled the Garden of Remembrance. Twice.

No parking space.

He shot up Gardiner Row, down Great Denmark Street and swung into Temple Street. A steel barrier blocked the Lidl car park entrance. He retraced his path, spotted a space in Nerney Court, and tucked the Merc between a Bedford truck and a Honda Accord. Swallowing a mouthful of antacid liquid, he checked the bulging A4 size envelope was in the briefcase and left it there for protection against the elements. He lit a cigarette, grabbed the case, and trekked back towards the supermarket.

Sleet and snow covered the ground in crusted slush. A skin-numbing wind, sharp as glass splinters, whipped along Temple Street, sweeping up fast food litter. Fog clung to the streets like a grey blanket, and the whole graffiti-ridden area looked derelict, apart from a bony cat rooting through a burst bin bag.

Ferdia glanced at the parked cars. A taxi, cleared of snow, fumes floating from its exhaust, stood out from the other ice-encrusted cars. His phone hummed as he watched a shadow shift around in the taxi. He was being watched. Ferdia crossed the street and rapped on the driver's window. The glass slid down, and the burned grassy smell of marijuana hit Ferdia's face.

'Whaddaya want?' The driver sniffed and rubbed a fingerless glove across his runny nose.

'You Dessie?' Ferdia bent and peered in at the small man, thin as a heroin addict.

'Who's askin'?'

'I've a package for him.'

'I'll deliver it. Where's McGuire?'

'Where you put him. In intensive care.'

'Defuk are you?'

'Postman Pat.'

'Let's see it.'

'What?'

The driver leaned towards the window. 'You tick or wha? Dosh. Dough. Moolah. Cheese.' He rubbed his forefinger and thumb together. 'Flash de cash.'

Ferdia's stare searched the interior. No Ciara. He flicked the cigarette butt away. Sparks flared as it scudded along the footpath.

The driver held out a gloved fist. 'Gimme money.'

'Gimme receipt.'

The driver eyeballed Ferdia and sucked his teeth. 'Funny man. Fifteen gran'.' He tapped the dashboard. 'Haven't got all nigh'. Cash on de dash.'

'Where's Ciara?' Ferdia asked.

'Wha?'

'Ciara McGuire. Where is she?'

'Dafuk ya onabout? Cash. Now.'

Fast as a striking rattlesnake, Ferdia reached in, grabbed the scrawny neck and pulled the driver's face out the open window. 'Where's. Ciara. McGuire?' His gruff growl resembled two rough surfaces grinding together. The man gagged. Behind him, Ferdia heard the heavy thunk of a jeep door closing.

Then another.

And a third.

Feck.

Ferdia released his grip, opened the briefcase and tossed an envelope onto the driver's lap. 'There ya go. Debt paid. Slán.' He wandered around the front of the car, memorised the number plate.

'Oi.'

Ferdia strolled on, wondering if he'd get time to get the credit card knife from his wallet. Not that it would be much good.

'Oi, mister.'

Ferdia felt his neck tingle, a presage to violence. He twisted his body around but kept walking. Out of the fog, three men bore down on him. The middle guy, big as himself, had shoulder-length hair. The other two were a little shorter. The man on the left wore a Stetson. Then Ferdia remembered he'd left his wallet in the car. Could he hoof it back to the Merc? Possible. At a stretch.

'Hey, bud.' The men bunched in, attempting to block any escape. 'Story?'

'No story, lads.'

'Wha' didja do to Decaf?'

'What?'

'Our mate. Decaf. Wha' didja do to 'im?'

'Nothing.'

'Ya throttled 'im. 'e can't breathe.'

'Huh. Smokes too much. Occupational hazard.'

'Whaja got in the case, bud?'

'Nothin' worth dying for.' Ferdia shouldered by and walked on.

'Give it 'ere.' A hand tried to prise the case from his grasp.

Ferdia twisted to face the trio, his back against a wall. 'Hold your whisht, lads. I've beaten better than ye just to get into a fight.'

The long-haired man stepped forward, the point of a V formation. 'Deadly, bud.' He reached into a pocket. A brief glint of light on steel, as the taxi headlights danced on the blade. 'You mentioned sumptin' 'bout a receipt. I'll tattoo it on yur back.'

The taxi drove away.

Ferdia pushed away from the wall, planted his feet, swung the briefcase up and caught the man under his chin. The jaw broke with a crack, sharp as a rifle shot. The thug's body locked, flopped, buckled and hit the street.

'Wha' de…?' Together, the other pair rushed Ferdia.

Ferdia stood his ground, dropped the case, gripped both men by their necks and used their momentum to lift. Two heads collided with a liquidy splat. He let go, and they collapsed in a heap beside their comrade. Ferdia looked around. No CCTV. They'd picked their spot well. He coughed, swallowed, let the acid roll back into his stomach, waiting for it to settle and the burn to pass. Then he squatted and paint-brushed the gang leader's face with a palm. 'Hey, bud. Wake up.'

'Mmmpfffff,' the man mumbled through a broken jaw.

Ferdia picked up the knife. A Bowie Fixation, with a twenty centimetres black blade. He pocketed it, zeroed in on the other pair. One was still out for the count. Stetson man groaned. Ferdia caught him by the collar and jacked him up against the sidewall. 'Name?'

'Mellon. Tommy Mellon.'

'Which of ye's Dolan?'

'Isn't 'ere. I shouldn't be either, mister.' Mellon rubbed his head. 'I'm jus' helpin' a frien'.'

'Me too. Where's Ciara McGuire?'

'Who? Whatcha on abou'? I haven't a—'

'Grand, so.' Ferdia's voice fell through the freezing air like an axe blade. He turned to the gang leader, wedged a knee on his chest, and hit the thug's nose with a hammer fist. The septum squashed flat as a ball of putty. Air whistled in the man's throat. Blood spurted, bubbled and dribbled into the slush. Mellon gawked as his mate's pulverised nose, and vomited.

'That's for Charlie.' Ferdia glared at Mellon. 'Well, *bud*, if you've nothing to say, you're no addition to me.'

'I'm new. Jus' obeyin' orders.'

'What orders?' Ferdia sensed movement behind him. He kept his eyes on Mellon and drove an elbow into soft tissue behind the third thug's ear, sending him back to dreamland. 'Well?'

'We go where Dessie tells us.'

Ferdia's mobile bleeped again. 'Who's this fella?' He nodded at the motionless lump under his knee.

'That's Jackdaw.' Mellon's eyes, wide as saucers, strayed back to his friend's flattened nose. 'You broke his fookin'—'

'Calcium deficiency,' Ferdia said. His fist thudded with the force of a battering ram into Mellon's ribs. 'Pay attention. I won't ask again.'

Mellon moaned. 'Crowe. Stevie Crowe. We call him Jackdaw.'

'Who's Decaf?'

'Nobody. Tommy Coffey. He's a driver. A bagman.'

'Where's. Ciara. McGuire?'

Mellon worked at breathing. 'Haven't come across any—'

'Ye took her. Where did—?'

'Swear ta God, I know nuffin' 'bout—'

'Where's Dolan?'

'Dunno. Haven't seen him. I—'

Ferdia's fist bunched. Mellon tucked elbows into his ribs for protection. 'Listen, willya? I swear, I met 'im once. Weeks ago. Everything's sorted around a middle man.'

'What middle man?'

'Tiny.'

'Argh, feck this.' Ferdia crashed a punch through Mellon's guard. The controlled power blow folded the thug sideways, and he puked again. Ferdia hauled him back into a sitting position. 'Last chance, *bud*. From the top.'

Mellon croaked, gasped for breath. 'Dessie's the front man. He gives orders to Tiny. Tiny's our contact.'

'What orders?'

'If a punter won't…they can be—'

'Squeezed? The way ye softened up Charlie McGuire?'

Mellon coughed, hawked and spat blood.

'Where does Dolan hang out?' Ferdia asked.

'In Whispers.'

'What's that?'

'A nightclub.'

'Where?'

'Off Stephen's Green.'

'Describe him.'

'Medium size. Longish blonde hair.'

'You're no help. What's Tiny's name?'

'Jus' Tiny.'

'Where can I find him?'

'Near Grafton Street. Hibernian Way to Stephen's Green. That's 'is patch.'

'Begging?'

'Um…yeah.'

'Dessie Dolan's the top man?'

'I *tol'* you, Dessie's our gaffer. Haven't a scoobies who the top man—' Mellon flinched when Ferdia drew back his arm. 'Don't hit me. Don't hit me.'

'Besides cash collections, what else ye mixed up in?'

'That's it. End of.'

'How many in his crew?'

'Seven. Eight.'

Ferdia's mobile hummed for the third time. He pulled it out, squinted at Malcolm's text:

Detectives are questioning a man named

Adam Styne...

Feck.

'Listen up, Mellon, you know what fear is?'

'Wha?'

Fear,' Ferdia said. 'It means Feck. Everything. And. Run. If I spot you again, ever, you'd better run or I swear to God, I'll...Make sure Dolan gets my cash. An' tell him to call his dogs off, far as McGuire's are concerned, or I'll shut down his game. Got it?'

'Yeah.'

Ferdia slapped the crumbled Stetson onto Mellon's head. 'We're done.' He picked up the briefcase and walked away. At the corner of Nerney Court, a wave of acid scorched his chest. He stumbled against a doorway, blinded by the fiery sensation, gagged, swallowed several times to suppress the sourness, and lurched on.

In the Mercedes, he gulped a half bottle of Gaviscon, let his stomach settle then pulled out a cigarette pack. The bile churned again. Ferdia threw the box into a water gully and drove out. Halfway along Gardiner Street, he felt the muscles in the back of his neck relax, and at the traffic lights beside Busáras, he re-read Malcolm's text.

'Feck.'

A car horn blared behind him.

'Feck. Feck. Feck.'

11

THURSDAY 17 JANUARY

MORNING

'HI. I'M RONAN. Um, Hugh asked me to…Hugh Fallon?'

'Hi. Thanks for calling.'

'Hi,' Ronan said again. He shook Sharona's hand. 'I saw you on telly. You were, I mean, you sounded cool.'

'Thanks. Coffee?'

'Erm, I don't want to bother—'

'No trouble.'

'Well, okay.' Ronan fumbled with a jacket button, glanced around the kitchen and missed what Sharona said. 'Sorry?'

'Milk? Sugar?'

'Please. Thanks.'

Sharona spooned coffee into two mugs.

'Hugh said you've a computer problem.'

'Yes.' She added milk, handed Ronan a mug and slid the sugar bowl towards him.

'Thanks.' His hand shook. The sugar spoon clattered to the floor and dinged like a tuning fork. 'Sorry. Here, let me.'

'It's okay. I've got it.'

Ronan's eyes flashed across Sharona's facial bruising. 'Sorry.'

'No problem. When did you meet Hugh?'

'Few months back. Had a gig with his crew until we were made redundant two weeks ago. I'm searching for a job, but may go abroad.'

'Oh?'

'Haven't decided yet.'

'Oh.' Sharona sipped coffee.

Ronan gulped his. 'Isn't my first option, but—'

'I see.'

A cat strolled in and rubbed against Ronan's leg. When he scratched under Cleopatra's neck, she arched her back and purred. 'So, um, is it a desktop or laptop?'

'Laptop. I'm convinced my email account got hacked.'

'Err, can I…?'

'Oh, sure.' Sharona powered up the laptop and inserted a broadband dongle. 'Can you tell me if I've imagined this?'

'Easy. Company email account or personal?'

'Personal.'

'Cool. Checked your email access logs lately?'

'My what?'

'Pop3 or IMAP?'

'No idea what you're on about.'

'Who's your email provider? Hotmail? Yahoo? Google?'

'Gmail.' Sharona logged in and pushed the laptop to Ronan.

'You scroll down here. See this box?' Ronan moved the pointer. 'When you click on "Details" it shows you the log-in history. If you notice a weird IP address, we can track it. Let's check "Recent Activity." Ronan scrolled and clicked.

'What's an IP address?'

'Internet Protocol. All machines linked to a network must have an identity number.' Ronan pointed. 'Here's the IP number for this laptop.'

'Oh, right.'

'What mobile do you use? Android? iPhone?'

'Nokia.' Sharona showed her phone.

Ronan stared. 'Wow.'

'Wow, what?'

'A Nokia 5610. That's—'

'I don't need to read emails the second they're sent or check social media every hour. If something's urgent, people can phone or text. You think my Nokia's ancient?'

'No, um, it's got a brilliant long-life battery. So, did you log into emails from an internet café last week?'

'Nope.'

'Sure?'

'Positive.'

'Ah.'

'Why?'

'Here's what we've got.' Ronan's fingers skipped across the laptop keys. 'Someone logged into your account last Saturday at four twenty-three p.m., and again at a quarter to twelve.'

'Wasn't me.'

Ronan thumb-flicked through his own mobile screen, found an app and tapped in the IP address. 'Ooookay. If I take *that* reference, copy and paste it into *this* lookup site, it gives me a location…That's quick—you've good reception up here. Voila!' Ronan pointed at the screen. 'Ganestown.'

'I was in Belfast. Can you see who the IP belongs to?'

'Yep, with a court order.'

'Crap.'

'You could buy an IP locator.'

'What's that?'

'Geographical locators. They give a locality. Reverse DNS, or Traceroute—'

'Sounds pricey.'

'Depends. Anyways, the gardaí'll put on a trace. Won't cost you a cent.' Ronan looked at Sharona. 'This is criminal. You *are* gonna get them involved?'

'Mmm.'

'Aren't you?'

'Yes. Of course. Can you see if my Facebook or bank account's got hacked as well?'

'Facebook? Easy peasy. Bank accounts? Best check direct with—'

'Okay,' Sharona said.

Ronan gazed out the kitchen window while Sharona typed in a password and gave him back the laptop.

'See, Facebook gives your history in the security section of "Account Settings." They notify you if your account gets logged into by a different device. Yeah, there's that IP again.' Ronan minimised the screens, maximised another window. 'Wonder if the hackers routed your emails back to themselves.'

'God, what does that even mean?'

'They can set up the person's mail, so the Inbox gets auto-forwarded to themselves if they believe it's worthwhile. That avoids the hassle of re-hacking the account. Less traffic reduces the probability of getting caught. Or noticed. What happens is, they create a...anyway, it's no biggie. Nope, it's clean. Whoever it is, dips in and out. An amateur I'd say. Maybe a jealous boyfriend.'

'Don't have a boyfriend.'

'Oh. So, yeah, it's good to browse Recent Activity on Gmail once in a while.' Ronan pushed the laptop across to Sharona.

'Can we gather evidence?' she asked. 'Put the culprit behind bars.'

'I'd say you've enough evidence already,' Ronan said, 'The gardaí will link the IP to the hacker, and Bob's your uncle.'

'I don't want this dragging on.'

'It won't. Guaranteed. Um, what's with your bruises?'

'A man kidnapped me Sunday night.'

'No! Wow. Bummer, dude.'

'Did Hugh tell you he rescued me?'

'All he said was you'd a computer problem. There's no way he'd brag about…you alright?'

'Bit sore. I'll survive. So, what way should I present this? Can you help me get the information together for the gardaí?'

'I'll go with you. If you like, I mean. Thing is, they might ask technical—'

'Fluffy bits?'

'Hmm?'

'Never mind. Bad joke.'

'I'm sure you can handle—'

'I'd appreciate your help. Thanks.'

'No probs, dude, um, Sharona. We can grab a coffee on the way. Discuss tactics, if you want, that is.'

'What, my coffee isn't acceptable?'

'No, it's—'

'What's wrong with it?'

'Your coffee's cool—'

'I'm messing. I'd love a decent coffee. After we've visited the bank and Garda station.'

'Cool.'

MID-MORNING

DETECTIVE MARCUS MULRYAN rang Hugh and asked him to call into Ganestown Garda Station for a follow-up interview and sign the official report. Again, it didn't sound like a polite request. En route, Hugh crossed paths with Sharona and Ronan. They'd given statements and handed in the laptop.

The interview took longer than he'd expected.

Mulryan quizzed Hugh, queried each minute, beginning when he'd phoned Sharona. He rechecked and cross-referenced Hugh's replies on pages of handwritten notes, until he'd exhausted his questions.

'Did Sharona's abduction lead you to question Styne about Ciara McGuire?' Hugh asked.

'Where'd you hear that?'

'Malcolm texted me last night. Has there been any news? Any sightings? Why is Styne—?'

The stenographer brought in the printed statement and gave Hugh a copy to sign.

'We've a way to go,' Mulryan said. 'Real life crime isn't CSI. It takes more than an hour to solve the case.' He looked at his wristwatch. 'Officials are speaking to the family now, and it'll be on the one o'clock news bulletin, so I'll give you an update: Styne was arrested earlier on suspicion of murder. We've found human remains on the farm.'

'What? Who's remains?'

'Not confirmed yet.'

'But you've an idea?'

'Ciara.'

'Ciara? Ciara McGuire?'

'Yes.'

'Ciara McGuire? Dead?'

'Yes.'

'On Styne's farm?'

'Yes.'

'Styne killed her? Adam Styne's a killer?'

'Possible serial killer. We've located other remains. Formal identifications will take a while.'

'A serial killer? Here? In the Midlands?'

'Huh-uh.'

'Jesus.' Hugh was glad he was sitting. 'Ciara. This'll kill Ciara's father, Charlie.'

'Yeah. Tough on all concerned.'

'What now?' Hugh asked. 'Will the farm be dug up? How long before—?'

'No, no. A specialist team with GPR equipment will search for soil disturbance.'

'What's GPR equipment?'

'Ground-penetrating radar. It transmits echoes wherever…' Detective Mulryan scratched his chin. 'Terrible ordeal for families, waiting for word. They're the ones who have to sew their lives back together. Crimes of this magnitude not only robs victims of their lives; it destroys families, neighbourhoods. One day, we'll get closure for relatives.'

Hugh thought on that. 'God. We read about the crimes people commit. In cities. You never consider them happening in your own backyard, involving neighbours and friends.'

'Happens in every town.' The detective changed position and rested an elbow on the desk. 'So, there you have it. A forged painting leads to a killer.'

'Christ.'

'The evidence gathering will continue for the foreseeable. Edmond Locard's exchange principle states every contact leaves a trace. It'll gel, in time.' Mulryan twirled a pen between his fingers. 'That aside, you left a few marks on Styne.' He pulled a report from a stack. 'Looks like he'll need a lot of screws and bridge plates. Must've been a helluva kick. You blew out his knee; he'll walk with a limp forever, and be on a liquid diet for a while. Are you a kickboxer, or always this reckless?'

'Never reckless,' Hugh said. 'But even if I knew he was a killer, not sure what I'd have done different. Sharona was in danger, and the element of surprise was on my side. Reckless? God, no. Pure self-defence. Scary to think evil operates so close to us. Hiding in plain sight.'

'By and large,' the detective said, 'evil people aren't the criminals locked up. Real monsters are seldom caught. You'd no *idea* what you'd find in Styne's house. You're a lucky man.'

Hugh said: 'Hadn't a clue whose house it was. Hard to imagine a psychopath can masquerade as a businessman—'

'Or vice versa,' Mulryan webbed both hands behind his neck.

'A psychopath in a suit,' Hugh said. 'I didn't consider the consequences; just reacted at the time. But why murder Ciara? And others.'

Mulryan shrugged. 'Greed's a motivator in most criminal acts. Or power. No one becomes a depraved serial killer overnight. Everybody *could* get involved in unlawful activity, but the majority stay within the law because they don't fancy the consequences if they're caught. A few ignore the penalties; get a thrill out of bucking the system.' Mulryan shrugged. 'Maybe Styne gets off on killing. Thinks of it as fun. A game. I can't explain what sparks these episodes.'

'Might feel the law's for other people,' Hugh said. 'That it doesn't relate to him. Thinks he's too clever to get caught.'

'Hmm. The people in white coats can decipher him.' Mulryan stood and jingled pocket change. 'But, the brain's peculiar. There's a delicate line between sanity and insanity;

teeny incidences can escalate and cause enormous consequences. Still, this points to you and Ruth in the spotlight with Sharona.'

'No, thanks. That's not for me. I'm happy to keep out of the limelight.'

'You mightn't have a choice.'

'I don't want to become the story. I prefer to remain in the background. One celebrity is enough in Ganestown.'

'It's a small town,' Mulryan said. 'This story will be major news. Your involvement will leak, whether you want it to or not. Prepare yourself.'

AFTERNOON

JUST BEFORE AFTERNOON coffee break, gardaí charged Styne with Ciara McGuire's murder.

Whether it was an official tip-off or Dorothy Ridgeway, Sharona's near-fatal miss grew wings when it got fed to the media. When an eagle-eyed hack recognised her with Ronan in Starbucks, Sharona got pulled into mainstream broadcasts again, and the media scrum began anew. Her wish of getting back to reality lasted fourteen hours.

By teatime, a communications village mushroomed in Ganestown's Square, with the speed and efficiency of a stage set. Camera crews swamped Sharona, exploiting the photogenic heroine they'd become acquainted with, and who could deliver concise sound bites. The multi-coloured discolourations got snapped and filmed at every angle to satisfy the media's thirst for drama. Editors sourced her as the cover story on the main bulletins, relegating other breaking news to second and third spots. Local politicians praised gardaí for their speedy intervention, and Hattinger's family solicitor issued a terse declaration of his client's innocence, urging the authorities to concentrate on arresting the actual killer. Ambrose Hattinger drew the shutters on all business units, closed ranks and the family withdrew into a bubble of silence.

To fill newspaper column inches, roving reporters went on a feeding frenzy, door-stepping Adam Styne's neighbours in Kilcormac and Tullamore. Outside Broadcasting Units looped the district, foraging for news. Hardened farmers scratched their heads, straightened peaked caps, listened to everything and said nothing. Grinning kids bobbled into camera range, making faces for the nine o'clock news. Housewives expressed disbelief at what they'd seen and read. 'Knew him since he was a youngster,' one said. 'Kept to himself. His father, God rest him, was a hard worker.'

'Can't blame parents' background or lack of education,' another added. 'They grafted hard to put him through university. Well-educated, he was.'

'He was odd,' a third noted. 'Bit stand-offish, like he was better than the rest of us. Distant, unless it suited him. Had high notions. Seldom mixed with us locals. I didn't know he'd a big job in Hattinger's. I thought he was a salesman.'

NIGHT

'ANY ISSUES TODAY?'

'No. Kathleen's tip-top,' Sarah said. 'We drove to Athlone, walked a little. Called into Ozanam House on the way back. Kathleen helped settle in a group of four that were evicted from their rented house. We're not long home. She's tired. Wanted to get to bed. Oh, I got a pill organiser. It'll help.'

'Great idea.'

'I'll give Kathleen her medication before I go.'

'Let me do it. Did Ma ask why you're chauffeuring her?'

'Seems content to sit in the passenger seat.' Sarah put on a coat. 'Did you hear they've arrested a man for Ciara McGuire's murder?'

'I caught it on the news bulletin. Um, I'm having a meal with a friend on Saturday night, and I wonder—'

'That's a coincidence. Kathleen and I planned to go to a Céilí on Saturday. Don't know what time we'll get back, so if it suits, I'll stay over...'

Sarah had organised a week's drugs in a twenty-one slot pillbox. Kathleen had stuck a handwritten note to a cupboard:

Dont forget to take tablets every day

Her immaculate handwriting was deteriorating.

Hugh hobbled upstairs with a thimbleful of tablets and a glass of water.

'Peter?'

'It's me, Ma. Hugh.'

Kathleen sat up. 'Peter. Thank God you're here. Get that woman out of our house.'

'Sarah's gone. She said you'd a wonderful day.'

'Indeed I hadn't. Nasty woman. Locked me in here and took my schoolbag. Tore up my homework—'

'Sarah—'

'Shhh. Don't let her hear you. Have you an hour free to deliver food parcels? We can't let people go without food on Christmas day.'

'Christmas is...Yes, Ma, we'll organise food later.' The front door closed. 'I've got your night tablets.'

Kathleen slapped Hugh's hand away. The pills strewed across the bedroom floor. 'You're poisoning me.'

'Ma!'

Kathleen cried.

Hugh held his mother, rocked her and babbled about nothing in particular.

No response.

He worked through the names of County Council representatives contesting the local elections in a few months, and asked who she'd vote for this time around.

No reaction.

He tempted Kathleen with another set of pills. Tried talking again, to distract her. 'Who'd you meet in Ozanam House today?'

No reply.

He coaxed and cajoled her to swallow the tablets, and never felt more helpless watching his mother refuse, lips tight as a vice, trapped in a world of her own.

It took two hours for the tension to ebb. Hugh crushed up the pills, blended them in ice cream, and Kathleen finally accepted the concoction. He stayed by her side until she drifted off to sleep. Hungry, but too fatigued to eat, he lay on his bed and dialled Ruth. 'Hope I'm not interrupting.'

'It's quiet at the moment. A young guy came in earlier, paralytic, but managed to hold onto a slab of beer, though. He's asleep now, cradling the twenty-four pack. Two mates with him, both pissed, described every ache and pain they've suffered, and I'm supposed to laugh hysterically when they ask for a sponge bath as if it's the funniest thing ever.'

'Give them a sleep-off-the-hangover injection.'

'I wish. What plans have you for tonight?'

'I'm chilling. Ma's upset. Took ages to pacify her. Wrecked my head. I cheated and stirred the tablets into ice cream.'

'That's good. Yoghurt works too. And a pill crusher might help. Chemists have them. You should consider short-term respite care.'

'Yeah, for myself.'

'Ha-ha. Seriously, even one weekend a month. Caregivers need care too.'

'I'll manage for the present. I've got Sarah 'til mid-February.'

'It'll get complicated if you've to travel for work. Think of your own health, Hugh.'

'The Mullingar job ended quicker than I thought. I'll—'

A monitor bleeped.

'There's trouble. Gotta go. See you Saturday.'

Hugh considered Ruth's suggestion. What *were* the choices? Will I find a job and be able to continue caring for Ma, he wondered. If I opt for a self-employment scheme, would it afford me more breathing space? What ventures work best? Would I make enough income to survive? Or set myself up for failure? How'll I anticipate and avoid the pitfalls? If it sinks, I'm finished.

His mobile buzzed. Ferdia.

'Ciara's body is being released tomorrow afternoon. Sealed casket, though. Bastard destroyed her face with acid. Funeral Mass Saturday, eleven o'clock.'

'I'll be there. How's David?'

'He's…' Ferdia turned his shaky voice into a cough. 'See you at church.'

12

FRIDAY 18 JANUARY

MORNING

NATURE'S CHOIR SANG in full chorus.

The sun cast a silver hue on the shimmering landscape. Kathleen and Sarah were in the kitchen. Sarah tidied and Kathleen doodled dreams on a sheet of paper. 'I'm off, Ma.' Hugh gave his mother a kiss and hug.

'I'm going dancing tonight,' Kathleen's eyes shone.

'Oh?'

'Tomorrow night, Kathleen.' Sarah said. She looked at Hugh. 'Still okay if I sleepover?'

'Sure.'

Hugh knew from Sarah's smile the cousins had talked.

'Where're you off to?' Kathleen's expression became anxious.

'Mullingar. To help out at McGuire's.'

'Will you be home soon?'

'Soon. I promise.'

'How long?'

'Three, four hours.'

'Where are you going?'

Mullingar, Ma…'

Hugh zipped across town to his own home for a change of clothes, passed the school where Eilish taught. Still closed.

In Starbucks, he spied Ronan and Sharona sitting face-to-face in a secluded corner. Ronan's boy-band smile had returned.

'Can anybody join in?'

Ronan jumped.

'Relax, man.' Hugh squeezed in beside him.

'We were gossiping 'bout you,' Sharona said. The inflammation had reduced, but make-up couldn't disguise the mottled bruises.

'God. I'm sure you could find a more stimulating topic.'

Sharona's mobile beeped. 'Another text from Dorothy,' she showed them the screen.

'She'll adopt you,' Hugh said.

Ronan nudged Sharona: 'Go on, tell him the latest.'

Hugh eyed them both. 'What?'

'No question, my email account got hacked,' Sharona said. 'Gardaí will monitor it for a few days, and if the person logs on…bingo. Then the file gets sent to the DPP, whatever that means.'

'Means if there's enough evidence, the court will convict the hacker,' Ronan said.

'And jailed, I hope.' Sharona looked at Ronan. 'Ron was fab.'

Ronan blushed.

'And in other news,' Sharona added, 'a TV3 producer asked me to audition for an investigative reporter's role in a true-crime series they're planning.'

'Wow. That'll set you up for life. Congratulations.'

'Thanks. They want me to screen test next week, but I've got my heart set on opening the art gallery.'

'No harm in going for the audition, anyway. Bet you'll ace it,' Ronan said.

Sharona made a face. 'The camera adds five kilos. I mightn't appeal to—'

'You will,' Ronan nodded.

'I enjoyed the craic around the TV crews over the last few days,' Sharona said. '*If* I got the job, I know what my first project would be. I could write the script now—'

'Wait 'til after the interview,' Hugh said.

'Hmm. But if I *showed* the interviewers I'm serious—'

'Still think you should wait.'

'If I go for it, I want to give it my best shot. Anything else on Styne today?'

Hugh shook his head. Hope he's locked up forever, or dies. I'm good with either. Any luck on the jobs front?' Hugh looked at Ronan.

'I've a dozen CV's mailed out. Hope I get an interview soon. You?'

'Haven't committed to anything, except—'

'Except tomorrow night.' Sharona flashed her impish grin.

'What's tomorrow night?' Ronan asked.

'Hugh's got a date.'

'Cool.'

'Not cool. Hot.' Sharona bounced her eyebrows.

Hugh rolled his eyes. 'Jesus. Add matchmaker to your list of talents.'

Sharona's mobile rang, and she moved outside to pick up a signal.

Ronan said: 'If you get any hint of work dude, keep me in mind.'

'Course I will, *Ron*, if you're still around. You're the guy who, and I quote, "Can't wait to get outta this poxy place. I'll give it a week. If I don't get a break by then, I'm outta G'town".'

'Yeah, well, circumstances change, dude.'

'That was Dorothy.' Sharona slid back into the conversation. 'Jana Trofimiack talked. The PSNI arrested a professional art forger in County Armagh. On the back of that, Europol arrested an art dealer in Spain, and two other people in France. This scam was massive.

'Did Dorothy get the McKelvey back?'

'They're tracking it. A Spanish collector bought it.'

'So, what now?'

'The police will hold both the genuine and forged pieces as evidence. The case will wind its way through the court. Dorothy said Jana and her son will get deported, once she gives the police all her information, and hands over the scam proceeds.'

'What happened to "Go to Jail? Do not pass go. Do not collect two hundred pounds"?'

Ronan shrugged. 'It's the prisoner's dilemma, dude. Little pawns sometimes wriggle free.'

AFTERNOON

MCGUIRE'S HAD the mood of a funeral home.

Customers stood in clusters outside; mourners alone, together. Inside, thrums of deep conversation, words clipped tight with anger, buzzed through the store as customers and staff comforted each other.

'Charlie's discharged himself. He's upstairs,' a checkout man told Hugh.

'Really? He shouldn't be here.'

'Yeah, he's fighting a tailspin at the moment, but who's gonna stop him? He looks rough.'

Hugh hobbled past empty shelves. Malcolm met him on the stairwell. 'Dad's distraught.' His voice dropped. 'He blames himself for Ciara's death.'

'I'm here for you both,' Hugh said.

'Thanks. But don't tell me that God wanted Ciara with Him, or He only gives these crosses to people who can bear them, or, it's His will, part of an eternal plan, and Ciara's in a better place now. I've listened to that crap for two days. It makes me puke. I'm fed up with people telling me the Lord meant it to be; that it happened for a reason.'

'Words spoke with good intentions, Malcolm.'

'They don't stop the pain or relieve the agony. We'll never have a chance to talk again. A detective showed me pictures of the room where he held her.' Malcolm gulped. 'Bastard threw acid or weed killer on her. And he kidnapped Sharona? I mean, what the——?'

'Yeah.'

'Hell's the matter with people?'

'Can't answer that, Malcolm.'

'Why's your foot plastered? And the head bandage? Did you crash?'

'No. I got tangled up in Sharona's rescue.'

'Oh? You rescued her?'

'I helped.'

'Did you see him? Styne?'

'Mmm.'

'I hope you hurt him. Bad.'

'Not enough.'

'I'll repay what I owe you, soon as this nightmare ends. You know I'm good for it.'

He looked over his shoulder and whispered, 'Don't mention it to Dad, he's got enough worries——'

'Sure. Keep the faith, Malcolm. Help him get through this.'

'C'mon, Dad's in his office.'

Charlie sat at his desk, head cradled between his hands.

'Hugh's here,' Malcolm said.

Etched lines of grief and faded buttery coloured bruises marked Charlie's face and forehead. His eyes were watery and bloodshot, their normal crispness dimmed to a pale tan.

The side of his mouth, Hugh noticed, drooped. In less than two weeks, Charlie had become an old man.

'I'm sorry for your loss, Charlie. I've no words, can't imagine how—'

'Thanks, Hugh. Your support means everything. It's Ciara's birthday tomorrow, you know.'

'Knew it was around now, but—'

'What happened to you?'

'Hugh helped rescue Sharona,' Malcolm said.

Charlie stared. 'How'd you get involved in—?'

'I'll tell you another time.'

Malcolm left.

'I dealt directly with Adam Styne once,' Charlie said. 'Knowledgeable man.' He sighed. 'Who can you trust nowadays, when the person who smiles most turns out to be the biggest villain?'

'If there's anything I can do—'

'Everybody's rallied around. The staff…Their offers of assistance…Genuine people. Thanks, Hugh. You've helped manage the fort.'

'I didn't do much—'

'All I ever wanted was a chance to be a first-class employer and leave a decent inheritance for my kids. I envisaged Ciara taking a role here after Malcolm grew into the business. They'd both run the company together. That's been my dream.'

'You've built a legacy. It can—'

'The business doesn't interest me anymore, Hugh. I can't focus. Passion's gone.' Charlie's eyes skimmed the walls. 'It's my moment to ride off into the sunset.'

'Today isn't the time to make life-altering decisions,' Hugh said. 'Viewpoints change. Business is in your blood.'

'Not anymore. For years, I neglected my kids in the belief I'd improve their lifestyle. That's what parents want

for their kids, right? Turns out I've built a memorial. Makes
you wonder what's the point? The one time Ciara needed
me, I wasn't there. That'll haunt me till I die.'

'You couldn't have done—'

'You can't say for sure. It's possible I'd have visited,
or…' Charlie exhaled. 'Doctor warned me not to get
stressed.'

'Have you to go for more tests?'

'No, unless something…Six months. I'll be on tablets
for the rest of my life, though. Keep my diet under control.
No salt. More exercise.' Charlie slumped in the seat. 'I'm
tired, Hugh. Tired of life. Old fogeys like me tend to stay in
the job way beyond our sell-by date. I'm out of ideas. It's
time to hand over the reins. Malcolm will inject new
enthusiasm into McGuire's. Companies demand vitality,
energy. New blood generates vibrancy.'

'Don't plan on spending your days on the golf course,'
Hugh said, remembering Sharona's words at the fundraiser.
'You're still needed, and you've heaps to teach him.'

'You too, Charlie said.'

'I don't work here anymore.'

'You found another job?'

'Not yet. Philip let me go. I appreciate money's tight—'

'*My* name's over the shop front. It's not the accountant's
decision which piece of the pie gets handed out or kept.
That's *my* choice, and I didn't authorise anybody to let you
go. Meant what I said. I'm taking a back seat. You've a few
years' experience on Malcolm; your management skills are
essential. Don't let me down, Hugh. You offered. I'm
calling in the chit.'

'Of course, I won't let you—'

'We'll talk again next week. Now, I've to go'—Charlie
took his coat from a wall hook—'and meet the undertakers.
They've collected Ciara. She's on the way to Ganestown.

We're taking her home tonight for a wake.' He looked at his watch. 'I've got an hour to teach myself to cry with a smile. Then tomorrow, instead of helping organise a birthday celebration, I'll bury my daughter.'

13

SATURDAY 19 JANUARY

MORNING

PARKING WAS IMPOSSIBLE around Ganestown Parish Church.

The sombre bong of the church bell reverberated, and the town square got crammed with vehicles. Throngs of funeral-goers ditched their transport on the outskirts and walked to the funeral Mass. Outsiders from the hinterlands, unacquainted with McGuire's, blended with locals in a show of support for the bereaved.

Hugh got one of the last spaces in Meadow's car park and hobbled to church. On the altar, a priest prepared a thurible for the Mass ritual. He spooned incense into the censer, blessed it with the sign of the cross, added charcoal, lit it and hung the chain on a stand. It swung gently to and fro, its scented haze shrouding the coffin and Ciara's framed photo. A male song-thrush perched on a cross-beam above the casket, and when the choir sang the intro hymn, the bird's fluty tweets chimed in poignant harmony: *'Cherry dew cherry dew cherry dew. Knee deep knee deep knee deep.'*

The organ music tailed off, and the priest spoke. 'The end of human life is a sacred moment. We want death to reach us at a measured pace, one that gives us time to accept the inevitable. But too often its arrival is unexpected, and it alters our world in a heartbeat. The tragic end to Ciara

McGuire's young life has shaken the beliefs of this community. Today, we struggle to make sense of—'

'Mammy.' David's wail masked the priest's words.

Sobs spread along the top pew, across the middle aisle, growing in volume. The funeral ritual had brought any ambiguity to an end, and Ciara's kin keened at their loss. Adam Styne had ripped the heart from a family, and left a trail of destruction in his wake.

Outside the church, Hugh spotted Sharona hug Charlie. She stooped to console David, still crying and clasping his grandfather's hand. A nosy neighbour stood on a low wall, scanning the crowd, taking a mental headcount. On the fringes, a small group shattered the dignified air with raucous laughs. Milo Brady lurked nearby. Ferdia's heavy hand thumped Hugh's shoulder. 'Sad day.'

'It is. Jesus, bad enough hearing about unavoidable deaths, but when you witness an unnecessary one, and someone you know, it's tragic. A life not lived.' Hugh shook his head. 'You okay?'

'Argh, an old dog for the hard road. It'll be strange not having Ciara around. Always thought of her as more my own daughter than a niece-in-law. One of the decent HR people. Had a genuine concern for staff.'

'She did.'

'Every death's equal, but not every death's the same.' Ferdia exchanged nods with a passer-by. 'Hard to accept when it's not in the natural order of things. Anyway, whether it's nine or ninety-nine, the loss is no less, and life goes on no matter what. The focus from here on is Master David. He's got a tough road ahead.'

Hugh glimpsed Charlie again, waxen skin stretched tight as a drum across his cheekbones. A queue of people were wrapped around the church exterior, waiting to sympathise.

'His scars are healing,' Hugh said, 'but it'll take him a long time to recover from this.'

Ferdia's eyes followed Hugh's gaze. 'Aye. He's bolloxed. Every way. Physical. Mental. Emotional. He'll live for another thirty years and that'll be his purgatory. We spent the night talking about Ciara. Remembering stuff we'd forgotten. He's holding onto a reality that no longer exists. All his dreams get buried today. She was his light, even in dark days. A broken heart's the heaviest thing to carry. What do they say? The more you love, the more you lose.'

'He blames himself.'

'Huh. That makes it worse. It's shot his conscience to shit. The combined weight of grief and guilt can cripple a man. It'll take a while for this to sink in. Visible wounds mend; it's the feckin' internal ones that cause real pain.' Ferdia rubbed an eye.

A man joined them. 'No parent should hafta bury a child,' he jerked his head in Charlie's direction. 'It's a dream crusher. Everyone liked Ciara.'

'She was easy to like,' Ferdia said. 'Forget the bullshit 'bout time's a great healer. It isn't. The loss goes on and the pain never ends in this vale of tears. Only way to cope is learn to live with it.'

'Still, it passes,' the man said, 'and pounds the shite outta you before it goes.' He wandered off.

Ferdia looked across at a plague of politicians converge on Charlie. 'See? They're out in force today. Visible for a change. I'd say the feckers never met Ciara. Don't see the accountant, Waldron. Chas said last night he'll offer you a management role. I hope you take it. It'll be a win-win.'

'We'll see what happens,' Hugh said. 'Charlie said he won't come back to the business. Malcolm's in charge, and he'll have different ideas about—'

'Three things wrong with that. One, it's a knee-jerk reaction. Two, Mal's not near ready to grab the reins, and three, Chas hasn't even *begun* to prepare an exit strategy, so pass no heed. You'll be grand. Reputation got you in the door, talent and ability will keep you there.'

'I'll see if I can fit in,' Hugh said. 'I don't even know how...'

'You'll learn. And don't worry about fitting in; it's better to stand out. When all goes well, praise the team. If all goes pear-shaped, take the blame.'

'Okay. You were sparring again.' Hugh pointed to Ferdia's scraped knuckles.

'What? That? I paid off the gombeen men. They wanted to force me into a dance routine. Had to convince them I don't tango.'

'Jesus, Ferdia. They? How many?'

'Three.'

'Jes—'

'Argh, they're amateurs. In boxing terms 'twas like flirting. Went off smooth as honey on a bruise.'

'I said I'd go with you. Why didn't you tell me?'

'I forgot. Mea culpa.'

'You're hilarious, Ferdia.'

'Sure, you're fighting enough battles.'

'Did you get hurt? Or hurt them?'

'Nah, not much. Spídógs, they were. Street goons, hopping about like grease on a hot griddle. What? Don't look at me as if I'd two heads. Honest, I didn't touch them, well, except for the fella who beat up Chas. I admit I might've given him a few extra whacks, by accident.'

'Reckless move, Ferdia. There'll be a comeback.'

'You reckon? Nah. Bullies back away when you stand up to them. They're wannabe gangsters throwing a few shapes like drunk uncles at a wedding.'

'You said yourself these are dodgy people. Remember?'

'It'll be grand. A summer breeze would blow them over. The fella I wanted, Dessie Dolan, didn't show, more the pity.'

'Dessie Dolan? I heard that name...Sharona mentioned it. He's a friend of Malcolm's. What's he got to do with Charlie?'

Ferdia scratched his head, balancing truth and lies. 'Argh, you feckin' can't fix foolish. Turns out Malcolm borrowed money. Got drawn into a poker game, an' lost. Didn't pay the debt fast enough, so Dolan twisted Chas's arm.'

Hugh stared at Ferdia. 'Christ. Sharona mentioned an addiction and that Dolan was low-life. I thought she meant Malcolm was buying some recreational drugs off him. Jesus. And Charlie wants Malcolm, a gambler, in charge of the company? How much did he borrow?'

'Smallish loan. But compound interest is a crippler.'

'You know impulsive habits lead to rash decisions, Ferdia. Managing a business—'

'He's family.'

'Yeah.' Hugh sighed.

'Anyway, 'twas a once-off. Dolan won't be back.'

'And you know that...how?'

'I'll warn him away.'

'How? Come on, tell me what your initial gambit will be.'

'I'll give Dolan a hard warning. A statement of intent. Frighten the bejesus outta him, an' run him and his goons out of town...when I find him, that is. He reminds me of a badger, well-known but seldom seen. But he'll pop up on my radar soon enough.'

'Forget it, Ferdia. Leaders never appear on the front line. He'll send more muscle men.'

'Let him send who he wants, 'long as he doesn't want 'em back. Nah, he'll stay away. I'll have to go looking for him. I won't be the first to walk into hostile territory. Attack's the best form of defence.'

'And fights lead to funerals.'

Ferdia shrugged. 'Sure, you never know.'

'Most times, you kinda do. Those type of people retaliate. They *have* to get even. It's a law, a code. Any sign of weakness, the rival gangs step in and—'

'No risk, no reward. Besides, I need a receipt for my accountant. Tax purposes, you know yourself.' Ferdia winked.

'Christ sake, Ferdia.'

'We are who we are, Hugh. You're a professional, a product of the system. I'm a rebel, a maverick, navigating on pure feckin' instinct. What've I got to lose?'

'Brain cells?'

'Nah. I'll be grand, and so will you. Think of the momentum you'll gain on the upswing from all this.'

'What momentu—?'

'Sort your auld banger out yet?' Ferdia changed the subject.

'It's in for a service, but I'll probably sell it. I can use Ma's car. She won't need it now.'

'Huh,' Ferdia said. 'Heading to the hotel after?'

'No. You?'

'Gonna catch up on paperwork. Wiseman wants me to figure out ways to deliver meaningful solutions. Whatever the feck that means.'

'Any blood tests back?'

'Aye. Doctor Dracula was in touch.'

'And?'

'Looks as if I've got diabetes. And the heartburn thing? He wants to do a biopsy. They're querying Barrett's oesophagus.'

'What's—?'

'Not sure, but turns out I could have it. Said I might need surgery. Has a name the length of your arm. Something reflux. Sounds like the make of a car.'

'Hmm?'

'The operation. Volvo, or Honda.'

'Volvo-reflux? Honda-reflux?' Hugh thought for a second. 'Never heard of it. When's the biopsy?'

'Said he was looking forward to seeing me Monday morning. I said I wasn't looking forward to seeing *him*.'

'What hospital?'

'Saint Vincent's.'

'The cancer hospital?'

'Aye.'

'No way.'

'Yes, way.'

'Jesus wept.'

'I'll be grand.'

'Why in hell do you keep these things bottled up, Ferdia? You'll be groggy afterwards. I'll take you.'

'Ah, good man. Oh, there's a lad I want to chat.' Ferdia whacked Hugh's shoulder again and gave a flea-swatting wave. 'Pick me up at nine on Monday, so. Slán.' Ferdia vanished, quick as a pickpocket on a busy street.

'Hugh?'

Now he knew why Ferdia disappeared so fast. Eilish was wrapped up in a full-length grape-green coat and cream gloves. Ray-Bans covered half her face. 'Hi,' he said.

'Hi,' Eilish used a tissue to dab beneath an eye. 'Thanks for the message.'

'I thought you'd want to know—'

'I did.'

They both studied the ground.

'Terrible loss,' Hugh said. 'You and Ciara were close.'

Eilish wrapped her arms around herself. 'Since we were kids. It's her birthday today.'

'I know.'

'It hasn't sunk in yet. I'm so numb, I can't call to mind the emotions to deal with this. It's…and I feel guilty because…I tried to contact her last weekend, and she didn't answer her phone. I should've known there was a problem. I could've driven out there and—'

'Yeah.' Hugh stirred a pebble with his shoe. 'School hasn't reopened?'

'Monday.'

'Well, take care.' Hugh moved away.

'Hugh?' Eilish caught his arm. 'I'm…can we meet?'

Hugh stared at the gloved hand until Eilish released her grip. 'Why?'

'I need…I want—'

'You need? You want? Me. Me. Me.' Hugh bit his lip. 'It's always about you. Some things never change.'

'That's not fair.' Eilish glanced around. 'Or true. Ten minutes? Coffee? After the burial?'

'For what?'

'I'd like us to talk.'

Hugh opened his arms wide. 'What can I say, when I don't have anything to say?'

'You owe me—'

Hugh stepped away, then turned back. 'Huh? I've taken nothing from you, so I *don't* owe you. If anyone is due anything, it's me. I'm sorry you couldn't appreciate what I…' He glanced around, swallowed his anger and lowered his voice. 'Anyway, now doesn't suit. I'll text you. Next week.'

'That's too…I…Okay.'

Hugh shuffled away, wondering what Eilish's urgency was. Must be important if she wanted to meet so soon after Ciara's funeral, he reasoned. Should I go for coffee? Where's the harm in that? He limped on. *Let it wait. Eilish wouldn't answer my calls, didn't ask how come I'm bandaged up. Never bothered to ask about Ma. Whatever it is, it's for herself. Focus on what I've gained, rather than remember what I've lost. I loved you so much, Eilish, and although we don't have a future, I'm grateful for what we shared. I regret it didn't work out, but the way you told me we're finished cut like a knife. You could've given me an explanation then. Now, I don't want it. I've got my memories, but I'm moving on; getting my life together.* What if Ma hadn't fallen, he pondered. Suppose Ruth wasn't on duty that night in A&E. She was becoming…well, he wasn't sure what, but he looked forward to seeing her tonight. He imagined her vanilla essence and strawberry scent. Next week he'd devise a long-term plan for his mother. Ruth would advise him and help pick the best solution.

His mobile buzzed. Ruth.

'Are you psychic? I was thinking about you.'

'Aww. Nice thoughts, I hope.'

'I've left Ciara McGuire's funeral. Contemplating how the unravelling of one life can sow the seeds of another.'

'And that's good?'

'Has potential.'

'We still on for tonight?'

'Can't wait. Oh, Ruth? Is there an operation for reflux problems called Volvo or Honda?'

'Um…No. You must mean Gastroesophageal Reflux,' Ruth laughed. 'The surgical procedure's called Nissen Fundoplication.'

'Is it a concern?'

'Varies from patient to patient. Not usually a cause for alarm, but it can be. Why?'

'Might be on the cards for a friend of mine. See you around eight?'

'Yummy.'

AFTERNOON

ADAM STYNE COULD barely open his mouth.

A nurse wheeled him into a day room and said an ambulance crew would be along to transfer him. She didn't answer when he'd questioned where. He watched the news bulletin on a small television, and endured waves of pain, still convinced the doctors were intentionally keeping him on low morphine doses. He wondered if he'd glimpse Slieve Bloom again.

Two paramedics peeped in and whispered together, discussing, he thought, what made him tick. He'd listened to guards talking outside the hospital room door. Heard them discuss the injuries they'd cause when they'd get him in a cell. A woman whispered she'd slam a dictionary on his head without leaving a mark. He'd find a way to capture their chats. Use them in evidence.

Styne used the tip of his tongue to explore the wire holding his jaw together, searching the gaps left by teeth extractions.

Why did I react so quickly to Ciara McGuire's snub? Stupid. Stupid. I'd covered my tracks; would've been impossible to trace me online. And I should've walked away from Sharona Waters. Needed time to plan.

His fuzzy brain perked up when the TV showed footage of Ciara McGuire's funeral cortège taking her sanctified remains to its final resting place. The screen cut to a miscellany of archived film, summarising Hattinger's business from its foundation to resurgence, before a camera shot showed the present-day Tullamore premises with its padlocked doors. At some point, a drone had swooped, capturing video footage of his house in Kilcormac, the aerial views now served up for public consumption.

A cut to a live camera feed. For a heartbeat, he didn't recognise the road leading to his house entrance.

Madeline's jeep.

A scoop of trench-coated reporters, intent on committing acts of journalism, waited at the automatic gates.

Drive through them, you stupid bitch. Mow them down.

The gates inched open; reporters and camera crews swarmed around. A scribbler opened the driver's door. 'Can you comment on the revelations concerning your husband?' Flashguns hosed Madeline's face. Her frozen expression resembled a rabbit caught in headlights. A recorder got shoved under her nose and snappers focused camera lens.

'How'll you cope, now he's charged with murder?' A woman pushed forward, persistent in her pursuit of a quote. 'Can you enlighten our readers—?'

Other voices chimed in:

'Were you shocked?'

'Have you any words for the victim's families?'

'Did you attend Miss McGuire's funeral?'

'Have you spoken to Charlie McGuire? What did y—?'

Adam Styne strained to make out the obscured shape on the passenger side.

'Will you visit your husband? What'll you say?'

'Did you have any suspicions?'

'Is it true you're planning to take over the Hattinger business?'

'You're trespassing on private property.' Madeline forced the jeep door closed. The gates were taking forever to open.

Run my business? She couldn't run a…And no declaration of innocence. No 'Adam is innocent'. She'll return to Paris and bury her head. Should've set up an alibi and had her killed there years ago. Soon as I get away from these chumps, I'll do it. But first, Fallon and the Waters woman. I bet Madeline will attempt to sell the farm. Let her try. The locals will think they're in for a land grab. No chance there either. Let them believe the town hero has become a lunatic.

Ideas swarmed through Styne's mind; lines of legal argument already forming.

The jeep nudged by the hollering horde, and a reporter grabbed the passenger door handle. A camera zoomed in.

Styne frowned.

Why's that northern battle-axe in my jeep? Going into my house?

'Mrs Ridgeway, will Hattinger's still be in charge of your auction? Do you have a date set?' The journalist thrust a microphone under Dorothy's nose.

Dorothy kept her eyes on the windscreen, hands joined in her lap. The jeep disappeared up the winding driveway.

Adam Styne gaped at the television screen.

I bet that cow is putting ideas into Madeline's head. I have to stop those bitches ruining my business. Maybe the barrister is right. We'll delay and defer, squeeze out a trade. If that doesn't work, I'll plead insanity; declare myself unstable, unfit to stand trial, too mad to assist in my own defence. It'll be up to psychiatrists to decide a suitable rehabilitation. I'll help them reach the correct decision. Easy to fool them: plead to a multiple personality disorder. Psychiatrists love that shit. Worst-case scenario? Three to five years. I'll win. Then there'll be retribution. Revenge and retribution. They'll all learn I can do anything to anyone, anywhere, anytime. And good luck trying to accumulate and piece together the evidence I've scattered across ten counties.

He thought about how far he'd come, from where he'd started, and vowed this glitch wouldn't see everything he'd worked for go up in smoke.

In three years, I'll buy Hattinger's outright.

'You shouldn't be watching that.' A nurse rushed in and turned off the television.

He ripped Madeline's letter into strips and tore the pieces into shreds. More ideas stacked up in his brain. He stored a few, rejected others and remembered he'd used the iPhone to find Sharona Waters' address.

Premeditated abduction. Something else to consider and find an explanation for.

EVENING
FERDIA FOUND A space in Brown Thomas's multi-storey car park.

His third trip to Dublin city centre in as many days. He pulled on a wool hat and strolled into Grafton Street. A saxophone honk echoed from an alleyway. Two women studied their reflections in the Marks and Spencer winter window, and applied mascara. Piles of frozen slush, heaped against walls, were melting. Ferdia sauntered through the Hibernian Way arch, eyes scanning as he dodged and ducked, camouflaged by crowds of shoppers.

No Tiny.

He hung a right onto Dawson Street.

On the corner of Stephen's Green, a Chinese busker sat on the steps of the old Anglo-Irish Bank premises, and played 'In the Hall of the Mountain King' on a homemade washtub one-string bass. Ferdia kept going, hunched and ponderous, looking at nothing, seeing everything. There was little to see, except pedestrians coming and going. He crossed the street, dawdled beside a Range Rover that took up two disabled driver parking spaces, and didn't have a permit displayed. He searched through pockets, forgetting he hadn't smoked since Wednesday night.

Now what.

He considered options, wondered if Dolan had scouts nearby. Spotters. He jammed the mobile to his ear, pretended to take a call. Should've squeezed Tommy Mellon for more information, he thought. Telling him to warn Dolan away from McGuire's was stupid. The message needed to be stronger. Personal. And taken seriously. Malcolm didn't need a vulture like Dolan adding to his woes. If Dolan approached McGuire's again, he'd retaliate. He walked along the Stephen's Green railings, to the Shelbourne Hotel and back again. Still nothing. He meandered to Stephen's Green Centre, turned down Grafton Street and pressed Niamh's speed dial number.

'Glad you called,' she said. 'I was wondering how you are?'

'Rough day.'

'Can't begin to imagine.'

'Yeah. And before you ask, no cigarettes, although my hands have searched pockets a hundred times. Once today's over, I reckon I've broken the habit.'

'And David?'

'Mentioned you before Mass.'

'Aww. Poor boy. My heart's breaking for him. You stopping by?'

'Aye. I've to see a few people first.'

'I'll cook dinner.'

'Keep feeding me, and I'll be like the stray cat you can't get rid of.'

'Hah. If you want, stay over, I'll take you to Saint Vincent's on Monday.'

'Thanks, but Hugh's volunteered. Hugh Fallon. He wants to meet up next time you're in Ganestown. I'll collect David tomorrow from Chas and drop him off at school Monday morning. No point having you drive to Ganestown, then turn around and go back again.'

'I've taken a few days off,' Niamh said, 'so I'll go to Ganestown Monday afternoon, and have a fire lit and the house warm when you get home. Maybe I'll meet Hugh then.'

'Grand. Mightn't be the best company after doc spends the day poking and prodding me.'

'Doesn't matter. I'll talk to the dog. Say hello to David for me.'

'Will do.'

'Keep next weekend free, Ferdia. I've booked us—'

'Aww, you shouldn't have.'

'It's your birthday.'

'I know, but still. Where are we going?'

'It's a surprise. See you later.'

Plan B, Ferdia decided, thoughts gathering pace with his quickening steps. Have a gander around Whispers nightclub. At some stage, Dolan will appear, and I'll warn him off, personally. I'll get Hugh to do a reconnaissance mission on Tiny. Another lead, back to Dolan. Hugh'll blend better, be less noticeable. 'Guerrilla tactics,' Ferdia muttered. 'I stand out too much to blend in. Attack and retreat. Between us, we'll feckin' smoke him out.'

NIGHT

HUGH REDUCED THE oven temperature.

He didn't want to burn their first meal together. Then he changed his mind and turned the heat up again. Worse if he undercooked it.

The doorbell rang.

Ruth's nose peeped out from beneath a cream Parka jacket with a faux fur-trimmed hood.

'Welcome,' Hugh said.

Ruth melted into his arms. Wine bottles clinked. 'Food smells delicious.'

'So do you.' Hugh twisted his head. 'Hear that?'

'What.'

'The ice. It's cracking. The Arctic spell's over.'

Arm-in-arm they went inside, leaving nature to itself. What had been solid ice for the last month, was now trickles of water. The thaw had finally begun.

Lightning Source UK Ltd.
Milton Keynes UK
UKHW012130060322
399669UK00003B/97